FROM THESE
BROKEN
STREETS

FROM THESE BROKEN STREETS

A NOVEL

ROLAND MERULLO

LAKE UNION
PUBLISHING

Published by Lake Union Publishing, Seattle

www.apub.com

Amazon, the Amazon logo, and Lake Union Publishing are trademarks of Amazon.com, Inc., or its affiliates.

ISBN-13: 9781542018968
ISBN-10: 154201896X

Cover design by Faceout Studio, Amanda Hudson

Printed in the United States of America

In memory of
Orlando Amadeo Merullo Sr.,
who was convinced, against his wishes,
to change his name

Courage is the price that life exacts for granting peace.

—*Amelia Earhart*

AUTHOR'S NOTE

Incredible as it may seem, the story that follows is based closely on historical record. This book is a work of fiction, the people and conversations are made up, but the main events described in these pages mirror, however imperfectly, what actually took place in Naples, Italy, in late September, 1943. Those events were so diffuse and complex that only a book of several thousand pages could do them justice. So I have had to compress time and alter certain details in order to give a sense of the essence of the Neapolitan rebellion, commonly called The Four Days of Naples. Given those constraints, I have tried to be as factually accurate as possible.

One

Having been caught in a sudden afternoon rainstorm and separated from his friends, Armando ended up spending the night on an awning-covered porch in the Chiaia neighborhood, a sleeping place he'd never used. There was thunder in the wet darkness and flashes of lightning, too, not so different from the years of Allied bombing. He woke at first light to find his legs in a puddle and a man standing over him—the owner of the house, he guessed. The man was as wide as a wine barrel, with thick arms and fat hands, an ugly mouth, and short, curly hair that came to a point low on his forehead. A silvery scar ran across the middle of his neck. He reached down and lifted Armando to his feet, not gently, and held him there—wet, shivering, too close. "You pay rent here?" the man said, the scar on his neck bouncing with each word.

Armando couldn't speak. His legs were shaking, his breath coming in gulps. After a few bad seconds, he shook his head.

"You have a name?"

"Ar . . . Armando."

"Last name?"

Another shake of the head.

"You sleep wherever you want to?"

"*Sì, sì* . . . On the streets."

The man ran his eyes—small, dark, merciless—over Armando's face and released his grip. "You're a *scugnizzo*."

Armando nodded, proud of the label. *Scugnizzo.* Street kid. He was slightly less afraid now.

"What do you do for food, for money?"

The boy narrowed his own eyes, didn't blink, didn't turn away. "What I have to."

The ugly man studied him, but he seemed to Armando to be partly somewhere else, to be thinking up a plan. "I'm burying my brother today," he said.

"I'm sorry."

"*Sorry* is a pleasant word."

"I am, though. I don't have a brother. Or a mother. Or a father. The nuns raised me."

"Too bad."

"Until I ran away."

The man kept moving his eyes across Armando's face, as if searching for something there, bringing himself back from wherever he had been. "You want to make two lire?" he said at last.

"*Sì, certo.*"

"Wait, then. Don't move."

Legs wet, his ragged shoes soaked, the awning dripping behind him and a line of cold nervousness running up and down his spine, Armando watched the man disappear into the house. He thought of running, but he was too proud to run, his stomach hurt from hunger, and two lire would buy him and his friends enough food to fill them up for a day or more.

When the man returned, he was holding a parcel the size of a loaf of bread. It was wrapped in brown paper and tied with yarn. "You know the Spagnoli neighborhood?"

"*Sì.*"

"Take this there. Vico Politi number eighteen. Knock twice on the door. A woman will answer. Tall. Red hair. Give her the package and leave, *chiaro?*"

"*Sì*, very clear. What is it, food?"

The man stared hard at him for a moment, and then a small, mean smile lifted the corners of his lips. "You sure you want to know?"

Armando nodded, suddenly afraid again.

"Three pistols. For killing Nazis. And if you steal them instead of making the delivery, I'll find you and break both your legs. Clear?"

"*Sì, sì.*"

The man gave Armando the package, then reached into his pocket and handed over two one-lira coins, beautiful pieces of metal, big bird on one side, some kind of prince or king with a curved nose on the other. "You remember the address?"

"Vico Politi. Number eighteen."

"Good. Now go. And never come to this house again. If I have more work, I'll find you. *Vai!* Go!"

Armando didn't move. His legs were shaking from the cold and something else, but a string of steely notes was sounding in his brain, a song, a street kid's anthem. "You know *my* name," he heard himself say in a steady voice. "But I don't know *yours*."

For a few seconds, he thought he'd ruined everything. The wide man was looking down at him, still as a closed garage door, not happy. The tiny smile was gone. "Zozo," he said at last, very quietly and slowly, as if it were an incantation. "Zozo Forni. Now go before I break you in half."

Two

A cloud of foreboding hovered around Colonel Walter Scholl as he climbed the steps of the German army headquarters in the south of Rome. He adjusted the monocle on his left eye, something he wore only for important occasions. The office to which he'd been summoned— to meet with none other than Field Marshal Albert Kesselring, commanding officer of all German forces in Italy—meant a climb of five stories, the ascent made on wide marble steps slightly worn at their centers. He was in good condition; the climb was no problem. The problem was the summons itself, coming as it did only four weeks after a reprimand for "personal behavior unbecoming an officer of the Reich." That reprimand had been issued not by Kesselring but by a jealous major general in Rieti, where he'd recently been stationed, and it was a stain—shameful but small—on what had otherwise been an exemplary military career. Straightening the jacket of his uniform as he went, Scholl wondered whether this meeting would be disciplinary in nature or something else. For a long time now, since his triumphant return from the Norwegian campaign in late 1940 (he was wounded in the battle for Narvik), he'd been anticipating a promotion. Perhaps the day had finally arrived.

He reached the top of the staircase, brushed a tiny crumb of bread from his left sleeve, presented himself at the desk in the outer room, and did his best to conquer a small facial twitch, a tic, that had afflicted him of late. Kesselring had been awarded the Knight's Cross of the Iron Cross with Oak Leaves, Swords and Diamonds! A giant among men and a personal favorite of the Führer. The annoying tic—how Scholl despised it—was acceptable, then, understandable. Anyone would be nervous before meeting such a man.

Kesselring summoned him with a single word. *"Eintreten."* Scholl stepped into a high-ceilinged office with elegant white molding, tall curtained windows, an enormous desk. He stood before the desk and saluted. Kesselring sat there, a handsome man, wide lips, alert eyes, a sense of dignity about him. Scholl had never seen the field marshal without his hat and was surprised to realize that Kesselring was balding on top. Still, a good-looking man, Luftwaffe veteran of the first war, now with the weight of an entire occupied nation on his shoulders. The field marshal gestured with one hand to a chair, red-upholstered, that would have been more at home in the parlor of a Viennese socialite than the office of a commander. "At ease, Colonel. Sit."

Scholl sat. Spine straight, monocle in place, eye contact steady. The tic had temporarily left him in peace.

"We have a situation," Kesselring began.

Scholl swallowed, perhaps too obviously, tried to maintain his composure. If the Rieti fiasco was being referred to as "a situation," he was in trouble. Assignment to the Russian front wasn't out of the question, and, from what he'd heard, since the surrender at Stalingrad in February, things hadn't been going well on the steppes.

After straightening the papers on his desk in an absentminded way, Kesselring looked up and said, "Do you know Naples at all?"

"Only by reputation, sir. After Narvik, I've been stationed in Rieti."

"Quiet there?"

"Fairly quiet, Herr Field Marshal. Some bombing."

Kesselring flexed his cheek muscles as if irritated and ran his eyes across Scholl's face, the medals on his chest, the placement of his hands on the chair arms. "Naples will soon fall into enemy hands."

"But how can that be?" Scholl let out. A huge error. Kesselring was already smirking. He'd taken it personally: a major city under his control was being lost to the Allies. Scholl bit down hard on the insides of his mouth.

"It simply is. To complicate matters, the citizens are . . . *unruhig*. Restless. You've never been?"

Scholl shook his head, afraid to speak another word.

"A dirty hovel. Ragged. Poor. Lawless. The Allies have been bombing it steadily for three years, and now, soon enough, they'll inherit it. They're welcome to the place, though the port is of some value."

It wasn't a personal discussion, then, had nothing to do with the reprimand. Despite his foolish remark, Scholl felt a wave of ease—almost confidence—move through him.

Kesselring blinked once, slowly. "We need a qualified officer to go there and subdue the city, collect the Jews according to Himmler's plan, and maintain order until the time comes for our troops to move north to new positions. Your name was suggested to me as a man who could be firm enough with the Italians to take on such an assignment."

Scholl allowed himself a single nod. A promotion, then. A new opportunity.

"I've assigned you an aide who's been there for some weeks, Captain Nitzermann. And a driver from our fleet here, also somewhat familiar with the place. Flying into the city has become complicated, so he'll drive you down there without delay. This afternoon. Two hundred kilometers. Do whatever you have to do in order to maintain a degree of subservience." Kesselring closed his eyes for several seconds, tiredly, Scholl thought, then opened them. "It may prove necessary to destroy the city entirely before you leave it. Willing?"

"Of course, Herr Field Marshal."

"Go then." Kesselring looked down and ran his eyes over the papers between his hands. "Lieutenant . . . Renzik is the driver. He'll meet you at the front door with a car and accompany you as your assistant. Pack quickly and go. The territory south of Rome is safely in our hands, so you should encounter no trouble. Questions?"

"None, sir."

"Go then. If difficulties arise, use your own initiative."

Scholl had to restrain himself from offering thanks. He waited a moment to be certain the interview was finished, then stood and saluted with a "Heil Hitler!" He turned sharply on his heel, marched through the outer office, and trotted down the five flights.

A promotion. In charge of an entire city! *"Use your own initiative,"* the field marshal had said. *"Maintain subservience."*

So much for the whims of jealous major generals. So much for a transfer to the Russian front.

Three

Despite the Allied bombing raids of the past three years, and now the dramatically increased German military presence in Naples, Rita Rossamadre had kept to her practice of making the long trip to the Monastero di Genovese once a week in order to confess her sins. Her half brother, Marco, had been a monk there nineteen years—from the day of his twenty-third birthday—and since women were not allowed inside the monastery proper, and since Marco wasn't allowed to leave the grounds, he performed the sacramental rite of absolution in a small stone shed against the outer wall of the enclosure, a place where the hired workmen kept their tools and, in better times, had enjoyed their lunches. This weekly arrangement—her brother stepping outside the walls to meet with a woman—had been going on for the better part of a decade, and it seemed to Rita perfectly in keeping with the Neapolitan habit of acknowledging rules without quite obeying them. In the old days, when there had been gasoline, men parked their cars, trucks, and motorcycles exactly where they wanted to—sometimes under **No Parking** signs—and women bought half their goods on the black market; people would take communion on Sunday morning and sleep with a mistress or a married man the same afternoon. Sometimes they paid their taxes; often they did not. It had always seemed to her that the city was filled with the best and worst of humanity, and that, no matter how much suffering it endured, Naples retained a sense of humor, a stylish independence, and, among the true Neapolitans, a reflexive generosity that showed itself in every interaction. Their Jesus was a kind, winking savior. Why would He mind if one of His monks left the enclosure for half an hour every week to give his sister spiritual comfort?

In order to reach the monastery, Rita had to walk one kilometer from her building in the Quartieri Spagnoli to the port, catch the A-622 bus to Ercolano—a half-hour ride south—and then make the difficult climb up the monastery access road, with the dark bulk of Vesuvius rising in front of her. Still, as complicated as the trip had become in wartime, it was the high point of her week, and all of it—the walk to the port and back, the two bus rides, the time with her brother—felt like spiritual nourishment.

On that day, the Spagnoli was unusually quiet. The terror of the planes and sirens had been absent from their lives for more than two weeks now, though no one knew for certain why the bombers had disappeared or when they might return. At about the same time the bombings stopped, news reached them that something had happened to Mussolini, and that the king and the head of the military, General Badoglio, had offered the Allies an armistice. Then that Italy had switched sides and would be fighting with the Americans! For one day, everyone thought the war was over—everyone, even the Germans. There were celebrations, Italians dancing in the street, even a few German soldiers joining them.

That brotherhood had lasted only a matter of hours before Hitler gave his men the terrible message: they had to fight. In the following days, he'd sent more and more of his army into Italy, because half the Italian soldiers had simply taken off their uniforms and come home. First they'd fought the Allies, now they were fighting *with* the Allies; what was the point? The bombs had stopped falling: that was the good thing. But the Germans had taken over the city, and no one besides the most devoted Italian Fascists thought that was something to celebrate.

As always, however, Rita went along her route without fear, protected by Saint Agata and by a mysterious feminine strength—a power, almost a magic—that had lived inside her for decades.

On this humid September day, the buses were running, the 622 almost on time—a miracle—and there were several empty seats, all near windows. In peacetime, in warm weather like this, window seats were prizes; now, the opposite. Passengers—mostly women heading out to the countryside to cut dandelions and hunt for mushrooms—huddled close to the middle aisle in case there was an explosion. Rita said a prayer to San Cristoforo, patron saint of travel, and took an empty seat by a rear window, her small purse held on her lap with both hands.

The bus lurched off. She considered her sins.

Except for one part of her life, it seemed to her, she was basically sinless. She believed in God without question, prayed daily to the Virgin Mother and to San Rocco, Santa Agata, San Gennaro, and San Cristoforo. She had money and some food and shared generously with poorer, hungrier neighbors and any child she happened to find on the streets, especially her little friend Armando. Never in her life had she intentionally hurt another soul, and before the war, she'd even made a habit of feeding the Spagnoli's dogs, cats, and pigeons.

Her one sin—and she sometimes wondered if *sin* was the right word—came from the way she'd made her living for twenty-two of her thirty-eight years, first as a teenage orphan who'd been violated in the most horrible way, and then as a single, childless woman: she allowed men to share her bed in exchange for gifts of various kinds. It had made her, by the standards of her poor neighborhood, quite well off. But even in the depths of her sin, as she'd often said to her brother, she endeavored to keep one hand clasped around the ankle of the Blessed Mother. She refused to sleep with married men. And though she'd been asked a thousand times and offered tempting sums, she refused to venture into what she thought of as the more perverse sexual practices. This personal code limited her clientele, but she had always wanted it limited. One man, sometimes two, was enough. For years now, since before the war, Aldo Pastone and the elderly Avvocato Cilento were her only sources of support. These days, there was no shortage of girls and women in Naples who sold their love—for money, to keep their children from starving, to curry favor with the German overlords or the Fascist secret police, Mussolini's OVRA. Rita didn't judge them. But neither did she consider herself one of them.

She would, for the hundredth time, discuss this complicated moral situation with her half brother and listen to his advice.

That morning, there were puddles in the gutters—it had rained the night before, thunder booming and echoing in the Spagnoli's narrow streets—and in places, the stone pavement was steaming in the sun. Through the bus window, she saw a pair of starving dogs drinking from one of the larger puddles. She turned her head to watch them, praying for them, and just then saw a German jeep go racing along Via Vespucci in the opposite direction, crashing through a puddle, soaking the dogs and sending them scrambling away. The jeep was headed toward the train station, she guessed, because there were two soldiers in front and a woman about her own age squeezed between them. All over the city, the Nazis were arresting Jews, taking them to the station, carting them off. Rita sent her prayers in the direction of the terrified woman and watched until the jeep was out of sight.

Four

Aldo Pastone saw it this way: when he'd been a boy, the Camorra had controlled Naples, killing just enough people to make everyone fear them, and taking more than their share of the proceeds of others' work.

When he'd been a young man, Mussolini and the Fascists had controlled Naples, killing just enough people to make everyone fear them, and taking more than their share of the proceeds of others' work.

Now he was in the middle of life—forty-three next week—and, thanks to the cowardice of the Italian Fascist generals and the foolishness of Il Duce, the German military had taken control of the city. They killed more people than they had to, and took too much pleasure in it. And they were greedier even than the *Camorristi* and the *Fascisti*, leaving no room for him and others like him to make a living.

He himself had never been, nor ever wanted to be, a member of the Camorra—though he had friends and business associates who were.

He himself had never been, nor ever wanted to be, a Fascist—though he knew a number of people who were.

And he himself never wanted to see another German uniform for as long as he lived.

Early in the morning on this warm September day—the air still humid from the previous night's rain—Aldo found himself sitting on the concrete wall at the Port of Naples, or what remained of the port after three years of British and American bombing raids: broken piers, a pocked street, the rubble of ruined storage sheds, and the rusting hulls of sunken ships. Hanging from the roof of a bombed-out building across the way was the chassis of a small car, thrown there, thirty meters up, by one of the thousands of explosions that had torn the city to pieces. He was hungry, nothing unusual there. To stanch the hunger, he was smoking the last of a cigarette—stolen, naturally—while watching for his daughter to appear at the corner near the hotel. Grand Hotel Santa Lucia, it was called, in honor of both the street that ran along its northern edge and the neighborhood behind it. But, in secret, Aldo liked to pretend it had been named for his only child, Lucia.

The Santa Lucia hotel was undamaged but closed. One block away, a sister hotel, the elegant Vesuvio, had months ago been reduced to rubble.

With his back to the water, Aldo could run his eyes over part of his enormous city. Its hills were carpeted with apartment buildings, old *palazzi* standing shoulder to shoulder, four and five and six stories of stucco walls, flat roofs, tall, narrow windows, and balconies protected by wrought-iron railings and supported by curved concrete gargoyles. He guessed that almost half the city's structures had been damaged or demolished in the raids, tens of thousands of Neapolitans killed. Here and there, the pointed tops of surviving churches showed above the roofs, and here and there, he could see gaps where the Allied bombs had obliterated an entire residential block. Since the recent armistice— a surprise to almost everyone: Italy was now no longer aligned with Nazi Germany—the bombing raids had abruptly ceased. He blamed the Allies for the destruction, and didn't blame them. Like most inhabitants of the city, he wanted the Americans to make an assault on Naples, and didn't want it. There would be more bloodshed, more ruin. But maybe there would be food again, and freedom, and an end to the reprisal killings—executions in cold blood, ten or twenty or a hundred Italians for every German soldier's death. The Nazis were more ruthless even than the Camorra. Their slaughtering of the innocent was worse even than the Allied bombs. Once every few days, it seemed now, the occupiers would find some reason to line up a group of men, women, and children, cut them to bloody shreds with machine-gun fire, and leave their corpses lying in hideous poses on the street. Lucia's boyfriend's mother and father had been among the recent victims. She'd told Aldo that she'd helped Giuseppe wrap and bury the bodies. It had left a mark on her. No father could fail to see it.

It occurred to him, as he waited for Lucia to appear, that in his time on earth, he'd spent exactly one night outside this city. He and Vittoria, Lucia's late mother, had gone to Caserta for a night of love. One night, most likely the night on which their only child had been conceived. The memory, a rare tender place in his thoughts, didn't fit the atmosphere of war, so he turned his mind away from it.

There was the clank and whir of a truck engine changing gears. He saw a German lorry, its bed crowded with shackled Italian men—Jews, perhaps—speed through the square and head off toward the Garibaldi station.

By reflex, he slid sideways so he was half-hidden behind a pile of stones and what was left of the fishermen's display boxes. Once General Badoglio and the king had announced the armistice—a little over two weeks ago—Hitler realized that most Italians would no longer fight for the German cause, so, in addition to the Jewish families, Christian men were being rounded up and shipped north to work for the mustachioed maniac, to build his tanks and airplanes, to die in his cold land. Another reason to wish for the Allies to make their assault as quickly as possible.

Aldo drew the last bit of pleasure from the cigarette and flicked it over his shoulder into the sea. He saw a skinny little street boy trotting along on the opposite sidewalk with a wrapped package under one arm. If it was food, he'd be chased and beaten for it.

Just as the boy disappeared around the corner, Aldo saw Lucia appear there, thinner than she'd been in the days when people ate more

14

than once or twice in twenty-four hours, but still as beautiful as her mother had been. Long legs, long black hair, a finely chiseled face, and a certain joyfulness to her walk, even now. He had a few small gifts for her, and his generosity (he avoided the word *love*) gave him a momentary feeling of peace. For two days, if they survived two more days, his daughter would have enough to eat.

But the peace was short-lived: behind Lucia, he saw another figure come into view, a German officer. Mostly hidden by the pile of rubble, Aldo watched with a deadly calm, already committing the man to memory—narrow shoulders, long, thin arms with a sharp bend at the elbows, and an awkward gait, the gait of a goat whose leg had been broken and hadn't properly healed. Aldo couldn't hear clearly from this distance, but the man must have called to Lucia, because she stopped, paused, turned to face him. The officer limped up and stood too close, spoke to her with his chin lifted in a gesture of superiority, almost of ownership, and with a touch of craziness to it, also. Lucia angrily shook her head, hair swinging. With one of his thin arms, the officer reached out, pinched the material at the front of her long skirt, and lifted it so that her calves showed, then her knees.

Lucia—fearless girl—slapped at the German's hand to make him let go. She stepped back, spoke words Aldo couldn't make out, then turned and hurried away—not toward her father, but around the corner of the hotel and up along the street that bore her name.

Aldo put his feet to the sidewalk, hands on the wall, ready to stand. The knife in his jacket pocket seemed to have a pulse. The German officer shouted something—*"Ricordami!"* was the only word Aldo heard. *Remember me!*

Lucia went half a block, then turned purposefully into a courtyard. She didn't live there, but the German wouldn't know that, wouldn't know who might be waiting for her: a father with a knife, a trio of fearless street punks, a Camorra boyfriend with brass knuckles and murderous friends. They were being harassed now, the Nazi occupiers: yelled at in shops, stolen from, even, people said, shot at with stolen guns—rumors were everywhere. The officer watched Lucia disappear through the archway, waited a moment as if deciding whether or not to follow, then limped off in the direction from which he'd come.

"You will live, then," Aldo muttered to himself, watching the man turn the corner and disappear. *You will live another day.*

Five

Lucia waited in the courtyard, mostly hidden behind a stone column, watching for the German to appear. On the chipped stucco of the column, just at eye level, the remains of a propaganda poster fluttered in a breath of sea air: Fascist Youth—a boy and a girl working the fields, their eyes alight with joy and confidence. The lower half of their faces had been torn away, a small Neapolitan rebellion. Despite two decades of Fascist songs, school indoctrination, propaganda on the radio, and posters like this everywhere they looked, the people of her city still mostly resisted the Fascist impulse.

Above her, two pigeons cooed on a concrete ledge. A rat scuttled across the courtyard tiles, so close that she could hear the *tick tick tick* of its nails. Paper flaps of the torn poster settled back against the stone, her heart leaped and slammed against her ribs, but, for several minutes, no man in uniform walked in through the arched entranceway.

Just as her heartbeat was settling, Lucia heard the sound of footsteps and shifted sideways, deeper into the shadows, pressing her back against the column. The footsteps moved closer. Shoes, it sounded like, not military boots. She risked a peek around the edge of the column and saw a woman of late middle age with her hair wrapped in a kerchief. She was carrying a cloth bag in one hand, and her long skirt was wet as far up as the knees. A small forest of greens burst out of the top of the bag as if growing there. *Dente di leone.* Dandelions. In normal times, in the days before the war, before the bombings, before the Germans came in such numbers, those greens would have been a pleasantly bitter addition to the evening salad; now, fetched from the city's weedy outskirts, boiled and served without bread, salt, or olive oil, they'd make one meal for a whole family.

When Lucia stepped out from behind the column, the woman turned away, her body curling over the bag.

We've become like animals, Lucia thought, protecting our food. She tried to make herself as unthreatening as possible, approached the woman slowly, asked in a soft voice, "Did you see a German soldier there, on the sidewalk?"

The woman narrowed her eyes, squeezed the middle of her lips upward in an expression of disdain, shook her head angrily. By the time she stepped through the archway onto the sidewalk—all clear—Lucia realized that the woman had thought she was asking about a German lover.

Standing there, looking across the boulevard at the seawall, she needed a few seconds before she spotted her father. He was half sitting, half leaning on the wall, still as the mound of stone in front of him, mostly hidden behind it and the ruined wooden stalls where fishermen had sold their catch in the days when this part of the port was alive with commerce. She remembered the smells, the cries of *Polpo! Polpo! Octopus, octopus!* Housewives planning the evening meal, studying the sea life packed in ice: glistening sardines, mackerel, swordfish, squid, bream, sometimes a whole magnificent tuna, the sight of which had always made her inexplicably sad, as if a great creature had been subdued and murdered by lesser souls. Now the stalls and display boxes stood in a broken line, empty and unattended, the street cratered months before by an errant bomb, the sidewalks silent.

Short and powerfully built, dark-eyed, dark-haired, wearing, even in the September warmth, the tattered black leather jacket that signaled his alliances, her father was watching her intently. He did not so much as raise a hand in greeting. There seemed to be no feeling in his face. Had she not wanted so badly, in a nation of large families, to have one relative she could love, just one, Lucia might have walked away. But she crossed Via Partenope and went up to him. He offered a nod, no kiss, the intense gaze.

"Walk with me," he said, standing, and they started off, north, along the port, past the windowless buildings there, the piles of concrete and glass and iron-reinforcing rods, the droppings of a horse.

"How are you, Father?" she asked, when he'd led her back across the oceanside avenue and down a narrow alley. "Still coughing?"

He lit a cigarette, blew out the smoke, said, *"Sono perfetto"*—*I'm perfect*—the words soaked in irony, the cigarette a boast in these hard times. "You?"

"I'm worried Giuseppe will be taken to the work camps. More and more men are being picked up."

A grunt. Her father turned away from her and spat on the stones. She thought she saw the stain of blood in his mucus.

"And there's someone new coming," she said, "a new Nazi. A colonel. I saw it on the teletype before I left work last night. Rosalia, who hears every rumor in the city, says he's supposed to be truly evil."

Her father sucked on the cigarette. "You should spy for the Allies. You work in the right place for it."

She said nothing. Above them on small balconies, a few shirts and pieces of underwear hung drying, shifting back and forth in the breeze like the flags of besieged nations. No potted flowers there now, no women exchanging gossip, no caged canaries singing in the sun. A small band of barefoot *scugnizzi* sprinted past them up the street, the urchins' laughter echoing against the facades of the houses.

"Giuseppe's making a map," Lucia went on, very quietly, trying, for the twentieth time, to change her father's opinion of the man she loved, to describe his courage, his determination, his goodness, his grief over the recent murder of both parents. "It shows every district.

German headquarters, Italian arms warehouses, the places the Nazis sleep. There's a book where he works, in the Archives. It shows the layout of the rooms and offices, the entrances, the stairways. When he's not doing that, he walks the whole city for hours and hours, making mental notes about the number of soldiers he sees in various locations, how many are guarding the arms depots, and so on. He thinks it might help the Allies when they come, if he can find a way to get them the information. If he's caught, the Nazis will kill him."

"If he's caught," her father said after another few steps, "he'll *wish* for them to kill him."

When they reached the door of the basement apartment where he now lived, a *basso* on Via Serapide, her father put a hand on her arm, a rare touch, a signal to wait, a sign that she should not dare to step into his territory. He went down a single step, unlocked and shoved open the squealing metal door, and disappeared. When he came back to her, he was holding a package wrapped in butcher's paper and tied in string. "Take it," he said, handing it over. "In a week, come back. The port. Same time."

And then he was hurrying away from her toward a steep set of neighborhood stairs, as if the thought of an embrace, a kiss, even a single moment of tenderness, terrified him more than any Nazi colonel. His walk—brisk, bowlegged, arms swinging—shouted, *Leave me alone!*

Lucia stood there, watching him until he was out of sight, then she walked for half an hour up Via Toledo, toward the center of Naples, crossed Piazza Dante, and, instead of going straight to work, went and sat in a back part of the Duomo for a few minutes. There was liturgical singing in one of the side altars and, in front of her, beneath the spectacular marble sculpture of Mary surrounded by angels, an old priest saying Mass to fifteen people, his words echoing against the high stone ceiling like the murmuring of the dead. She thought of the arguments she and her father had endured—why did she have such a temper?!—all the times she'd been ashamed of him for the way he earned his money . . . even when that money was paying for her food, her schooling, her clothes. She'd confessed it more than once, the ingratitude, the adolescent feistiness. She had prayed, scores of times, for him to suddenly turn into the warm father of her imagination. When the war came, she'd hoped it might change him, soften him. Now she knew how foolish that was: war softened no one.

After a time—no one else in the rear pews—she loosened the string of the package and lifted the paper to either side. Six small dusty potatoes in a cardboard box, four one-lira notes, a very small bar of soap, and two condoms—American, it seemed—in their silvery packets. The condoms felt sinful there, in church, and brought tears to her eyes. On the one hand, it was a sweet gift, thoughtful, respectful, even tender. Giuseppe would be glad. On the other, the message seemed to be: *Don't do what I did. Don't bring into this world a child you do not want.*

Six

Having fed his uncle from their tiny supply of food, and having helped him downstairs so he could sit in the sun of the Naples morning, Giuseppe DiPietra started off on foot toward the National Archives. These days, he wasn't required to be there at any specific time; no one checked on his comings and goings. His boss, Riccardo Filangieri, had moved the most precious historical documents to a villa twenty-five kilometers from the city center in order to protect them from the bombing raids, and he now spent all his workdays there. Giuseppe wasn't doing his actual job in any case, and Filangieri probably knew that.

As he often did now on this morning walk, Giuseppe was thinking of his mother and father, murdered in cold blood along with twenty of their neighbors. For hours at a time now, he couldn't get the images out of his mind—bodies strewn like mutilated rag dolls across the steps of the Ministry of Health, faces twisted in the terror and agony of death, the fingers of his mother's left hand clutching the cloth at her husband's shoulder, the pools of bright-red blood, edges drying in the sun. Night and day the images haunted him, and they fed a slow-burning fire of hatred. It was everything he could do not to let the fire burst into a roaring blaze and consume him, not to attack every Nazi soldier he saw and beat them to a bloody pulp.

His street, Via Telesino, was choked with mountains of rubble, as if a sloppy Neapolitan stonemason had piled truckloads of material there and was preparing, next day, to rebuild his ravaged city. Although the bombs of the most recent raids had fallen several kilometers to the east—in Capodichino, near the airport, he guessed—the air even here tasted of dust and smelled of smoke. From inside one of the buildings, he could hear a child wailing, not the usual frustrated cry, but a wartime wailing, filled with unbearable anguish and confusion, not really childlike at all. For almost three years, from November of 1940 until two weeks ago, the Allies had targeted Naples with their raids. First the British at night, then the Americans during the day. Not only military installations—the port, the airfields, the armories—but shops, theaters, residential neighborhoods. Six-hundred-year-old churches obliterated. Ordinary people strafed on the sidewalk. And then, suddenly, the bombings had stopped, and there was no explanation until the secret armistice was made public, five days after it had been signed.

Everyone knew the Allies had landed troops on Sicily, everyone knew they were fighting their way up the peninsula, everyone knew the Nazi choke hold on Italy was loosening. But no one could be sure it wouldn't tighten again, or how much suffering people would have to endure before liberation came . . . if it came at all.

Now that Mussolini had been deposed, and King Vittorio Emanuele III had signed an armistice with the Allies, the Germans, long a presence in Axis Italy, had taken over more and more of what had once been called "law enforcement duties," and turned from barely tolerated occupiers to vicious fiends. Bad as the Fascists had been, they were nothing compared to these new rulers. Now there were mass public executions, Gestapo torture cells, Jews and former Italian military men being sent north to the work camps. And all that on top of terrible hunger, cases of typhus and malaria, and wartime shortages of everything from salt to soap.

It seemed to Giuseppe that he could hear the death rattle of the Neapolitans' patience. Of late, there had been several small acts of rebellion in the poorer neighborhoods—Nazi soldiers attacked, military

23

vehicles damaged—and one protest at the university that the Germans had disrupted by using tanks and machine guns. Five killed. Five more killed! Each death made the wound of his parents' murders bleed all over again. But he could sense something in the air, almost as if there were about to be an eruption of Vesuvius, the temperamental mountain that hovered over all of them like a fierce god. A pressure, a hot fury, he could sense it. He wondered where it would lead.

Officially, his work was to curate the documents in the National Archives, to aid scholars in their research. He'd been there almost six years, and some months a small salary still trickled down to him through the labyrinthine corridors of Italian bureaucracy. Unofficially, secretly, since two days after the murder of his parents, he'd been occupied with a different kind of work. If the pair of German officers walking past him now in the other direction, one of them arcing a huge load of spittle onto a pyramid of stone and dust, had any idea of that, he'd be taken into custody within the minute.

But no, they strode past with barely a glance—high black boots, black belts, black-lidded gray hats, and evil, narrowed eyes that showed, it seemed to Giuseppe, both the old superiority and a new wariness.

A few blocks away, in the direction of Piazza Dante, Giuseppe heard two quick rattles of what sounded like machine-gun fire. A faulty engine, it might have been. Or another killing.

At the corner of Via Materdei, he came upon a man sitting on the sidewalk with his back against the wall of a building that no longer had any glass in its windows. The man's left leg, blown off below the knee, was stretched out in front of him, the stump wrapped in a blood-stained scrap of undershirt. Gaunt, unwashed, obviously starving, the man raised a hand without even looking up.

Giuseppe reached into his pocket. One coin there. He leaned down and without a word handed it over.

Seven

Colonel Scholl found it hard to believe that flying into Naples had been rendered impossible. For most of the past year, after being transferred from Rieti, he'd been stationed at Gestapo headquarters in Rome, filing reports, taking part in interrogations, supervising an antiaircraft battalion, dying of boredom. There had been some raids on that city, true, but the main airport, Roma Pratica, had consistently remained open, and the damage done by the supposedly brilliant English—and then American—pilots and navigators had been limited mainly to civilian targets, as if they didn't like the Italians, either, and preferred to fly the safer routes and kill the dark little men, women, and children, rather than risking German antiaircraft fire around the airport and important military installations.

After being wounded in Narvik (rifle bullet to the outside of his right thigh), he'd been brought back to Berlin to recover, then sent to Rieti in central Italy to oversee operations there: manage the antiaircraft squads and four companies of Italian soldiers, track down and execute the few partisans they could find, keep the local people cowed and obedient. Scholl had spent almost two full years in the landlocked industrial hub, and during that time, he'd developed a deep disdain for the Italians, a sentiment he made no effort to hide. Just the opposite, in fact: in Rieti, he'd found that, military men and civilians alike, the more roughly the Italians were treated, the better they behaved. Not that their performance ever rose to the level of any German or Austrian soldier he'd trained with. On Sicily, for instance, where the Allies had staged a mistake-ridden landing two months ago, reports filed by combatants there indicated that some Italian companies had surrendered en masse at the first glimpse of Allied forces. Simply dropped their arms and walked, singing songs, toward the beachheads. Singing songs! It was impossible to imagine any German warrior doing such a thing.

And then, of course, once Mussolini was deposed, the Italian king and his generals had (a) agreed to an armistice with the Allies, and (b) kept it secret for the better part of a week! *Armistice* was hardly the word. *Surrender* was more like it. *Surrender*, or, even better, *betrayal*.

Worst of all, it seemed that, especially since the betrayal, the Italian preference for indolence had infected some of the Reich's own forces. Immediately after his meeting with Field Marshal Kesselring, Scholl had requested a folder of informative briefs—everything he needed to know about the city of Naples. It took him fifteen minutes to pack his bag, but two full hours for the briefs to be delivered to his office—two hours! When they finally arrived, they contained reports of sporadic uprisings and small acts of resistance in Naples. *Resistance*—another fine word. Resistance to what? The very troops who had been defending them!

And what kind of resistance could there have been? Once the betrayal had been made public, half the Italian Army disappeared into the hills. Uniforms and equipment abandoned, whole companies dissolved into thin air. So who was resisting? The local pizza maker? The whorish women? The schoolgirls?

He tapped the tip of a finger on the top of his desk, pressed his teeth together. He'd seen bits of resistance in his Rieti posting and knew exactly how to quell them: one German dead meant a hundred Italians dead. Lined up in the street, shot like beasts. There was nothing complicated about it. He fit the folder into his bag and carried it out into the sticky Roman air.

As promised, Kesselring had given him a staff car, and also assigned him four armored vehicles and six motorcycles to make the trip to Naples, a distance of 226.2 kilometers, most of a day's ride. These vehicles weren't for his protection—the terrain separating the two cities was, as Kesselring had said, securely in German hands—but rather to demonstrate to the Neapolitans that a new overseer had arrived, a kind of local king to replace their half-size Emmanuel, who'd run away, south, after signing the surrender. Fled to Bari, fearing for his life. What kind of leader did such a thing?

Lieutenant Renzik was behind the wheel of the jeep. Young, nice-looking in a girlish way, sitting at attention. The plan was for them to travel in the jeep for most of the distance, then the convoy would stop, Scholl would get out, and enter the city in more impressive fashion.

Through the streets of Rome they went, passing one church after the next—how poorly these people had been protected by their Jesus!—and then onto the main road. Renzik kept silent, eyes straight ahead, both large hands gripping the wheel. Highway A1 ran alongside the sea for a time, with mountainous terrain to the left, and then slid inland along a flat plain with the mountains now to their right. Halfway to Naples, it occurred to Scholl—an unpleasant thought—that there might be another reason behind the new assignment. Instead of an honor, as he'd first assumed, perhaps it was a veiled punishment. During his time in Rieti, certain personal matters had come to light. A habit, a preference, an amusement he should long ago have abandoned. First, there had been the transfer to Rome, and now one farther south. So perhaps he'd been assigned to Naples, that much closer to the fighting, not because he was of particular value to the Führer's forces, but for exactly the opposite reason.

The thought upset him. Even in the midst of it, though, he couldn't keep from turning and looking at Renzik—young and healthy, a perfect specimen. Married, it seemed, judging by the ring. But who knew the inner workings of men, their dark precincts, their secret desires? War, with its constant proximity to death and long absences, was famous for straining marriage vows to the point of breaking. "Wife at home?" Scholl asked him.

Renzik turned his blue-green eyes from the road and nodded. Sadly, perhaps.

"Missing you?"

Another nod.

"Let's hope we can get home soon and the two of you will have a fine victory celebration! A week of doing nothing but wrestling in the sheets!"

A third nod. No spark of excitement there, as if the man—sleepy-eyed, soft-faced—had long ago given up the dream.

Scholl turned forward, the bad thoughts assailing him again. From two directions. A kind of body hunger on the one side, urgent, pressing, whispering. And guilt on the other, mixed with the sour taste of regret. He would banish them both, bring a strict discipline to his own behavior and to the people of Naples . . . and happily destroy the place, if the order came. The fate of an entire city—a million people—in his hands. He felt capable, optimistic, already making plans. The hungry ones were so easy to control.

Eight

Armando found the house without trouble—Vico Politi, number eighteen. He knocked twice on the door, and it opened immediately. A tall woman with red hair. He handed the package across the threshold; she took it in both hands, looked him up and down—from his ragged shoes to his matted hair—and closed the door in his face.

Feet still wet, stomach grumbling, he fingered the coins in his pocket and started down the sloping street toward Via Toledo. On the way, he passed one of the yellowish sheets of paper the police had pasted to walls everywhere in Naples:

RISPETTATE IL PANE:

ORGOGLIO DEL LAVORO,

POEMA DI SACRIFICIO

MUSSOLINI

If he hadn't been so painfully hungry, the words would have made him laugh out loud. *RESPECT BREAD! Pride of Work. Poem of Sacrifice.*

As if, he thought, anyone would *disrespect* bread these days. And as if half the people he knew could even read! He sent up a silent prayer of thanks to the orphanage nuns who'd taught him, and walked on, imagining food, feeling it in his mouth, tasting, chewing, swallowing.

He was supposed to meet his friends in front of the Duomo. He'd lead them up the street, halfway to Via Foria, where a café there was open most days and where the two lire would get them something delicious: stale crackers and perhaps a little cheese, a bag of roasted chestnuts, or whatever the café owner had been able to find on the black market or buy with his ration coupons. They'd slip into an alley and eat their food in safety, and his friends would ask where he'd gotten the money, and maybe he'd tell them and maybe he wouldn't. Zozo, the man's name was. He'd remember it.

Stomach swirling in anticipation of his first meal in twenty hours, Armando had crossed Toledo, the wide main street, and was hurrying along Via Capitelli when he heard shouting just around the next corner. Two men yelling. German words, rough, angry. And then the horrible sound of a woman screaming, *"No, no! Per favore, no!"* He felt a prickling of fear run along the skin of his arms, but the woman sounded like she needed help. The building at the corner to his left had been reduced to a shell of stone walls surrounding rubble, the doors and windows gone, sky for a roof. Hoping to cut the corner and get to the woman more quickly, Armando climbed through what had been a ground-floor window, made his way across a landscape of stone and dust, and was about to exit through an open doorway when he saw the backs of two German soldiers on the other side of the street. Funny helmets, gray uniforms, rifles. They were forcing three people to stand against what was left of another ruined building there. An old man, an old woman, a girl who looked to be five or six. The woman, the girl's *nonna*, Armando guessed, tried to grab the girl's hand and run, but one of the soldiers clubbed her over the head with his rifle. She was lying against the base of the wall and the man and little girl were bending over her, reaching down, when the second soldier opened fire. Armando flinched and slipped behind one side of the doorway. It was over in seconds. Two quick *at-at-at-at* bursts, the three bodies twitching, a thin river of blood running into the gutter, and the Germans were in their motorcar and gone.

Armando peered around the edge of the doorframe, frozen, breathing in gasps. He saw a weeping woman go up to the bodies and make the sign of the cross, and he started in that direction but then saw the ruined face of the little girl, and he turned and sprinted, blindly, as if he might outrun the awful sight, keep it from being etched into his memory. He'd seen dead bodies before; everybody had. He would come out of the air-raid shelters to find buildings on fire, people lying facedown in the street, horses cut in half by the explosions. But the girl's face had been turned into a mask of bloody flesh. He sprinted along the street but could not stop seeing it.

Nine

The climb from the bus stop in Ercolano to her brother's monastery was long and steep, a paved road at first and then gravel, but, accustomed to walking, Rita managed it without trouble. Once past the buildings of the town, there were only old pine trees to either side, small vineyards and orchards, a few large cactus plants lifting their spiny arms toward the sun. The air here was as fresh as it had been in peacetime, but she wondered what it must have been like for the monks to watch the bombs falling on Naples. They would have had a clear view, seen the Allied planes in formation, then the bombs tumbling, the explosions and smoke and fires. How horrible that must have been for men of prayer and peace.

She could see the gray tops of the monastery buildings—the color of an old woman's hair—and the stone bell tower standing proudly against the enormous dark-green pyramid of Vesuvius behind it. It sometimes seemed to her that the monastery's founders had built their sacred, walled-in village there as a statement, proof that they weren't afraid of the volcano, weren't afraid of death. Their focus was on the world to come.

That morning, she'd eaten one small, partially rotten apple, so she wasn't too hungry. A precious apple! Brought to her by Avvocato Cilento, once a powerful lawyer with a beautiful wife, now an old widower with no work. Cilento claimed to have been a faithful husband,

and she believed him. His body no longer permitted him the pleasure of making love, but he came to her once a week in spite of that, took off his clothes, and lay with her all night in bed, skin to skin. "I cannot live without the touch of a woman," he'd confessed to her once. In payment—irregular but generous—he brought portions of food or objects from his home: solid-brass candleholders, a small tapestry from his travels to Morocco, old coins, old stamps, china dishes and cups. He'd carry these objects through the streets in a worn alligator-skin carpetbag, little by little emptying the rooms of his glamorous two-story apartment in the Vomero. "When there is nothing left," he told her, "I shall stop visiting you."

But she'd never allow that.

On his most recent visit, he'd said something about helping a scientist friend interfere with the German radio communications, giving the man money and food to keep him healthy enough to perform his secret work. Rita wondered if it was true, or just an old man's boasting.

She turned sharply right, onto the narrow walled street—Via Luigi Palmieri—and saw the monastery buildings directly in front of her, one thin metal cross, a meter tall, standing up from the tallest roof. Her brother—a half brother, really (but what was the difference? God had placed them in the same womb!)—would be expecting her.

To the north, beyond the buildings, was a paved road used by delivery trucks, another way to get from here to Naples, but not one that was part of any bus route. On this side, the dirt road had become only a path paved in pebbles and weeds. She followed it almost as far as the wall of the enclosure, pushed through the metal door of a windowless shed there, and sat, as always, on a wooden crate. She took out her rosary beads, set her purse aside, and waited for her brother to appear.

She hadn't been there three minutes when she heard the tap of his sandals on dirt. Marco came through the door, carrying a worn leather satchel. They embraced without a word, and he sat on a crate opposite her. Behind him, workman's tools—hoe, scythe, shovel—hung neatly from a row of rusty spikes. Marco's face was drawn, sun-darkened, hair clipped very short, green eyes alert. Around him floated a sense of peace.

First the business of confession—her same sins, his same absolution. Then, from the satchel, he brought out their simple lunch: a thin bread made from chickpea flour, four roasted chestnuts from the monks' own trees, and one piece, barely larger than a child's fist, of mozzarella—made from the milk of water buffalos that lived in the marshland to the south. They ate slowly and with reverence, mouthful by mouthful, and drank from a single wine bottle filled with tepid water. In these terrible times, all of it was luxury. For centuries, the monks had been largely self-sufficient: living off their animals, their trees, their own gardens. Before the war, Rita had pitied them their meager life. Now, that life seemed like it belonged to a side room of Paradise. So far, at least, the Germans had left the monastery alone, and the Allied bombs had not fallen here.

"Walking here today, I was thinking," she said, "that my life of sin has given me a deep understanding of men."

"Your 'life of sin' has more love and goodness in it, Rita, than the lives of a hundred so-called sinless women."

She nodded, indulging him, and reached out for the bottle and drank, then went on. "When I think of men, I think of things with hard shells—chestnuts, clams, eggs. But always the inside is soft. Men have their strength, their titles—*capitano, avvocato*—"

"King, *duce.*"

"*Sì, sì*, exactly. Their fighting, their wars. But behind that is the soft boy, which they hide."

"But not from you?"

"Not in my bed, no. Not always."

"And women?"

"Women can be hard, too—like pasta, like grains of rice—but life cooks us, love cooks us, and we go soft. When you see a mother loving her child, there is always a softness."

She watched her brother turn his eyes to one side, afraid perhaps to show pity for his childless half sister. She wondered if he missed a woman's love (one of the other monks, made bitter by years of abstinence, had accused Marco of meeting her for sex! As if he would break his vows! As if he would sleep with his own flesh and blood!). She thought of what Avvocato Cilento had said about the need for a woman's touch, and wondered if these weekly meetings weren't only for *her* benefit.

Love, she was thinking. *Love, men, their hard disguises.* She drank from the bottle and said, "Aldo, the other man who—"

"I know, Rita. You've told me about him many times."

She nodded, still half-ashamed. "Aldo speaks of his daughter the way you speak of Christ, the way I think of Mary and Santa Agata. But when I see him on the street, he has around him a wall like yours here." She gestured out the door. "Lucia is her name, he says. A beautiful girl, he says. I hope one day to meet her."

"He's had a troubled life."

Rita nodded. "A brutal life. A life hard enough to build a crust around any soul."

From the monastery church, the first bells sounded, calling the monks to prayer. Her thirty minutes with her brother were over for another week. He stood, the brown robe swirling at his ankles like a woman's dress.

Rita saw one surprising wrinkle of concern form on Marco's unwrinkled face, then watched it pass away. He said, "I have a secret for you to hold. And something to ask you."

"I hold so many, my brother. Ask me anything."

Marco paused, the green eyes fixed on her intently, one cloud showing in the peaceful sky behind them. "We have someone new with us now, a soldier, an American, a brave man. A few nights ago, he slipped through the German lines and found us. We are keeping him safe. He said that the Allies are preparing to attack the city, and asked if we have information about the situation in Napoli. Where the Germans are, what armaments they have, where are the headquarters. Do you know?"

"I can find out," Rita said. It seemed to her that she'd seen this moment in a dream or a vision. Strange as it was, coming from a man of prayer, she'd somehow expected it. "I can find out and come here next week and tell you."

Her brother almost smiled. "Sooner, if you can," he said. "If you don't mind doing this, my sister. But please tell no one."

Marco made the sign of the cross over her and then, outside, where anyone with evil thoughts could see, held her in a long embrace.

Ten

With great care, Giuseppe spread the handmade map across his desk in the Archives' basement level and spent all morning painstakingly drawing in more of the streets and landmarks of the Vomero neighborhood—Via Ribera, Via Vincenzo Gemito, the Stadio Arturo Collana. Set up on a hill as it was, the Vomero seemed to him the most poorly guarded of all the city's neighborhoods, at least as far as the Italian armories were concerned. According to his on-foot research and things Lucia had told him, some of those depots were just converted schools or warehouses, not surrounded by barbed-wire-topped walls, guarded by only two or three German soldiers now that so many Italian military men had been called away to foreign battles and so many others had deserted. As Giuseppe worked, the map pressed flat by his left hand, he thought about his boss, the superintendent of the Archives, Riccardo Filangieri. Days after Italy's entrance into the war, Filangieri had had the foresight to move the most precious materials out of this building. Nearly nine hundred cases of documents and books—Giuseppe knew, because he'd spent four days loading them onto trucks and driving them the twenty-five kilometers to San Paolo Bel Sito—were housed now just outside the city proper, in the Montesano Villa, a beautiful box of a building surrounded by chestnut and eucalyptus trees. Foresight, yes, but were the irreplaceable treasures truly safe there? The bombs hadn't damaged the villa, but if the Nazis found out about the documents, wouldn't they burn the building to the ground, as Filangieri had told him they'd burned libraries all across Europe? Giuseppe shook his head at the thought and tried to concentrate on his work, but a film of disgust remained. Why burn a library or an archive, hardly threatening from a military standpoint, unless you were intent on eliminating all traces of goodness and knowledge in the world, creating a new history of blood and hatred? Why would any human being do such a thing, not to mention kill unarmed civilians in cold blood?

He'd just drawn and marked the schoolhouse where he'd seen the Nazi guards when he heard what sounded like boots on the stone stairs. He had time only to roll up the map and toss it onto the floor at his feet, push his glasses back against the bridge of his nose, then step away toward the stacks. He was looking down a narrow row formed by shelves of bound documents. A German officer appeared there, straight in front of him, backlit by a shaft of sun in the stairwell. Just as the officer started toward him—his gait awkward, as if one hip were locked and the other moving freely—Giuseppe saw Lucia appear there, too, halfway up the flight of steps, a silent apparition. She was holding her shoes, one in each hand, so as not to make any sound. She'd been coming to warn him and had arrived a few seconds too late.

The officer was in front of him. Three green bars with one set of green oak leaves, two stars on the epaulettes. A captain, Giuseppe realized. Part of his work now, part of the assignment he'd given himself, was to know the ranks. *"Che fai qua?" What are you doing here?* the Nazi captain demanded in his horrible accent, staring down into Giuseppe's eyes. Taller. Not hungry. Not afraid. Using the *tu* form of address, as if the man were his boss. *Altezzoso* was the word that came to Giuseppe's mind. *Supercilious.* Out of the corner of his eye, he saw Lucia, a shoe in each hand and a bag over her shoulder, tiptoe down the last two steps and disappear behind one of the stacks.

"Look at me!" the officer commanded. "What are you doing here?"

It seemed to Giuseppe that the German had brought a stink into the room. Not a moral stink, a literal one. "I work here," he said.

"Doing what?"

"Cataloging. Caring for documents. When scholars are doing research, I—"

"Not man's work!"

Odd as the comment was, it sounded a familiar sour note in Giuseppe's mind. At times, he'd had the same thought. He loved his work but, especially since the war had started, had felt vaguely ashamed doing it. With his small, straight, Aryan nose; strong, dimpled chin; and perfect posture, the German standing a meter in front of him seemed the embodiment of masculinity. A brutal, unforgiving masculinity but, all the same . . . Along with the smell, there was a gust of shame in the air between them. These people had murdered his parents, and he'd been unable to do anything about it.

The man leaned his face closer, and now there was an obvious lunacy in the eyes, and something else, a particular breed of evil Giuseppe couldn't name. "And you're not in uniform. Why?"

Giuseppe thought he heard something behind the stack, and wondered if Lucia—who sometimes exhibited an explosive temper—was going to step out and hit the German over the head with one of her shoes. Giuseppe had a terrible urge to spit into the haughty face. He wanted to answer the question this way: *Because, years ago, my uncle convinced a friend in a certain office to certify my work as being of critical national importance so I wouldn't have to serve in the army of the madman Mussolini!* which was the truth. But what he actually said was, "Health problems."

"What kind?"

"Epilepsy. I sometimes have fits."

The German ran his eyes over Giuseppe's face, as if searching for signs of the illness, then said, *"Senza senso!" Nonsense!* In the man's mouth, the words became *"Tensa tensu!"* He took hold of Giuseppe's left biceps and squeezed. "You're strong. If you can't fight for us, you can work for us, epilepsy or no!"

The German didn't release his arm, but—and this was strange—when the soldier squeezed his biceps, all fear seemed to drain out of Giuseppe. He *was* strong. As a boy, he'd worked with his stonemason father, hours and hours carrying stone and shoveling mortar. He was still on the thin side, not tall, but, even though he'd lost weight, his arms, shoulders, and back were thick with muscle. He knew he could have picked up the German like a tree branch and broken him in half against the bookshelves, but, of course, that would have been suicide. The man had a pistol in his holster, a knife on his other hip. And an entire sadistic army behind him.

Without letting go, the German walked Giuseppe backward toward the desk. From this angle, the map was invisible, but if they went a little farther—two more steps—they'd see it there on the floor. A hand-drawn map of Naples's neighborhoods on a rolled sheet of light-brown paper, three-quarters finished, but already with two arms depots clearly marked, one in a schoolhouse in Vomero, the other in a small armory next to Santa Lucia. The existence of that map was a certain death sentence, but what place could be safer, he'd thought, than the basement of the National Archives? Why would any Nazi soldier venture here? Now he cursed himself for his carelessness.

Instead of going around behind the desk, the German stopped in front of it. Still holding Giuseppe's arm for balance, he lifted one leg and kicked at a half dozen books in bookends there. They tumbled onto the floor. The captain scraped the sole of his right boot down twice against the desk's front edge.

Giuseppe saw the moist brown substance on the metal. The smell was stronger.

"Italian horseshit," the German said, releasing him. And then, over his shoulder as he turned and limped away, "Epilepsy or no, you'll be sent to the Fatherland and you'll work for us."

Giuseppe listened to the boots in the stairwell, glanced to the left to make eye contact with the half-hidden Lucia, then crumpled up a piece of newsprint and began to clean.

Eleven

Lucia waited until she heard the German's boots reach the street level, then she went and stood at the base of the stairwell and listened to be sure. A pause, as if the man were looking around for someone else to torment. The sound of the heavy front door banging open and closed. She returned to the desk and helped clean up and set the books back in place. Together they traced the steps to the stairwell, but the trail of manure thinned out and disappeared there. It wasn't exactly the kind of lunch hour she'd had in mind when she'd left work and walked over to the Archives.

"I'm surprised there are any horses left on the streets, with the hunger," she said.

Giuseppe nodded, not looking at her.

They tossed the soiled newsprint into a wastebasket, and Giuseppe carried the basket to the base of the steps and told her, "I'll take it when I go."

Lucia reached up on her toes, kissed him, and held him tight against her. She could feel the humiliation. Hard enough for the man she loved that, in a city of *Camorristi*, street toughs, and wizened fishermen, he was an intellectual. So much worse to be orphaned and then bullied by a sadistic occupier. It often seemed to her that Giuseppe didn't understand that precisely what attracted her to him was his intellect and sensitivity, the fact that he *wasn't* a fisherman, or a fighter, or a black-marketeer like her father. The fact that he preferred playing the piano and studying English to machismo posing on the street corners, that he loved words and artwork, not knives and fists and stealing. He was man enough for her, more than man enough, without puffing up his chest like a rooster or pummeling someone's face to prove his power. But holding him against her now, she could feel that the moment with the Nazi officer had reawakened the doubts he had about himself.

She knew how to chase them away.

In the days when the government could afford it, there had been a night watchman in the building. At the rear of the basement level was a storage room with a cot, a sink, and a rust-stained, seatless toilet. Not the most romantic place for a tryst, but, since she rented a tiny ground-floor apartment with a curious landlady above, and he lived with his uncle, it was their only hope of privacy these days.

She led Giuseppe there by the hand, stopping on the way to pick up her canvas handbag. "My father gave me some gifts today," she said. "Let me show you."

Twelve

As the column of military vehicles sped south toward Naples, Colonel Scholl chewed absentmindedly on a piece of sausage and read over a copy of the manifesto he'd sent by telegraph to the Italian officials there. The tone was exactly right. The key was to be ruthless, unyielding, to set the rules in place and back them up with merciless force. The Italians were a weak people—overly emotional, cowardly, too fond of the sense pleasures. And as they'd recently proven, all too ready to flip sides, to betray, to run.

Lieutenant Renzik shouted over the noise of the motor, "I was stationed in Naples for a while. You'll be staying in the Hotel Parco, Herr Colonel. A fine place. Close to the water. Should I take you there or to the office where you'll work, the former *Amministrazione?*"

"The office," Scholl answered, keeping his eyes away from the handsome face, holding his gaze forward. "This isn't the time for rest."

Field Marshal Kesselring had said the goal was to *"subdue"* the city, and that it might very well prove necessary to destroy it once it had been subdued. On the long, tedious trip south, Scholl found himself imagining the different ways that task might be accomplished: squads of soldiers lighting fires in residential sections; the artillery brigade established at Capodimonte, one of the city's high points, raining down barrage after barrage of 150-mm shells from their Nebelwerfer 41s; a fleet of tanks rolling through the main avenues, firing into the foundations of famous museums and churches; before-and-after photos taken, to be shown later, at high-level meetings in Berlin. The beauty of it, the power: to be in charge of wiping an entire three-thousand-year-old city off the map. How many colonels, even how many generals in history had ever been given such an honor?

Though the field marshal had never quite said so, the implication was that, in the unlikely event the Allies continued to advance, the forces of the Reich would fall back to a line of positions halfway between Naples and Rome, just about where his entourage was at this moment: east of the Sperlonga headquarters, a short distance from the sea. The flat plain across which they traveled now was flanked by mountains—through the windows of the jeep, he could see them, three thousand meters at the tallest peaks, he guessed—and, with the holding of that high ground and the Reich's superior air power and superior generals, the advancing Allied armies would be cut to shreds. All that would be left to them and the Italian traitors would be a retreat through thousands of hectares of ash and rubble, to their former Napoli. Burned, blown up, rendered uninhabitable, Naples would stand as a monument to Nazi power, a warning to the rest of Europe and the world. *"Pockets of resistance,"* the reports in the files had said. The Italians would see what happened when there were pockets of resistance: a flattened city. Smoking ruins, blood, nothingness.

And his name would forever be associated with that.

Thirteen

Aldo disliked ceremonies of any kind—birthday celebrations, weddings, wakes, anniversaries—and he had a particular dislike for religious services . . . not that he'd seen very many of them. Still, it would have been unwise to avoid attending the funeral of Giovanni Forni. It would also have been an act of the purest ingratitude, because Forni, the notorious leader of one of Naples's most powerful Camorra clans, had helped him more than any person he'd ever known. Saved him from the consequences of the one truly violent deed he'd ever committed, given him decades of good-paying work, watched out for him at the edges of the illegal world—no one on this earth had helped him more.

So, a few hours after his brief visit with Lucia, four days after the Germans had executed the man who'd run the whole, once-lucrative stolen-goods distribution for the Camorra, Aldo put on his only suit and only felt hat and walked halfway across the city to the Church of Saints Demetrio and Bonifacio near the Piazzetta Monticelli. The church's saffron facade had been damaged in an Allied bombing raid— he could see the pocked stucco and one soccer-ball-size hole in the front wall—but, unlike the much larger, much more famous, and completely ruined Santa Chiara two blocks away, it was still functioning. And now, thankfully, there were no raids at all. No sirens, no droning airplane engines or winged shadows flitting across the streets like

scampering devils, no deafening crashes, no collapsing apartment buildings, no fires, no screams of people whose child or parent or spouse had
been trapped in the rubble or mutilated by a truck-size piece of flying
stone, no crews of elderly firemen trying desperately to free them. He
wondered if it was because of the king's armistice, as people said, or
because the Allies had heard of Forni's death and were keeping their
planes away from Naples in his honor. Stranger things had happened.
It was rumored, for instance, that the famous American mafioso, Vito
Genovese, fleeing a murder charge in his own country, was working
with the Allied generals in Sicily—running spies, procuring necessary
goods, intimidating key officials. And everybody knew what the Sicilian
mafia—La Cosa Nostra—had done to help with the Allied landing on
their island in July.

Musing, wondering, running every possibility through his mind,
Aldo removed his hat, stepped into the piazza, and went through the
church's large green metal door.

There were hundreds of people in the Church of Saints Demetrio
and Bonifacio, every pew filled. Old men, young women, street kids,
even one or two groups of *carabinieri* in their policemen's uniforms.
For all the evil deeds Forni had committed—and his viciousness was
legendary—the *Camorrista* had littered the city with favors, providing
jobs, protection, food. All these people hadn't come to his funeral out
of curiosity.

Aldo hoped he might see Rita among the mourners and ask her the
proper etiquette. He stood near the back, ill at ease, unsure, until a trio
of friends noticed him there and waved him into a pew. Mario, Luca,
and Angelo had been his Neapolitan brothers for thirty years, since
their days as twelve-year-olds in the cells of Nisida. Aldo sidled in close
to them, handshakes and embraces all around. Following their lead, he
stood and sat and knelt at what seemed the appropriate moments in
the service. The order of the Mass made no sense to him. The prayers,

hymns, and readings left him cold. Only the sermon—too long!—was of some small interest. "If we have been baptized into the faith," the monsignor said at one point, "Christ looks upon our transgressions with one eye, and our kind deeds with two. He does not wish to cast us into the eternal flames. Like any good father, he wants for his children not suffering, but happiness."

Kind deeds with two eyes, Aldo thought, *transgressions with one*: it was the opposite of the way humans behaved, the exact opposite, and he found himself wondering if the monsignor had been paid to offer this foolish idea in front of Forni's family, if he'd been threatened, or if—the least likely possibility—he actually believed what he was saying.

The father's love made sense. But he wouldn't let himself think about that part.

When most of the other mourners went up for communion, Aldo followed his friends' example and remained in the pew. When they bowed their heads, he did the same, watching them out of the corners of his eyes. Instead of praying—an alien act—he remembered his fight with the older, bigger Giovanni Forni on his second night in Nisida. A brutal affair it had been. He'd held his own for a time, and then Forni had knocked him down. He'd leaped to his feet, bleeding from the mouth, been knocked down again. He'd gotten up a third time, bloodied, barely able to see, swinging wildly. Forni had knocked him down again, then pounced on him and beaten him unconscious. Two broken teeth and the scar beneath his left eye were the mementos of that fight.

After their battle, a cautious friendship had evolved, a mix of wariness, respect, and something else, too, the kind of history that linked him even now to the three men kneeling beside him. The broken-up families they'd been born into, the harsh life of the streets, the months in Nisida with its moldy bread, damp walls, and sadistic guards—one of whom, as Aldo knew all too well, would later meet a hideous end. It toughened them, cemented them together. And then, years later, Forni had climbed the bloody ladder of the Camorra, learned to kill and scheme . . . and given all his old friends jobs, money, and food for their tables.

Part of Aldo—a small, buried part—wished he'd been able to make a life for himself without Forni's help, without the Camorra. That small part swelled like a blister whenever he so much as walked past a church, and sometimes, late at night, when he paid his visits to Rita. He wouldn't think about that, either.

At last, the service seemed to be ending. Here came the monsignor, marching slowly down the center aisle like a well-fed king, with priests holding the tails of his robe so they didn't drag on the red carpet. Angling in through the hole in the wall, a ray of sunlight touched the young, dark heads. And here was Forni's casket, carried by six of the most vicious men in southern Italy, including the Dell'Acqua brothers, Vito and Ubaldo, professional assassins. Behind them came the mourners, family first. As Forni's brother walked past—Zozo, another killer, heir to the blood-soaked throne— he reached out to shake Aldo's hand and leaned his mouth close. "Meet me at the Castello after he's buried," he whispered into Aldo's ear, then walked on.

The Castello Restaurant's back room, Aldo thought, when he'd left the pew and was mimicking the others and crossing himself with holy water at the marble font near the doors. Forni's lieutenants would be there, Zozo first among them. If they approved of his decades of work, they'd find something new for him now, with the port ruined and the Allies rumored to be closing in. If they wanted him out of the way—for any reason, sensible or no—they'd have Ubaldo Dell'Acqua kill him, an assignment the monster would fulfill without the smallest twinge of guilt or regret.

Stepping into the morning sun, adjusting his expensive felt hat, Aldo spotted Rita there in the crowd. For some reason, the sight of her—black hair, almond-brown skin, huge, dark eyes—caused him to remember the monsignor's sermon. God's supposed forgiveness. Aldo didn't know about that, but he knew that the woman he visited every week had a kind of street holiness to her, the ability, no matter what he'd done in his life, to make him feel like a good man. As he walked toward her, she turned a beautiful smile in his direction, and a thought occurred to him: *But I've never been baptized.*

Fourteen

Full-bellied for a time, with the horrific scene of that morning still burning like a dark secret behind his eyes, Armando let the others go off on their own explorations while he headed toward the Vomero with Tomaso.

Of the boys in his *coro*, Armando felt closest to Tomaso. While not the oldest or the largest, the two of them were the quickest, the most daring, maybe the smartest, and the only two who admitted to being virgins. It was possible—likely, even—that at least one of the others was lying, that the stories of glamorous introductions to the world of sexual pleasure were embellished, maybe completely made-up. Still, the details seemed accurate (and how was he to know if they weren't?), and the expressions on their faces as they told their tales made Armando, even when he was sleeping in the corner of a cold alley or in his secret place at the tire company warehouse, dream of delicious foods and warm baths.

He and his *coro* met up every day and roamed the city, from Sanità to Chiaia, from Materdei to Poggioreale, from Arenella to Vasto, but there were certain favorite places that always seemed to draw them. The Castello Restaurant's waiters, for example, would sometimes leave food near the side door in a covered dish, so that was a regular stop. And on their rounds through the Vomero, he and Tomaso would always swing by the Café Sangiuliano, one of the eating places that had remained open. The owners, an elderly couple named Lena and Salvatore, would usually have a bit of food set aside for them. The café's offerings were limited now to polenta with a few wild mushrooms, watered-down coffee or tea, white rice with olive oil, and the occasional plate of horse-meat, rabbit, or fish. Nazi officers had requisitioned a house on the same block—simply thrown the owners out and moved in—and they would sometimes occupy one or two of the café's outdoor tables, which had the effect of keeping other customers away. Whenever Armando and Tomaso saw German soldiers at the Sangiuliano, they did whatever they could to torment them.

But Armando wanted more than that now, more than torment: after what he'd witnessed this morning, he wanted revenge.

As they climbed the hill from the stadium and sauntered toward Piazza Vanvitelli, Tomaso winding a newly discovered length of yarn around his wrist, both of them alert for all possibilities, Armando noticed a German officer sitting alone at one of the Sangiuliano's tables. The sight of the uniform lifted the memory of the dead girl into his inner eye and almost made him vomit. He and Tomaso glanced at each other, the only signal either of them needed. The officer had taken off his black-lidded hat and set it on the table. He was sipping from a cup, apparently waiting for his food. While Armando hovered nearby, creating a distraction by singing a Neapolitan song—*"C'e La Luna"*—loudly like a crazy boy begging for coins, Tomaso crawled up behind the officer's chair and tied the loop of twine loosely around the chair leg and the officer's ankle. A second later, Armando, still singing, ran past, grabbed the hat, and he and Tomaso sprinted to the corner and were gone. Behind them, they heard the crash of a falling chair and angry German words that meant nothing to them.

Safe in a favorite hiding place where the mouth of a storm drain had been cut into an ancient stone wall, they sat examining their new acquisition, turning the souvenir this way and that, handing it back and forth. Unlike some of the others they'd seen, this cap had a band of thin green thread along the top and what appeared to be a metal sunburst above the lid, two narrow braids of rope there. The boys took turns trying it on and guessing what the insignias meant. "Worth anything?" Tomaso asked.

Armando shook his head. "A pistol would be. Next time, we should try for the pistol or a knife. But this"—he twisted the cap around on his head and angled it down rakishly over one eye—"a gift, maybe. For *Nanella*."

"Or for a girl so we could have sex with her."

"We?" Armando said, and his friend laughed.

For a little while, sitting there making sure the coast was clear, Armando thought of telling his friend about what he'd seen, about the terrible events of the morning. Twice, he opened his mouth to speak, but the words wouldn't come. Watching from the bombed-out building, he'd been afraid, and he was ashamed of being afraid. But it was more than that. Bad as the German occupation was, before this morning, part of him had been able to laugh at the soldiers with their turtle-shell helmets and muddy language. Not anymore, not now. Now some strange new feeling was boiling over inside him, in his brain and belly, in his hands. He'd used the word *hate* before, many times; now he knew what it actually meant.

He thought about the way his day had started, on the puddled porch in the Chiaia. He wondered what it felt like to have your legs broken, wondered who the scary man and the red-haired woman might be, and what the pistols would really be used for. *"To kill Nazis,"* the man had said. The words filled Armando with a peculiar excitement, an excitement that wrapped itself around the fear and shame and hatred inside him, holding it there, preserving it. He wondered if the ugly man was sane. The Nazis had tanks, machine guns, rifles, huge wheeled artillery on the Capodimonte Hill. They lined up Neapolitan grandparents and little girls in the center of the city and killed them in cold blood. They sped through the streets and strode down sidewalks like owners, like gods, superior, untouchable . . . and red-haired Italian women were going to kill them with pistols?

Instead of describing the murders to Tomaso—he did not want to relive that scene—he told him about the ugly man on the porch, and the pistols, and he said, "That's where I got the money for our food."

Tomaso kept his eyes on the street, pretending to be unimpressed. "People are stealing rifles all over," he said. "People are hiding Jews. People are making hand grenades."

"We should get some."

Tomaso nodded, kept his eyes forward. "Who was the ugly guy, do you know?"

"He told me his name. Zozo Forni."

At last, Tomaso turned and looked at him. "You're kidding, right?"

Armando shook his head.

"You don't know who Zozo Forni is?"

"Sure, I know," Armando said, even though it wasn't true. "Everybody knows him." He didn't like his friend's tone of voice, and didn't want to hear any more on the subject. *He* had gotten the money for their food, not Tomaso. *He* was the one who'd delivered pistols that would kill the Nazis. He took the soldier's cap from Tomaso's hands, slipped it up under his T-shirt, and walked out into the street, unafraid. Tomaso followed and let the subject drop. They made their way back down the long, zigzag staircase that led to the Spagnoli and went looking for the rest of their friends.

Fifteen

Lucia had dated Giuseppe for almost a year before they made love for the first time. These days, when no one knew if they'd live another hour, and people grasped for every pleasure they could find, she often wondered why they'd waited so long. But that was their story, two twenty-year-old virgins falling in love, and she was proud of it.

They'd met by the purest accident (or, as her friend and coworker Rosalia liked to say, *Thanks to the hand of God*). Lucia had been walking through Piazza Cavour on her way to the university when she saw a young man stop and give a roll with what looked like salami and cheese in it to an old woman begging on the street. It wasn't an unusual sight—there always seemed to be beggars, Neapolitans were famous for their generosity, and in those days, meat, cheese, and bread were still available. But the young man was nice-looking in an unusual way, with a shock of black hair parted on one side, a large, straight nose holding up a pair of eyeglasses, strong shoulders, and a wide forehead and wide mouth. Something in his movements, an unselfconscious tenderness, struck her as the mark of a gentleman. Unafraid—from girlhood, it seemed—to take the initiative with boys, she decided to stop and say a word to him.

It turned out that they were both heading to the building where music and language classes were taught, so they walked there together, making conversation about nothing for three or four minutes, then saying goodbye with a studied casualness. It was more than a month before their paths crossed again. She saw him at a café, sitting at an outdoor table beside a pretty young woman. A girlfriend, she supposed. Lucia nodded, risked a *"buona giornata,"* and he recognized her and said "good day" in return. Several more weeks and a third encounter: Giuseppe walking straight toward her across Piazza Dante, smiling sheepishly, stepping through the crowd near the Porta Alba archway, where the tables of people selling used books and posters were always set up. They talked for a bit; he asked her out for a meal—not too shyly, but not with great confidence, either. That meal began a long, slow courtship: concerts, dinners, Masses, kisses. Giuseppe taking her to the music room at the university and playing Bach or Chopin, his beautiful hands dancing over the keys, his handsome face set in calm concentration.

The arrival of the war complicated their courtship, too, as it had every other aspect of life. As did the fact that, when her father finally met Giuseppe, he disliked him from the start: a professional black-marketeer meeting a lover of books and music—how could it be otherwise?

Very slowly, their kissing moved them toward lovemaking, but finding a private space was a problem, and the need to avoid becoming pregnant was a problem, and their Catholicism was a problem, too. Then Giuseppe took the job at the Archives, and then he discovered the watchman's closet. The watchman disappeared and, with him, their Catholic reticence.

Now she lay beneath him, their clothes stacked neatly on a chair, and let him—tender and generous as always—help her forget the war for a little while. They had to move slowly and gently, otherwise the cot's old springs squeaked like the cries of outraged nuns, but Lucia discovered she enjoyed lovemaking even more that way. A slow building of pleasure, almost a torment, and then release.

Afterward, a patina of sweat on their bodies, and a supernatural calm.

She lay there with him in that calm, not wanting to speak and disturb it.

But it had to be disturbed; she knew that. Terror or ecstasy, nothing lasted. Time shifted the world out from under them, their bodies changed, the days passed. Even the shape of the war, it seemed, evolved by the hour. From British bombers above to American troops in Sicily; from Mussolini boasting of victory from his balcony at Palazzo Venezia to Radio London describing German losses in Russia; from Fascists strutting around as if they owned the world to soldiers fleeing their posts and hiding their uniforms and Blackshirts suddenly scarcer than flour and quieter than ants. Before the September 8th armistice, the Germans had been there, of course, a noxious presence, but no worse than Mussolini's thugs. After the armistice, with Italy now officially aligned against them, their numbers swelled by the day and they turned into uniformed devils. They'd slaughtered Giuseppe's mother and father in cold blood; she'd helped him wrap the mutilated bodies in blankets. Together with his uncle and a priest friend, they'd brought the bodies to the cemetery at Poggioreale and buried them there. You could not forget such things.

Lucia sighed quietly. Giuseppe was so still, one shoulder against her bare left breast, that she wondered if he'd slipped into sleep. She thought of telling him that the same German who'd wiped his boot on the desk had been following her for a week now, bothering her, that when she'd gone to meet her father near the port that morning, the man had taken hold of her dress and lifted it over her knees, that perhaps he had come to the Archives looking for her, not him. But she decided to hold the information inside. There would be time for those reports. "Two things I know from the office," she said quietly, afraid she might wake him.

"What?"

"First, the Allies are very close. Another week and they might reach us."

"A good thing . . . unless the fighting is so fierce that everyone is killed and what's left of Naples totally destroyed. And the second?"

"A new German is coming to take over the city. Walter Scholl is his name. A colonel."

"How do you know?"

"I see the teletype every morning. He sent a sort of manifesto, too, and wants it posted all across the city. The whole upstairs office is scurrying around trying to find a printer who'll agree to make copies."

"The Nazis are desperate to hold Italy now. Naples especially. They won't send someone gentle."

"A terrible man," she told him. "Judging by the office gossip—as usual, Rosalia has all the inside information—a vicious man. Even the Fascist generals were overheard saying so."

"With admiration, no doubt."

"More or less."

Giuseppe was quiet for a few seconds. She believed she could hear him thinking. At last he spoke. "We have each other. The Nazis can't take that away."

She knew, of course, just as he did, that it wasn't true. The Nazis could take anything they wanted, ruin anything they cared to ruin. But she only reached for his wrist, and held on, and kept those thoughts to herself.

Sixteen

As he entered the building, Aldo was greeted in a surly manner by the only waiter the Ristorante Il Castello still employed, a man Aldo had always suspected of being a fanatical Blackshirt, one of Mussolini's men. The waiter—tall, nose like a hawk's beak, unsteady eyes—pointed him to a door at the back of the back room, half-hidden behind a curtain, and informed him that, instead of holding the meeting in the restaurant, as he'd done in the past, Signor Forni had decided to hold it underground. "For reasons of safety." The waiter accompanied Aldo into the back room—too closely for Aldo's comfort—pulled the curtain aside, unlocked and opened the door, and Aldo stepped into a shadowed, downward-sloping tunnel in which he had to crouch as he walked. At the end of it—forty steps—lay one small section of the vast Neapolitan underground, city beneath a city, hundreds of subterranean rooms, thousands of years old, linked by a honeycomb of tunnels. As he made his way along the dark slope, moving toward a faint light below, he thought: *The perfect place to be killed.*

These days, Mussolini's UMPA, his civil defense organization, was making use of Naples's underground tunnels and caves for bomb shelters, and, during the worst of the raids, it wasn't uncommon for whole families to spend weeks in those shelters without seeing the sun. Showers had been set up, makeshift toilets arranged; in some of the shelters he'd seen, there were even working kitchens powered by an ingenious arrangement of wires and batteries.

The space he entered now was secret, of course. The UMPA and OVRA wouldn't know about it and likely wouldn't venture down here even if they did. Mussolini had done everything humanly possible to eliminate the Camorra, the Cosa Nostra, and the 'Ndrangheta, but like some kind of slippery, many-legged underwater creature, speared, hooked, slithering through nets, the various underworld organizations—Neapolitan, Sicilian, and Calabrian—had stubbornly survived, fed by wartime necessity and disorganization, and Italy's ancient tradition of putting local loyalty above any kind of national interest.

In the center of a circular cavern with a rough-hewn ceiling, a table had been set up, a single bulb hanging over it, and four short, round stools evenly spaced around it. At the table sat Zozo and his two lieutenants, the Dell'Acqua brothers, Vito and Ubaldo. Every adult in the city knew who they were. Merciless executioners and two of the stupidest men Aldo had ever encountered. They were good at two things: taking orders and taking human life, and over the years he'd done everything possible to keep his distance from them. As he stepped out of the tunnel and into the circular space, Aldo felt their eyes on him and realized he'd arrived a few minutes late. Zozo Forni had been kept waiting. Not good. And the presence of the Dell'Acquas was a bad sign. Without the tiniest twinge of conscience, they could kill him here, cut his body into pieces, and carry it out in a box to be thrown from a fishing boat into the sea, or buried beneath one of the thousands of piles of rubble that dotted the city now like freckles on a face. Lucia would think he'd abandoned her, and would possibly starve. His life, worthless as it was, would end like an animal's life: no grave, no stone, no explanation, no funeral in one of Naples's many churches. Nothing.

He decided to face his fate with as much dignity as he could summon, not to beg, not to quiver, and, hopeless as it would be in any case, not to try to run.

Zozo gestured for him to sit on one of the stools. In front of him was a plate with olives and cheese, beside it a glass of red wine. A last meal.

"Eat something. Drink," Zozo commanded, the scar on his neck making small jumps as he spoke. Aldo obeyed. Under the weight of the three sets of eyes, he was struggling to think of what he might have done wrong. For fourteen years, he'd overseen the theft of goods from the freighters that docked in Naples's busy port. *"Our tax,"* Zozo's brother, Giovanni, had called the larceny. At night, and sometimes even in daylight, the dockworkers would siphon off boxes of American liquor or German beer or British batteries, or soap or cloth or shoes that were either arriving from abroad or being sent there. He'd been told that somewhere around 5 percent of the goods was a fair tax, enough to make a healthy profit but not enough to anger the Fascist police, who—themselves the recipients of bribes—expected a certain amount of Camorra bounty to be taken, but wouldn't stand for the wholesale disruption of legal trade. Aldo had been instructed to keep the dockworkers in line by using a mixture of payment, favors, and fear, and over the years he'd become an expert at striking that balance, allowing them, in turn, to take their percentage. From time to time, one of them would have to be roughed up for stealing too much, or kicked off the dock entirely.

In the years leading up to the war, he'd done a good job—Giovanni himself had told him so more than once—but then, November 1940, the bombings had started. The port—from which soldiers and military equipment were being sent to the Libyan front—was a prime target. Soon the waters were littered with sunken ships, the docks and nearby roadways pocked with craters. Workers killed. Power and sewer lines destroyed. Trade brought almost to a standstill. Lately, the Germans didn't seem to want even fishing boats to set out to sea, as if the old fishermen with their wrinkled skin and scarred hands might be spies paid by Churchill or Roosevelt, or as if they could ferry the entire population of Naples over to Capri or across the Atlantic to New York. This most recent stage of the war had all but suffocated Aldo's livelihood. Giovanni Forni had given him small jobs—carrying cash to a contact behind the train station, buying horsemeat on the black market and delivering it to certain favored cafés, once, traveling by donkey-drawn cart to the Capodichino Airport at midnight, meeting some Roman stranger there, a silent man with an enormous white mustache, and accompanying him to the San Cristoforo Hotel. He'd become a charity case, his management skills put to the side.

Then, along with nineteen others, Giovanni had been grabbed from a restaurant, at random, and executed by the Nazis in revenge for the ambush and killing of one of their men. Aldo mourned him, of course, and worried there would be no more work, none at all. Through old contacts, people who owed him a favor, he managed to scrounge bits of food and other essentials, half of which he passed on to his daughter. But he was basically adrift, without a patron, powerless, and as hungry as everybody else.

He finished the last olive, the last sip of wine, and raised his eyes to the men for whom he'd become a liability. He contributed nothing now. He had secrets they wouldn't want others to know. He had a daughter who worked in the government offices alongside the Italian Fascists, supervised by the new Nazi overlords. None of it was good.

"*Allora,*" Zozo began. "So . . . are you happy working for us, Signor Pastone?"

Aldo hid one trembling hand beneath the table. "Yes, yes, of course. For all these years, I—"

Zozo didn't seem to be listening, so Aldo stopped in midsentence. Maybe the question had been a trick. Maybe whether Signor Pastone was happy or not didn't matter at all.

"As of two weeks ago, the bombs stopped falling. Can you guess why?"

Aldo shrugged, swung his eyes to the brothers with their thick black brows, and then back to Zozo's fat cheeks and large ears.

"No guesses?"

"Maybe the Americans have run short of fuel for the planes. They're waiting to be resupplied, through Sicily. Or they're setting up their bases there, now that—"

He stopped again. Zozo's lips had stretched into a smile. The smile said, *You are as stupid as the Dell'Acquas.*

Aldo watched him, waited. He was pretending to be unconcerned, but already mounting a defense. He'd mention the things Zozo's brother had said, the compliments. He'd say how flexible he was, that he had other talents, that he'd always been loyal, that, over the years, he'd brought in a great deal of money.

Zozo belched quietly, and the smile disappeared. "Mussolini is gone. The king signed an armistice. We're fighting alongside the Allies now."

"I knew . . . about the armistice. We thought it meant the war was over. Even the Germans thought so for a day."

Zozo looked away. The light bulb suddenly went out, throwing them into darkness. Aldo clenched his hands into tight fists. The other three men laughed, and in ten seconds, the bulb flashed back to life. Vito Dell'Acqua, the taller of the two, perhaps slightly more stupid, spoke up, and Aldo shifted his eyes there. "The boss has a job for you. If you want it."

"I want it," Aldo said, too quickly, then cursed himself again. Fear brought trouble. Showing need brought more than trouble.

Zozo plucked an invisible something—lint, dust, a speck of blood—from the cuff of his long-sleeve shirt, pursed his lips, reached up, and squeezed the end of his nose between thumb and second finger. "Now," he said, drawing out the word. Aldo felt a coating of sweat on the back of his neck. He didn't move. "Now, the British and the Americans have come to our doorstep, all the way from Sicily. Think about that. They landed in July, it's September. They've already fought their way from southern Sicily almost as far as Napoli. Seven hundred kilometers. In two months. Let's say they keep coming. Let's say the Nazis run away, north. Let's say that, in their haste, our German friends leave behind . . . *materiale*. Bullets, rifles, blankets, the tires on their damaged trucks, the uniforms on their dead."

He paused, and the quieter brother, Ubaldo, the true killer of the trio, picked up the conversation as if speaking lines he'd carefully rehearsed. "One day these things could be value."

"*Of* value," Zozo corrected him.

Ubaldo grunted and averted his eyes.

"What's my job in it?" Aldo asked.

Zozo squeezed his nose again, as if trying to make it smaller. "You have your men who used to help you at the port?"

Aldo shook his head. "Old, dead, disappeared."

"Find new ones. We can tell you where these valuable objects might be located. Even now, before the Allies come. Trucks at the edge of the city. Two lonely soldiers on the road. You can take your men and . . . *liberate* the Nazis of their weapons and clothing and other supplies, liberate the trucks of their tires. Guns, grenades, and bullets are especially welcome. You will work mainly at night. You will be told where to find the material and then where to bring it."

Aldo squirmed in his seat. The three men were watching him. A drop of sweat streamed down his left side, armpit to hip. The plan sounded suspicious to him. Where was the market for German military equipment? It was one thing to take tires from a stranded truck, but German soldiers weren't going to give up their arms voluntarily. And, with a single exception—many years ago and completely justified—he was not a killer.

Still, what were his options?

"You accept?"

"I accept."

Zozo nodded. "The pay"—he rubbed his right thumb against two fingers—"will be generous."

Aldo nodded his gratitude, but something wasn't right, he could feel it.

"Go, then. You'll be contacted. Tomorrow. Next day. Day after. Find at least one other man. We'll give you something to help you in your work."

"I have a knife."

Again, the twist of a smile.

Another *stupidaggini*, Aldo thought. A knife would be nothing against German soldiers. By this point in life, he should know when to keep his mouth closed. He stood and thanked them; shook each hand, one after the next; then turned his back and felt their eyes upon him, a line of electricity running up his spine. He started to say more, but in this company, it was important to act with confidence. The fewer questions, the better. One thank-you was enough. He strode toward the tunnel entrance, the hair on his neck standing at attention, a tingling in his fingers. And then he was crouching and climbing the stone ramp in darkness, guided by one sliver of light showing at the edge of the door in the back room of Ristorante Il Castello.

Still alive.

Seventeen

It was late afternoon by the time the entourage entered Naples. Although many of the street signs had been destroyed in the bombings, Colonel Scholl was able, using a military map, to see that they were driving down Via Duomo, then turning left onto Tribunali, and pulling up in front of Castel Capuano, a long, boxy, four-story building with a square clock tower in front. He climbed down from the armored car, told his driver to find some food for himself and the rest of the men, brushed the dust from his uniform, and looked up. Four officers, standing in a neat row, saluted him. He returned their salute. One of them, a captain, thin-hipped and elegantly tall, led him through the front door, through an elaborate marble foyer, and up four flights of stairs. The office that had been prepared for him offered a view out over a thin slice of the city, all the way to the port, and boasted a pair of glass doors that opened onto a balcony from which he had a more expansive perspective. Once Scholl was set up there—shown the desk and files, the telephone and teletype—the handsome captain who'd accompanied him up the stairs, Nitzermann, he said his name was, asked permission to leave.

"No, stay with me a moment, Captain. And no need to stand so stiffly at attention like that. We'll be spending a lot of time together. I want you to tell me something."

"Anything, Herr Colonel."

"The women of this city, are they . . . available to our men?"

He tried to ask it in as casual a way as possible, a superior officer worried about morale, but Nitzermann, whose skin was as smooth as a baby's and nicely tanned, seemed already to be regarding him with suspicion.

"I wouldn't know, sir. I haven't been here that long. I was in Africa, then Sicily."

"Yes, of course. I wondered if you'd heard anything. Diseases and so on."

The young captain gave him a blank look, as if he couldn't imagine where the diseases might come from, or what kind of diseases they could be. His mouth, somewhat crooked, was twisted further in puzzlement. At last, he said, "I've heard there is typhus and malaria, sir. That's all."

"Fine, fine. Not among our men, I take it?"

The captain shrugged, causing Scholl to wonder, not for the first time, if intelligence could exist alongside good looks. He adjusted the clasp of his belt, thought of pressing on with the inquiry, then changed direction. "Tell me, what else should I know about Naples? What should I know that the briefings and books don't tell me?"

The captain's confusion deepened, his cheek muscles pinched into dimples, eye contact unsteady. "I don't know what you mean, sir," he said at length.

"Your impressions. Of the people here, the people who have now switched from friends to enemies at the direction of their little king. Speak freely. What have you heard about them?"

"Hungry, sir. I've heard they are hungry."

"Beaten down?"

The captain's neck twitched. "Some of them, yes, sir. From what I understand."

"Then what's this I hear about pockets of resistance? Are those reports accurate?"

"Scattered and small, sir, but yes, there have been skirmishes. Nothing we haven't been able to handle to this point."

"Really? Then why was I sent here? If these things could be handled without me."

"Because the Italian generals, sir. They . . . the Fascist generals. Mussolini's men. They . . ."

"Speak freely."

"I sensed, after the . . . the surrender, the betrayal, that the Italians could no longer depend on their troops to keep order, and that we could no longer depend on them and the other officers to . . . act correctly."

"And the generals are where now?"

"Coming later today to hand over to you, officially, authority over the city."

"And their soldiers?"

"Many have deserted. Some remain loyal."

"And their arms? Depots? Armories? Have we secured them?"

"Some, yes."

"Some?"

"Yes, sir. Most."

"And the others?"

"There seems to be some confusion, sir, as to where they are, exactly, and how many. Some of the soldiers who deserted were guarding those places—their own storage facilities and so on—and we've never had an exact—"

"Captain," Scholl said, slapping one palm against the top of the desk for emphasis, "first assignment: secure the arms storages, wherever they may be. Every one of them. Second assignment: have the proclamation printed up—it was received here?"

"Yesterday morning, sir."

"Printed up and posted everywhere across the city. Everywhere. As soon as possible. I'd hoped they'd be visible by now. Third assignment: if you haven't done so already, identify every Jew in Naples and the surrounding areas. Names, ages, addresses. Of every single one, and have that information ready for use. You're aware of *Reichsführer* Himmler's plans for this coming week?"

"Yes, sir. To arrest the Jews and bring them to the train station for shipment north."

"You've been collecting names?"

"Yes, sir, and some Jews have already been shipped. The files are kept at the Municipio, at Castel Nuovo. Marshal Bruni is in charge there."

"An Italian?"

"An Austrian-Italian, sir."

"Trustworthy?"

"Absolutely, Herr Colonel."

"Good. Make sure no one is missed in the collection. Fourth assignment: once the proclamation is posted, begin arresting Italian men who fail to report. Summarily execute anyone who resists in any way. Anyone, man, woman, child, old, young. Anyone and everyone who resists. Hold the men we can use, for shipment. Bring deserting soldiers to the Gestapo. Shoot the rest. Clear?"

"Absolutely, sir."

"Dismissed, then."

Nitzermann saluted and left.

Alone, Scholl stepped out onto the balcony and studied the sunbeams angling through a line of purple clouds out over the bay. Soldiers deserting. Arms depots unsecured. Pockets of resistance. Fleeing generals turning over their authority. All of it had the scent of disaster. If the reports were correct, the Allied forces were moving up steadily from the south and were within a hundred kilometers of where he now stood. Perhaps closer. It made no sense to wait. He'd spend a day, two days at most, getting a better sense of Naples, subduing whatever resistance he encountered, collecting as many Jews as possible, and then he'd ask permission to burn the city to the ground.

Eighteen

Walking home from the Archives that afternoon, Giuseppe marveled at what a good day it had been—the lovemaking with Lucia, her gift of food (he carried a potato in each pocket), the continued absence of bombing raids, the fact that "Captain Horseshit," as he thought of the man, hadn't seen the rolled-up map on the floor behind the desk. Amazing how little it took now to make a perfect day, compared to what it had taken in the past, when there would be lovemaking *and* three meals, no threat of arrest or death, no concern about bombers overhead, when Via Foria would be alive with couples and friends having an *aperitivo* at the cafés at this hour, not littered with the rubble of blown-apart homes and offices.

The air was already growing cooler, smelling of the sea—*la bell'aria Napoletana,* his mother had called it, *the beautiful Neapolitan air*—but at the same time, there was something odd about the afternoon. It took him a few minutes to realize what it was: the streets were almost completely empty. He glanced up and to his right, instinctively, to see if the sky above Vesuvius had darkened, if the volcano, quiet for the last fourteen years, had suddenly decided to erupt again. But no: the sky there was blue and quiet.

Rumors and real news always raced around Naples like swirling flocks of birds, touching down here, rising into the air and changing shape before touching down in another neighborhood. He wondered if the Allies had reached Ercolano at the southern edge of the metropolis, and everyone else had heard the news and was in hiding. He saw one little boy—barefoot, filthy, naked except for his sagging underpants—run out of a doorway as if fleeing a bath. A woman appeared, captured him in her arms, and carried him hastily back inside.

He turned a corner onto Via Degli Scalzi. Quiet even here, on a busy avenue.

But then, ahead, close to the western edge of the Stella, he saw a cloud of brown dust, a line of vehicles. For a few seconds, he remembered what Lucia had said and allowed himself to believe it was the Allies, making their assault at last. But there was no sound of gunfire, and when they came, they would surely come from the south, not the northeast.

Something else, then.

Moved by a peculiar premonition, he ducked into a doorway and stood there, motionless. Motorcycle engines. The low rumble growing louder and louder until it was a deafening roar. His back was to the wall of the entranceway, and he couldn't see them until they were even with him, and then past. He leaned out, following them with his eyes. A line of black cars, swastika flags flapping, three motorcycles to each side. Behind the cars, a German military vehicle—like a tank without guns. The top was open, and standing there like a prince, a god, stiff-backed, hands on the metal near his hips, was an officer in a German uniform. For two seconds, given the amount of fanfare, Giuseppe thought it might be Hitler himself.

The caravan raced on, toward the German headquarters. One starving brown dog appeared, trotting along in the vehicles' dusty wake as if hoping to be thrown a scrap of bread. Giuseppe waited until the noise of the motorcycles could no longer be heard, then he stepped out onto the sidewalk and turned in the direction of home.

Nineteen

That afternoon, Lucia left the office later than usual—the long lunch hour with Giuseppe and then extra translation work and an extended conversation with Rosalia—and decided to take a different route back to her tiny ground-floor apartment, her *basso*. Ordinarily, she'd go along Via Medina and through Piazza Cavour to Via Miracoli, off which her short alleyway curled to a dead end. But on that afternoon, with the sun dipping behind a flat bank of clouds and casting a lavender light over the bay and the city's western edge, she wondered if the hideous German captain might somehow have learned of her regular route. He had followed her as far as the Santa Lucia hotel when she went to see her father that morning; he'd likely followed her on one of her visits to Giuseppe at the Archives, and that's why he'd shown up there at lunch. If he trailed her to the *basso*, she'd have to start staying elsewhere, and so many buildings had been destroyed, so many families made homeless, that nearly every person she knew already had a house full of friends sleeping on their floor. Staying at Giuseppe's might be an option, but there were complications: first, unless it was unavoidable, neither of them wanted to move in together until they were officially married, and they weren't yet even engaged, and second, the room where his parents had slept had not been touched for the past two weeks, since their murder, and Giuseppe and his uncle had single beds, so whatever sleeping arrangements they agreed on would mean a constant awkwardness of one kind or another.

She decided to take a roundabout route and walked toward the Spagnoli neighborhood, a detour that would take her past the Ristorante Il Castello, where her father could sometimes be found. Set on a slope that led upward from the Centro toward the Vomero district, the Quartieri Spagnoli—the Spanish quarters—was a maze of narrow streets and alleyways and, even in wartime, usually a jumble of activity: kids running in the street kicking soccer balls made of taped-up cardboard, or digging through piles of rubble looking for treasure— a flashlight, a fountain pen, a pocketknife. This evening, though, for some reason, the Spagnoli seemed strangely quiet. She saw a few old men and women sitting in chairs on the sidewalk, staring blankly at what was left of their world, their wrinkled faces bathed in the day's last light and reflecting a sorrow so deep, it seemed nothing would ever be able to erase it. At an intersection, one horse-drawn cart came toward her, the ribs of the horse pushing out from its shrunken belly, the cart itself empty, the man in the seat looking like he hadn't eaten in weeks. *A skeleton leading a skeleton,* Lucia thought, and she wondered if he was on his way to fetch a casket and carry it across the city to Poggioreale for yet another burial.

She wasn't really expecting to see her father—it was more a hopeful impulse than anything—but as she turned onto Via Speranzella, she thought she did see him there, far ahead, a man in a dark leather jacket just at the corner of the main road, Via Girardi. She decided to draw closer and make sure. Even if it did turn out to be her father, she knew there would be no conversation, or none of substance, or that she might decide not to call out to him at all. Still, a ferocious curiosity drew her on, something she could feel in her midsection. The truth was that she knew very little about the man who had fathered her, and nothing at all about her mother—except her first name, Vittoria. When she was a small child, her father had found a series of women—lovers, friends, hired help; Lucia would likely never know—to care for his daughter. She remembered countless nights when he hadn't come home, when the woman of the month would cook for her, read to her, tuck her into bed, all the while making up reasons why Aldo couldn't be there. That he was involved in important work. That he was visiting a very sick friend. That he'd gone to Rome or Milan on business—a weak lie for a man who never spent a night away from the city of his birth.

Lucia had a handful of memories of spending time with her father, and she cherished them like emeralds or rubies. Once, he'd taken her on a fisherman friend's boat to the island of Capri, where they'd ridden up to the city on a funicular and had pizza and gelato. Once, he'd brought her by train on a day trip to Rome, and they'd seen the Pope being driven through the city in a magnificent car. A few times, when one of the women hadn't been available, her father had walked her to school or accompanied her home after classes.

As she grew older, as she made the slow, difficult transition from girl to young woman, her father had drifted even further away, into his duties, his meetings, his friends, his secrets. The first time she'd found the courage to ask about her mother, his face underwent a terrible transformation, the eyes squeezing into slits, the lips twisting down, the voice turning into a growl. "She's gone," he'd said. "Dead. Don't ask again! There are some things a person should never talk about!" That odd and terrible response had been enough to keep her from asking a second time, and made her wonder if her father was telling a lie. But when he wasn't around, driven by a visceral curiosity, she'd taken to asking the women about her mother. None of them knew anything or, if they did, they pretended not to. A mystery woman, Lucia decided she must be, and as she moved through the teenage years, desperate for the guidance of a mother figure, she concocted all kinds of imaginary explanations: that her mother wasn't dead at all but alive, a prostitute, a nun, a gypsy. Or her favorite: that her mother was actually a princess, Princess

Vittoria, and her parents, a European king and queen, had so hated her choice of the uneducated Italian Aldo Pastone as a boyfriend that they'd forced her to give away the love child and never speak of the girl again.

In one early conversation, Giuseppe had asked her what had brought her mother and father together, where they'd met, why they hadn't raised their daughter as a couple, how and when Vittoria had died. Lucia had no answers. Before the most recent chapter of the war, a few months that had turned her father from a prosperous port boss into a man who had to sell pieces of furniture in order to eat, she'd promised herself she'd find the courage, and the right moment, and demand that he give her at least a few facts. She did try, but it had led only to another explosion and the worst argument they'd ever had. She'd left his apartment the next day, found, with Rosalia's help, the inexpensive *basso*, moved her things there, swore she'd stop speaking to her father forever and try to stop wondering about the woman who had brought her into this world. It took him less than one day to find her, and about that long for her to change her mind about her wondering. He knocked on the door, handed her a small package of food, and stood there, looking as if he wanted to say something else. "Come in, Father," Lucia had said, but he pressed his lips tight, turned, and walked away.

Little by little, they'd managed a tentative reconciliation. She refused to move back in with him, and he'd changed apartments, but she met him now, every few days, accepted his gifts, asked about his health. He was spitting blood from time to time, looking hungry. With all the other pain that surrounded them, the last thing she wanted was to provoke another fight.

Even so, the desperate curiosity remained, an unquenched thirst. Not a day passed when she didn't wonder if, in spite of what her father said, her mother was still alive, someone she passed on the street. Or if she might be living far away, in Sicily, in Calabria, in the northern mountains, wondering about the man she'd once loved, and the girl she'd abandoned.

When Lucia turned another corner, there he was, far ahead of her, recognizable by his fierce walk.

A Nazi soldier passed her, going in the opposite direction, and offered a pleasant hello. She nodded once, turned her eyes down, hurried on.

She kept herself at a good distance from her father, staying close to the buildings in case he turned around. But he didn't turn around. Hands in the jacket pockets, head slightly bowed, he went along at a steady pace, like a man thinking through some great problem, a man who didn't want to be bothered. Halfway to Via Pasquale Scura, he stopped at one of the few working street-food stands in the city. She stopped also, hid behind a light pole, watched. He was making a purchase—she couldn't see what. He handed over something, money perhaps, though with her father you never knew, and the man in the stall handed something to him in return, a paper bag. Her father tucked it under one arm and went on.

When she reached the stand, she saw that the man there was offering roasted chestnuts, but at twenty lire for half a kilo! A ridiculous price. She loved chestnuts, but in peacetime they were one-tenth that cost. She walked on, wondering if the chestnuts might be a gift for his lover.

A left turn onto Via Splendore, then right, onto a narrow alley, a *vico* with no name on the corner, then onto Vico dei Bianchi near what remained of the Spirito Santo church. Lucia hurried to make up ground and then stood at the corner and watched him turn left into a house in midblock. The door, painted bright yellow, opened and closed. She made a mental note—Vico dei Bianchi, the yellow door, the two-story building with no balconies but what appeared to be a terrace on the roof. She stood for a few minutes, wondering if he had a woman there, or if he was just visiting another of his Camorra friends, then she turned and went on her way.

Twenty

When Giuseppe arrived home, he didn't see his uncle in front of the house, and didn't see the rusty metal garden chair in which he usually sat and received visitors. A neighbor must have brought the chair inside. His uncle was probably up in the apartment, writing in his notebook . . . or maybe the Germans, knowing of Donato the Hunchback's value to the people of the city, had taken him away as one of their perverse punishments. They slaughtered the innocent, they buried people alive, they burned libraries and blew up apartment buildings and raped women. He hated them with every fiber of his being.

He mounted the three flights of steep stairs, the soles of his shoes scuffing dusty stone, opened the door, and was happy to find his uncle there, sitting at the kitchen table filling his precious notebook with tiny script. Though Donato rarely spoke about it, Giuseppe knew that his uncle was writing an informal history of the war in Naples, documenting the day-to-day struggles, and planned to mail it to his brother, Orlando, who'd emigrated to America before the war. No doubt, if the Germans discovered it, the notebook would be enough to condemn Donato to execution, but he was a fearless man, a seer, a sage. As was the case with all male hunchbacks, Neapolitans considered him to have been particularly blessed by God, and he sat out in front of the house every day when the weather allowed, and let himself be touched by strangers. He loved Lucia as much as Giuseppe did, and she loved him in return.

In order to look up at him, Uncle Donato had to lean far back in the chair. *"Hai notizie,"* he said, as if he knew.

"Yes, I have some news." The water was running on that day. Giuseppe poured himself a glass from the faucet, checked to see that it wasn't cloudy, and sat opposite his uncle. He described the visit of the limping German officer, the manure, the threat of being taken north, his made-up story about epilepsy, everything but the love-making with Lucia. His uncle listened silently, attentively, expressionless. "And then on the way home, Uncle, on Via Scalzi, I heard a commotion of motorcycles. I hid in a doorway. A German armored car raced past, surrounded by the motorcycles, swastika flags flapping, a man standing up in it like a king. I thought, at first, it might be Hitler."

His uncle blinked, then nodded as if he'd already heard that particular piece of news. Giuseppe waited. There were times when his uncle seemed to be looking through his nephew's skin and the bones of his forehead, directly into his brain. The man ate very little, said perhaps a hundred words a day, and yet, bringing food and small gifts, people came from all over the city not only to touch him, but to consult with him on all kinds of issues—medical, marital, spiritual—secretly these days, stepping into the shadows when the Germans drove by. He could see now that there were two apples on a plate at his uncle's elbow. That would be their evening meal, that, the potatoes Lucia had given him, and a small bag of fresh figs on which Giuseppe had spent half a week's salary.

"There will be an eruption," his uncle said, slowly and quietly, but with his usual air of certainty, as if he had plucked the truth from his private orchard and was presenting it, indisputable, for his nephew's consumption. "This will happen very soon. You will be asked to play a role."

"The volcano? Vesuvius?"

His uncle shook his head and went back to his writing, a dismissal. But then, eyes downcast, tip of the pencil touching paper, "I love you as I loved my brother and sister, and I thank you again for taking care of me."

Later, with the apple, one small boiled potato, two figs, and two glasses of water in his belly, Giuseppe removed his clothes, turned off the lamp, and lay in his dark bedroom, listening. Normally at this hour on a warm, late-September night, there would be voices in the street, the sounds of forks against plates, of corks being pulled from bottles, children playing, women singing, accordion notes, the steady muttering of engines on Via Salvator Rosa. Normally, the city was a festival of noise. Now, all was silent. Then one *pop*, perhaps a block away, a strange sound. Perhaps another Neapolitan had been shot.

A few seconds passed, and Giuseppe heard raised voices, too far off to decipher the words or language.

And then what sounded like two or three people running along the street below his windows, a door slamming shut. Silence. He waited, listening for more, but the night did not speak.

Half the time, his uncle's predictions were correct. Half the time, they were not. An eruption. *Eruzione.* Unless he was speaking metaphorically, which Uncle Donato sometimes did, it could mean Vesuvius. His uncle had said that he, Giuseppe, was supposed to play a role in this eruption. What role exactly? Helping people flee? Rescuing documents? Bandaging burned limbs?

He became aware of an engine in the street, certainly a German truck this time. No other vehicles would be out after dark. Brakes, slamming doors, the hurried slap of boot soles, as if the soldiers were chasing someone, or running to hide. One more *pop*, much closer now, but were they shooting or being shot at? He heard a voice right below the window, a single German word, shouted: *"Vorsichtig!"* Then the truck revving up again, tires on the paving stones. The soldiers gone, the night quiet.

Vorsichtig.

He thought it meant *careful*. He'd have to remember to ask Lucia.

Twenty-One

Rita wasn't surprised when she answered the knock on the door and saw Aldo there, the old scar on his left cheekbone, package under his arm. But the look on his face—sorrow, regret, worry?—wasn't typical of him, not when he visited her, at least. Not at all. In fact, over his decades as an orphan, a street boy, a prisoner, a dockworker, and then a man who worked for Giovanni Forni, Aldo had learned to keep all expression from his handsome face. The fine forehead and beautiful dark eyes, the straight nose and dimpled chin—he managed the muscles there the way her downstairs neighbor, Joe, managed the muscles of his fingers when he sewed. She'd seen Aldo at times when he was in physical pain, times when he'd just had a stretch of luck at the docks and made a sack of money (he'd always bring her a special gift then), times when he was worried about Lucia to the point of being unable to sleep, but very little of that ever showed on the features of his face. She had to draw it out of him with hours of companionship, with talk, a meal, wine, lovemaking. Even then, there were times when what he was actually feeling appeared only in a parting few words the next morning. *"Going to the hospital later for this pain when I breathe,"* he'd say. Or *"Lucia's office has been taken over by Austrian Nazis."* Or, removing a small gold brooch from his pocket, *"Things have been good lately—here, take this."* And then out the door he'd go. She'd give him a moment to hurry down the stairs, and then she'd step over to the window and watch him walk away, striding along with his arms held out from his body as if a thief were about to reach for his wallet.

He has tight control over his heart muscle, too, she often thought, as she watched him go, and it filled her with sadness. She knew that heart of his, knew what he felt for his daughter, and suspected what he might feel for her. But he was afraid to show any of it, afraid that the hard men he'd dealt with all his life would see it as weakness and make their assault on his livelihood. Maybe, she mused, that's what jail time in boyhood does to a man. That's what having no parents does: for the rest of your days, you walk through the world feeling like a hungry dog with a piece of meat in its mouth, turning your head this way and that, worried every second that it will be taken away.

Something was different on this day, however; she sensed it immediately, embraced him warmly, and pulled him into the room. It was early for his visit, but she'd been thinking about him all day—a sign that there had been some important event in the life of the man she cared most about on this earth. She reached up and kissed him on each cheek, then pulled the little table closer to her bed and sat on the edge of the mattress. Aldo drew up the only chair and sat across from her, unable, for some reason, to meet her eyes. She let him be.

For her beloved Aldo, words were like coins in the pocket of a poor man. He'd hold them tightly, spend them carefully, and only after great thought. Once, Avvocato Cilento had asked who was her true love in life, and she'd demurred. But if she had been willing to answer, she would have said it was the man sitting opposite her now, handing over a paper bag that held a dozen precious roasted chestnuts, lifting his eyes out the only window, with its curtains half-drawn, one loose shutter tapping there. She supposed he knew how she felt, but they'd never discussed it, and she'd never heard him use the word *love*, not about her, not about Lucia, not about anyone alive or dead.

From the bag, she took six of the chestnuts and put three on his side of the table and three on her own. For a little while, instead of speaking, they pinched away the dark-brown shells, a cross cut into each of them (*"to remind us of Our Lord's suffering,"* a nun had told her once, but Rita thought it was simply to make it possible to allow the delicious nuts to be roasted without exploding). Inside the shell was a thin, furry film, a kind of skin or lining, and beneath that skin the succulent meat, soft and deeply ridged, color of the paper that beef had been wrapped in, during the years when there had been beef for sale.

When they'd finished the food and scooped the sharp pieces of shell into the wastebasket, she brought him a glass of water from the kitchen sink—clean and drinkable today—and when he'd eaten and drunk, she got up again, turned the lock on the hallway door, and said to him, *"Andiamo a letto."* Let's go to bed.

He didn't object—in the history of the human race, what man had ever objected?—but took off his clothes like a laborer at the end of a hard day, and lowered himself on top of her. She was naked and had the palm of one hand against the bones of his back, the other in his hair, holding his head in the crook of her neck. They found their comfortable rhythm, her feet hooked over the back of his strong calves, his lips against the skin of his neck, her large breasts pressed between them. But the feeling today was different. He moved against her with a certain soft urgency, as if there were something he was supposed to accomplish but he did not want to accomplish it; as if he were waiting for some sign from her, permission to break out of the comfortable pattern they knew so well and reach some new understanding. She could feel every particle of his skin against her, and she did something she had never done with him: turned and lifted his head so they were kissing. Softly. Almost like teenagers kissing for the first time. They had kissed before, yes, but only briefly and never during the actual lovemaking.

The touch of his tongue seemed to push aside the frail wall she'd always held between them, much frailer and weaker than the wall she held between her and other men, but a wall all the same, or perhaps, with him, just a curtain over a doorway. It surprised her, and the surprise took the form of a new heat that radiated up the bones of her back. She had to move her mouth to the side in order to make what she'd once heard called "the opera of pleasure," quiet sounds she'd long ago learned to make but that had never come from the middle of her like this, a deep current of joy that moved up from the place where she and Aldo were joined and through her lips and out into the air. Always at the moment of ecstasy, he squeezed her tight, but this time she was squeezing him tight in return, making the sounds. Her first experiences with men had been violent, and the pain and humiliation of that had cast a long, dark shadow over every act of love since then. Twenty-two years that shadow had lasted. Now, it seemed, after so many acts of love, it had finally moved aside and made way for warm light.

They lay breathing hard against each other, a species of relaxation in her arms, legs, and torso that she did not ever remember feeling. Aldo rolled onto his back, and she was left looking up at the cracks in the tall ceiling, the lamp there hanging from its dusty metal chain, a spider crouching in one corner. From the street below, she could hear the squeal of a cat, then the happy cries of boys, then the bass voice of her neighbor, Leopoldo Fontana, the Fascist, shouting one word. *"Basta!" Enough!*

"Something different," Aldo said at last.

She thought he was referring to the lovemaking, because she could still feel it in her toes and fingers, a gentle thrumming, and the emotional part of it—so different, too—seemed to have occupied a corner of her mind. It was setting up house there, furnishing the space, throwing open windows that had long been closed. She turned her head halfway toward Aldo.

He said, "I went to Forni's funeral."

"I saw you there." She looked up at the ceiling again and tried to hide her disappointment from herself.

"And then, afterward, to a meeting. A secret meeting. Zozo and the Dell'Acquas. Down below. Below the Castello."

"Something good?" she asked. Though the lovemaking had never been like this, there had been times, countless times, when she'd felt a connection to Aldo that went beyond their friendship, or their arrangement, or whatever word fit the weekly meetings that had gone on since long before the war started. He was, for her, so much more than a man who helped her survive, and she was certain she was more, for him, than a vehicle for his sexual pleasure.

"Good and not good," he said, and then he was quiet for a time. "Good, because I have work again. New work. Selling military equipment. Guns, tires, blankets."

"And the not good?"

"Because . . . because of something I've never told you."

There was a long silence. Instead of breaking it with words, she brought her right leg up and over his left, resting the calf on his shin. And she waited.

"I," Aldo began, then there was another pause. "I killed a man. One man. Long ago."

She was surprised and not surprised, but the air between them seemed now to be trembling, and she was afraid of speaking a wrong word into it, of closing the door that had just opened.

Aldo coughed a deep cough, sighed, went on. "He was a guard at Nisida, and he used to . . . do things to the boys there. The other boys. The most terrible things. One night, many years after I was out, I saw him. On the street. In Vasto." Aldo fell silent again, his body rigid. "I choked him with my hands."

Rita dared not move or speak.

"I can't describe the feeling of it, Rita," he said at last. "The taking of another life. I've done some bad things, stolen, cheated, lied, fought. But the life of that man, evil as he was, lives inside me even now."

"You saved others from being hurt. Other boys."

"*Sì, certo.* But still . . . I work with killers. I've always worked with killers, around killers, but on tiptoe. Serving them, earning money for them, being paid by them, but it was always just taking, stealing, but never stealing from an individual. I've never done that. Always from the big ships. From countries, from companies I couldn't see."

"And you always shared."

He grunted, coughed again, lay still. "But now I think . . . now there are going to be times when I am asked to kill."

"Germans?"

"Human beings. Men."

He fell silent, and Rita reached out and took hold of his forearm, the tips of her fingers squeezing the powerful muscles there. "Can you refuse?"

Aldo let out a sorrowful laugh, one syllable. An answer as clear as any word.

When they'd been quiet for another little while, she decided to offer a secret to match his secret. "I visited my brother, the way I always do."

"The monk."

"Yes."

Another cough. "I didn't think the buses were running there anymore, the way you go."

"Sometimes, they run . . . He told me something I'm not supposed to tell you." She took a breath and said the first words of the Hail Mary, silently. "There's an American spy living with them in the monastery. He's gathering information so that when they come, when the Allies reach the city, they'll know where to attack. Where the Nazis are. Where their guns are. You can't tell anyone."

"And you can't tell what I told you, either."

"I keep secrets well," she said.

He ran his fingers across the top of her thigh. "The Allies are that close, then. Forni and the others will be glad. Once the Germans are gone, they'll make a fortune—you'll see. Everything will be for sale to the Allies, everything from women to Nazi souvenirs to gasoline."

She nodded, five, eight, ten times, her chin pressing down against her neck, a new bond between them now, after all these years, with their tattered pasts. "Our secrets," she said. She felt like she was reaching back for the new place that had seemed, for a few seconds, to have opened between them. More than anything, she wanted him to offer some words that acknowledged that new place, to speak about feelings, not facts, not money. But after a short while, she heard his breathing change, felt his right leg twitch once in sleep.

She got up and went over to the window in order to latch the tapping shutter back in place. Just at that moment, the lights of the city went out.

Twenty-Two

By the time Colonel Scholl left his new office in Castel Capuano, it was long after dark. The day had been a tiring one—the trip from Rome, the official transfer of power from the two Italian generals, news that one of his men had been killed by a sniper on the city's outskirts, first meetings with a series of captains and majors to get a sense of the situation in Naples and of their responsibilities and attitudes, the pile of paperwork to read (he still carried some of it in the briefcase beside him on the seat)—and he felt a certain weariness come over him as he climbed into the front seat of the staff car. He'd hoped Captain Nitzermann might join him on the ride to the hotel—anything to offset the company of the tiresome Renzik—but Nitzermann, he remembered, had been sent to coordinate with some of the city's tank commanders and check on persistent troubles with the radio frequencies. If it were true that the Allies were soon going to attack the city, their approach would have to take them through one of two routes: along the coast in Ercolano or farther to the east, on the other side of Vesuvius. Tanks and the Capodimonte artillery would be the first line of defense.

Lieutenant Renzik started off through the dark city, gripping the wheel tightly with both hands, like a teenager.

"Do you know the best way?"

"Yes, Herr Colonel. I've spent a little time here. And I've been looking at the map."

Good that you can read one, Scholl thought. As they went, he turned his head out the window and studied the streets. All but lightless at this hour, they were a maze of shadows. The Allied bombing had ceased weeks ago and, along with it, apparently, the rules about illumination. Here and there, from buildings where the electricity was still functioning, he could see a lit window or storefront, sometimes the headlights of a lorry or other military vehicle coming in the other direction. Based on what he'd seen on the way in, Naples was a mess, a jumble, a city that looked as though a child had organized it in the schoolyard dust and then, in a fit of anger, taken his small hand and knocked parts of it to pieces. He'd seen the cone-shaped Vesuvius. He remembered reading about it as a Stuttgart schoolboy, seen the photos of . . . what was the name of the ruined city? *Pompeii.* That was another maze, the wooden roofs burned away, brick walls still standing in places and broken apart in others. Naples would look like that soon, he mused, though not because of a volcanic eruption. Perhaps, years into the future, the modern Neapolitan ruins would be a travelers' destination, tourists from Berlin and Vienna making the trip to remember one of the important moments of the war.

Instead of taking what seemed to be a direct route, Renzik turned this way and that, choosing smaller side streets and moving along at a snail's pace. "Why the rush?" Scholl asked, and he could see that it took the lieutenant a moment to realize the question had been sarcastic. The best drivers had been sent to the front, the rest left behind to chaperone officers.

"Because, Herr Colonel," the man said after a pause, "the other drivers told me that some of the streets are blocked."

"By what?"

Another small fit of confusion. Did the man not speak German?

"By the stones, you know. From the bombs, you know . . . and some unofficial . . . barricades."

"And we can't clear the main roads well enough for our own vehicles to pass? How do the tanks get through?"

Renzik shrugged, blinked, clutched the wheel. Scholl looked away. Here and there, he could see a few old men and women sitting out in front of their buildings, as if waiting for a bus that would never come or sons who would never return. One ragged palm tree, looking underfed. A street sign dangling from its pole. Small bands of half-dressed urchins, not yet old enough for service, but too old, apparently, to be at home with their parents after dark. The whole scene seemed to him the precise opposite of orderly. No wonder the Italian Army couldn't fight; the men had been raised in whorehouses.

At last, Renzik pulled to a stop in front of a building with **ALBERGO PARCO** in unlit letters out front, then hurried around to open the passenger-side door. "I'll wait," the lieutenant said.

"For what?"

"F-for you, Herr Colonel."

"I'm living here, as you yourself told me," Scholl said, holding back a last word of the sentence—*idiot*—that climbed into his mouth. The man's eyes were blue-green encyclopedias of stupidity. "Be here tomorrow at seven."

Scholl carried his black leather briefcase through the front door— no one there to hold it open—and encountered no trouble at the registration desk. They knew who he was. A nod, a key to a third-floor suite, an apology for the broken elevator. Between the desk and the bottom of a curving marble stairway, Scholl had to cross a carpeted lobby with an enormous vase—empty—sitting not quite in the middle of a round table. To one side of the lobby were a sitting room and a small bar, and as he passed, he looked through the arched doorway and saw a collection of sordid souls, nursing drinks, a few standing at the bar, others occupying the tables. Sordid, perhaps, but they were meeting his eyes with a certain familiar eagerness. Men and women both. Young. Looking fairly well-fed and fairly well-dressed, the men in tight pants with shirts open at the neck. He let his eyes linger for a few seconds—too long!—then snapped his face forward and mounted the steps to his floor.

Two upholstered chairs and a sofa in the front room. A pair of doors with paned glass backed by a curtain. Beyond them, bed, bureau, bath. *Adequate* was the word he'd use. Clean enough. He removed his boots, washed the city dust from his face, and lay for a time on the oversize bed looking up at the light fixture. On the endless drive between office and hotel, a particular kind of agitation had taken his body prisoner; a particular voice had begun sounding quietly in his thoughts. It plagued him most often when he was tired like this, and it was sometimes—now, for example—accompanied by the annoying facial twitch. He tried to silence it, but the images of the men and women in the bar had amplified both the agitation and the voice, and they haunted him now. The people there were nice-looking in a dark, exotic way. There for the taking. The cost would be minimal, a few lire notes stuffed into a hand.

It was exactly what had gotten him into trouble in Rieti, but how wrong his superiors had been to judge him for that! From the many tales he'd heard, other officers sought their pleasure in similar ways, and they'd never suffered any kind of censure. And how many of them carried the responsibility for subduing an entire city—a million people!—and caring for an essential section of the southern front?

The voice made its case, arguing persistently, persuasively. He stood up, took off his jacket, and loosened the top button of his shirt. He looked in the mirror, smoothed his graying hair, grimaced at the thinning front edge. "A man does not live by work alone," he said aloud, but the line only half convinced him. The facial twitch clicked once, again, then subsided.

He went into the outer room, put his hand on the doorknob. Filled with a familiar anticipation, he opened the door, stepped out onto the ruby-red hallway carpet . . . but then something about the decor—the carpet; the garish wallpaper, lime green with gold stripes; the ceramic

91

lamp sconces hanging every few meters, adorned with naked cupids prancing; the photo of Mussolini in a cheap yellow frame—it was the Italian aesthetic, too much of everything, and it muffled the persistent voice long enough to allow him to turn back. Muttering a curse under his breath, he locked himself in his rooms, took off his clothes, ran a bath. There seemed to be no hot water. The Italians couldn't even manage that.

He sat on the edge of the tub, naked, and was staring at his bare feet when the electricity died and the world went dark around him.

Twenty-Three

Lucia worked in the Municipio on Via Imbriani, a grand five-story building that, before the war, had housed the offices of various functionaries and served in part as a collection area for not very important paperwork: parking and traffic fines, the recording of minor infractions—a fisherman tying up his boat in the wrong place, a teacher missing two days of school without an excuse, an old man written up for pissing on the street, drunk. In those days, her office had been presided over by an enormously obese man named Pasquale Lotesani, a harmless bureaucrat, unmarried, poorly schooled, who collected his paycheck and smoked his foul cigarettes, and who habitually thumbed through the stacks of papers on his desk as if the true meaning and purpose of life were hidden there, and, one lucky day, he might accidentally find it.

But then, with the start of the war, everything changed. The Fascist police, always a nuisance, burst through the front entrance one afternoon and came stomping down the long hallways, suddenly intent on instituting a machinelike efficiency. Lotesani was made to stand up and explain what he was doing, what his office was doing. Lucia saw him there, wobbling on his fat legs, his belly hanging down over his belt like a living creature, his chubby hands holding on to the edge of his desk and trembling. "It's imp-imp-important work!" he managed under the questioning.

After that interview, Lotesani had been sent away—to some fly-infested outpost in the Basilicata, Rosalia told her—and a new man, Marshal Pierluigi Bruni, was installed on the top floor. Northern Italian. Perhaps half-Austrian, she couldn't be sure. Suddenly, everyone in the building was required to arrive promptly at eight thirty, to cut their lunch break to forty-five minutes (she obeyed this order for only three days), to stay until exactly five o'clock. Germans in plain clothes came in and rifled through the filing cabinets, looking for what, Lucia couldn't at first guess. And then she'd been promoted, moved upstairs to an office presided over by short-haired men who spoke Italian with an Austrian accent and who filled the drawers and cabinets with the files of Italian soldiers and government workers—photo, date of birth, place of residence, marital status, children, criminal record if any, religious background, physical condition. All that was required of her was to file these in a particular order, to answer the phone, to endure the compliments and the flirting, the occasional unwanted touch—things she'd long ago learned to deal with.

But then, when Mussolini was deposed and the German grip tightened, things changed again. Bruni himself summoned her and instructed her to go through the files looking for what he considered "signs of Jewishness"—certain names, facial characteristics, kinds of education. She did the job as haphazardly as she possibly could, misfiling people, slipping sheets of paper into drawers where they'd never be found. She was moved again, to a desk closer to his, where she still had responsibility for some files but also answered the phone for Bruni, kept his appointment book, supervised a regular flow of Fascist operatives who waited, straight-spined, in the hard chairs until they were called, then went into Bruni's office and closed the door.

The place revolted her, but she needed the money to survive and, unlike some of the second-floor officers, Bruni left her alone. Didn't touch her. Didn't ask her to eat with him. Didn't comment on her dress or her hair or her "soft, lovely voice." Didn't "accidentally" run one hand over the backs of her shoulders or brush against her buttocks as he walked past.

Until the murder of Giuseppe's parents, she'd been able to maintain a separation between the woman she was at work—efficient, cooperative, and obedient only on the surface—and the woman she was the rest of the time. She told herself that so many other Neapolitan women were surviving by selling their bodies, that what she was doing didn't really help the Fascist cause. But when Giuseppe's parents were killed, that rationale withered.

She'd been walking with him hand in hand on Via San Biagio when someone he knew from the Archives ran up and told him that his parents—out scrounging for food on a Saturday morning—and a group of others had been arrested at random, pushed into the rear of two trucks, and brought to the Ministry of Health. There, they were being made to stand in three lines on the front steps while the Germans assembled an audience.

She and Giuseppe had set off at a run—the Ministry was a kilometer away—and made it three-quarters of the distance when they heard, first a muted applause, then screams, then machine-gun fire.

By the time they had turned the last corner, the German trucks were driving away and the Ministry steps were littered with bodies and blood, the single most horrific scene she had ever witnessed. Chests blown open, hands severed, faces reduced to raw red ovals, all presided over by a trio of black-uniformed Nazi officers with rifles at the ready. A stunned crowd milled about in the street, and someone—a man, a woman, she didn't remember—had told her that the Nazis had forced them to kneel and applaud the execution, that the whole thing had been filmed for propaganda purposes.

Before he was allowed to approach the bodies, Giuseppe was made to show his papers. Made to show his papers! He found his mother and father lying together and knelt and wept, and what followed were the very worst hours of Lucia's life. She'd hurried back to Giuseppe's house for blankets and to summon Uncle Donato. Giuseppe had borrowed a wheelbarrow. They had wrapped the bodies, loaded them into the wheelbarrow, and taken turns walking them, with a helpful priest, in broiling heat, all the way to the cemetery, a three hours' march.

After the burial, after that hideous day and the hideous night that followed, a change had come over the man she loved. How could it not? Giuseppe started to spend his days in the Archives' basement, working obsessively on his secret map. And a change had come over her, as well: she began taking risks she never would have taken before the murders. When Bruni was out on one of his three-hour lunch breaks (lunches that, in a lustful irony, reportedly included a tryst with a Jewish lover), she'd slip into his office on the pretext of dusting and organizing and would peek at his notes and recent correspondence. She'd go through the files, and if she found a soldier or an arrested citizen who was Jewish—or even who might be suspected of being Jewish—she'd remove the file, tear the papers into tiny pieces, hide the pieces in the cups of her bra, and, at home, burn them with a candle flame in what had become a ritual for her, a religious rite. It was, of course, impossible to remove every file or even spy in his office every day, but she did what she could.

It was on one of those clandestine errands that she'd seen the telegram announcing the imminent arrival of Colonel Walter Scholl. He was coming, the telegram said, "to restore order to the city of Naples and its environs."

Lucia's closest friend in the building was a single woman named Rosalia DeLamentalla, who came from a large family that lived together in the Vasto section, just southeast of the Centro, and that included one sister who'd become a nun. Rosalia's only annoying habit was that she continually commented on Lucia's attractiveness. "I'll never find a husband, never ever," she would say, "and you're besieged by admirers!" or "It's fitting that you've found your Giuseppe, a prize, a prince, the most handsome man in Mezzogiorno! And you, like a princess, like a queen!"

Rosalia was, in her own right, a queen. The queen of news. Lucia could never understand where she got her information—perhaps from one of her many siblings—but it was unfailingly accurate. Before anyone else heard the reports, Rosalia whispered to Lucia that the Allies had landed on Sicily and Italian soldiers were surrendering by the thousands. Then another burst of whispering just inside the bathroom door: that Mussolini had been taken from office, kidnapped, and couldn't be found. Then that an armistice had been signed. Then that the Germans were pouring men and supplies over the northern border. Then that there were reprisal killings. Then that the Jews—who, despite his vituperative "racial laws," Mussolini had never sent north—were being taken by train to Germany to be worked to death. Then, an hour after Lucia saw the telegram, Rosalia told her that she'd already known about this colonel and that he was reported to be a beast, a sadist. She said that, angry at the Neapolitans for their failure to be suitably welcoming to the new German troops, Hitler had hand-chosen one of the most vicious men at his disposal and assigned him to take charge of Naples.

When Bruni returned from lunch that day—Lucia could smell the perfume on him—he handed her a long sheet of paper of a texture she wasn't used to seeing and told her to roll it up very carefully, take it to the printer, and have posters made, "like the circus uses," he said. "The kind you can stick up on buildings and light poles. Two thousand copies. And tell no one."

Lucia rolled up the paper, collected her purse, walked down the four flights and out into her ravaged city. Although she'd been seeing this same view for years now, every morning and every afternoon, it still caught her and made her stop and stare. Across the street, where a *tabaccheria* had once stood, an elegant *palazzo* rising above it, there was nothing but a pile of debris, as if a tooth had been ripped out of a mouth by an amateur dentist, leaving only remnants of porcelain and gum: stones and great chunks of concrete, electric wires, shards of glass twinkling in the sunlight, a girl's white shoe, and what appeared to be part of a wheel, bent almost in two, that had once belonged to a bicycle. The buildings to either side remained standing, window shutters closed, one tiny pot of flowers on one fourth-floor balcony, a woman there, her fleshy arms crossed on the wrought iron. She was staring across the street and down at Lucia. As their eyes met, she lifted the second finger of her left hand in a feeble greeting. Lucia waved back and walked on, the rolled paper held under her left arm, the purse on her right shoulder, some new dark cloud sinking low over her thoughts.

A pair of German soldiers passed her going in the opposite direction. She cast her eyes down and pretended not to understand when one of them said, *"Schöne Brüste." Beautiful breasts.*

Why she'd decided to study German at university, Lucia would never quite understand. The complex grammar had interested her, and the sound—which, even before the war, so many of her friends had mocked—had reminded her, in a positive way, of a sad hymn in a minor key, all mournful notes and jagged changes. Her abilities with the language had landed her, not so much the job she'd originally been hired to do—the Germans weren't in control then—but the promotion from that job to Bruni's office. She could read the telexes and telegrams and file them properly, and even though some of them contained information she perhaps should not have seen, Bruni didn't seem to mind. And his recently arrived "associates" didn't seem to have thought to bring secretaries with them when they traveled from Vienna or Berlin.

As she went along, carrying the rolled-up poster now in both hands, she passed a restaurant that had remained open, a place called da Carmela on Via Tribunali. Sitting at one of three outdoor tables was the black-haired, blue-eyed German officer she sometimes noticed around the office. When she looked up and saw him, she realized he'd been staring at her, watching her walk along the curving, narrow street. He had a plate of food in front of him, which made her realize how hungry she was. He lifted a hand in greeting, a small, friendly wave. And then, "Join me?" The voice was kind, the invitation seemed harmless, the crooked smile sincere.

She nodded once, curtly, as if she hadn't understood, moved her eyes in front of her, and went on her way. If they knew what we were doing, she thought. What we were thinking. If only they knew.

Twenty-Four

One day a week—usually the day after Aldo visited—Rita made a trip to the Poggioreale Cemetery. The war had made everything more complicated, including the cemetery visit. More than a year earlier, the buses that used to go in that direction had stopped running, either because so many streets were no longer passable or because so many buses had been damaged or destroyed in the bombings. So, unless she was able to catch a ride with one of the wagons carrying caskets, she was required to walk: two hours each way.

She had no relatives buried at Poggioreale—none that she knew of, in any case. In the old days, she'd make the journey simply as a religious pilgrimage, to pray for the dead and to keep the gift of her own life in perspective. She'd bring flowers and place them next to graves that looked as though no one had tended them in years.

Now, however, there was one particular grave she cared for and at which she prayed every week. Merchants selling cut flowers were as scarce as soap, but she'd sometimes find a flowering weed growing from a pile of rubble, and she'd bring that along and place it near the plain round stone—no name engraved—that marked the burial plot.

On her walk that morning, trudging along what had once been a street of elegant homes—Via Arenaccia—but was now a kind of cemetery of buildings with huge piles of stone and glass blocking the roadway every fifty meters, she thought about how strange it was that she'd met two of her beloved young people in air-raid shelters.

In the days when the bombs had been falling, Rita and everyone else in Naples headed for the shelters as soon as the sirens sounded. If she were home when the horrible wail screamed out over the city, she'd hurry down the stairs and rush to the shelter on Largo Concordia—the same place where she'd first met little Armando. But if she happened to be out and about, she simply followed the crowd to the nearest refuge and ended up in all kinds of different bunkers and tunnels with all kinds of different people. Most of the shelters were underground, in the city beneath a city that had been carved out there thousands of years before. Some, especially near the Stella and Ottocalli, were caves that, centuries earlier, had been cut deep into the limestone cliffs, incredible places. One had a ceiling that must have been twenty meters high. People had actually built houses there, several of them two stories tall! Children had been born there; grandmothers and grandfathers and the wounded and sick had died there. Some of the shelters were filthy; others were cleaned according to a rigorous schedule arranged by the people of the neighborhood.

Of them all, the worst she'd ever seen was a concrete-walled, aboveground shelter behind the Garibaldi station, a place she'd run to once, only a few months earlier, when she was caught out on the streets later than usual, returning from a visit to a friend in Nola. The shelter was filthy, rank with the stink of human waste, but some of the people she'd met there had no place else to go; their homes and the homes of their relatives had been obliterated.

Rita believed she possessed an almost bottomless tolerance for the sight of human misery. From a very early age, long before Italy's involvement in the war, she'd seen and experienced things that would have sickened or destroyed most people. But her faith was strong, her belief in the existence of another dimension unshakable, and she'd found that helping and giving were the perfect antidotes to hopelessness.

That night in the fetid shelter, she'd come across a young girl named Anna who was trembling in fear as the bombs fell and the concussions rocked their concrete refuge. The bombs Rita could deal with—she'd had years of practice—but the sight of the girl's trauma had been almost too much to bear: the terrified young creature reminded her so vividly of herself at that age, though their terror had different sources. The frantic eyes and trembling mouth, the *no! stop! no!* that seemed to shiver wordlessly from her skin. It was like looking in a mirror that showed her worst memories.

Rita clasped the girl against her bosom, rocked her there, talked to her, called on the saints and angels to give her peace and keep her safe. When the all clear finally sounded, she accompanied the girl to her wreck of an apartment on Via Venezia in the Vasto. Anna lived with her grandmother, who'd been too terrified to leave. The inside of their apartment was all unwashed dishes and clumps of dust. It was obvious that the girl and her grandmother were close to starving, so Rita had started going by there every few days, sharing some of her rations, doing what little she could to keep them alive.

On the fifth or sixth visit, she'd noticed a strange rash on Anna's body, red spots that covered her midsection and legs but left her palms and the bottoms of her feet untouched. At first, Rita thought it might be the measles or chicken pox, but Anna had an extremely high fever and a cough, and seemed disoriented. Against the wishes of the elderly grandmother, who had no other company on this earth, Rita lifted the girl into her arms and carried her all the way to Palazzo Fuga, where the poorest of the poor were housed and treated. Half-starved as she was, Anna weighed less than a sack of potatoes, and her fever was so strong that Rita's skin sweated where it came in contact with hers. In better days, the Fuga had enjoyed a reputation for excellent care, but its finest doctors were at the front now, conscripted into Mussolini's army, and the place was staffed by volunteers, three doctors and a handful of nurses too old for military service. The emergency room was as crowded as some of the bomb shelters, with men, women, and children of all ages lying about in postures of exhaustion or agony. The smell, the cries and moans, the faces of the toddlers who'd been mutilated, blinded, or deafened by the bombs or whose arms or legs had been cut by flying glass or stone, the old women in ragged clothing and the old men without shoes—it might have been a scene from a painting of hell.

After the better part of two hours, when a nurse had finally arrived to examine little Anna, she couldn't disguise the look of horror that crossed her face. The girl was brought into a back room, a closet really, and kept alone there, her clothes stripped off and her body washed as carefully as it could be washed given the shortage of soap. *"Tifo,"* the nurse had whispered to Rita in the hallway outside. Typhus. "Go home, destroy the clothes you're wearing, wash yourself, and pray to God you won't be infected."

Rita did as she was told, confident that the saints would protect her, and she went back to visit Anna every day, watching and praying at the bedside as the girl burned up and trembled, and finally, after hours of agony, succumbed. They buried her in a simple grave in the poorest corner of the Poggioreale—Rita paid for the plot.

On this morning, after sending Aldo away with a last embrace, Rita set off to say prayers for Anna's soul. The trip was long, but it soothed her tired soul. For the last part of the journey, instead of staying on the streets, which had been so thoroughly bombed in that part of the city that it was more like mountain climbing than walking, she cut through a corner of a field, following a narrow path at first and then losing herself momentarily in the grassy remains of a small orchard. Not long before she emerged, near the cemetery gates, she ducked under the branches of a tree and, to her astonishment, happened to see a single peach hanging there, hidden by the pointed leaves, perfectly ripe. The orchard owner and the starving vandals had somehow missed it. She plucked the peach, slipped it into the pocket of her dress, and went on to the grave site.

After her prayers there, after clearing a few weeds from the lump of dirt that marked Anna's grave, Rita made her way back toward the Centro again, her stomach aching, the peach tapping against her thigh with every step. The temptation to take it out and eat it was almost overwhelming, but she knew there was food at home, and she suspected she would come across someone who needed the nourishment more than she did. As it happened, her route took her close to the old tire warehouse on Via Casanova. There was little use for tires now; the building had been abandoned, its large front windows covered with metal grates, its front doors locked. Armando had told her that he slept there sometimes in the warmer months, in a repair shed the mechanics had used. "It's safe and quiet there, *Nanella*," he told her. "No one knows about it."

She found the building without trouble, went along the alley beside it, and saw the mechanics' shed, a rectangular wooden box that was missing a section of one wall. There was her young friend, his head resting on an old motorcycle tire, as sound asleep as any prince in any luxurious bedroom. Careful not to awaken him, Rita took the peach from her pocket and set it beside him on the wooden floor, then, tired and hungry, hurried back up the alley and turned toward home.

She'd gone only as far as Corso Garibaldi—two blocks—when she heard a commotion in front of her. Shouting, at first, and then the most horrible screams. By instinct, she stopped and looked for shelter. A ruined tram car sat there, frozen on its tracks, right in the middle of the street. No glass in the windows, the roof caved in. Rita ducked behind it, heard the shouts again, the cries of a child. She placed both hands on the warm metal of the tram's front end and peered around its nose. Halfway up the block, two German soldiers were dragging a pair of children out of a house, their heels scraping on the pavement, the girl's right shoe falling off, the boy swinging his arms wildly, the soldiers holding them by their shirt collars. Jews, the children must have been; it was unlike the Nazis to take children away unless they were Jews. Rita watched, horrified, as the boy and girl were squeezed into the front of the truck from both sides, one soldier shoving them through each door and then climbing in after them. She focused all her attention there, willing something miraculous to happen, willing the children to escape, the soldiers to have a change of heart, the truck to stutter and stall.

Before the engine could be engaged, she heard gunshots, and then the whole scene in front of her went suddenly chaotic, a photograph cut into puzzle pieces, the pieces flung into the air. She ducked down closer to the street, but couldn't keep herself from pushing her head out past the tram's front end and watching, praying. It took her a few seconds to understand: someone was firing at the truck from the top floor of one of the houses on the left side of the street. The soldier on the driver's side started firing back, the long, dark barrel of his rifle pointing out the truck window. There was a series of loud exchanges, then the rifle sagged and fell. She could see the man's arm hanging limp over the edge of the truck door. A second passed, two seconds, and she saw a line of bullet holes—from a machine gun?—moving along the truck's rear fender like the small, circular footprints of an invisible animal. One tongue of flame erupted at the end of the line of bullets, and suddenly the truck was burning, the passenger door thrown open, one soldier sprinting away, the children screaming as they tumbled out and then, tripping and falling, raced back into the house. Small tongues of flame licked over the truck fender, and then there was an explosion, and a piece of the truck went flying up in the air and came crashing down against the back end of the tram just as a blast of air knocked Rita onto her back. She lay there for a few seconds, stunned but unhurt, mouthing a Hail Mary, the smell of smoke and burning rubber, the scene already replaying itself in her mind's eye like a bizarre dream.

Someone, some ordinary Italian, had a machine gun in a third-floor apartment and had used it to shoot at German soldiers! One soldier was dead, the other running for his life.

Impossible.

Twenty-Five

Aldo was sitting alone in his apartment, nursing a glass of lifeless beer and going over every facial expression and tone of voice from the underground meeting and his visit to the Spagnoli, every word that he, Zozo, and the Dell'Acquas had spoken, every word he'd said to Rita, and every word she'd said to him in return. This was his compulsion, and had been for as long as he could remember. It was as if his mind didn't work fast enough to process interactions on the spot, so he had to go over them time and again after the fact, to see if he'd embarrassed himself, given too much away, made himself look foolish or vulnerable, or if there had been some secret meaning, some bad intent, in the things people had said to him.

With Rita, of course, there was no worry about bad intent, but there had been something new between them yesterday, something so different and puzzling that he couldn't find the right way to think about it. With Zozo and the Dell'Acquas, it was similar in this one way: something unspoken and unfamiliar had lurked beneath the conversation. That loaded question: *"Are you happy working for us?"* could have been a threat. And the new job smacked of a cover for something else, a disguise, a trick. How were he and his helper going to steal German military equipment? What would they do, lure Nazis into the woods, slit their throats, then remove and sell the tires that had been on their cars, or the boots that had been on their feet, the pistols and rifles they'd been carrying? Then he was supposed to sell it to the Allies, but the Allies were still probably a hundred kilometers away. It made no sense. It was a trick of some kind, but, though he replayed the meeting a dozen times, he couldn't penetrate to the heart of it.

As he sipped and pondered, there were three quiet knocks on the metal door. Afraid of nothing and proud of being afraid of nothing, Aldo opened it without hesitation, and as if his thoughts had summoned the man, there, a meter in front of him, stood Zozo Forni, feet spread wide, a grin on his unshaven face. The lightweight dark jacket. The curly hair and low forehead, the narrow eyes that made him look, always, as if he'd just been awakened from a dream in which he was arranging to make someone disappear. The large, straight scar glistened in the middle of his neck, a razor cut from childhood; people said his own father, a small-time criminal, had tried to kill him in a fit of drunken anger and nearly succeeded.

"Permission to enter," Zozo said, and the grin—a boss's grin, a killer's—widened.

Aldo had rented the ground-floor apartment in a dark mood, after the big argument with Lucia, and it was a dark place. Two rooms. One small, chest-high window on each side of the door that led to the street. A tiny kitchen and tiny bathroom crammed together at the back, with another window there—a glassed slit in the wall—and a bedroom half as large as the cell he'd shared with three boys in Nisida. Strangely enough, though, the furnishings (he'd had to sell two of the three lamps) were old and elegant, the chairs upholstered and heavy-legged, a half-broken chandelier hanging over a mahogany table it would have taken four strong men to move. In one corner of the room where he ate, the previous owners (he imagined them as an elderly couple whose fortunes had withered as they aged, but who'd retained, for sentimental reasons, a few pieces of furniture from their ritzy villa in the hills) had set two armchairs at an angle to each other, both covered in purple upholstery and lined with decorative brass pins. Aldo sat often in one of them. In his time there, no one had ever sat in the other.

Zozo was the first. Aldo had one bottle of beer left. He opened it, poured it into a glass, handed the glass to his visitor, and sat opposite him. It took him a quarter of a second to notice that Zozo had a pistol in a holster at his ribs. The *Camorrista* had small, chubby hands, fingers like sausages, and nails, even in wartime, kept in impeccable condition. He was overweight, not grossly so, but even with the hefty belly, he moved like an athlete and somehow always seemed perfectly relaxed. He blinked, and Aldo thought the man might fall asleep.

"To your new assignment," Zozo said, lifting the glass. When they'd drunk, he tapped the pistol beneath his jacket and said, "This is for you," but made no move to take it from the holster and hand it over.

"I've been thinking about the job," Aldo said.

Zozo laughed, one note, a kind of amused grunt. "And you have questions, correct?"

"*Sì.*"

"Take my advice: don't ask them."

"*Sì, certo.* Fine."

Zozo ran his eyes around the room. "My suspicion," he said, "is that no woman has put her foot in this place in the past century."

Aldo forced a smile, waited, watched. If Zozo had come to kill him, there was no use in trying to escape. Escape where? Out the front door into a part of the city that, even with the German presence, the man basically controlled? The Germans only *seemed* to run things. They did, in fact, have power in a certain way. They could stop you on the street, arrest you, bring you to the torture cells, kill you for no reason. But their authority was like a heavy gray quilt over a mattress covered with a thousand spiders, each with its own web and territory. With the quilt over both of them now, the most powerful spider of all was sitting in the chair opposite him, holding the glass of beer loosely between thumb and forefinger and keeping on his face an expression that no one on earth could read. Amusement? Stealth? Fury? No one could read it. "You have your Rita," Zozo said.

Aldo nodded, only partly surprised. He'd never mentioned his visits to Rita, not to anyone. The big spider's associates had followed him, checked on him, made sure Aldo Pastone wasn't working for the Fascists or the Nazis or one of the other families, then made their report.

"And your beautiful daughter."

Another nod, a stiffening.

"Who we watch out for always."

"That matters to me."

"I imagine it does." Zozo drained the glass in a single long gulp and set it on the marble-topped side table to his left. "Someone is following her. A German soldier. Did you know? *Lo zoppo*, we call him. *The lame one.*"

"I've seen him."

"And wanted to kill him, no doubt."

"Right."

"For the things he's done bothering Italian women, your daughter and others, he *should* be killed. He's a would-be rapist, a snake. Perhaps soon some unpleasant fate will befall him."

At the word *rapist*, the ugliest of words—*strupratore*—Aldo felt the skin on the backs of his shoulders rippling. At the same time, he realized the true purpose of the visit: Zozo was about to recruit him to become an assassin, using the safety of his own daughter as leverage.

"He follows your Lucia about the city as if he has no other job."

Aldo sat still, watching, waiting for the order.

Zozo sighed, shifted his weight in the chair, started to say something, stopped himself, moved on to another subject. "People have had enough," he said. "Things are changing now in the city."

"In the country," Aldo ventured.

"*Sì, sì, certo.* First we are fighting against the Allies. Now we are fighting with them. Our *duce*, our king . . ." He waved a hand as if the two men operated on another planet, which, in a sense, they did. His eyes closed another fraction. "They pretend to rule us but serve only themselves. What we have is our family, our city, those close to us. The rest is illusion, a mirage of power, am I correct?"

Aldo nodded.

"When the war is over," Zozo went on, "we'll have our city again. It will be completely ours. And the Hitlers and Mussolinis and Roosevelts and Churchills and Stalins will have"—another wave of the hand—"*un vuoto. An emptiness.* If they're even still alive."

"I was sorry about your brother. He was kind to me."

"Kind to many people, yes. And not so kind to others. You had his respect."

When Zozo paused again, hands on the tops of his thighs now, it occurred to Aldo that the conversation must be a test. The Camorra was loyal to one thing: the Camorra. If the Fascists enabled them to make money, then they supported, or at least tolerated, the Fascists. If the Allies were good for business, they backed the Allies. It occurred to him that, at some point, Zozo might have taken sides, might have become, for mysterious reasons, a supporter of Mussolini and his Blackshirts. Mussolini was gone now, but the Blackshirts remained, the OVRA remained, the spies, the ambitious bureaucrats, Fascists who would torture fellow Italians by forcing them to drink castor oil, shit their pants in public, and die of dehydration. They remained, and perhaps they were thinking that power awaited them again, in another form, once the Germans disappeared and the Allies had come and gone. Maybe they were intent on purging the city of any potential resistance, and Zozo was here to find out how his employee felt about Mussolini's departure, and where he would stand when the air cleared again and business flourished. Maybe the mention of his daughter was a veiled threat: *stand with us or we'll ruin her, carry her off in a car and ruin her forever.*

He'd heard the stories.

"You had my brother's respect," Zozo repeated. He drew the pistol out of the holster, tilted it this way and that in his hand for a few seconds, then reached it across the small space between them, handle first. "Loaded," he said. "You know how to use it?"

Aldo nodded.

"The clip has six rounds. We'll get you more."

"Fine."

Zozo pushed his weight to the edge of the chair as if to stand, then hesitated, palms on knees. He lifted his eyes and met Aldo's, and some of the pleasant disguise fell away. "It's a good thing to have a weapon now. There has been a series of . . . *incidents* in various parts of the city. Have you heard?"

"Yes, rumors anyway."

"Facts," Zozo corrected. "Some of our Nazi friends have met a sudden end of life. Which opens up for us certain opportunities. Tonight, the Dell'Acquas will come by here and pick you up in a car. The car has a large trunk. They will take you out the Avellino road, and there will be a German vehicle disabled on that road, at the thirty-two-kilometer mark. There won't be any soldiers guarding it. It will be disabled, abandoned. Your task will be to strip it as quickly as you can of anything that seems of value, anything you can fit into the trunk of the car. Weapons are first priority, understood?"

Aldo nodded.

"Don't put them in the back seat but in the trunk. Take a man you trust, if you want to, for companionship." He laughed at his own joke. "Once you've cleaned out the car, they'll drive you to a place near the church in Vasto. Do you know it? Near Corso Novara."

Aldo nodded, watching, trying to see what was behind the plan.

"That's all. And here . . ." Zozo fished into the inside pocket of his jacket, brought out a folded envelope, and set it on the table. "A first payment. We all have to eat."

Aldo nodded his thanks. Zozo stood and went to the door, opened it himself, and left without looking back, without a handshake or a goodbye. Aldo closed the door, waited a moment, then lifted the flap on the envelope and thumbed through the bills there. Four fifty-lire notes. Enough to feed him and Lucia for weeks. He lifted the pistol from the table, gingerly, and checked to see that it did, in fact, have a magazine with bullets in it. His mind was working and working, running through a dozen possibilities that might warrant such a generous payment. The Dell'Acqua boys would take him out on the Avellino road in darkness. He'd strip a German jeep that would have been abandoned at precisely the thirty-two-kilometer mark, carry back the contraband in the trunk of a car. Weapons especially. Bring the car to the Vasto.

It made no sense. There was something Zozo wasn't telling him. A missing piece.

Twenty-Six

Armando didn't like to sleep during the day—he always awoke sweating or shivering and tormented by the thought of missed opportunities—but sometimes it was unavoidable. Sometimes the nights were broken up by exploding bombs, or by the wails and screams from apartments; sometimes it was too cold, or too hot, or raining hard, or the only potential sleeping places were noisy with the squeals of rats. So he stayed up, walking and walking, or sitting with his friends by the port or in a piazza, waiting for their luck to change. After a night like that, if he found himself anywhere near the tire store on Via Casanova, he'd sneak into the deserted workshop and lie down for an hour or two, wooden floor for a bed, old tire for a pillow. No one bothered him in that place. He'd never seen a rat there, only a scampering mouse or two, and enough of the roof remained to block out the direct sunlight and most of the rain. For whatever reason, the dreams he had when he slept there were especially vivid, and on this day, he'd awakened from a long sleep speckled with visions of the nun who'd been so kind to him, Sister Marcellina. In one of the dream-moments, she was handing him a banana—he hadn't seen a banana in many months—and asking him to pray with her. He agreed, and was even going to kneel down next to her in a church pew when something, some sound or movement, caused his eyes to open.

For a time, he lay there, wide awake but not moving, thinking about the dream for a while, then thinking about the little girl the Nazis had shot with her grandparents, then staring across the littered floor at a greasy red rag that lay discarded beneath a workbench. These days, he liked to look at objects, even simple things like the yarn Tomaso had used to tie the German's ankle to a chair, and imagine ways they might be used. It came from his years on the streets, where a nail or stone or an abandoned belt buckle could become a weapon, where a coin might be discovered in the gutter. He was used to scavenging for food, but, important as that was, he enjoyed even more the hunt for materials. The greasy rag was useless, he decided, and then, remembering the German hat, he reached down to the shirt at his midsection and felt it, safely in place.

As he took his hand away, his fingers grazed something. He looked down. On the dusty floor, just in front of his navel, he thought he saw a peach. He closed his eyes and opened them, shook his head, afraid to reach out and touch what he was certain must be a mirage. He'd seen the crazy ones—men and women, old and not so old—who'd been driven over the edge of sanity by the war, and for a moment, he worried the months of hunger and the horrors of war were causing him to lose his mind. He stared at the peach, unmoving, and then at last reached out one finger and gingerly touched its skin. The peach tilted sideways, then righted itself when he took his hand away. It seemed real. He reached out again, propping himself up on one elbow, and touched it with two fingers and his thumb. Definitely real! He sat all the way up, still staring at it as if it might suddenly mutate into a hand grenade and explode in his face.

At last, he wrapped his fingers around it and lifted it to eye level. The fine dusting of fuzz, the mottled pink and orange and red and yellow skin, the stub of a stem and one small bruise on the side facing him. He brought it to his nose and smelled it. Ripe. Unbelievable. Instead of biting it, he licked it, once, the skin lightly scraping his tongue. He looked around again, opened his mouth, and took a small bite, the sweet flesh tugging back gently against his teeth. There was juice on his tongue and lips, an absolutely incredibly delicious taste in his mouth. He rolled the small bit of peach flesh around and around, sucking on it, still unsure that he was awake and sane, and then he squeezed it between his back teeth—more juice—and swallowed. Though he knew it was impossible, he looked up, through the hole in the roof, as if there might be a tree growing right above him in the tire company lot, or as if an angel might be hovering there, smiling down at him, nodding, waiting for a gesture of thanks. Nothing but sky, blue, with one fat, bubbly cloud sailing across it, but it seemed to him now that there might, in fact, be some spirit looking out for him. A mother spirit, perhaps. Or the spirit of that little girl. He spoke a word of thanks and took a second bite, then heard a muted noise from the direction of Corso Garibaldi. A small explosion, it sounded like. He decided to go out and investigate.

Twenty-Seven

At the close of the workday, his precious map stored safely in the watchman's room, rolled up tight and squeezed between the wall and the bed where he and Lucia had made love, Giuseppe left the National Archives building and wandered, almost like an aimless man, in the general direction of the Duomo. He was, however, the furthest thing from aimless. According to what he now thought of as the most valuable book in the entire Archives, *The Directory of the Public Structures of the City of Naples*, there was a building not far from Piazza Cavour that, during World War I, had been used as an armory for the Italian military. He knew where the storage facilities were, and suspected that this one had fallen into disuse. But, upon waking that morning, he'd had the thought that the Germans might have resurrected it for that same purpose. While it might not be their main storage area, they could be keeping small arms there, or vehicles, or even a few of the thousands of men who had been stationed in the city since the retreat from Sicily and Mussolini's mysterious departure from Rome. The Allies would want to know.

So he wandered, hands in his pockets, looking, to any casual observer, like nothing more than another hungry Neapolitan young man in his wrinkled brown pants and scuffed brown shoes, searching the city for a cheap bowl of soup or a pretty young woman. Up past the huge cathedral he went, dodging the piles of rubble and scavenging dogs and scaring flapping pigeons into the air. He heard a gull cawing above him and thought of the times his parents had taken him to the shore when he was small. Before the onset of war, he'd made this walk hundreds of times, varying his route home, and always the air had been filled with rich smells: tomato sauce simmering in an upstairs apartment, meat cooking, warm bread being taken out of an oven, small pizzas, calzones, and *sfogliatelle* just made and on display in glass cases on the sidewalks. The brisk scent of lemon, the rich fragrance of basil, the earthiness of just-harvested mushrooms sitting in boxes on a stand at the corner of Via Foria.

Now, only the smell of smoke and dust, perhaps a hint of the sea.

He saw a boy go past, dressed in the unofficial uniform of a *scugnizzo*—the dirty clothes and ragged shoes—his face triangular and smudged, one hand on his midsection, as if he were hiding something there beneath the T-shirt.

Giuseppe went left on Don Bosco, past a row of beggars, men and women to whom he had nothing to give. For some reason, the sight of them stimulated his own hunger, a clutching in his stomach, a radiating ache. It was like a companion to him now, and he knew that a million others shared the feeling. He turned right onto a side street—no sign, but he knew it must be Viale di Quaresima, the Alley of Lent. That word caused him to remember his boyhood Lenten fasts, his mother and father and he and his uncle forgoing meat and, for the forty days leading to Easter, each of them giving up something they loved, as a spiritual discipline—veal for his father, mushrooms and peppers for his mother, chocolate for him. It was almost impossible to recall being sated enough to voluntarily give up any food for a day, anything, for one day, never mind meat, never mind a favorite food for six weeks.

The memory sparked another, harsher one: the sight of his parents' bloody bodies lying in grotesque positions among thirty or forty of their fellow Neapolitans. His mother's hand on his father's shoulder. The place they'd been executed—on the steps of the Ministry of Health (the Germans seemed to find the location ironic and amusing)—was a hideous display of body parts, raw flesh, pools of blood. Men, women, and several teenagers arranged in a montage of agony. The Nazis had made surviving family members show their identification—as if it mattered, as if the soldiers knew the names of the victims—and then wait half an hour before collecting their loved ones' remains. With Lucia, his crippled uncle, and a local priest named Father Carvelli, Giuseppe had loaded first his father's body, and then his mother's on top of it, into a wheelbarrow—what choice did he have?—covered them with a blanket from their own bed, and wheeled them all the way to the Poggioreale Cemetery. The trip, made in scorching heat, lasted three hours. Even his uncle had taken a turn with the wheelbarrow and had managed a hundred meters before collapsing. They'd paid for the plot, dug the grave themselves, and then, wrapping the two bodies in the blanket and lowering them into the hole, knelt and listened to Father Carvelli say the burial prayers. And then Giuseppe alone had been able to shovel dirt into the hole.

He shook his head violently, as if the memory could be thrown from his temples into the afternoon air.

He went past the church—Madonna delle Grazie—and there was the armory, just ahead and on the opposite side of the street, covered now in long shadows. At the front gate stood a guard in German uniform, and, in the courtyard beyond, Giuseppe could see two soldiers crouching, at work on a vehicle. One of the soldiers wasn't wearing a helmet and had a white bandage wrapped around his head. Giuseppe could see an uneven red circle on the bandage. Fresh blood, a strange sight on a German soldier. Casually, almost accidentally, he looked up as he passed, but his eyes took in everything. Three floors, few windows, the guard, the bandage, the damaged truck.

Giuseppe walked on, turned a corner, and there a man coming in the other direction caught his eye. He didn't know why at first, since the man was dressed in a most ordinary way, much as Giuseppe himself was dressed. Something was different, though. The felt hat, the long-sleeve white shirt, the brown pants, the shoes . . . something didn't seem quite right. It wasn't until he'd gone to the end of the block and glanced back that he was able to understand what it was: the man didn't walk like an Italian, and the clothes were new, as if they hadn't been worn in a year. Some kind of visitor. Perhaps a spy.

Twenty-Eight

Armando made the peach last as long as he could, holding each bite in his mouth and moving it around, licking the juice from his fingers, sucking on the pit as if it were a piece of candy until the taste turned bitter and he reluctantly spat it out. He stood up and brushed the dust from his shirt, pants, and hair and walked down the alley to the street. The peach, he realized, had not fallen from a tree, nor had it been sent to him by an angel. It must have been brought by Sister Marcellina, and that must have been why he'd dreamed of her. Somehow—maybe she'd seen one of his *coro* and asked where Armando might be found—she had discovered his favorite sleeping place. She'd been given a peach and thought of him. Guilt was an alien emotion to him, but he felt a twinge of something similar, the realization that he had never gone back to the orphanage to thank her for all she'd done. The reason for that was partly embarrassment and partly the worry that one of the other nuns would see him and pull him back into the building, force him to go to Mass, try to convince him to become a priest. Some of the other *scugnizzi* had started a rumor that the nuns would turn over orphanage escapees to the guards at Nisida, and they'd spend a year there, paying for the trouble they'd caused.

Untrue, probably, but, loving freedom as he did, Armando had never wanted to take the chance and had always given the orphanage— set a hundred meters to one side of the church in Materdei—a wide berth. But the peach filled him with a bloom of confidence and softened his heart and he decided to seek out Sister Marcellina and thank her. The motivation wasn't completely selfless: maybe she had a connection to an orchard keeper in the hills near Avellino. Maybe there would be peaches enough for the *coro*.

Armando prided himself on a kind of sixth sense, and as he went along—using the side streets, which seemed safer—cutting past Piazza Cavour and toward the rear of the Archeological Museum, keeping an eye out for opportunities and wondering what his crew was up to without him, his sixth sense told him there was something odd about the afternoon. For one thing, for a few minutes there was a strange smell in the air—burning rubber. And there was next to no traffic on the streets, not even the occasional bus or tram when he crossed the busy Don Bosco. No German lorries or jeeps hurrying past. For another, with each day that passed without bombs falling, a strange tension had begun to seep into the broken streets and rubble-choked alleys. From his friends, he kept hearing stories of small rebellions, a report of several *carabinieri* being killed because they'd exchanged gunfire with a carful of Germans. Something would happen soon. Either the bombs would start falling again, the Allies would march into the city behind their tanks and guns, or the Nazis would grow ever more vicious and simply kill people at random, without even the excuse of revenge.

As he was thinking this, he found himself walking past the armory on Via Stella, two soldiers in German army uniforms lingering in the courtyard, one of them with a bloody bandage on his head. Armando shifted the hat inside his shirt so that it flattened against his left hip, hidden from the soldiers. What good was it? What was the right thing to do with it? Was it wrong not to share it with Tomaso, and let *him* carry it around? He held on to it like a trophy and wondered how the officer would explain its absence to his superiors. The strange sense of trouble, almost an anxiety now, followed him like a bad smell. He looked away from the soldiers, turned the corner, went another block, and saw, coming the other way, a man with too-clean clothes and a strange way of walking. As the man approached, Armando stopped, made his face into a mask of self-pity, and held out one hand, palm up. *"Sto morènd e' famè,"* he said, Neapolitan for *"I'm starving."* The man seemed to understand dialect, but he only made a face and walked past. Armando turned to watch him go. Something wasn't right. *A spy,* he thought. *American, maybe. Or maybe a Nazi searching for Jews and hidden weapons. A Nazi who understands Neapolitan.* He was tempted to run after him, place the stolen hat on the guy's head, and sprint away.

But on he went, climbing the rise of Via Materdei. With its neat houses—most of them now damaged by the bombs—and patches of park, it had always seemed to him a strange place for an orphanage. But there was the Church of Santa Maria, where they'd been forced to attend Mass. And there, not far beyond it, the orphanage itself. To his horror, he saw that, while the corner facing him was intact and the facade still standing, the whole rear half of the building was simply piles of stones and pieces of broken furniture. A tall chimney stood up out of the nothingness, miraculously untouched. He circled around back and picked his way carefully through the ruins—stones of every shape, chunks of concrete, scraps of bed linen, table legs, one dented pot—until he was standing where he guessed his own bed had been, ten steps from the chimney. He wondered if Sister Marcellina had been killed, if any children had been. He prided himself on never crying, never, not after a beating, not while sleeping out in the cold, not from hunger, but now he could feel tears rising into his eyes. He remembered—two or three years old he must have been—standing obediently in line for soup, a spoon in one hand, the plain orphanage uniform covering him from shoulders to knees. He thought of his friends, boys and girls both, and how, one by one, they'd been taken away. *"Adopted,"* Sister Marcellina had said. *"Given to couples who are unable to have children of their own."* But he was never adopted, and he'd grown to believe it was because of something in his face, a devious look in his eyes, his sly smile. In time, he forced himself to exaggerate those things, to be proud of not being given away, of being the favorite of the prettiest nun in the building. He stood there for a minute, thinking of her, wondering where his friends were now, where she was, if they'd all been killed, and then he turned and picked his way carefully through the rubble, back out to the street.

He walked over and up the steps and made himself place a hand on the big doors of the church. After a slight hesitation, he pulled one side open, went through, and stood in the rear of the nave for a few minutes, letting his eyes adjust, taking in the smell of incense and candle smoke, running his gaze over the dark, empty pews, hoping to see a nun's habit. He noticed that the huge old paintings had all been removed from the walls, and he remembered staring at one of them—the Virgin's robe a beautiful blue, like the color of the sky, and a small child at her feet, clutching its hem with one hand—during the most boring parts of the Mass. Now, bare walls. The wooden confessionals, the white marble altar, all of it still a bit frightening. He sat in one of the rear pews. The stolen hat burned against the skin of his belly. He lifted his shirt and removed it, turning it this way and that, admiring again the fine tailoring and brass insignia, wondering what the green line of thread meant, wondering if it was a sin to bring a stolen piece of the Devil's uniform into the sacred space of a church.

He heard a footstep on stone and looked up to see a familiar face there beside and above him.

"*Lu skutchamenz,*" the priest said. *The little pest.*

"*Padre.*"

"You've come to confess, yes?"

"Ah, I have nothing to confess, Padre Paulo. God loves me more than you! You should confess to me!"

The priest settled himself in the pew next to Armando and wrapped an arm around the boy's shoulders for a moment, sighed, reached out, and touched the stolen hat. "You made this yourself, I suspect."

Armando smiled. "Yes, it took me a long time."

"I'm sure."

"And a mysterious angel left a peach for me this morning. I was sleeping. I woke up, and the peach was there. A perfect peach. I ate it very slowly."

"Good, good. A peach. I haven't seen a peach since . . ." The priest waved his hand and looked up at the altar. "I've missed you," he said.

"What happened to the orphanage?"

A sorrowful shrug. The old man met Armando's eyes for a moment, then looked away. "The bombs."

"Were people killed?"

Another sad shrug. "With God now," he managed, but without much enthusiasm.

"Sister Marcellina?"

"Miraculously unhurt. She went to stay with her family. In the Vasto, they live. Took one boy and one girl with her. She comes to Mass every week. If you have the time, you might do the same."

Armando studied the wrinkled, spotted face, recalling a thousand acts of kindness. The memories were almost enough to make him consider going to Mass again. Almost. "I thought she was the one who brought me the peach. At my secret place on Via Casanova. The store that used to sell tires."

"It's possible," the priest said. "She lives not far. Many strange things are possible . . . that a boy your age could learn to make such a beautiful hat, for instance."

"Can you hold it for me, Padre?"

"Of course. I'll hide it in the room where we change. We have some other things hidden there."

"Guns?"

The priest put a finger to his lips.

"Really, Padre?" Armando whispered.

The slightest nod, then a pause and the priest said, "When the war is finished, this hat will be some kind of . . . trophy. You can sell it."

"When will the war be finished?"

"God alone knows that, my *skutchamenza*. But when it finishes, you will study for the priesthood, yes, as you promised?"

A smile stretched the muscles of Armando's face. Their running joke. "And you will live on the streets, Padre. I'll show you all the tricks." He handed over the hat and, just as the brim left his fingers, felt his mood change. "I saw something terrible yesterday, Padre. I saw a little girl and her grandparents shot in the street. I can't forget seeing it. I can't clean it out of my mind."

Padre Paulo wrapped his arm around Armando's shoulders again and pulled him close for a moment. "Sometimes," he said, "I pray to forget the things I've seen and the things I've heard."

"Does it work?"

The priest shook his head, reached beneath his robe, ruffled the cloth there for a few minutes, then produced a single coin and pressed it into Armando's palm. "For food," Padre Paulo said. "If you find another peach, buy it."

"I'll bring you half."

The priest tapped him on the shoulder, and Armando left the pew and slipped silently through the heavy front door, making the sign of the cross as he went, something he hadn't done for many months. Outside, he glanced at the orphanage again, and was about to cross the street when he heard a truck speeding along the stone pavement. He worried it would be driven by a hatless Nazi, come to send him to the cemetery to lie forever in the cold dirt beside the murdered girl, but it was an Italian Army truck, its open bed roofed in green canvas. The truck skidded to a stop just before reaching him. He saw two men in civilian clothes climb out of the back and caught a glimpse of them carrying something down a short set of steps and through an open doorway. A casket, he thought at first, because what they were carrying was long and thin and wrapped in a white sheet. But the contents of the package rattled, like metal against metal, and the men were hurrying.

Another few seconds and they reappeared and climbed into the truck. As it went past, the driver turned and looked at him. Out of a street kid's habit—anything to torment the authorities—Armando made a vulgar gesture, grinned, and hustled away in the opposite direction. He'd gone half a block before he realized that he'd recognized the mean-looking man in the passenger seat. He remembered the name, too. Zozo Forni. He hoped Zozo hadn't seen him.

Twenty-Nine

On her way home, wondering what would become of the Jewish children who'd barely managed to escape, Rita heard what sounded like bombs or huge guns going off. Near the airport, she guessed. Four quick explosions, then nothing but the odd quiet of the streets. She was grateful that, as the sun dipped behind the buildings in front of her, the air at last began to cool. It had been a very long and tiring day, a day filled with surprises, as if the stars were aligning in playful fashion, taking the expectations of simple human beings and tipping them upside down.

On warm evenings like this, life had always been lived on the streets. In better times, when the men hadn't been sent off to Russia or Africa, Albania or Greece; when women and girls hadn't been forced to sell their bodies for food; when wine and pasta were plentiful; when the magnificent jumble of humanity that went by the Italian name Napoli had been able to work and laugh and make love and endure life's ordinary sadnesses and struggles; when the five- and six-story palaces that lined the main streets, with their wrought-iron balconies and rows of elegant windows, and the six-hundred-year-old churches with their stained glass and gold had stood intact and undamaged; and when the German army had stationed its soldiers north of the border; the tables of the city's sidewalk cafés had been full; the children had invented games and roamed the alleys; and neighbors had sat in circles, sometimes well into darkness, gossiping and arguing, telling tales, laughing, breaking spontaneously into Neapolitan songs like *"C'è La Luna"* and *"Torna a Surriento"* and the wonderfully erotic tune that always made her a little sad, *"Comme facette mammeta"*—*how your mama made you.*

Like almost everyone else she knew, Rita mourned those days. The festivals, rituals, and parades, the amusing superstitions and elaborate church services, the lavish meals and magnificent funerals, the only very occasional sound of an ambulance Klaxon and the prayers that would be sent after it for the suffering soul—she missed all that richness. Acting upon some unwritten instruction, the people of Naples had tried to keep the shops and cafés open, even the movie theaters, but the schools had long been closed. She tried very hard to hold on to some small semblance of that happy past, even now. She still visited her brother at the monastery, made her weekly trip to the cemetery. She entertained her men. And if she was alone as the day faded, she carried a chair down from the second floor, set it out on the sidewalk, and sat there enjoying the light on the housefronts, the smell of the sea air, the children at play.

She pulled open the yellow door, climbed wearily to her apartment, put a little food and water into her mouth, and then, intent on bringing something familiar back to the surprising day, she carried a chair downstairs and sat there, watching the kids.

Their games now had more shooting and soldiering in them, but boys and girls alike, they still raced and flirted, climbed on piles of rubble even though their parents warned them not to, still came back to the house weeping if they fell and hurt themselves or endured a verbal insult. From time to time, she managed to buy some small candies—nothing like what she'd once been able to find—and the boys and girls would swing by her chair, make their selection, then race off again, their lives touched by the war, of course, but not always with the same heavy hand that touched their parents' lives.

Soon, her neighbors joined her there on the sidewalk—the saintly Eleonora, mother of eight, and her husband, Joe, a tailor of the first order, a man who'd gone to America before the war to make money, and come back (keeping the American name), a man who could repair anything with his delicate hands; Gina and her grown daughter and the grown daughter's four-year-old girl, the two adults sniping at each other constantly and complaining about every manner of thing from the smell of sewage to the scourge of lice.

And then, alas, another addition: Leopoldo Fontana, the next-door bachelor Fascist, the man from whom they'd first heard the name Benito Mussolini. Since those long-ago days, they'd heard it from him again and again, in every conversation. According to Leopoldo, Mussolini was never wrong. Mussolini was a genius, a loving father, a hero. Victim of the sly Roosevelt or the boastful Churchill. Now he'd also become the victim of General Badoglio and the king, traitors both, snakes who'd swept Il Duce from office, against the will of the Italian people.

Leopoldo was fond of shouting at the children—it was almost a hobby of his—perhaps because he had no wife to shout at and no children of his own. He seemed to expect them, at age four and six and thirteen, to behave like little soldiers. "Stand up straight!" he'd yell. "Stop that weeping!" "Pull that dress down!" "Your parents need to instill some *disciplina!*"

More than anything, Rita found his tirades boring, though, since Mussolini had been deposed and the Germans had come to the city in greater numbers, Leopoldo seemed emboldened, and even tried to tell Eleonora how she should behave. Once, having heard enough from him, Eleonora, never known to utter a bad word about anyone, looked at him with a fierce eye and said, *"Leopoldo lu strunze." Leopold the turd.* And that moment had been replayed a dozen times since, often in Leopoldo's presence, to a concert of laughter.

This evening, he was at it again, telling Joe he should find tailoring work, when there was simply no work to be found. Complaining about disorder. Reminding them, for the fiftieth time, that for three years, the bombs had been dropped, not by the Fascists, not by Hitler, but by the British and Americans. "Too cowardly to fight like men, hand to hand."

"Did you fight?" Joe, a veteran of the first war, asked him.

Leopoldo hadn't fought. Instead of answering, he told a little girl that her dress was up over her knees. "Cover yourself! Cover yourself!" he called out in his deep voice. "What's wrong with you!"

And the reason *why* the bombs had been dropped by the Allies was something Leopoldo seemed unwilling to consider.

As Rita sat there—feeling the heat of the afternoon moving slowly toward the cool of night, and listening to Leopoldo grumble—she caught sight of a beautiful young woman coming around the corner and walking slowly along the other side of the street, as if she were searching for something or someone. As the woman came closer, Rita could see that she had long legs, long hair, a lively stride, a face Michelangelo might have considered placing on one of his statues of the Virgin Mother. Her footsteps echoed in the quiet street. All the assembled neighbors were looking at her. And now the beautiful young creature seemed to be looking back at them. After a moment's hesitation, she crossed the street, wound her way through the children, touching one girl on the head the way a mother might, and approached the adults. "I'm looking for someone who knows my father," she said, running her eyes from one end of the row of chairs to the other. "Aldo Pastone."

Leopoldo snorted, turned his face away, hooked his thumb in Rita's direction. "You could say this woman knows him."

"I'm his daughter," the beautiful stranger said. She had a purse over her right shoulder and a strand of hair falling across her face.

Leopoldo snorted a second time, started to make another comment, then stopped himself, got up, and strode away.

Rita stood. "Come with me," she said. She held open the yellow door and led the way up to her apartment.

Mounting the stairs she'd climbed so many times on so many other occasions, now on very tired legs, Rita felt a kind of shifting inside her, as if her new feelings for Aldo, sparked by the most recent visit, had magically manifested themselves in the arrival of his spectacularly attractive daughter. At the top of the stairwell, she opened the door and led her guest to the kitchen table. She told the young woman to sit. "I have a little wine," she said. "But not much to eat. A bit of rice and fish if you want. I'm sorry."

The girl shook her head. "I'm sorry not to have brought anything."

They both knew it was merely a dance of politeness, a delicate Southern Italian choreography drawn up centuries ago and remembered from better days. Rita stood and busied herself cleaning the glasses twice and holding them up to the light, then pouring the plum-colored war wine, something that would have been tossed in the sink a few years ago.

She sat facing her guest as she had faced the girl's father just the day before. Strangely enough, the daughter looked nothing like Aldo. He was dark, but she was somewhat light of complexion with hair that was a shade this side of black. He was handsome enough, but she was stunning, with bright-green eyes, prominent cheekbones, and a lovely mouth. What a beauty the mother must have been, Rita thought. From the street below, she heard Leopoldo's guttural laugh. She got up again, closed the door tight, and pulled the windows closed.

"I'm sorry if I'm bothering you," the girl began, using the formal *Lei* instead of the familiar *tu*.

"Dammi del tu," Rita told her, and her guest smiled shyly and nodded. "I'm not that much older than you. Thirty-eight, and you're . . ."

"Twenty-six next week."

"Ah. Please. There's no one left on earth who uses the *Lei* with me, and I prefer it that way."

"Yes, fine. I . . . ah . . . I followed my father here yesterday. I saw him come in the door downstairs. The yellow door. I feel dishonest doing that, but I have no mother. I never knew a mother. And he . . . he's . . ."

Rita thought the girl was about to burst into tears. "You haven't told me your name."

"Lucia."

"Yes, I remember now. He's spoken of you a hundred times."

"Really? With me, he is as distant as the moon."

With me, also, Rita almost said, but it wouldn't have been true anymore, and something in the young woman's presence seemed to require the truth. For a moment, she could think of nothing to say, and then she remembered what she'd told her brother: the masculine exterior, the shell, and so she repeated it the same way.

A sad smile caught the corners of Lucia's lips. "Not all men," she said.

"No, but these are terrible times."

"He was like that in the easy times."

"I don't see him as ever having known easy times."

"Some of that is his choice."

"*Certo.* And for each of us, our choices grow out of a certain soil. If the soil is not healthy, how can a healthy tree grow?" *How can it bear good fruit?* she was on the verge of saying, but she realized that, in Aldo's case, whatever arid soil his own choices had grown from, the fruit he'd produced seemed . . . *radiant* was a word she might have used. The woman sitting opposite her had a certain glow that went beyond the physical beauty, a brightness that Aldo showed only in the rarest of moments, and even then only for a second or two, a flash of some hidden courage. Rita wondered if she might be looking at the person she wished she'd become, the woman she might have been, had her early life been other than it was.

Lucia shrugged and looked away.

"I can't tell you how happy it makes me for you to come here."

Lucia nodded, brought her eyes back. "You aren't married?"

Rita shook her head.

"Then how do you live?" she asked. "How do you earn any—" She stopped, as if the answer had suddenly occurred to her.

"I live because I sleep with men," Rita said. "I've lived that way for a long time. My father was a Moroccan trader, here only long enough to plant his seed inside my mother, who had an older son by another man, and who abandoned me when I was young. I never feel ashamed," Rita said. "It's strange. But now, for a moment, I do."

"I'm sorry, I shouldn't have—"

"No, no. Your mention of your father made me think of it. He's distant, yes, but at least you see him sometimes. I never saw my father. My mother was also abandoned by that man, and she had an older child, a son in the seminary. She left me at the orphanage when I was eight, and died a month later. Or so I was told." Rita sat there, staring at Aldo's daughter. Something about the girl had lifted the heavy cover from a box inside her. The words, held there so long in darkness, seemed to leap out toward the light. "From the orphanage, I was adopted. Sent to live with a family. Near the train station. Very poor people. Troubled people, with very troubled friends. Men . . . *used me* from the time I was twelve, one after the next. And then a priest rescued me. I lived in the rectory next to the Duomo from the time I was fourteen until I was sixteen, and the priests there treated me well, but great damage had been done to me, to my mind. I felt too unloved by God to remain with them, and so I made the decision to leave, and I found a man who was kind to me and gave me gifts. Then another man. Then another. I have tried, always, to be with them with love. I kept some of the gifts they gave me, and some money, and I . . . Thanks to my brother now, I—"

"Please stop," Lucia said. "I don't judge you. Please."

Rita stopped, tears welling up, but she held her eyes steadily on Lucia's and refused to let herself cry. "For the past six years, I've been with two men. Your father and a famous lawyer. The famous lawyer can't make love, but with your father, I . . ."

"Is he kind to you?"

"Perfectly kind. In his fashion."

"From as far away as the moon is the way he's kind to me. He paid for my schooling, my clothing. He hired women to care for me, but I barely saw him, and he won't ever speak of my mother."

"Nor with me."

"Now he gives me gifts of food and . . . other things. I think he's embraced me twice in my life. Once when I fell and hurt myself and we had to go to the hospital. And one other time. We were walking. He heard a certain song. There were three seconds when he was warm to me. I loathe what he does."

"I think he loathes it also."

"I can't believe that. No brothers, no sisters, no mother. What I wish for is one family connection with some warmth in it. Everywhere I go, I see it, but not in my life."

"There are things I also see everywhere that are not in my life."

Lucia drank most of the wine in two long gulps and pressed her lips together. "Am I bothering you?"

"Not the smallest bit. Some day you will have children, and then all the love you wish for, you will give them and they will give you."

"Do you have children?"

"I do not."

"Do you want them?"

"More than anything on this earth."

"Can you? You're still . . . of the age."

"It seems not."

Finally, a tear that had been holding itself behind Lucia's eyes climbed over the lid and trickled down along one smooth cheek. As if in answer, a tear bubbled over in each of Rita's eyes. She swabbed at them with the back of her forearm.

"I'm sorry," Lucia said. "I work at the Municipio, under the supervision of the Germans now, though my boss is Italian. We received a proclamation from the new German colonel, and today I carried it to the printer to have two thousand copies made. I feel so guilty."

"The proclamation said what?"

"That he's declaring a state of siege, the colonel. That anyone found with weapons will be shot. That all men between the ages of eighteen and thirty-three should report and be sent to Germany to work in the camps. I have a lover," she said. "Giuseppe is his name. Both his parents were executed. On the steps of the Ministry of Health, two weeks ago. He'll surely be taken and sent to Germany. I'm hoping to ask my father for help, but he hates Giuseppe."

Rita traced the pain on Lucia's face, thought about what she had said. "The proclamation . . . it's the deed of the Devil."

"Yes, exactly. My boyfriend is making a map. Of the city. Of the places the Germans keep their men and guns and so on. He's hoping to give it to the Allies, so that when they come, if they come . . ."

"I'll speak to your father. He has friends. They can help."

"I didn't come here to ask you that. I don't want the help of those men."

Rita watched her, thinking how impossible it was to hold on to purity in a world at war. To hold on to it at any time. Purity, for her, had never been a possibility. Perhaps not for Aldo, either. It was possible that her brother, Marco, had clung to it, but in order to do that, he'd had to wall himself off from life and its temptations. "You should let your father try," she told the girl. "This paper will be posted around the city?"

Lucia nodded.

"Then your boyfriend will surely be taken, and you'll never see him again. You should let your father try to help. He's a good man."

The girl looked aside, unconvinced. She took a last small sip of the wine, only to be polite, Rita thought. Another second and she burst into tears and was weeping openly.

Rita reached across the small distance between them and put both her hands on Lucia's forearms. She held them there, squeezing gently, then drew in a breath and brought her mind down into the very middle of her own soul, the one place untouched by everything that had been done to her. That place contained a secret well that had kept her alive even in the harshest of times. She drew from it now. Love, comfort, healing. And passed it through her fingers. Two strands of Lucia's hair were held against her face by the tears there. Rita reached up and moved them aside, right, then left, then rested her hand on the top of Lucia's head until the girl raised her wet eyes and managed a smile.

"The map your boyfriend is making," Rita said quietly. "Can you bring it to me?"

Thirty

Stevie Spinelli was confident he could pass for a Neapolitan. His commanding officers had believed it, too: the dark hair and large nose, the fluency in the language and familiarity with the dialect, the advantage of having grown up with parents *"right off the boat,"* as his commanding officer had put it, of having been a boy who learned to sneak and deceive on the streets of New Haven, Connecticut. Dressed in the rough brown worker's trousers, felt hat, and long-sleeve white shirt they all wore, he'd walked down from the monastery into Ercolano like any stonemason or gardener on a day off, and taken the bus into Naples as if going in search of food, or to see a relative. The assignment had been simple enough: slip through the German lines in darkness, take refuge in the Monastery of the Genovese, where a contact had been made through a Vatican priest sympathetic to the cause. Make two or three trips into the city and get a sense of the places where German forces were concentrated and artillery positioned, the streets that could accommodate tanks, the places to avoid, the mood, if possible. Simple. Then return to the monastery for his pistol and knife and slip back through the lines—the most dangerous part of the whole thing—using the password, and make the report.

He loved the work. It was dangerous, yes, but no more dangerous than fighting up the ankle of the boot, facing Nazi snipers and mortars and their P40 tanks. A quarter of his company was already dead.

On the walk downhill to Ercolano and the ride into the city, no one spoke to him. It seemed that no one looked at him. The concern, of course, was that he'd be stopped by Nazi patrols, who'd want to know why he wasn't serving in the Italian Army. He had papers for that. A false passport identifying him as one Eugenio Ucellino, a false document from an imaginary doctor, signed and stamped, declaring that, while it would allow him to perform certain small physical tasks like painting and gardening, his weak heart would not permit any real soldiering, nothing that made him anxious or caused his pulse to rise.

Fifteen minutes on the bus through rolling countryside—a few places cultivated, one large crater from an errant bomb—then the bus turned downhill, sputtered across a flat plain (he was making mental notes all the while, looking for high ground from which the Germans could fire artillery, looking for defilade, studying the bridge over one narrow river and calculating how difficult it would be for the engineers to build something there quickly if the retreating Nazi supermen destroyed it), and made a right-hand turn onto a street right out of a fairy tale, a European Oz. In ruins, but still beautiful. Incredible. He searched for a sign, and there, on one of the buildings, twenty feet above street level, he saw it: **VERGILIANO**. Vergiliano Street. Half the buildings on the street had been reduced to piles of dust and chunks of mortar and stone. As if it were a cutaway in a book on interior decorating, he saw a surviving bottom floor, sliced open, tilted sideways, a piano and a dining room table exposed to view. Out front, the skeleton of a horse. Two beggars sitting side by side, crutches leaning against a concrete post beside them. An ambulance going the other way, in no hurry, no hurry at all. Trolley tracks. Another corner—no one paid any attention to the traffic lights, most of which weren't functioning in any case—the bus veered around a bomb crater in the middle of the street (the pavement was composed of enormous, flat-topped purplish stones) and then entered a block that looked as if it might have looked before the war, five- and six-story buildings glued together side by side, like Manhattan town houses but with more elegance and style, with balconies on every floor, tall windows, most of them shuttered against the day, the stucco dusty and chipped but colored in pastels—lemon, pumpkin, peach.

For a few minutes, he forgot to think about any kind of military analysis and just marveled at the feeling of the city. *"Palaces,"* the Italians called them, *palazzi*. In other places, they might simply be called *apartment buildings* or *town houses*, but *palaces* was the right word. Now a row of shops along this part of the block, a few open, a line of women in front of one of them, another line at a water fountain, another at some kind of municipal building where he guessed meager rations were being handed out. The bus stopped there. He stepped out the rear door and walked away from the long line as if in a dream. Napoli was tattered, ruined, yes, but magnificent all the same. Rife with malaria, typhus, and dysentery, he'd been told; the people on the verge of starvation; the Nazi soldiers—here came a trio of them, looking scared—killing indiscriminately, grasping to keep control of a country that was slipping away from them by the hour. They were doomed; they knew it. Italy was lost. It was just a question of time . . . how long Hitler would insist on fighting and how much blood would be shed.

Up and down the blocks he went, from time to time glancing very subtly back over his shoulder to make certain he wasn't being followed. The people had hunger and death on their faces, but there were kids playing here and there in the debris, one person singing in an upstairs room, sparks of life on the ravaged landscape. How, he thought, how on earth was any army going to enter this place, with its alleyways and balconies and rooftops, its crooked avenues? How were they ever going to chase the Nazis from the city without losing thousands of men to artillery and snipers, squads of machine gunners packed into the upstairs rooms and on the roofs, having had weeks to prepare for an assault?

As he was thinking this, he turned a corner and saw, on his right, a fence with barbed wire on top, two German soldiers standing inside the ten-foot-tall gate. He looked without appearing to look, studied the soldiers' posture—alert, wary, nervous. One of them had a bloody bandage around his head instead of his goofy Nazi turtle helmet. Spinelli sauntered past; turned a corner, ignoring the pleas of a little black-haired boy who had his hand out and was wearing a T-shirt that read: "DRINK MOXIE"; briefly met the eyes of a man about his own age coming the other way.

By the time he returned to the bus stop, Spinelli was sorry to discover that the 622 to Ercolano had stopped running for the day. This information was passed on to him by a very old man sitting on the bench there, a homemade cane between his knees and gnarled hands resting on its curved top. *"S' 'e fermat 'o Pullman,"* he said in the dialect. The sound of those words cast Spinelli back to Wooster Square, the *"New Haven Ghetto,"* some called it. *"Guinea Town,"* others liked to say. The words stung, yes, but here he was, a corporal, on his way to master sergeant, and then . . . ? He knew it like he knew his own name, knew that he'd survive the war, knew he'd be decorated and promoted. He didn't know where the confidence came from—sports, maybe—but it had always been there, and it was surely part of the reason he'd been chosen for an assignment like this. Confidence, fearlessness, fluency in Italian and a fair ability in the Neapolitan dialect, both. And something else, besides: the shine of good luck, good fortune. He was blessed and knew it.

Spinelli sat down beside the old man and for a while just gazed out at the hills of San Sebastiano. He could see a small orchard of olive trees there, the limbs heavy with fruit not yet ready for harvest. It seemed to him that everything had been provided to the human species—food, water, the company of others, every imaginable invention, from screened windows to penicillin. All people had to do was keep from letting greed or the hunger for power take over their lives. But we can't manage even that, he thought, can't seem to agree that the suffering a human life automatically includes is enough; we have to add to it. The Mussolinis and Hitlers and Hirohitos have to add to it.

"Lei, dove abita?" he asked the man after a time. *Where do you live?*

"A farm," the man said. "Mancini Farm. I am called Domenico Mancini."

"Stefano Spinelli," he said and held out his hand. The man's palm was calloused, the grip firm.

"My farm is a long walk from here," Domenico said. "A very long walk."

"We could try for a ride."

"Try." Domenico lifted his face toward the road, as if to say: *it's useless, but try.*

In fact, Spinelli thought, it might very well be useless. He could walk back to the monastery, he knew that. Eight miles. But old Mancini would never make it, and the man reminded him of his uncle Carmine, the same peaceful eyes, the same narrow, pointed shoulders and large hands.

He stood and stepped to the edge of the road and waited. Nothing. The crickets chirping, the silence of the end of day. Over his left shoulder, the sun was just setting. Soon darkness would envelop them, and then the old man would be stranded here until dawn.

Five minutes passed. Ten minutes. The better part of half an hour. Twilight was wrapping its shadows around them. And then, a pair of headlights in the distance. Spinelli stepped onto the edge of the road and held out a thumb, and by the time the vehicle came close enough for him to realize it was a German military truck, it was too late to back away. The driver saw them at the last minute and hit the brakes hard, and the old man was on his feet and walking into the road in the dust and darkness. Spinelli reached up and opened the door wide, saw the German soldier there in the interior lights—so young and tanned, he looked like he might have come from a party at the beach. A captain,

Spinelli was surprised to see . . . if he was reading the insignia correctly. Smooth-faced, clear-eyed, a crooked mouth, somehow unthreatening. Spinelli helped Domenico climb into the seat and then climbed up beside him, squeezing against the door so the old man's legs wouldn't be pressed against the shift. The German soldier started off without a word.

After a mile or so, the captain broke the silence. "Ercolano?"

"Sì, sì," the old man said.

Spinelli was perfectly happy to let Domenico do the talking, but the driver leaned forward and looked at him. *"E tu?"* he said. Decent accent.

"Same, same," Spinelli said. *Lo stesso, lo stesso.* "We live with each other." And then, to the old man, in dialect: "Please pretend."

Domenico nodded. They bounced along. Because he couldn't stop himself, Spinelli pushed his luck a bit and asked the driver, "Miss home?"

He glanced across the seat and thought, for a moment, that—barely out of boyhood, really—the captain might start to cry. *"Certo,"* he said. "I hope I survive to see my mother again. My father is fighting now in Russia, but I hope to see my mother."

"You will," Spinelli told him.

"Sì, sì," the old man piped up.

"You shouldn't tell anyone I gave you a ride."

"Never."

"I'll let you off on the outskirts. I know the Allies are close. Everyone knows it. I'm supposed to speak with a tank commander about what to do. Please don't tell."

"Never," Spinelli repeated. *"Mai."* But he was thinking: *So there are tanks in Ercolano. Loose lips sink ships.* Along they went in the darkness, figures appearing here and there at the side of the road, women in long dresses walking along, holding a bucket or balancing a basket on their heads. Once, a man on a bicycle, navigating in darkness.

Just shy of Ercolano, the German pulled to the side of the road. The old man thanked him, Spinelli thanked him. Before Spinelli closed the door, the driver said to him quietly, "Starting tomorrow, don't show yourself. You'll be picked up and sent north."

Spinelli stood there for a second, one hand on the door, looking at the young face. *And you and I are supposed to kill each other,* he thought. He nodded his thanks, closed the door, bade Domenico Mancini farewell, and started off on the long climb up to the monastery.

How on earth, he wondered as he walked, *how on earth are we going to bring the Allied armies into a city like Naples and not lose twenty thousand men in the process?*

Thirty-One

From her tearful visit with Rita Rossamadre, Lucia headed straight to Giuseppe's house. For the start of that walk, east along Via Toledo, the sun was directly behind her, casting a coppery September light that dusted the fronts of the buildings on the south side of the street, turning the windows there into flashes—of hope, it seemed to her—but sending long shadows in front of the people walking on that side. She was very hungry, but food was secondary now.

In the heart of the Materdei, she turned left onto Vico della Calce and climbed up to Giuseppe's street, and wasn't surprised to see Uncle Donato sitting outside in his regular chair. She loved that man, loved the way he dealt with his physical limitations, loved the dignity with which he accepted the daily visits of people he didn't know, people who believed that a man with a hunched back—*un gobbo*—had been touched by God and so putting a hand on his back brought a blessing (for women it was the opposite: their hunched backs were thought to be bad luck). They came not only to touch him but to seek counsel from him. Sad as it was to see such a brilliant and compassionate spirit imprisoned in a troubled body, Lucia felt, in his presence, something that went beyond the superstition, something like what she'd felt with Rita—a deep goodness, an actual sense of holiness.

Seeing Uncle Donato there didn't surprise her. What did surprise her was the sight of the limping German, his back to her, walking toward the other end of the street, not half a block from the front of Giuseppe's building. Reflexively, though he couldn't see her, she ducked into a doorway and peered after him. She watched him swing his bad leg in an almost circular fashion as he went. He was following her everywhere. Asking people, tracking her—the port, the Archives, now here.

When she felt certain he was gone, Lucia stepped out onto the sidewalk again and approached Uncle Donato. He offered her one of his rare smiles, thin-lipped and sorrowful, as mysterious as the *Mona Lisa*'s.

"*Come stai, bella?*"

"All right, Uncle." She tilted her head toward the end of the street. "Did he speak to you, the German?"

"In his fashion."

"Was he asking for me?"

"No, *bella*. He said this, exactly: *'Queers, Jews, and cripples, we'll send you all to the work camps.'* And then he spat to one side."

"Did he upset you?"

"Nothing upsets me, my beautiful one. Half of me resides in the next world. Giuseppe is upstairs, preparing what passes for our dinner. Eat with us. Tell him I'm in no hurry to come inside. Spend time with him alone. I will wait here until you fetch me."

She reached down and kissed Uncle Donato on the top of his head. A man, she thought, who had most likely never known the joys of physical love, making it easier for others to enjoy them. Tonight, though, lovemaking was not what she had in mind. She considered telling Donato about the proclamation, then decided against it. He didn't need another person pouring troubles onto him, and she wanted to tell Giuseppe first, in any case.

She went through the open entranceway and up the stairs, tapping on the apartment door—which stood partly open—then stepping inside. Giuseppe greeted her with a warm embrace and, after one glance into her eyes, "What's wrong?"

"I just came from the printer. Two thousand copies of a poster. Tomorrow it will be put up everywhere in the city. A proclamation. It's the new Nazi, the colonel I told you about. Scholl is his name. He's declaring martial law, saying that any Italian found with a weapon will be shot on sight, and that all men between the ages of eighteen and thirty-three must report to the headquarters at Castel Capuano day to be sent to Germany to work! You have to hide!"

"Sit, sit," Giuseppe said, pulling two chairs out from the kitchen table and sitting beside her, one hand on her knee. "They can't take me. I have a job."

Lucia stared through the lenses into his eyes, wondering how it was that such an intelligent man could, at times, think in such a twisted fashion. She could feel the pulse in her throat, feel a burst of anger rising inside her. She tried to speak calmly, but couldn't. "Nonsense, Giuseppe! They don't care about the Archives! They'll take you to Germany, to the camps. They'll work you to death!"

Giuseppe held up one hand and then placed it on her shoulder and squeezed. "All right."

"You have to hide!"

"I have my map to finish, Lu. I saw something today that I have to include. I thought the place might be unguarded, but there were soldiers there, Germans. And there are still a lot of places I haven't—"

Lucia slapped both hands down hard on the tops of her thighs. "Giuseppe!" she yelled.

"What? It's all right. I just—"

Tears in her eyes now, the familiar tightening of her neck muscles, the pulse thumping there. She had to squeeze the material of her dress in both fists to keep from waving her arms around, finding a glass and smashing it on the floor. She loved Giuseppe, loved him, but he could be maddeningly stubborn. "Stop, Giuseppe, stop! Listen to me! They're going to be taking men from the streets—not just one here and there but everyone. You'll be ordered to report. Not next month or next week, tomorrow!"

He was staring at her sadly, the way he always did when she let the temper get the best of her. But how else to get through to him? She took a long breath, relaxed her hands, looked down at the floor and then back into his eyes. "Let me go and get the map. Please. I know someone I can give it to now. She knows someone she can give it to. A spy. An American. You have to hide!"

"Hide where, Lucia?"

"My father knows places, and has friends who can take you there. Go see him, ask him. He'll help you."

"Your father despises me."

"He doesn't know you, that's all. He can change. He'll change. You'll see. He'll help you."

"For your sake, maybe."

"Go see him, please." Lucia slammed a fist down on top of her right thigh and felt the tears rising up again. "Please, Giuseppe! Twenty-one Via Sospiri, in the Santa Lucia. Bottom floor. Please go. Now."

"I know where it is. You took me there that one time, remember?"

"Please, Giuseppe. For me, please."

"I'll go, I'll go. Come with me."

She shook her head. "I make him uneasy. And my boss, Bruni, is—"

"You're his daughter."

"I make him uneasy. Go alone. Please," Lucia said, the words bursting out of her in a fast stream. "I'll find him tomorrow after work— Bruni is forcing us to come in on a Saturday—and ask him where you are, and I'll come to you. I saw a message on the teletype, in German. *'Take the young men and the Jews,'* it said. *'Reduce the city to ashes and mud.'* I'm leaving work after tomorrow. Not going back. I went to see a woman, the purest of women. My father's friend. When I was sitting with her, I realized I can't work there anymore. I've been trying to destroy some of the files—the Jews—and if they find out, they'll arrest me, or kill me."

"You can spy on them without doing that."

She shook her head violently. "I'll go in tomorrow, then simply disappear."

"You'll starve."

"We're starving anyway. Please, give me the key. Let me take the map to her before it's too late."

Giuseppe turned his eyes left, in the direction of the room his parents had slept in. The door was closed, and Lucia was almost sure that no one had set foot in there from the moment she'd been sent to get the blanket off their bed and bring it to the Ministry so it could be used to wrap their mutilated bodies. She watched Giuseppe breathing, watched his chest rise and fall. It sometimes seemed to her that his obsession with the map was the only thing that had kept him sane after his parents' deaths, that, without it, he'd have done something crazy to avenge them—savagely beaten a German soldier in the street, found a gun and killed one of them, lit their headquarters on fire. She knew that asking him to hand the map over to her before it was finished was like asking him to pull the heart out of his chest and lay it on the table, and she knew that asking him to go and seek help from her father was even more painful to him. They were the kind of favors, she thought, you could ask only of a true love. The kind of sacrifices only a true love would offer you in return. She breathed slowly, watched him, tried to keep herself from saying anything else.

After one long, terrible minute, Giuseppe leaned sideways, pulled the key out of his pocket, and handed it to her. "The front door," he said. "The lock sticks sometimes."

Lucia jumped up and kissed him, then held on to him after the kiss, held him and held him. "I'm sorry I yelled. I love you. I'm sorry."

He was nodding, saying, "Yes, yes, same, same. I'm stubborn, yes, go."

"I can trust this woman, I know I can. I love you so much!"

Just as the last syllable was out of her mouth, they heard a tremendous crash.

"The bombs again," Giuseppe said. "My uncle!" He was on his feet, heading out the door, Lucia one step behind.

But there had been no siren, and when they reached the street, they saw immediately that, instead of hiding in shelters, the few people on the sidewalk had turned in the direction of the sound, west, toward the sunset. Uncle Donato was looking that way, too. Lucia saw a plume of smoke there, bubbling up lazily into the evening light.

"Uncle," Giuseppe said. "We have to get inside."

Donato turned and looked at him, then shook his head. *"Non ci sono aerei, Giusepp',"* he said. *"There are no planes, Giuseppe.* It didn't come from the air."

"What, then?"

"The *Nazisti.* They have begun the destruction of Naples."

Thirty-Two

Giuseppe held Lucia for a long time, pressing the fingers of one hand against the top of her back and holding her against his chest. From their first kiss, they'd had some kind of electrical bodily connection. He could feel the current running between them now, feel the intensity of her love vibrating in every place they touched. She kissed him deeply, turned, and walked away, saying, "I love you so much, Uncle," to Donato, and nothing else. Giuseppe stood there, watching her go, trying to find a way to measure the force of her affection, the depth of it, trying to imagine a place she wouldn't go with him, an expression of love she wouldn't be able to summon. He'd been romantically involved with three women before meeting Lucia, three very nice-looking, very fine young women. Though he'd never made love with them, there had been a real compatibility there—in terms of personality, intellectual interest, physical attraction. But he'd never met anyone with Lucia's capacity to love. It was almost visible in her, sometimes calm and mild, other times fiery, something so much a part of her that it seemed to emanate from her eyes. He watched her, hoping she'd turn around and show him those eyes, offer one last gesture of support or affection, but she turned the corner onto Via Fontanelle and was gone.

A thought appeared and reappeared in his mind like a needle being drawn through a piece of cloth, dragging after it an old thread of shame, piercing him, then leaving a sour feeling. Piercing him again. He hadn't fought in the army, hadn't been able to save his parents. And now his girlfriend was protecting him, taking the risk of delivering his map to a woman she barely knew, a risk that carried with it the very real possibility of torture and death.

And his job? To hide.

Once, not long after the burial of his parents, still tormented by grief, he'd confessed these feelings to his uncle: men were fighting; he wasn't fighting. Was he then not a man? Men were often loud and aggressive; he didn't like being loud and aggressive—just the opposite, in fact. Was he then not a man? His father had made a living laying stone, a man's work; he, Giuseppe, filed documents and advised scholars.

His uncle had listened with his head slightly lowered and without making eye contact at first. Then he'd raised his eyes, peered into Giuseppe's, and said, *"The danger here is that, in trying to prove to yourself something you do not need to prove, you will behave in a way that is untrue to you, and place your soul in danger."*

Now, watching Lucia turn the corner and disappear, Giuseppe did what he could to banish the dirty strand of thought. He tried to tell himself that the courage of kindness was his manhood. That his true identity was rooted, not in violence, aggression, and hatred, but in kindness. He was half-convinced.

For another hour, he sat there with his uncle—the smell of smoke and stone dust in the air, the sound of fire engines, the raw, creeping sense of terror at knowing their city was very likely in the process of being destroyed, building by building. Though he didn't want to believe what Lucia had told him about the proclamation, Giuseppe found himself looking up and down the street for German army trucks or soldiers. Would he run if he saw them approaching? Would he stand and fight? Should he go to Lucia's father, as she'd begged him to do, and ask for a hiding place, a gun, the protection of some Camorra killer?

There was a second explosion, larger, farther away, a muted *ba-boom-boom-boom* that reminded him of the days of the Allied bombings. His uncle turned his head in that direction and muttered something under his breath, a prayer or a curse, Giuseppe couldn't tell. "I may have to hide, Uncle, if they start arresting young men."

His uncle nodded. "Hide until the eruption," he said, and Giuseppe let the words hang in the air between them.

After another few minutes, he helped Donato up the stairs and fed him. (A feast: rice with a few boiled baby carrots, all of it gifts from the people who visited the hunchback and, in exchange for his wisdom, brought what amounted to offerings.) Though it really wasn't necessary, when his uncle went to the bathroom, Giuseppe waited outside the door in case there was a problem, and then walked with him to the bedroom and kissed him good night because Donato liked to go to sleep not long after darkness fell, early in winter and late in summer. (Nature meant for this to happen, he insisted.) There was water in the pipes. Giuseppe cleaned and dried the dishes, forks, and glasses, set them on the counter, closed and fastened the window shutters, then sat for a time, wondering what he should do. No more explosions broke the night quiet. He sat in his father's armchair and, in the yellow lamplight, tried reading a few pages of a favorite book—Lampedusa's *The Leopard*. For a little while, captivated by the novel's rich language and depth of feeling, he was able to focus on the words—*Their certain marriage, though not very close, extended its reassuring shadow in anticipation on the parched soil of their mutual desires.* But the needle kept piercing him. The residue of shame wouldn't leave: Lucia was resisting, he was hiding.

He placed the bookmark (one of his father's old playing cards), set the novel aside, and turned out the light. Starting the next evening, Lucia had warned him, there would be a curfew. Martial law. Anyone found with a knife or gun, anyone resisting the proclamation in any way: shot dead. Every young man must report. If he went to the Archives, the Nazis would come for him, load him into the railed back of one of their trucks, carry him and others at gunpoint to the train station, and ship them north. God knew what they'd require of him there. God knew what they were requiring of the Jews who'd already made that trip. He'd seen them himself, families huddled outside the Napoli Centrale train station surrounded by soldiers with raised rifles, carrying small children against their chests and cloth bundles in their hands. They were being sent north to work, the Nazis claimed. But no one had ever received a droplet of news from this "north." Friends, neighbors, coworkers—no one had gotten a telegram, a letter, or a phone call from Germany talking about the conditions there or asking about things at home.

Death camps, they were, then, not work camps. It would be the same for him and his friends.

The only option was to do what Lucia had asked him to do. Go to her father. Ask for help.

He stood, and quietly, in order not to wake his light-sleeping uncle, went through the door, down the steps, and out onto the street. A memory followed him as he moved, haunting him, mocking him. He knew where Lucia's father lived because she'd taken him there. Once, one time, two months ago. *"He can be gruff,"* she'd warned as they walked along holding hands. But when he was finally introduced to Aldo Pastone, Giuseppe realized that *gruff* was the wrong word. *Ice* was the word, colder than cold. A scarred, blocklike face and powerful body. Camorra friends. Little interest in his daughter, it seemed, and even less in the man she loved. Aldo had met them at the door, holding one arm against the jamb at shoulder height, as if to block even the idea of them entering his dark lair, or as if there were someone inside he didn't want them to meet. He'd shaken hands, at least, with a crushing grip, run his eyes across Giuseppe's face, and then looked at his daughter and uttered this line of love: *"Why did you come?"*

Giuseppe remembered the route—down Toledo and west toward the warren of the Spagnoli. Even though, now that the bombings had stopped, they weren't required to keep their houses dark, there were few lights in the windows and fewer people on the streets. He could sense the moon rising behind him—full, it would be on this night—but not yet see it. One or two older men straggling home late from a day job somewhere in the countryside, their backs bent and their clothes filthy. One or two women grasping to their chests small paper or burlap bags—containing rationed food, no doubt, or something purchased at outrageous prices on the black market—and keeping their eyes down. It was unusual, on such a long walk, not to see German vehicles or soldiers, but Giuseppe supposed they were resting in their barracks at this hour, preparing for the hard work of capturing Italian men.

In the Spagnoli, a lively, poor, densely packed district that sloped up from Via Toledo toward the Vomero, he heard the sound of voices from inside those houses that had not been destroyed, and came upon a trio of men about his own age sitting out in the darkness, sipping what he guessed to be wine from coffee cups. He nodded to them, and as he passed, one of them called after him, "Careful tomorrow, brother."

West of the Spagnoli, almost to Santa Lucia now, he passed a group of four street kids sitting on the concrete posts at Piazza del Plebiscito. He found a coin tucked into a fold in his pocket and flipped it in their direction. One of them caught it and made a show of dancing around in front of his friends, celebrating.

Little bits of life remained, Giuseppe thought. His feelings for Lucia, the quartet of *scugnizzi*, the guys on the sidewalk, those grand old buildings that had not been bombed. The Nazis hadn't been able to take away *everything*. Not yet, at least.

Wondering what kind of reaction he'd get this time at Lucia's father's door, distracted by the apprehension and so not as careful as he might have been, Giuseppe turned a corner onto Via Solitaria and ran chest to chest into a German soldier. The man was staggering drunk, the top collar of his uniform unbuttoned, his hat on sideways. After he recovered from the first contact, he put his hands to Giuseppe's shoulders and shoved him back, saying something in his own language and then *"Merde Italiano!" Shit Italian.*

For a few seconds, the two men glared at each other, one sober, one not. The street was dark; there was no one else around. What had been building up inside Giuseppe—the limping officer and his horse manure, the shame of Lucia's courage set against his own need to hide, the sounds of his city being destroyed, the image that would never leave him of his mother and father on the steps of the Ministry of Health— was like a huge pile of kindling soaked in gasoline. The German's hands against him had sparked it into a blaze. Giuseppe stared through the smoking hatred for one more second, then took hold of the man by his upper arms, turned him, and smashed his head back against the wall of the corner building. Already wobbling from the alcohol, the soldier sagged, half-unconscious. Giuseppe straightened him up, smashed him against the wall a second time, let him drop there. And then he ran.

It was only a few hundred meters to Lucia's father's house, a straight sprint through the Palazzo Calabritto and right onto Via Bisignano. Then down Via Sospiri, little more than a crooked alleyway, a street so narrow that, even before the bombing, a single vehicle could have blocked it. Aldo Pastone's metal door, the bad memories. Gasping for breath, praying that Lucia's father was home, Giuseppe pounded his fist on the metal. Nothing at first, no response. He looked to the corner, expecting soldiers with rifles raised. He pounded again. The door was thrown open and there was the face, the scar, the icy block, the steely eyes.

"I'm . . . I'm Giuseppe," he said between hard breaths. "I just—"

"I know who you are," the man replied, staring. Two miserable seconds of nothing, and then Giuseppe saw the door open wider and heard Lucia's father say, *"Entra."*

Thirty-Three

On Via Gennaro Serra, not far from Piazza del Plebiscito, where Armando and Tomaso had agreed to meet the rest of the *coro*, they came upon two German army trucks parked one behind the other at the curb. Without saying a word to each other, they stopped walking and studied the scene. The cabs and open beds of both trucks were empty. Ten meters in front of the forward truck, on a stone bench tucked into a circular alcove, the drivers sat smoking. While Tomaso slipped around to the street side of the rear truck, out of view, Armando walked up to the soldiers with his hand out. He turned down his mouth and squeezed his eyes partly closed, making his face into a mask of supplication and speaking a steady stream of words designed to disguise the sound of air being let out of a truck tire. "Please, please, men. Please. I'm so hungry. A coin, a few coins, please. I know you're generous, please, men!" One of them waved him away, but Armando kept pleading—"Look at me. Look at how hungry I am"—until the other soldier reached out and tried to extinguish the cigarette butt on the boy's palm. Armando pulled his hand away in time, and by then he could see Tomaso going past, down the middle of the street at a fast walk, and he joined him. They looped around the block and onto the huge cobblestone square, hid for a few minutes until they felt they were safe, and then, still ready to run, sat there on one of the concrete posts. They were facing the great church with its columns and rounded roof, the two curving parts to either side that always made Armando think of the wings of a giant stone bird. More so even than Naples's other big churches, this one seemed to him like the House of God. Or at least what the House of God must look like in heaven. He'd never been inside.

"Completely flat?" he said without looking at his friend.

"Almost. They can probably drive it, but they'll cut up the tire. Plus, I bent the thin metal piece, the little tongue, the way I showed you last time, so they won't be able to fill it up again."

"We're tire experts now."

"Right," his brave friend said, and Armando wondered again if he should have let Tomaso keep the German soldier's hat. He shrugged, spat, watched the corner.

"Do you ever want to do more?"

"Always."

"Any ideas?"

Tomaso shook his head, and they saw their other two friends striding toward them across the cobblestones.

Armando was thinking about the murdered girl and her murdered grandparents, about the package the men had carried off the truck in the Materdei, about Zozo Forni. There were rumors of fighting in the streets, small battles in different neighborhoods, one against one, two against four, quick exchanges of gunfire. But he hadn't seen the evidence with his own eyes and didn't know whether the stories were true. People kept saying the Allies were close, but they'd been saying that for a month now and nothing had happened, and he could feel a kind of nervous itch in his arms and hands. He wanted to do something more than carrying a few pistols to a woman's house and flattening truck tires. He wondered if he should take a risk and lead his boys back to Zozo Forni's place in the Chiaia and see if the man had other work for them.

Up beyond the Spagnoli, they could see the light cast by the rising moon. *"Piena,"* Armando said, as if to himself. *Full.* Sister Marcellina had always told him that *la luna piena* was a reminder that one day they would see the Lord's face, not merely reflected in the people around them, in the clouds, in the birds, but full and close and massive. *"The blinding light of love,"* she had said. Armando tried to imagine it.

As they sat there, a young man walked past. *Guaglione* was the word in dialect. *A guy.* They eyed him, as they eyed everybody, and, as always, Armando made his judgments. Somebody you wouldn't want to fight, he thought, with those shoulders and arms, but he was wearing glasses, too, so maybe he wasn't so tough after all. As they watched, the man reached into his pocket and flipped them a coin. Armando made the catch, nodded to the man, then taunted his friends with a victory dance. They watched him and laughed: they'd all benefit. The two lire from Zozo, the mysterious peach, the coin from Padre Paulo, and now this—good things were falling into his hands; the saints were smiling on him.

But the mood dried as quickly as a shallow puddle on an August day. By then, eight o'clock on a Friday night, news had spread of the arrival of the Nazi colonel and about the new rules he'd announce the next day, and, though they pretended otherwise, Armando knew that all four of them were worried what it might mean.

"He's going to make us all dress up like Nazi soldiers, and he's going to kill anyone who refuses," Roberto said.

"Doubt it," Tomaso told him. And then to Armando, "Where's the hat anyway? What'd you do with it?"

"I left it."

"Where?"

Armando shrugged. "I'll let you have it for a while. Have you eaten?"

Tomaso nodded. "Not much."

"Nothing for me," Roberto said.

"Me also," Antonio chimed in. "Nothing."

Armando held up the coin. "This will get us something. What's open?"

"The Sangiuliano."

"Let's go."

They set off toward the Vomero, alert as foxes to the stirrings of the night: a seagull crying out, a man scolding a child, from far off, in the direction of the Arenella neighborhood, a strange echo, as if someone were snapping a stick at regular intervals.

"Shots," Roberto said.

This time, no one disputed him.

They walked in a loose formation, spitting, swaggering, looking from side to side as if seeking out enemies to snarl at, attack, destroy. From off to the east came a deep, muted *boom* that echoed through the streets like thunder. They all flinched and then pretended they hadn't.

Thirty-Four

As she hurried through the Naples night, key in hand, Lucia realized that she was walking along the same route Giuseppe had taken to work for the past six years, though not, of course, in the light of a rising moon. Because he loved the city, and loved *places* in general (it was part of the reason he'd decided to make his map), he'd described the route to her many times: west along the main road—Santa Teresa; down Enrico Pessina into the Centro and as far as Piazza Dante, where he'd first asked her to have dinner with him, then south along Tribunali as far as Via San Gregorio, a right turn there, down the curving Vico Figurari, to the door of the National Archives.

She held the key in her left hand, her lucky hand, and could feel that her palm was coated in sweat. The nervousness had such a hold on her that, until she'd actually set foot on the square and started approaching the statue of Dante at its center, she failed to notice the clique of German soldiers standing around two motorcycles in the corner to her left. They were everywhere, everywhere. You couldn't look out your window, walk three blocks; you couldn't sit in a piazza watching the sunset without hearing their trucks or seeing their uniforms or feeling their eyes upon you. Too late now—if she made a sharp right turn, they'd see her, sense her fear, and it would draw them like hungry wolves. Instead, she decided to walk as close to them as would seem reasonable.

Go past them, through the dark, covered passageway at Porta Alba that led toward Piazza Bellini, then down Tribunali as far as San Gregorio.

She went along steadily, heart slamming in her chest. She glanced up at them, then away. Very strange—the soldiers were standing close to each other, two of them with rifles at the ready, conversing in low tones. From the years of their presence in the city, she knew their habits well enough to sense the oddity of the scene. Usually they'd be spaced farther apart, standing tall, fearless. And if they were speaking to each other, their voices would be loud, as if they assumed no Neapolitan would understand their language, or as if they didn't care. She wondered if the arrival of the evil colonel had cast fear into their hearts, too. Or if it was something else.

As she walked past, one of them whistled at her between his teeth. She heard the word *Dirne. Whore.* She kept walking, same pace, eyes up and forward, the slippery key against her left palm, a slow-burning anger in her belly. When she stepped into the covered passageway—in better times, it had been busy with booksellers and strolling couples; now it was dark and quiet as death—she listened intently, worried one or more of the soldiers would be following. But she was alone, out the other side into moonlight again, past the church of Purgatorio ad Arco with the brass skulls—polished by a million touches—that stood on concrete posts in front of it. She ran her palm over one for good luck, then turned right onto San Gregorio, then right again on the curving, downward-sloping Vico Figurari, and right a third time at the end of it. There, directly opposite the ancient church of San Filippo, stood the square bulk of the *Archivo* building. Just then she heard the loud report of a motorcycle engine and wondered if one of the soldiers was following her after all. But the noise faded in the opposite direction, and only a single pair of footsteps—her own—echoed against the walls.

Ten meters shy of the door, she paused, pretended something had gotten into her shoe. She leaned against the building and bent one leg up behind her, took off the shoe, and shook it. There was only silence at first, then a sound, repeated eight or ten times, that might have been shots in a distant neighborhood. She lifted her head and listened. One more report, from off toward Arenella, and then, in the quiet that followed, she was at the Archives' front door. The lock stuck, as Giuseppe had said it would, but she worked the key for a few seconds, opened the door, and closed it quickly behind her. In the lightless hallway, she had to stop and breathe deeply until she'd calmed down.

Without turning on a light, she crept past what had once been the desk where visitors registered. She felt her way along a row of stacks. The watchman was long gone, the cleaning people gone; the books she touched had a coating of dust on their spines. At the end of the row, she waved one hand around and found the iron railing, worked her way carefully to the edge of the top step, her eyes adjusting somewhat, the stairs faintly illuminated by moonlight from the one large window, unbroken, undamaged, cut into the exterior wall between the basement and first floor.

From there, it wasn't difficult to find the desk where Giuseppe worked, and from the desk, easier still to locate the place where he told her he'd hidden his map: squeezed between mattress and wall in the maintenance room where they'd made love. For a moment, she rested one hand on the mattress, for luck, then she drew out the map as tenderly as if it were filled with fresh eggs. Two-thirds of a meter long. As wide, in its rolled form, as the drain at the bottom of her kitchen sink. At first she tried to push it up under her long skirt, along the outside of her left thigh. But that made walking difficult, so she tugged free the hem of her blouse and slid the paper tube up the side, against her ribs. If she tucked the blouse back into her skirt tightly enough, the map would stay in place and she could swing her arms in a more or less normal gait.

The touch of the map seemed to cause a physical reaction, as if it were coated in acid. A small confusion took hold of her, a gust of doubt. For the trip back upstairs, she decided to remove her shoes so as to make absolutely no sound. What sense did that make? There was no one in the building. But she did it anyway. She decided, too, as she slipped into the shoes again at the top of the stairs, not to take the time and make the noise required to lock the front door: no one would come here at night, and if they did, what difference would it make now? Giuseppe wouldn't return, and who would want to steal the books and documents that remained?

Outside in the air again, she was gripped by the most terrible anxiety—the thumping pulse, the sweating hands, the conviction that she'd be caught with Giuseppe's map and sent to the Gestapo torture cells. She thought of carrying it to Rita's immediately, but it was farther to Rita's house than to her own, and she'd have to cross streets busy with German vehicles. No, she'd do that tomorrow. In daylight, on a Saturday morning, especially, she'd be less likely to be stopped.

She listened—no sound; and watched—no soldiers; then she drew in two short, ragged breaths, calculated the route least likely to have Germans on it, and started off. She'd gone most of the way home before she remembered that Bruni was forcing them to report for work the next day. *"First thing,"* he'd said. And on a Saturday. Some urgency with the posters, with the collection of Jews. If she didn't show up, they'd be suspicious, possibly send someone out to look for her. She'd bring the map to the office then, secretly of course, and concoct a plan with Rosalia's help. That was the wisest move . . . or was it procrastination?

Thirty-Five

Rita sat out in front of her house until a later hour than was customary for her. Leopoldo the Fascist had gone off on one of his secret errands, reporting on his talkative neighbors, perhaps, or being treated to a meal in the German barracks or the OVRA headquarters, where he might trade his worthless information for a piece of tough beef or a plate of potatoes. She and Eleonora and Joe were careful around him, of course. But it didn't really matter what you actually said: they could make up whatever they wanted, claim you'd told a joke at Mussolini's expense or expressed a longing for the quick arrival of the Americans. These days, however, beyond execution, there wasn't much available to Leopoldo and his friends in the way of punishment. People were suffering to such an extent that the threat of prison or murder carried half the weight it ordinarily would have. Let Leopoldo tell his lies and spread his venom. She wondered if he'd run when the Allies finally arrived, or if he'd beg her and the other neighbors to tell *gli Americani* that he'd only been *pretending* to support Il Duce, that he was actually a lover of democracy and freedom and not really a Fascist at all.

Even with the hunger, sorrow, duplicity, disease, and death that surrounded them, Rita thought it was a beautiful September night, with a full moon—color of the inside of a peach—rising to her left. She sat with Joe and Eleonora and the next-door neighbor, old Ugo, speaking quietly at times and, at others, sitting in the silence and feeling the warm embrace of the city around them. A soft, salty breeze wafted in from the port and brushed at the skin of their arms and faces. After a stretch of silence, Ugo said, quietly, "I heard someone say today that there are Allied spies in the city."

Rita didn't speak. She'd already told both Aldo and Lucia about the man hiding in the monastery—a sin of lack of trust that she'd have to confess to her brother, who had specifically asked her to keep it secret—she didn't want to hear herself say the words again.

"When they arrive, they'll come with bombs again," Ugo went on, his voice thick with fear, "then artillery, then tanks. That's the order of things: bombs, artillery, tanks. Then the soldiers. Until two weeks ago, we were the enemy, and we expect them now to have mercy on us! If I were a young girl, I'd run."

"Run where?" Eleonora asked. There was no answer, so she went on. "The *Fascists* were their enemy, not us. Not people like us."

"Yes, but they can't aim their bombs so they hit only Leopoldo and the others."

"Nor can they treat the young girls any worse than they're being treated now."

Rita sighed and stood up. She was tired of the fear. She felt it, yes, but it had been in the air so long—almost three full years now they'd lived in the grip of war—that it was like a bad smell everyone had almost gotten used to. A rat's carcass rotting in the gutter. Sewage from a broken pipe. Old sweat on clothes that had been worn for weeks without a washing.

She bade her friends good night and climbed the stairs, thinking, for some reason, of Aldo's daughter and wondering if she'd ever see her again. Wondering if she'd bring the map her boyfriend was making. There was no way to get in touch with the girl, except through Aldo, and Lucia had specifically asked that her father not be told of her visit. Having mentioned the spy, not once but twice, Rita thought this was one secret she ought to keep.

She'd undressed to her underwear and bra when a knock sounded at the door, harsh and quick. She wondered if it might be Aldo's daughter, needing a place to hide. She wrapped an old shawl around herself and opened the door. A tall man in a German army uniform stood there, leaning to one side like a building whose foundation had been damaged in the bombing. Without saying a word, he shoved her back into the room and slammed the door closed behind him.

"How much?" he demanded in bad Italian. "I know what you do. How much is the cost?"

She could smell her own sweat. The man was insane, or drunk, or both. The words weren't slurred, but his head bounced as he spoke, and it was as if his eyes were being pulled side to side by a puppeteer's strings.

Without waiting for an answer, he pushed her back and down onto the bed, and in a second had unbuckled and lowered his pants. There was a gun in the holster. It banged loudly against the floor as the pants fell to his ankles, and for an instant, Rita thought someone might hear it and come to her aid. But Joe and Eleonora were old and half-deaf, and not unused to hearing a man's footsteps on the stairwell this late. Ugo wouldn't enter the building and, even if he did, wouldn't have the strength to climb the stairs. She reached up and took hold of the cross around her neck, a gift from Avvocato Cilento. Another second and the German was on top of her, pressing his weight down on her. His breath against her cheek and neck, his wet lips there, his hands grasping the cloth at her hips and tugging.

She had no choice but to call forth the spirits and work the curse the old gypsy women had taught her, the magic she held in reserve for the most dangerous moments. It was only the dialect that summoned them, not standard Italian, and so she turned her face to the side, squeezed her legs together, pushed hard with both hands against the man's shoulders, and laid the curse upon him, a curse she'd learned from women who'd come to her aid half a lifetime ago: *"Acqua cheta fa pantan' e fet'!"* she whispered. *Stagnant water becomes a quagmire and stinks!*

The soldier pressed his weight back down against her, pried her legs apart, tried to pull off the rest of her underwear, was making small grunting sounds as if he had penetrated her, which he had not. And he wouldn't. The water was stagnant. The machinery had been cursed and wasn't working, and wouldn't work. Press and twist as he might, the man's manhood was failing him and would fail him. Rita no longer fought; she simply kept her arms tight against her hips and pressed her legs together as hard as she could and focused on the next world, the spirit world, drew its strength to her and repeated the phrase aloud. *"Acqua cheta fa pantan' e fet'."*

The man worked and worked, then realized what was not going to happen and began cursing violently. He pushed himself away from her, slapped her hard across the face, and stood, pants around his ankles. He spat a spray of saliva that touched her bare chest, her chin. She watched him, holding tightly to the spirit world. "Whore, whore," he said. "No wonder." But there was more than anger in the words; there was a shaking, trembling, blind hatred that had its feet in the world of lunacy. The man had been cursed by other women, Rita thought, there was no doubt. Helpless in his fury, he reached down and, instead of pulling up his trousers, stood tall again, still bare-legged but now with the pistol in his fingers. "Hail Mary full of grace," Rita said aloud, because this was the moment her spirit would be set free.

But instead of pointing the pistol at her, the man pointed it at his own right temple. "Whore . . . whore . . . whore!" he said, as if counting to three, then pulled the trigger. Nothing happened. He pulled it again, *snap, snap, snap snap snap*, then flung the pistol against the wall. It bounced off the stone and dropped onto her belly. The soldier yanked up his pants and fled, leaving the door open wide.

Rita closed her eyes and waited for the sound of the front door, then she lay quietly, sending her gratitude out into the other worlds.

The metal of the gun lay cool on her belly, in the place where a child would have grown, had she been able to bear a child. She put one wet hand upon it, as if it were, in fact, an infant who needed comforting. And then, from eyelids to toes, her entire body started to shake, tears coursed down across her temples, and she tried with all her strength not to remember, not to remember, not to remember the things that had once been done to her.

Thirty-Six

If Aldo had made a list of the thirty people he might expect to find knocking on his door at that hour on a Friday night, Lucia's boyfriend would have been at the bottom of it. He had let the boy in, at first, simply because he didn't want to stand there with the door open and didn't want to let him stand out there for the Dell'Acquas to see when they arrived. But as soon as Giuseppe stepped across the threshold, breathing as if he'd just run all the way from Ercolano, it occurred to Aldo that the bespectacled visitor was a gift. If it was true that the Dell'Acquas were taking him out into the countryside to kill him, then it was at least possible that having another person along would deter them. Possible, not likely. Ubaldo would kill two as easily as one, but it might complicate things for him, this second person. The assassin might ask himself: *What kind of connections does the young man have? What kind of friends?*

It was a gift.

But then something occurred to him: "Lucia's not hurt?" he asked, looking out the window and not at Giuseppe.

"No."

"Not in trouble?"

"No."

That was all the information he needed. "I have an errand to do. You're coming with me," he said over his shoulder. The boy didn't answer. Aldo turned around and glanced at him, said, "Pretend to be tough." And almost laughed.

Another three minutes and a car pulled up in the narrow street in front of Aldo's door. A shocking sight in these times. Black in color. A long hood, pointed nose, and rounded passenger compartment, the type of car certain Italian officers had ridden around in before the war, and some German officers still used. Aldo had never seen this particular car before, but he'd seen the men in the front seat many times, and didn't like them. He suspected they didn't like him, either, but what were his options? He motioned for Giuseppe to join him, and as they left the house and stepped closer, he saw that the Dell'Acqua boys were wearing uniforms. On the epaulettes, one thick stripe, two thin ones, and the empty oval. Lieutenant colonels in the Italian Royal Army! There was something comical about it: dressed that way, the brothers seemed about as natural as a priest in soccer shorts. But Aldo supposed that, if you didn't know the men in the brown-green cloth, they might have been able to pass.

He and Giuseppe climbed in.

Vito glanced in the mirror and grunted, as if the idea of a stranger sitting behind him made him nervous. To his right, Ubaldo was still, quiet.

It was no small matter, Aldo knew, to have enough gasoline to run a car in the midst of war. No small matter to have a car out on the streets at all, where any German patrol might stop you and ask for papers. The car and uniforms were obviously stolen. After all these years of looting almost every other ship in the busy port, the ones that arrived and the ones about to depart, maybe the Forni family had an entire warehouse of stolen vehicles and clothing, disguises for any eventuality. As for safe passage on these streets, money had changed hands, Aldo was sure of that. But if they were going to the city's outskirts to steal from a disabled German vehicle, then who had been paid off? The Germans? Mussolini's OVRA? The remains of the Italian Army? He didn't ask. Zozo would no doubt have a hundred mysterious connections. It was simply none of his business.

He and Giuseppe sat on either side of the back seat—an American car it was, a new Ford. They bounced and swerved out of the Santa Lucia neighborhood, up Via Console and past a pair of German army trucks parked near the Piazza del Plebiscito, two soldiers struggling to repair a flattened tire. They stayed on the main roads for only a few minutes, and then Vito Dell'Acqua took them into the maze of side streets, the narrow, winding *vicoli* of the Spagnoli neighborhood, dodging piles of rubble and downed electric wires, running with the parking lights only, taking rights and lefts that made no sense . . . unless Vito happened to know which streets had been rendered impassable by the bombings and which had not, or which streets were more likely to have German patrols and which were not . . . or which Fascist officers in charge of which neighborhoods had been paid off. Twenty minutes of this and they passed the Santa Maria hospital, then, instead of taking the main road beyond the Sanità bridge, went along more winding side streets north of the Capodimonte Hill, where there was an artillery encampment from which the Nazis were prepared to obliterate the city—everyone knew it—and where Aldo saw six German vehicles parked, grille to bumper, almost like the circled wagons on the Westerns they used to watch when he was a boy. Opel Blitz trucks, and Kübelwagens, one Krupp Protze like the kind he'd seen near the port when he'd been waiting for Lucia. Two of them had desert markings and had clearly been at the front in Egypt and Libya, and then Sicily. Now here. Soon, he thought, if the Allies kept pushing them north, the Nazis would be using their desert camouflage in the Italian Alps. A knot of soldiers stood nearby, all of them heavily armed.

It was all so puzzling—that Zozo would risk sending a vehicle out on such an errand; that the Germans would be huddling together, not marching about; that the Dell'Acqua brothers, famous for other kinds of operations, would be put in uniform and sent out to steal.

Idiot that he was, Vito beeped the horn as they passed, and his idiot brother waved out the window to his German comrades. They turned their heads to stare at the car but did not wave back.

As they went along, no one speaking, Aldo worked the whole operation through in his mind but could find no answer to the puzzle. Beside him, Lucia's boyfriend had sense enough, at least, to keep quiet—though, if he was trying to look like a tough guy, it wasn't working. He looked like what he was, a soft-handed, bespectacled *guaglione* who played with papers all day long and received a paycheck for it. Nice-looking enough, and with strong shoulders and arms, but with the eyes of a dreamer. Aldo tried to guess what Lucia saw in him. Safety, maybe. This boy would never hurt her . . . and perhaps he'd stay around longer than other Neapolitan men, pay more attention to her than her own father had done.

Beyond Capodimonte—unchallenged all this way—they descended into the outskirts, the *periferia*, through a neighborhood where he'd once courted a girl, in the past century it felt like, a district called La Scampia. Flat as a table, it was, with poorly built two-story houses standing a little ways apart from each other like top hats placed haphazardly on a shelf, one tilting this way, the other that.

"Word is," Vito Dell'Acqua said after a time, speaking, as he always did, as if there were soup in his mouth and he was trying not to let it leak out, "there's a new boss now. Nazi boss. Word is, tomorrow he starts taking all the men north. Not just a few like before, a truckful here and there. All the men in the city. Everyone strong enough. To work."

"To die is more like it," Aldo said, and beside him, he felt Giuseppe flinch.

"Word is," Vito went on, "two German soldiers got attacked on the street today in Arenella. One got his ticket paid to hell. People say it was *carabinieri* attacking them."

"So then two hundred of us die."

Vito wrestled with the steering wheel as if it were an animal trying to escape his grasp, jamming his foot down on the clutch and wrenching the stick through the gears.

"It's true about the boss," Giuseppe piped up in a thin voice. "Someone I know saw the proclamation."

Aldo ignored him. Vito glanced in the mirror again. Ubaldo looked out the side window for a few seconds, then said, "True about the shit Nazi being killed, too."

Ten minutes more and they were in real countryside. In the light of the moon, Aldo could see fields of what he guessed to be tomatoes. Plants but no fruit. A sharp right turn and they crossed a narrow, flat bridge, the river beneath it showing a wavering line of moonlight. Another turn, left, and there by the side of the road, like a dark grave marker, stood an abandoned car with a swastika flag flying from its right front fender. "Two minutes," Vito said. "Take what you find. Hurry."

Aldo jumped out, listening to Giuseppe open and close the other door behind him. Here it is, then, he thought. A bullet in the back of the neck. Not only would he be dead, but his body would be found beside a disabled German vehicle, and word would go out that Aldo Pastone had been a collaborator. He approached the car, waiting for a shot—not the sound but the concussion. His skull exploding. He'd shit his pants, be found beside the car, gone forever. Giuseppe also. Everything he'd tried to do for Lucia—the women to watch over her, the schooling, the clothes, the food—and she'd be left with no relative in the world, no boyfriend, no nothing.

But, second by second, there was no shot. He hurried over to the disabled car, an officer's, he guessed. In the front and back seats, he saw nothing. They'd given him no tools, so how was he supposed to remove the tires or parts of the engine? With his bare hands? In two minutes? Giuseppe went behind the car, turned the T-shaped handle, and lifted up the trunk door. "Guns," he said quietly.

Inside the trunk, to Aldo's shock, he saw a small armory: three rifles, a portable machine gun, and three pistols. What kind of officer would drive around carrying weaponry like this? Someone had set it up all along, then, some spy, maybe, or a *Camorrista* who owed Zozo a favor. He took the machine gun, one rifle, and three clips of ammunition. Giuseppe slipped one of the pistols into his pocket and took the other two and the two rifles. They hurried back to the Ford. Vito had opened the trunk there. They deposited the bounty, slammed the trunk closed, and were off immediately, bouncing down the road in a different direction and then turning back toward the city. Aldo looked across the seat and saw Giuseppe staring straight forward. The boy had kept one of the pistols, held it in his pocket instead of putting it in the trunk. And he was riding directly behind Vito Dell'Acqua. He was crazy, then. A *pazzo*. A *fool*.

The whole adventure still seemed inexplicable to him. Guns, he could see. Guns had value. But why hadn't the Dell'Acquas simply gone on their own and retrieved them? Certainly it had all been planned to the minute. An ambush. The German driver killed an hour earlier, his body carted away. The car had been filled with weapons and left in a certain spot, at a certain hour. But why hadn't the guns just been left in the woods, in a culvert, behind a hut? And why had Zozo needed an extra man, two extra men, for what was really a very straightforward job?

And then part of the answer came: if they'd been caught on the way, the Dell'Acquas—in Italian uniform—could claim to have been working for the Germans all along, arresting these two, taking them to the railway station, or out into the countryside to be shot. The Germans wouldn't know any better and would be happy to have two more men to send to the labor camps, and Zozo, never putting himself at risk, would have lost basically nothing. The Fornis hadn't climbed to the top of the bloody ladder by being stupid. Or by risking their own skins when they could just as easily risk someone else's. As for the car, maybe it had been stolen from the streets, no one killed after all. Or maybe one of Zozo's contacts worked in a military garage and knew there were weapons stored in the trunk of that particular car, and he'd been paid handsomely to risk his life and pass on the word. Maybe the thief had driven the car out into the countryside just to torment the Nazis, who would have to spend more time searching for it. Maybe weapons were being stolen and hidden all over the city, and Zozo knew all about it but didn't want to say yet what they'd be used for, and had made up the story about selling boots and uniforms because there was something much riskier going on.

Aldo looked across the seat at Giuseppe, who sat in silence, not moving a muscle. He wondered what he'd gotten the boy—and himself—involved in.

On the outskirts of another poor neighborhood, the northeast corner of Vasto, near the agricultural market, Vito pulled the car in past the church on Corso Novara, then cut sharply behind a garage that sat beside a broken-down one-story block of a house. His brother carried the guns and ammunition into the garage, making two trips, not asking for help, disappearing for several minutes at a time.

You took a pistol, Aldo wanted to say to Giuseppe. *You're completely crazy.* But Vito was sitting behind the wheel, the collar of the uniform loose around his enormous neck. Aldo watched him, waiting, looking for any indication that he knew.

Ubaldo returned, and they were off again. Ahead, on Corso Meridionale, there was something that looked to be a checkpoint. Aldo reached inside his jacket and kept his hand on the pistol there. They approached slowly, Vito waving to the soldier at the side of the road, Aldo wondering if Giuseppe would use the gun he'd just stolen, or if Vito would take one hand off the wheel and grab the weapon he surely carried. The car slowed down a bit more. The soldier followed them with his eyes, started to raise one hand, but made no signal for them to stop.

Back in the heart of the city, the Dell'Acquas dropped off their two passengers, without explanation, in front of the Archeological Museum. "That's the job for tonight," Vito said. "Sleep like after you have sex."

Without a word, Aldo and Giuseppe were out of the car and walking down Costantinopoli, toward Piazza Bellini, two kilometers from home. Aldo relieved but still puzzled, Giuseppe quiet, swinging his eyes around as if he expected to be arrested any second and thrown into the back of a German lorry. They passed a wall on which someone had painted a message in large, irregular letters:

IL DUCE HA SEMPRE RAGIONE!

THE LEADER IS ALWAYS RIGHT!

But someone else apparently disagreed, because the graffiti had been partly covered over with black paint.

Near the piazza, Aldo said, "What do you think you're going to do with the pistol?"

"You saw me," the boy said, surprised, stupid.

"Of course I saw you. You should hope no one else saw you. What were you thinking?"

"In case the Nazis try to grab me."

Aldo shook his head. "The Nazis? You should worry about the Dell'Acquas. Do you know who those men are? They're killers. You don't steal from killers, and if they saw you, don't expect me to protect you."

"I won't. I don't expect anything from you. Lucia doesn't, either."

Aldo stopped and took hold of the boy by the collars of his shirt. He shook him once, hard enough to make the glasses wobble on his nose. "Don't ever speak to me about my daughter. Do . . . not . . . ever."

"No one else will," the boy said into his face, unafraid. "You're her father! You act with her the way a stranger would act! Worse than a stranger!"

"Don't tell me how I act. You're an idiot. You stole from the Dell'Acquas!"

"You're her *father*!" Giuseppe said again.

Disgusted, Aldo pushed him away, hard, turned his back and started walking. The idiot followed him.

"Tomorrow," Giuseppe said from just behind, "they're going to start rounding up men between the ages of eighteen and thirty-three and taking them north to work."

Aldo couldn't keep himself from emitting a short, bitter laugh. "I'm forty-two, next week. That doesn't worry me."

"Lucia asked if you could hide me, but I don't want to hide. I want to fight."

Another short laugh. "Fight them?" Aldo said. "With what, your hands? Your one stolen pistol?"

The boy reached out and took hold of Aldo's wrist, and Aldo found that, strong as he was, he couldn't twist it free. He stopped and turned. The boy's face was twitching. "My parents were slaughtered by them," Giuseppe said. "I cleaned up what was left of my mother and father and wheeled the remains all the way to Poggioreale and buried them there with my own hands." He squeezed Aldo's wrist in a grip tight enough to break bones. "I love your daughter, and I tell her so, something you have never done. So if you want to tell your friends I stole the pistol, and take away the one person in her life who treats her well, go ahead."

Giuseppe released his grip and for a long moment, they stood facing each other, eyes locked, moonlight on the boy's face. Aldo thought about the knife in one jacket pocket, and the pistol Zozo had given him, in the other. How easy it would be, and how horrible.

"Let me stay at your place tonight," the boy said. "One night. Tomorrow, I'll find my own place to hide. If not, do what you have to do about the pistol. Tell them if you want. Slice me up if you want. But think of what you'll be doing to Lucia."

Thirty-Seven

Colonel Scholl woke from a turbulent sleep, six restless hours wracked by a parade of lurid dreams. He lay in the comfortable bed for a time, letting the possibilities play in his mind, postponing the duties of the day, nursing a loneliness so subtle and so familiar, it felt like the whispering of a friend.

Eventually, the duties—his actual life, not the imaginary one—could be postponed no longer. He washed, shaved, put on his uniform, and by then his mind had cleared and the images set safely aside. In a flash of insight, the colonel understood his purpose for the day. All along, good soldier that he was, he'd been waiting for specific orders; now, good officer that he was, he realized he'd been assigned to Naples not to take orders but to give them. Hadn't Kesselring said *"use your own initiative"*? In all the city, there was no officer senior to him (the Italian generals—Pentimalli and Del Tetto—had, shortly after his arrival, turned over their authority and fled the city. Where, he wondered, did they intend to go?).

At breakfast, sitting alone at a white-clothed table in a private enclave of the hotel dining room, he drank his Italian coffee and ate his Italian egg and waited for the annoying Lieutenant Renzik to report for duty. It wasn't until 7:13, nearly a quarter of an hour late, that Renzik appeared at the door of the dining room, casting his eyes about as if watching for birds nesting in the corners. Eventually, he looked toward the enclave, saw his colonel, and practically sprinted across the empty main room.

The salute, the obligatory "Herr Colonel," the sloppy posture.

"You're late, Lieutenant."

"My apologies, sir. There has been a small problem."

Scholl watched him, almost amused. "Describe it, please," he said when Renzik held to a trembling silence. "Has the proclamation not been printed?"

"No, sir. It has. They, the posters are ready, they—"

"What then?"

"Sir, the jeep in which I was supposed to drive you this morning has been . . . sabotaged."

"In what way?"

"In the way in which it has been . . . Two tires were flattened and one sustained damage that made it hard to refill, sir."

"Where had it been left?"

"In the usual parking garage, sir. Near the university buildings at the port. Which, I was told, has always been safe. A guard—"

"And you tried to drive it with the flattened tire, am I correct?"

"Correct, sir, because I couldn't fill it with air, and I was late, because the nipple—"

"What nipple, Lieutenant?"

"The tire nipple, sir. Where you attach the hose. It was bent."

"And how did you get here?"

"I drove the jeep, but the tire is ruined now, sir." He took a sharp breath. "Shredded."

"Lieutenant, listen to me. By the time I take the last sip of my coffee and walk to the front door, have another vehicle ready. I don't care what it is, as long as it has four wheels with inflated tires. Has the proclamation been posted?"

"Everywhere, Herr Colonel."

"Good. How many men do we expect to collect?"

Roland Merullo

"I don't understand, Herr Colonel."

Scholl leaned closer and peered into Renzik's eyes, as if searching for something behind them. "If all the Italian men in this city," he said very slowly, "between the ages of eighteen and thirty-three, report to us as required, approximately how . . . many . . . will . . . there . . . be?"

"Captain Nitzermann said thirty thousand, sir. He was wondering where to put them all. We—"

"Tell Nitzermann to bring as many as possible to the train station and the rest to the stadium. In the—what is the neighborhood called? The Vomero?"

"Vomero, yes, sir. It's—"

"Go!"

Renzik saluted and hurried away. The obsequious Italian waiter—spying on them, no doubt—approached the table to inquire if the colonel had any other needs, now or later in the day. That was the way he put it. The "other needs" weren't specified, but the look on the man's swarthy face was one of sly awareness, suspicion, even superiority. Scholl shook his head, no, wondering if the waiter had been watching him, if he'd noticed the German colonel staring too long into the bar sitting room the night before. Or if, somehow, the German colonel's reputation and choice of amusements had preceded him. *Now or later in the day.*

Scholl stood, leaving no money on the table, and walked toward the front desk. "Would you have matches?" he asked the pretty young clerk there, in German.

Without need of translation, she reached under the counter and handed him a thin box. Scholl nodded his thanks.

On his way to the door, squeezing the box of matches in one fist, Scholl couldn't keep himself from risking a glance, filled with some longing, into the side room with the red-upholstered chairs, as if, even at this hour, he might see the pliant young women and trim, eager men. The room stood empty. He turned his eyes away, but a whisper

180

of regret followed him: Would a bit of pleasure have been so damaging to the great cause? Would it have interfered with his duties in any way? Wouldn't it have made the night more enjoyable, his hours of sleep more restful? And why was it that certain types of attraction were shameful and others not?

He shook his head to clear the thoughts, and stepped out into the day. A bit cooler this morning. Perfect. He'd be happy to contribute some warmth.

A minute's delay, then Renzik pulled up to the entrance in, of all things, a flatbed truck with a machine gun mounted in back. Italian, it seemed. It would have to do. Scholl climbed into the cab's passenger seat. "Do you know how to get to San Paolo Bel Sito?"

"I think so," Renzik said, engine running, both hands on the wheel, his face turned so that he was looking squarely at Colonel Scholl. "That's where they brought the—"

"I know very well what was brought there. Why else would I be going?"

"I don't know, sir. Because of that and the . . . the incident from yesterday, sir."

"Drive. The villa there. Whatever it's called."

"You know what happened there yesterday, sir."

"Of course I know! I don't have to sit with the radio every minute. Everything that happens in this city finds its way to my desk."

The route out of Naples took them past the enormous burial grounds—Scholl wasn't sure how to pronounce the name—and as they passed, he saw some kind of shabby funeral cortege, men, women, weeping children, dressed in rags, shuffling along in an uneven formation behind a casket carried on a horse-drawn cart with huge wheels. It looked like a scene from the fifteenth century. He spread the map on top of his thighs and did his best to identify the towns as they passed them: Monte Oliveto, Caravita, Romani, Passariello, Muli, Scisciano. Despite the time in Rieti and Rome, his Italian was still only passable, and he found the ugly names next to impossible to pronounce. What point was there in becoming fluent in the language? Let the Italians learn German.

He stared out the side window, wondering how the collection of the Jews was progressing and when he could write up a report for Himmler. A few unattractive stone houses stood along the roadside, the low hillsides behind them dotted with even lines of olive trees, the topography dry but pleasant enough in a Mediterranean way. What he thought of as "the body fever" was upon him again, a vibrating warmth that turned his thoughts, the way a rider turned a horse's head and led it in a certain direction. By and large, the Italians were a good-looking race, he had to admit it. He recalled the night in Rieti that had led to his censure. The tangled limbs, the juices, kisses, and moans, the soft beginning, then the frenzy, the giving up of all control. Afterward, the calm. The touch. The sleep.

Most likely, one of the lovers had reported him—currying favor, perhaps, or avoiding punishment. The man, he'd thought at first. And then, the woman. And then both of them, a team of Italian betrayers, collecting secrets that could be used to pay for their lives or their freedom. Foolish of him to be involved, and yet the memory itself was altogether fine, a respite from the loneliness and from the terrible tension of war.

Before they reached the city of Nola, Renzik, who'd been absolutely silent during the hour-long ride, spoke up. "Montesano, the villa is called, sir. The valuable papers have been moved there. From the Archives in the center of—"

"You are telling me things I already know, Lieutenant."

Renzik retreated into silence. Another few kilometers and Scholl saw a pond the size of a soccer pitch, surface untroubled. Beyond it, gates, a long driveway, and a square three-story villa with a columned entrance and a crenellated roof, as if it were a castle whose sharpshooter guards had once been stationed there, high up, to protect the prince from kidnappers.

"Strange place to bring documents," he mused aloud.

Renzik hesitated, turning through the gates and up the driveway. "Because of the bombs . . . in the center."

A tiresome companion, this Renzik. "And who killed our man here?"

"He hasn't yet been caught, sir. A sniper. One shot."

By the time they reached the columned entrance, Scholl could see that a civilian had come out to greet him. The man, middle-aged, short of stature, was wearing a worn black suit and dark necktie, knot loose, the top of his shirt unbuttoned. High forehead. Mustache. An intellectual.

Scholl climbed out of the truck and ignored the man's greeting. He stood with his hands clasped behind his back and let his eyes wander across the front of the building. He saw two of his soldiers just inside the door.

"I am Riccardo Filangieri, the archivist," the man was saying. "We regret the death of your lieutenant. I can tell you his killer was not someone who works here. We have only—"

Scholl reached out and hit the man hard in the middle of his chest with two bent fingers. The archivist stumbled backward and nearly fell. Scholl walked past him into the tiled foyer, on each side of which stood crates of documents and books piled higher than his head. He took the box of matches from his right front pocket and twisted them this way and that between his second and third fingers.

The archivist had recovered, and followed him inside. "Colonel, please," he heard the man say. Begging. "These are precious historical documents, some dating to the thirteenth century. Irreplaceable. Kindly—"

"My man also was irreplaceable," Scholl growled, turning to stare at the archivist, who was almost a head shorter. He had his hands clasped together now, pleading, begging, shaking them this way and that, his mouth trembling. Over what? Old papers. Meanwhile, an actual officer of the Reich, sent here to ascertain the location of the documents, had been killed in cold blood. Scholl turned to his two soldiers, standing beside Renzik near the door. "Any of our men elsewhere in the building?"

They shook their heads in tandem.

Scholl walked over to the nearest pile of boxes. He used his combat knife to cut one box open, and with the pleading Filangieri beside him, going on and on, Scholl tugged free an ancient-looking leather-bound folder, tore out a handful of pages, and perused them.

"The Order of Malta documents," Filangieri said. "Seven hundred years old."

Scholl could make no sense of them. He crumpled the pages into a ball and pressed the ball partway back into the hole he'd cut, then opened the matches, took one out, and struck it.

"Please, we beg you," the archivist said. One of the soldiers came over and, holding the man by both arms, pulled him backward toward the door.

Scholl struck the match and held it up in dramatic fashion, then reached out and touched it to the ball of paper. For a few seconds, he watched the flames catch and leap upward, watched them spread backward into another pile of boxes, and then to the front of the nearest box to the left. He let the match burn until it singed his fingertips, then tossed it into the fire. Filangieri seemed actually to be weeping now, or perhaps it was the smoke in his eyes. Scholl stood there until the air became thick with it, then turned on his heel and walked out. His men dragged the struggling Filangieri into the fresh air, where he stood wringing his hands and kept on with the pleading and weeping. When they could feel the heat from the fire, when the smoke started to billow out the front door and one open window beside it, Scholl turned to the man and said, "Go in now, if you like. Perhaps you can rescue something irreplaceable."

He instructed the two soldiers to climb onto the back of the truck, and Renzik to take it halfway down the drive and stop there. Scholl walked slowly after it, then turned to watch. For a few minutes, it seemed the fire might magically have been contained, or that the archivist had gone in and extinguished it with his bare hands. But then, one after the next, two of the paned front windows cracked and fell outward, and clouds of smoke poured into the morning. Scholl stood there for the better part of an hour, captivated by the sparks and smoke, watching flames licking out the windows, listening to the upper floor collapse. Just as he summoned Renzik—who seemed troubled by the blaze and was staring at it openmouthed—he caught sight of the archivist. The *Verrückte* had, it seemed, actually gone into the burning building at one point, because he was squatting on the ground a safe distance away from it now, fluttering some rescued pages in both hands. He seemed to realize he was being watched, and turned his head to Scholl and stared. Something in the expression there—not anger, not hatred, but a type of profound disappointment that bordered on disbelief—cast the colonel back for a few brief seconds to the stone house near Walchensee with a view of the lake. He was three or four, and though he couldn't remember what transgression he'd committed, he did remember his mother looking at him precisely like that, disappointed, incredulous. Her beautiful face—black hair, dark eyes—was turned toward him from across the room, the Bavarian summer sunlight angling in through a window behind her, the sense that her affection for him had evaporated and would never return.

Thirty-Eight

When he awoke at first light, Giuseppe wrestled for half a minute with a terrible sense of disorientation. He was lying on a carpet, covered by a threadbare blanket, with a seat cushion for a pillow. He was hungry and thirsty, and the room was lit only by deflected sunlight filtering in from two small windows near what he assumed to be the exterior door. He sat up. Beside him on the floor lay a German pistol, black as the darkest night, with a short, thin neck and a handle of raised pyramid shapes that made him think of his mother's cheese grater. A table, two armchairs. In one back corner, a small refrigerator and half-size stove. He shook his head, and the night's events came back to him. The drunken soldier. The German car with its stash of weapons. The two mustachioed killers, creatures from a violent nightmare, taking him and Aldo into the countryside. The stolen gun. The argument that had led to Lucia's father grudgingly allowing him to spend the night.

He stood up and peeked into the bedroom. No one. On the counter stood a clean glass, as if it had been left there for him. He filled it with water from the tap—only a trickle was coming through—drank it down, and then for a time paced the apartment, not spying, not rummaging through what few objects lay on the table and counter, just waiting. He waited for half an hour. Nothing. Finally, he jammed the pistol into the top of his trousers, covered the handle with his shirt, opened the door, and stepped into the day. Whatever terrors the streets of the city had held for the past few years—bombs, teetering build-ings with cracks running through them like the outline of a staircase, German soldiers, Neapolitans crazed by hunger or carrying typhus or malaria on their skin or in their blood—it had always felt like his city. But now that Lucia had described the proclamation to him, now that the threat of being snatched up and shipped north was right here, in the paving stones, in the morning sunlight, he picked his way along the dusty sidewalk like an alien. The city belonged to the Germans now, to this Colonel Scholl, who was telling them what time to go to bed, and what they could carry, and that they could be picked up like slaves and shipped off to die.

To heighten the feeling, even as he turned onto the usually busy Via Monte di Dio, he saw very few people on the street, and no young men at all. Not one.

He wanted to go back to his home and wash and change clothes and check on his uncle, or to his office and be sure that Lucia had found the map, or to the building where she worked and signal her through an upstairs window to come down and speak with him, but any of those things would have been madness. Then where to go? Aldo's door had locked when he'd closed it, and he didn't want to go back there in any case. A feeling of the utmost conspicuousness and vulnerability had come over him, as if he were walking along, naked, and might be spotted at any moment and arrested by the *carabinieri*. But it wasn't the Italian police who worried him. Brutally efficient as the Nazis were, they had no doubt started posting the proclamation at dawn, and sent out their squads and trucks to find Italians, and here it was, close to ten o'clock. He shouldn't have slept later than Aldo, shouldn't have waited for him to return home. He should have been up before the sun and . . . and what?

Not knowing what else to do or where else to go, he decided to climb to the Vomero and nurse a cup of coffee in the Café Sangiuliano's back room. One of the owners, Salvatore, had been friendly with his parents and knew him, and the back room was mostly hidden from the street and far enough from the cash register and entrance that Salvatore could warn him if the Germans appeared. The other advantage to this plan was that the shortest route to that part of the city was up the ancient Pedamentina stairway, which zigzagged from the Spagnoli to the abandoned monastery and the old fort at the southern edge of the Vomero hill. There would be less chance of patrols wandering that far from the roadway, and from the top of the stairway to the café was a distance of only a kilometer or so.

On the long climb, he passed two women. They looked at him with such horror that he at first thought they'd seen the pistol tucked beneath his shirt. But it was well hidden there, and he realized they must have seen the proclamation and were afraid for his safety; the arrests had begun. He reached the top of the stairs, glanced back and forth to either end of the street, crossed, hurried along in the shadow of Castel Sant'Elmo, and was within a block of the Sangiuliano when he heard the truck engine, the squeal of brakes, shouted German words. He grabbed the pistol with his right hand and dove onto a patch of grass behind a concrete bench and lay there, visible to anyone who happened to look in that direction, but as still as a dead body. Beneath the bench, he had a view of the street. Not fifty meters away, two German soldiers were wrestling an Italian man to the ground. They punched and kicked him until he stopped struggling, then dragged him to the back of the truck and lifted him into the bed, where another soldier sat with a rifle across his knees. The Italian lay like a captured fish on the floor at the soldier's feet. The doors slammed, the truck sped off. Pistol flat on the grass, Giuseppe rested his head on his arms and didn't move for the better part of five minutes.

At last, not seeing or hearing any more trucks, he got to his feet and, keeping close to the sides of the buildings, made it safely to the café. Salvatore greeted him in a worried way and led him, not only into the back room, but through a door there into his kitchen, and then through the kitchen, through another door, to a table where, Giuseppe guessed, Salvatore took his own meals before and after work.

The old man brought him a cup of weak coffee and a stale pastry, and when Giuseppe apologized for putting him in danger ("I'm sorry, I hadn't even thought that—"), Salvatore waved the apology away.

He sat there for two hours, taking tiny sips and tiny bites, listening for sounds from the street, wondering where he might possibly go. He'd been so careless. What hadn't occurred to him was that, wherever he went—back home, to Lucia's, to Aldo's, here—he'd be putting not only himself but other people in jeopardy. If the Nazis found someone hiding him, they'd both be taken or killed. Where, then?

Late in the morning, he heard the door open. He had one hand on the pistol, ready to fight. But it was Salvatore again, leading Avvocato Cilento. The old man was walking with the aid of a cane, dressed in an expensive suit, his eyes alert, his manner that of a respected elder who contained within himself a great wisdom. He was a kind man. Wealthy, but generous with his wealth. On a few occasions—when Giuseppe's uncle Orlando had needed official papers to get to America, for instance—the famous attorney had helped the family with legal matters, mostly without payment, and had been to their home scores of times for a meal or a glass of wine. His first name was Massimo, but everyone referred to him by his title, *Avvocato*, attorney. Avvocato Cilento.

He joined Giuseppe at the table. Salvatore set a coffee cup there, at his place, and went back to work. "You've heard about the proclamation, yes?" Cilento asked in his slow, elegant way of speaking. Even that short question was posed as if he were arguing a case before a magistrate, the grammar and pronunciation perfect, the eye contact exquisite, the shock of white hair combed neatly back and the cheeks cleanly shaved. He seemed unconcerned about being found in the presence of a young man who hadn't reported.

Giuseppe nodded.

Cilento took a sip and rolled his lips together as if trying to squeeze more taste from the diluted liquid. "Who is this madman Scholl?"

Giuseppe studied the wrinkles around the old man's eyes, wondering if he, himself, would live long enough to show the marks of age on his face, if he'd one day be able to tell his children or grandchildren what life had been like in Napoli during the war. "They're all madmen," he said, the words bursting from his lips with a fury that surprised him. "I saw him when he was just arriving. He was standing in the car like a king surveying his kingdom, surrounded by soldiers on motorcycles. Lucia had the job of taking the proclamation to the printer."

Cilento nodded somberly. "The tone of the thing: 'If you obey and stay calm, we will treat you well. If not, you shall be punished.' As if we are little children. Or dogs." He paused and sipped again from his cup. "I have a secret to share with you," he said quietly.

Giuseppe watched him and waited.

"Did you ever hear of a Dr. Giacomo Sarno? He taught for years at the university. A scientist."

"No."

"A friend." Cilento looked to either side, as if there were others in the small space, then leaned closer. "He's now working with some brave colleagues to disable German radio communications. The Nazis use certain frequencies, in the thirty-thousand-kilohertz range he said, whatever that means. Sarno is aware of them and perhaps knows how to disrupt them. Tell no one."

"Of course," Giuseppe said, but something in Cilento's face and tone of voice made him wonder if it was true, or if the old man was simply trying to hold on to some imaginary coattails of heroism.

They sat quietly for a while, a few street noises—a truck engine, a loud voice—reaching them through the walls. Giuseppe's parents had always been fond of the Vomero district—set up on a hill as it was—and referred to it as *"the countryside." "Pretty houses, but why would anyone want to live so far away?"* he could hear his mother asking. The air was clear, the nights a few degrees cooler, and from certain places—three blocks from this café, for instance, near Castel Sant'Elmo—you had a glorious view down across the city to the bay. Giuseppe supposed that, if the war ever ended, the Vomero could turn out to be the part of Naples where rich people lived. In that way, Avvocato Cilento might be ahead of his time.

Aside from Uncle Donato—who Giuseppe might never see again—Cilento was the closest thing he had to a father now, to an adviser. He held the words inside for a few minutes, then said, "Something strange happened last night."

Cilento took another sip of his coffee, wiped one finger delicately across his lips. "Tell me." The old face, the spots on his skin, the sagging flesh at his jawline, the furrowed forehead . . . all seemed to say, *It couldn't possibly be anything I haven't heard.*

So Giuseppe told him almost everything—the map, Lucia's panicky fear for his safety, his decision to abide by her wishes and seek out Aldo Pastone, his encounter with the drunken soldier, the errand in the black Ford. The only thing he failed to mention was the pistol. He could feel it pressing against the muscles of his stomach. *Stolen in the course of stealing* was the way he thought of it, hardly a transgression, but perhaps, as Aldo had said, foolish nonetheless. Still, if he were about to be captured, he wouldn't hesitate to use it. If it was a choice—die in Naples or die in Berlin, avenge his parents' death with the death of one Nazi soldier or surrender meekly—the choice would not be difficult.

Something new showed on Cilento's face, a twist of emotion. Disdain, fear, a bad memory—Giuseppe couldn't tell. It passed, and Cilento asked, "Aldo Pastone is your girlfriend's father?"

"*Sì.*"

"I know him, and some of his history. And we have a mutual . . . friend. You are in difficult company, did you realize that last night? Perilous company, I would say."

"I knew it, yes."

"Pastone ran the port. For the Camorra."

"Lucia told me. But he's not a member, she said."

"Perhaps not. But he was in prison with many of them as a boy. And over the years, he's made a fortune for them. He's valuable to them, to the Forni family, at least."

"Forni's dead."

Cilento nodded. "One of them. His brother runs the family now. Zozo. Am I correct?"

"I don't know anything about it, Avvocato. I've heard the name, that's all."

It had always been incongruous to Giuseppe that Lucia—such a straightforward and law-abiding soul—could have any connection at all, even a secondary or tertiary one, to the Camorra's evil and viciousness, that she could even know a man who worked for them, let alone have one as a father. Of course, in Naples, one never knew who had Camorra ties. The group—unlike the hierarchical Sicilian Cosa Nostra and Calabrian 'Ndrangheta his father used to tell him about—was splintered into a dozen families, each with its own power structure and territory, the families regularly at war with each other, seeking an advantage, moving in on a market, avenging this insult or that death. He knew about the Camorra; everyone in Naples learned of it, probably at the same age they learned their street address, but for the most part, his family and friends had always kept a distance, tried to live legally, to avoid buying stolen items, to avoid certain cafés, certain streets and neighborhoods at certain times of night. The war had changed all that, naturally. No one could be concerned now with where a pair of shoes or a bag of flour came from. If you had the money, if something became available, you made the purchase and were grateful.

Where the Camorra was concerned, he'd always been at pains to keep his hands clean. Now, in the course of one night, the nails were filthy.

"I care more about the Germans, Avvocato. The Camorra didn't kill my parents, the Germans did."

"*Sì, sì*, and what are you going to do? If you show your face on the street, you'll be carted away. What can you do against tanks and trained soldiers, against men with no souls?"

"I don't know, Avvocato . . . Last night I felt something different, another side of me. I stole a pistol and have it now in my belt." Giuseppe moved and lifted his shirt so the gun was visible.

"You stole from the Camorra?" Cilento asked quietly.

"Not exactly. It was German property."

"A distinction they'll fail to make, Giuseppe. A distinction they'll fail to make. What were you thinking? To become a man of violence like Aldo Pastone? To impress your Lucia? To die a martyr's death on the streets, killed by one group or the other, and leave her to weep for you?"

"Something," Giuseppe said, caught suddenly in a hot confusion. "I feel something. The Allies are near."

"And the Allies are going to save you from the Dell'Acqua brothers?"

Giuseppe shrugged and looked away. It had been a reflex, unconscious, unplanned. Not anything he cared to, or could, explain.

Cilento leaned back, a painful flex around his old eyes. "In any case, my suspicion—everyone I know suspects this now—is that, before the Allies arrive, Hitler will give his thugs the order to burn our city to the ground. Your Archives will be high on the list. You'll see. The Allies will arrive to a Napoli in ruins."

Giuseppe was half listening, half–lost in thought. "I think what happened, Avvocato, is that I reached the place where I can't live like this anymore. My parents' deaths, the constant worry about food, a Nazi comes in and wipes horseshit on my desk and I can't do anything about it. And now the evil colonel and his so-called proclamation. I've reached the point of not being able to say yes to it anymore. *Yes, all right. It is as it must be. There's nothing we can do.* I'm past that point now."

"And where does that leave you, my son? You have a pistol, they have tanks."

Giuseppe shrugged and looked away. He felt Cilento reach out and put a hand on his arm. "Stay with me tonight at least. You'll be safe at my place. I have food. It's very close to here."

Giuseppe shook his head at first, but without conviction. "Lucia," he said, and, though he tried, no other words came out, no other idea formed in his mind. He felt the pistol against his skin and wondered, hopelessly, what his father would have advised, what his uncle might suggest, and if he'd ever see Lucia's lovely face again.

Thirty-Nine

Early that morning, when the posters were delivered, Lucia watched the printer himself carrying them in with two helpers. Flat stacks of them wrapped in thin brown paper. Through the office door they went for inspection by Bruni, and then, five minutes later, down the stairs they went, into the hands of a dozen day workers, men so hungry and desperate that they'd do anything for a few lire or a basket of fish heads.

The posting of the proclamation seemed to her the second important thing that happened that morning. The first occurred almost as soon as she'd arrived for work, when she'd been ordered to carry into a second-floor office an armful of files—the Jews she hadn't been able to save. She handed them over to the officer on duty there—the same black-haired, blue-eyed man with the crooked smile who she'd seen eating at the café. He set them on the desk and escorted her to the outer door. That was normal enough. But then the officer glanced behind him, closed the door, and followed her down the hallway and as far as the stairs. He took hold of her left shoulder and turned her toward him, and she expected him to grab a breast or force a kiss: the Germans didn't ask. But he only leaned in, blue-eyed, clean-faced, and said in Italian so quiet, it was almost a whisper, *"Seskind ti segue."* Seskind is following you. He pantomimed a man lifting a heavy, dead leg from the hip. "Do you know who I mean?"

She nodded, frozen.

"A rapist, a fiend. Protect yourself," the soldier said, and then he was gone, a gray-shirted mirage shimmering at the end of the hall, stepping through the doorway and into his other life.

Descending the stairs, Lucia felt she was about to burst into tears. "A rapist, a fiend." Following her! And she'd told herself he was just another German overlord, a bit crazier than some, a nuisance. Her first thought was that she should tell her father, but she immediately buried the idea. Her father would pay someone to have the officer killed, or do the deed himself, and then he'd be hunted, or a hundred more Neapolitans would be executed, or both.

"A rapist, a fiend." She needed to set the fear aside. She had a task to perform, and she couldn't let thoughts of the crazy limping Nazi get in the way. Giuseppe's map was in the drawer of her desk, still tightly rolled. Unwilling to leave it in her apartment, to be separated from it for the whole day, she'd carried it to work that morning, the same way she'd carried it from the Archives, in the side of her blouse. The task now was to get it to Rita, her father's friend, and not be caught doing it. Early that morning, she and Rosalia had formulated a whispered plan. The plan had seemed so sensible then; now it seemed like a road map to a Gestapo interrogation.

She went back to her desk, spent the day with her teeth pressed together and a peculiar roiling in her stomach, waited until five p.m., carried the map into the toilet, placed it inside her blouse, and walked out the door with Rosalia beside her. Just two young Italian women, they looked like, leaving jobs so urgent that they had to be called in on a Saturday, jobs that enabled the Nazis to perform their evil deeds, but each carrying an empty water bucket and deadly secrets.

By the time they stepped out into the air, the proclamation had long ago been pasted to the sides of buildings. Rosalia saw one immediately and pulled Lucia toward it by the arm. The paper was dry, bubbling from a hasty gluing job. A small crowd had gathered, eight or ten men and women. One of them was reading it aloud:

FROM COLONEL WALTER SCHOLL, ARMY OF THE THIRD REICH

I ASSUME ABSOLUTE COMMAND OVER THE CITY OF NAPLES AND ITS ENVIRONS.

1. EVERY CITIZEN WHO BEHAVES CALMLY WILL ENJOY MY PROTECTION. ANYONE WHO ACTS AGAINST THE GERMAN FORCES WILL BE EXECUTED AND THEIR HOME DESTROYED. WOUNDED OR MURDERED GERMAN SOLDIERS WILL BE AVENGED ONE HUNDRED TIMES.

2. A CURFEW IS HEREBY ESTABLISHED FROM 8 P.M. TO 6 A.M. EXCEPT IN CASES OF BOMBING ALERTS.

3. A STATE OF SIEGE IS HEREBY PROCLAIMED.

4. ALL WEAPONS MUST BE HANDED IN WITHIN 24 HOURS. AFTER THAT TIME, ANYONE FOUND TO BE IN POSSESSION OF A WEAPON WILL BE IMME-DIATELY EXECUTED.

5. ALL MEN BETWEEN THE AGES OF 18 AND 33 SHALL REPORT IMMEDI-ATELY TO THE LOCAL GERMAN AUTHORITIES. THOSE WHO DO NOT REPORT SHALL BE ARRESTED.

6. PEOPLE MUST KEEP CALM AND ACT REASONABLY.

Rosalia and Lucia stood there listening, watching the faces in the crowd, a new fear there, or another dimension of an old fear. And then they set off for the water fountain near Rosalia's house, a fifteen-minute walk.

"It's so risky, carrying that map," Rosalia whispered as they went, her voice running beneath the sound of their footsteps. "You're so amazing, so brave! I think the plan is really wise, though. I do."

"Maybe I should just go there like this, in these clothes."

"No, no," Rosalia said. "I heard that a soldier was badly beaten there last night, near that woman's neighborhood. The Nazis will think nothing of stopping and searching a laywoman. They'll enjoy it."

Lucia couldn't think of anything to say. The risk seemed to have become part of her, to be trembling in her veins. And what was the option? Keep working in an office where they sent Jews to the camps, and put out proclamations designed to enslave the rest of the population? Sit quietly by and starve while waiting for the Allies to arrive? Spend every waking hour looking over her shoulder in case the *fiend* was following her, tracking her like an animal?

She reached out her free hand, felt the rolled map moving beneath the fabric, and squeezed her friend's forearm. "You're as brave as I am, Rosalia."

"I wish I had my sister's faith."

"You're doing more than she's doing. But tell me something: How do you always know what's going to happen before anyone else does? The landing on Sicily. The armistice. The proclamation. Now you were the first to know about the beaten soldier. You're at least a day ahead of everyone."

Rosalia walked along silently for a bit, holding her eyes forward. "I'm not pretty," she said. "I've never had much good fortune with men."

"What does that have to do with anything?" Lucia asked, but by the time the last word was out of her mouth, she had a sense of the answer. Before Rosalia could say anything else, Lucia asked, "Who is he?"

"The Italian officer on the second floor. An intelligence officer who . . . But I don't, you know . . . I don't do everything. Just some things. He's kind, not like the rest of them. And lonely. He gives me some information and I do things for him."

"Talk about a risk."

"Him or me?"

"Both of you. And you trust him?"

"He tells *me* things. He has to trust *me*, Lucia. I don't tell him anything. I give him . . . companionship."

"Where? How?"

"We find places," she said quietly. "A few minutes at a time." And then, "Don't judge me, Lucia. He's a good man."

"I don't judge you. Not at all. I just wonder how we could get the information he gives you to someone who could use it."

Another few steps of silence, and then, "I already do that."

Lucia stopped and turned her friend to face her. "I won't ask you who you tell."

"Better not to. It's no one you would guess."

"And you call me brave!"

The comment brought a smile to Rosalia's plump cheeks, quick as a flash of sunlight through storm clouds. Lucia shook her head in amazement.

On Via Miracoli, there was a line of women at the fountain, all of them with pails or pitchers. Lucia and Rosalia waited their turn, filled their buckets to the brim, held their mouths under the spigot for a drink, and then carried the heavy pails down the last block, the thin metal handles cutting into their fingers. As she went, worried constantly about the map, Lucia tried to imagine the shy Rosalia passing on information from a Fascist soldier! And her father's lover, Rita, passing a map to a spy! And the monks at Genovese hiding an American! And Giuseppe drawing his map! How many other people were secretly risking their lives?

Rosalia lived with her parents, two of her six older siblings, and, she said, two adopted orphans in a glamorous apartment on the second floor of one of Naples's nicest *palazzi*. The building was undamaged, the stairwell clean, the ceilings high and edged with fine molding, the furniture polished, heavy, hearkening back to the years before the first war, before Mussolini, before hunger.

But, for a week now, Rosalia said, there had been no water. A sink, a stove, a toilet, a bathtub, but no water. A bit of what they carried in their buckets was poured into the toilet, most of it into glass jars for drinking, and some into pots so Rosalia's mother could cook the

potatoes she'd managed to find . . . and then used a second time for
nettle soup. Little that she had, the woman invited Lucia to stay for the
meal, but Lucia shook her head. She saw the two orphans—a boy and a
girl—sitting in a corner paging through a book, and the last thing she'd
ever allow herself to do was to eat some of their food. She hadn't come
for a social visit in any case. In one of the small, elegant bedrooms, she
found Rosalia's sister Marcellina sitting in prayer, as calm and beautiful
as a linden tree in bloom, her hands loosely clasped, her eyes raised to
the window. Lucia stood there, waiting, until Marcellina bowed her
head, made the sign of the cross, and stood up to embrace her. She was
wearing ordinary clothing, a long skirt and pale-blue blouse, but the
clear skin and calm, alert eyes, even the way of standing, marked her as
a woman of the cloth.

She took Lucia by the elbow and led her to a closet. There, hanging
on a hook, was Marcellina's habit—the tunic, coif, and wimple—the
oddly shaped pieces all black or all white, a kind of puzzle. Without
saying a word, Lucia took off her work clothes, setting the map carefully aside, and, without saying a word, Marcellina began to dress her
in the habit, placing the tunic first. Then came the white apron, the
coif and wimple, a complicated process that made Lucia wonder how
long it must take nuns to get dressed in the morning and undressed at
night. At the last, Marcellina took the small wooden cross from around
her own neck, kissed it, and draped it over Lucia's head. Despite
Rosalia's reassurances, Lucia worried that Marcellina would consider
it a sacrilege—using her sacred outfit as a disguise—but the young
woman worked without hesitation, carefully, like a mother dressing
her daughter for a wedding, her immaculately groomed hands fitting
the wimple tight against Lucia's cheeks, tucking a loose strand of hair
beneath it, then standing back and almost smiling. "With God," was
all she said, pressing her hands against Lucia's shoulders and helping
her fit the map up into the folds of one loose sleeve.

Outside, in the living room, Rosalia's mother gasped when she saw Lucia in the habit, and Rosalia came over and gently hugged her, then held her hand. When Rosalia was upset—Lucia had seen it many times—her lower lip quivered. But, quivering lip and all, Lucia saw her in a different light now. "You'll go there tonight?" Rosalia asked.

Lucia shook her head. "Tomorrow, I think. If I go now, I'll be too close to the curfew on my way home. Tomorrow morning will be safer. I'll wear this home to get used to it. Thank you, Rosalia. Your sister—"

"Be careful, please," Rosalia said. "We'll be praying for you. Please come back as soon as you're done so we'll know you're safe."

On the first flight of steps, carrying her work clothes in a small bag Rosalia's mother had given her, Lucia nearly tripped over the long skirts of the tunic. She caught herself, and in a moment was out the door and going along the sidewalk in the direction of the Sanità, her stomach filled with nothing but water and pain, her mind a spinning wheel. Even in the cool evening, her whole upper body was coated in a thin film of perspiration. From time to time as she walked, she found a pretext for looking behind her. No limping fiend. No one at all.

At the corner of Via Mario Pagano, an elderly couple going the other way nodded at her. The couple was holding hands. The woman whispered, "Pray for us," as she passed. Keeping one arm pressed tightly against her side, Lucia promised that she would.

Forty

Armando's visits had become, for Rita, the best moments of the week. She called him *Skutchamenza, the pest*, and he called her *Nanella*, a word of great affection that fell somewhere among *grandmother, mother, sister*, and *best female friend*. No one, including Armando himself, knew how old he was. Eleven, twelve, a young-looking thirteen—no one knew. He told her he'd been left at the door of the Duomo, an infant wrapped in a blanket, then handed over to the nuns in Materdei and raised in the orphanage there before running away to live what he called "the free life" of the streets.

She'd met him three years earlier, when the bombs had started falling. She'd been walking through Piazza Bellini with a bag of tomatoes and peppers—those were richer times—when the air-raid siren sounded and she and everyone else hurried to the nearest shelter. They were down in one of the tunnels below the square, hundreds of men and women crowded in there together, all of them smelling of a rancid, fear-brewed sweat, all of them cringing at the muffled *boom*s and the concussions, one after the next, that seemed to go on endlessly. Two thousand kilograms, someone said the bombs weighed. Two thousand kilograms! The weight of small trucks falling out of the sky and exploding when they landed. When the worst of the bombing had finally passed, she felt a movement next to her and turned to see a small hand reaching into her bag of vegetables. Reflexively, she slapped at the hand, only a second later seeing the face connected to it. The face was small and pinched, almost triangular, topped by a filthy rug of dark hair. A boy. Thin and in old shoes, dressed strangely in ragged pants but a new-looking T-shirt that had something printed on it in English. The boy pulled his hand away, but when he turned his eyes up to her, she could see, in the life behind them, several things. Hunger, a deep sorrow, years of struggling to survive, but at the same time an impish, almost spiritual playfulness that was reflected, too, in the tiny smile at the corners of his mouth.

The all clear sounded. The people around her started to file back out into the light, but Rita stayed squatting there, looking at the boy. And he remained there, too, looking at her. She'd seen plenty of these street urchins in the city—*scugnizzi* was the word for them. They lived by stealing and tricking, sleeping under railroad trestles and in the corners of abandoned buildings, eating whatever they could grab from garbage bins, a plate on an outdoor table, or a merchant's display. Plenty of times, she'd taken pity on them and bought something—a slice of pizza, an apricot, a few pieces of candy—and given it to one or two of them. But there was something different about this vagabond child. Even by the elevated standards of the *scugnizzi*, he seemed older than his years, a man spirit in a thin boy's body.

"Here, take," she said, handing him two tomatoes and two peppers. He bit into the tomato immediately, hastily, the way an animal would eat, the juice and seeds sliding down his dirty wrist, his eyes darting around as if someone might reach out and steal it from him. There was no thank-you, not even a nod. Before she stood to leave, he stuffed the peppers into his pants pockets, held the uneaten half of one tomato in his mouth and the other in his left hand, and scurried away.

It wasn't until several weeks later that Rita saw him again. She'd walked to the port and was waiting for the bus to Ercolano, and there he was, crouching behind a line of bushes on the other side of the street, watching her. She had one small stale roll and a little cheese with her, something she intended to eat on the bus ride, and she clawed the air with the fingers of one hand, summoning him. He fixed his black eyes on her but didn't move. She clawed the air again, held up the roll, gestured with it in his direction.

When he stood, there was nothing servile about him. Shoulders back, head up, he strode across the street, a miniature man. He approached her, sauntering, wearing the same clothes he'd worn in the shelter, hands in his pockets.

She gave him the bread first and told him her address. "241 Vico dei Bianchi in the Spagnoli. I live there, but often you can find me where I pray, in the Church of Perpetual Mercy."

"Misericordia Perpetua," the boy said, echoing her. "A nice name."

"My house is near the Spirito Santo, which was bombed. The house has a yellow door, and I am up two flights of stairs. My name is Rossamadre. Rita."

"I'm Armando. I don't have a second name."

"Come see me."

The boy chewed the bread and kept his eyes on her. When she handed him the cheese, he was gone, sprinting for cover, disappearing past the bushes and down a narrow alley where, just before the bus arrived and blocked her view, she saw two taller boys chasing after him.

From that day, she watched for Armando everywhere she went, watched for him through her second-floor window, watched for him when she sat out on the sidewalk in the evenings with Joe and Eleonora and the others. Several more weeks passed before she finally saw him a third time, prowling like a cat in the shadows at the end of her street just as darkness fell. She went into her house and emerged again with whatever she could find—a little bread, a tomato, a mandarin orange—wrapped in a sheet of newspaper one of her men friends had left behind long ago. But the boy was gone.

When the others went inside, Rita sat in her chair, holding the parcel of food in her lap and praying to Saint Francis. After a long while, she heard a sound, a pebble moving against stone, and in another second, the boy had crept up without her noticing and was standing now, not with his palm up, but with his hand on her shoulder. He squeezed, said, *"Grazie, Nanella,"* took the wrapped food, and disappeared.

She had close friends, and in her life she'd had lovers who were kind to her, but there had never been a touch like that hand on her shoulder. Never. The touch of the child she would never have. She felt a sob swelling inside her breast but held it there, and gazed up the street at nothing. Shadows. Metal and stone. A slanted spill of rubble from the one nearby house that had been bombed.

Every day for the next week, she sat outside longer than usual, a small box of food on the ground beside her chair. No *scugnizzo*. But on that Saturday, late again, there he was, the thin shadow, the proud walk this time—no sneaking—and then his black eyes fixed upon her. He was standing directly in front of her, not holding out a hand, and, for once, not in any hurry to sprint away. There was a droplet of dried blood on the top of his right ear—his or someone else's, she couldn't know. *"Nanella,"* he said, "why don't you chase me away?"

"Because I know you."

"No one knows me, *Nanella*."

"If you have a name, someone knows you."

"Armando is my name, I told you that. And no one calls me anything else who wants to keep living."

The boy seemed suddenly to grow weary of holding up his manly disguise. He squeezed the edges of his lips into a smirk, took the food from her, and walked away. After a few steps, he turned, pronounced one quiet *"grazie,"* and was gone.

Since then, his visits had become a more or less regular occurrence, so much so that, on those weekends when he failed to appear, Rita spent the next days fretting, looking for him, imagining that he'd been killed by a bomb or a speeding military truck or that he'd been set upon by murderers while he slept beneath the bridge or in some abandoned warehouse. If there were other people on the sidewalk with her, he wouldn't approach, so she'd fallen into the practice of sitting out late, alone. Sometimes he'd sit there beside her for a few minutes in one of the chairs a neighbor had left out, and on those nights, they had conversations that ranged from conditions in various parts of the city to the lives of the saints. He was barely educated, but intelligent—the nuns had taught him to read—Rita saw that right away, and it linked them. She'd left school when she was ten, but the priests she lived with after that had given her books and lessons and complimented her on the way she thought and talked, and, although many of her friends now had little schooling and, unable to speak *Italiano*, used only the dialect, she enjoyed reading the newspaper and enjoyed her long conversations with Avvocato Cilento, one of the city's most educated men, and sometimes engaged in philosophical discussions with her brother, Marco. She'd long ago recognized this peculiar part of her: she liked being seen as less than she was. People regarded her as a not-quite prostitute, a big-breasted woman who liked men and sex and spent hours feeding the birds and muttering prayers. Beneath that unpolished exterior, she felt, not holy, of course, but close to the Blessed Mother and her Son. Not brilliant, of course, but thoughtful and, by the standards of her neighborhood, well-read.

Her *skutchamenza* was the same: you looked at him and it was easy to think: *street kid*. But scratch that deceptive surface and there was a sharp intellect and spiritual curiosity. A goodness.

Though he seemed to be perpetually hungry, *Skutchamenza* managed to grow. Though manly even in his boyhood, he managed to retain a childish playfulness, even when the bombings were at their worst and the hunger at its worst. He told her he had what he called *"un coro," a choir*. His choir consisted of himself and three or sometimes four other boys who lived on the streets. Once in a while, he said, if they couldn't live by stealing, they worked, an hour here or there, sometimes a whole day, cleaning manure from the stalls in Campo Diana, shining the car of a rich man, running errands for the *Camorristi* who frequented certain cafés and restaurants. "For my choir, I would die," Armando said. "And they would die for me. No one else matters. Only my choir, *Nanella*, Sister Marcellina, and Padre Paulo. No one and nothing."

"God matters," she corrected him, happy to be among those who mattered.

A spasm of pain or doubt squeezed his face, but he didn't dispute her. "Sometimes in winter I go into a small church, near the orphanage in Materdei. Madre di Dio, do you know it?"

She shook her head.

"The one with Padre Paulo. You can walk to Piazza Dante from there in fifteen minutes. If it's cold outside, Padre lets me sleep in the pews. Once, when I was sleeping there, a voice spoke to me. The voice of Jesus."

"Saying what?"

"Saying, *'Armando, you will soon die. There is no need to go to school.'*"

She thought he must be joking, but when she turned to look at his face in the darkness, she saw the muscles there set in the mold of an elderly man. It seemed to her that he was right: he would not live even to her age.

"After dying," she said, "the angels embrace you. You've never felt love like that, never. The angels embrace you and carry you up to the Lord, and you are given a task."

"What kind?"

"You have to help those suffering here on earth. As many as possible. Using the skills God gives you."

The boy turned his face away and wouldn't say anything else.

On that Saturday night, with the proclamation posted on walls everywhere she went, with occasional *pop*s and *boom*s in the distance, she wondered if the limping captain would seek her out a second time. Probably not, she decided. Pushing the fear to the edges of her mind, she sat outside in the cooling air, waiting for her little friend. It seemed to her that the anxiety she was feeling must be identical to what a mother felt for her child. It sent a worried warmth through her, a stream of love that even the voice of Leopoldo, reciting some Fascist anthem in his bedroom, couldn't spoil.

At last, she saw the moving shadow at the end of the street, *Skutchamenza*'s legs being thrown out in front of him by his proud stride.

Without a word of greeting, he came up and took the seat to her right, his thin arms resting on the metal, his shoes just touching the sidewalk. "Now everybody who lives near the port will have to move."

"Says who?"

"The new boss. The Nazi. The one who put up the posters."

"How near?"

"Three hundred meters. How far is it?"

"Twice as long as this street. That's impossible. Many thousands of people live that close to the water."

Armando made a manly shrug. "They say he's going to blow up the port."

"It's already blown up. I go there to get the bus every week."

"Yes, where I saw you. But the Americans could still land with their ships. People say he's going to wreck every pier, bring more boats in, and sink them."

"That means he's afraid now."

"They're all afraid now, *Nanella*. You can see it on their faces. A *carabinieri* shot some of them who were trying to steal from a store. In Arenella. Three of them got killed near another roadblock, in the Vasto. Listen, hear that?"

The *rat-a-tat* of a machine gun, another muffled *boom*.

Rita nodded. "I saw people shooting at them from a house."

"See, it's true! And they know the Allies are coming. Everybody knows. I saw a man on the street who looked like a spy. An American, maybe, but not with a uniform. A spy. I could tell right away."

Mature as he could be, Rita knew that, like most boys, *Skutchamenza* was prone to exaggeration. Still, the stories weren't so different from gossip she'd been hearing around the city for two weeks now, since the armistice. She'd noticed that, whereas earlier the Germans would make their patrols in pairs, now there were, at all times, three and four of them standing together or sitting in cars with their guns pointing out the windows. And the sound of shooting, once a rare event, had become common, something she heard every day. She remembered the street battle that had saved the Jewish children—in the middle of the afternoon, in the middle of the city—and wondered where the gun had come from. Maybe the Italian soldiers had brought their rifles home when they left the front, or maybe the Allies had already sneaked arms into Naples ahead of their invasion, or maybe people had stolen them from the armories and hidden them in churches and shops. When Aldo came, she'd ask if he knew anything, if the Camorra was involved. If anyone could get guns into people's houses, they could.

"When the Allies come, Armando, you stay with me, because there will be fighting everywhere. I have an extra room. The bed is covered now with things, but we can clean it off, and you can sleep there."

"Maybe, yes," the boy said. "It would be nice to sleep in a bed again. And I'll make sure they don't hurt you."

This time when he stood, he leaned down and kissed her on one cheek before hurrying away. She watched him go until he was out of sight, and then, for a time, couldn't keep herself from thinking about the past. Past touches. Past kisses, and the absence of them. She wondered what kind of man he'd turn out to be . . . if somehow, against all odds, he survived into manhood.

Forty-One

Lucia awakened lying on her left side. The first thing she saw when she opened her eyes was the nun's habit, the black dress folded neatly on a chair with the white wimple on top of it. The sight of it, the realization of what she was supposed to do that morning, made her literally sick to her stomach. She stood up quickly and hurried into the tiny bathroom and, leaning on the sink with both straight arms, barely managed not to vomit. How could Giuseppe keep working on his map every day? How could Rosalia stay sane, meeting her secret lover and delivering the information he gave her? How could the American spy cross German lines and hide out in the monastery? She washed, went back into the bedroom, and stood next to the chair looking at the clothes, then the rolled-up map leaning against the wall like a ticking bomb. Terror, raw, brutal, merciless terror, was the price those others paid for a chance to regain their former lives, but for a few minutes, she wasn't sure she could manage it. Part of her wanted to get dressed in her own clothes and go off to Mass and leave the map where it was.

But it was too late. She'd taken the map and held it as long as she could. She had to deliver it.

It required the better part of half an hour to get the habit on correctly, to pin up her long hair and arrange it beneath the wimple, to convince herself, really force herself, to walk out the door. In the early-morning light, she went along close to the fronts of the buildings, ready to duck into a courtyard or doorway at the first sign of anyone in a German uniform. Every half block, she glanced behind her. No one. The streets were nearly empty, eerily so for a Sunday morning. From time to time, she'd hear a truck engine off in the distance, a familiar rattling rumble. Sometimes a voice from the windows above, though most of them were shuttered. Once, she thought she heard a scrap of piano music, just a few tinkling notes. It made her think of Giuseppe and caused her throat to tighten. How long had it been since she'd heard him play, watched his fingers moving over the keys? Music, books, the kind of laughter that wasn't at someone else's expense—these were things the Nazis hated. She pressed his map against her ribs with the inside of her left arm, the long sleeve flapping against the back of her hand, the heavy black skirts feeling like burlap against her legs.

Going past the Duomo, feeling guilty at missing Mass and guilty to be dressed as a nun, she turned a corner and found herself face-to-face with a trio of Nazi soldiers standing beside their jeep. One of them jumped when he saw her, as startled as she was. Embarrassed, perhaps, he became the most aggressive of the three, stepping directly in front of her and blocking the way. "You're out of your convent, Sister," he said in surprisingly clear Italian.

"*Sì, sì,*" she told him in an apologetic tone. The terror had hold of her throat. Her legs were suddenly unsteady. The map in her sleeve seemed to be alive. "*Sì,*" she managed to say again in a voice that didn't belong to her. "It's an emergency. A spiritual emergency. A parishioner of Santa Maria is dying of typhus, and the priest, Father Carvelli, is unable to come. I've been sent to comfort her in her last hours."

"Typhus," the soldier said. *Tifo.* He was running his eyes across her face as if tracing the movements of a scampering spider, or looking for symptoms. "You'll catch it."

"I am under the protection of the Lord."

The man grinned. His two colleagues watched. "We should arrest you and take you to the barracks," one of the others said at last. "And see if the Lord protects you then."

For what? she wanted to ask, but she knew it would be useless. The Nazis didn't need a reason to kill; they certainly didn't need a reason to make an arrest, or to rape, or to torment. "It's an errand of mercy."

"We don't believe in mercy. Your people who are killing us don't seem to, either."

She waited, sweating now under the habit, holding the map tight against her side.

"It's not the clergy killing you," she said. "And this woman, a mother, is suffering terribly and of no danger to you. She wants only to have someone from the Church with her in her last hours. Kindly let me pass."

"For a kiss," the aggressive one said. "I can go home and tell my friends I kissed an Italian nun."

Lucia stared at him, the fear now being replaced by a smoking fury.

"Let her pass," one of the others said.

"A kiss first." He pointed to his lips. "Here." He was standing half a meter in front of her. He leaned forward, reached out, and took hold of her shoulders.

Lucia paused, then lifted her face to him, clasping both arms tightly to her sides. She felt his lips, then his tongue probing around against her lips and teeth, but she kept her mouth as tightly closed as she could manage.

The soldier stepped back, away from her, and spat. "Not much fun, Sister," he said. "Now go on about your errand of mercy."

They parted, and without speaking, Lucia walked past them, head slightly lowered, the anger simmering in her belly, the awful taste of the man's tongue lingering on her mouth until she turned another corner onto Via San Biagio and felt it was safe to spit and rub a sleeve back and forth across her lips.

And they want us to love them, she thought.

But maybe that wasn't true. Maybe, she thought, they have so much disdain for the Italians—our food, our music, our God-given happiness, our warmth—that they want, not to be loved but only to prove their own superiority. There must be decent ones among them, men like the soldier who'd warned her about the rapist. Surely there were thousands of young men who'd never wanted to be in Hitler's army. But it was the vulgar and violent ones who left an impression. It was the killers and torturers, the rapists and sadists, the Gestapo monsters. Hitler's boys. And Mussolini's, too, because there was no lack of Italian Fascists with the same appetite for violence and humiliation, the same need to prove to themselves and everyone else how right they were.

Strangely, the fury inside her seemed to have sucked away some of the fear. Walking along, alert still for patrols but now into the Spagnoli and almost to Rita's street, Lucia understood all too well that, if it hadn't been for that same strain of violence and sadism in certain Italians—men and women both—they never would have allowed Mussolini to draw them into the war, never would have brought him to power in the first place and kept him there for twenty-one years with his Roman salutes and Fascist marching songs, his code of *credere, obbedire, combattere—believe, obey, fight*—that had been drilled into the head of every schoolchild for the past two decades. How many times had she seen the graffiti: "THE LEADER IS ALWAYS RIGHT" and "MUSSOLINI FOREVER!" No, the Italians were at least partly to blame, no matter what people liked to believe. A kind of madness had infected half the country. She wondered how much suffering it would take to cure them of it.

As she turned onto Vico dei Bianchi, Lucia immediately caught sight of Rita sitting out in front of her house in a strip of shade, dressed as if she'd just come from Mass. Perhaps the woman actually saw the future, as some Neapolitans claimed to be able to do, and had been waiting for her to deliver her secret treasure. Not far in front of where Rita sat, a dog was walking in small circles, around and around, deranged by hunger, nipples dry and drooping, waiting to die. Something about the sight of it—dirty brown coat, long muzzle lowered almost to the ground, legs working automatically—seemed to Lucia as sad as anything she'd seen in the last few terrible years.

A splash of surprise and then concern went across Rita's face when she realized the nun walking up the street wasn't a nun at all. She made the sign of the cross and stood. Lucia hugged and held her and whispered into her ear, "I have something for you. Can we go upstairs?"

Forty-Two

At Avvocato Cilento's beautiful two-story apartment, there had been a mattress to sleep on and a private room, and the lawyer had apples and a little tough beef. And now, tea for breakfast. Unaccustomed to the luxury, Giuseppe ate the morning meal with a shroud of guilt hanging over him. He knew his uncle could take care of himself for a day or two, that their neighbors Carlo and Ravenna would help him up and down the stairs and check on him. But they'd wonder if Giuseppe had been caught in Colonel Scholl's web, or shot on the street. And if Lucia happened to pay a visit, she'd worry, too. He'd have to find a way to connect with her, to find out if *she'd* been caught or hurt, if she'd been able to get the map. But the phone lines had been undependable for months, and, given the proclamation, any thought of making the trip across the city to her tiny Via Maresca apartment seemed like a kind of surrender. If he were picked up en route, they'd never meet each other again. Trying to see her at Mass—she liked to walk down to the Duomo for the Sunday service—would be just as risky.

So he hid in Cilento's apartment for the entire Sunday morning while the elderly lawyer, too old to be worried about being captured for a work detail, was out in the city, attending Mass, or searching for food, or visiting the places he'd liked to go with his wife, Elisabetta—who, he told Giuseppe, he missed *"more than one misses eating."* As the hours wore on, Giuseppe felt himself held more and more tightly in the grasp of impatience. There was food, yes, and books, and he managed at one point to tune Cilento's round-topped, mahogany-trimmed Belsentire radio to a scratchy report from Radio London—it claimed that the Red Army had recaptured a place called Smolensk, and promised the Allies would be in Naples soon. A few days. A week at most. But by the time Cilento returned home for lunch, carrying a small bag of carobs and one of mushrooms, and by the time the soft morning sunlight had turned into the yellow heat of a typical September day, Giuseppe had reached the end of his patience. He thanked Cilento, but said he couldn't stay another night.

"And where will you go?" the old man asked.

"Back to Lucia's father's house first, to see if she's been there. And then, I don't know, to her place."

"Which is where?"

Giuseppe waved an arm. "In the Sanità, near the bridge."

"On foot, most of an hour. Someone will see you for certain. You'll be taken."

Giuseppe knew the truth of this but saw little choice: he felt like his legs were filled with bees, his mind with a bad mix of fear, guilt, shame, and a boiling anger. The pistol tucked into his belt seemed alive, his protection against being sent to the camps, but, at the same time, another death sentence if he was caught with it. "I'll try Aldo's first," he told Cilento. "And hope."

"The den of trouble," Cilento offered, almost under his breath, but he handed Giuseppe a small bag of carobs and mushrooms, told him he could stay there any time he needed to, and wished him well.

On the street, hot sunlight scorched the walls and windows of the apartment buildings, and the few brightly colored objects—a red shirt hanging from a clothesline, a strip of green tiles above a doorway—shone weakly, as if intimidated by a stronger sibling. It was a few minutes before two o'clock, but there were no other men his age to be seen. Here and there, he saw an old man or a woman scurrying along—he handed one of them the bag of food—and, once, a ragged band of *scugnizzi* hustling up an alley. The Germans would ignore such people, wouldn't even see them. What they cared about were men his age—between eighteen and thirty-three—as if anyone a year older or younger must necessarily be unfit for the superior people's labor camps. So he went as quickly as he could, darting from one shadow to the next, hyperalert for the sound of boots on the pavement, German voices, a truck or jeep or motorcycle. He'd made it to the bottom of the long stairway and almost into the Santa Lucia when he heard the sound of a speeding truck.

He was right in the middle of a long block of undamaged houses that stood against each other, side by side. No alley to duck into, no half-destroyed wall to slip behind. The truck was very close now; one more turn and it would be on this street. He tried one front door—locked tight—pushed hard on a second, and it flew open and he found himself in the living room of an elderly woman with a loop of rosary beads in her hands. Her face was a mask of bones and huge, terrified eyes.

"Hide me, please!" Giuseppe said. "I won't hurt you."

He closed the door behind him, and the woman motioned him into a back room. He crouched there, hand on the pistol, watching her back. She was standing at a front window, looking out at the street. He heard the truck turn onto the street, slow down, stop near the front of the house with the engine idling. Shouted German words. His breath was coming in quick bursts. If they pounded on the door and opened it, he'd start firing, kill as many as he could. And then he realized, again, that he'd put an innocent person in grave danger.

Behind him in the room, he could hear a grandfather clock ticking off the seconds. He was hyperventilating, eyes glued to the door. If it opened, if he could kill them, she might somehow escape. More shouts, a horrible minute of quiet, then the truck engine in gear again, moving away.

He waited only another few minutes, thanked the woman four times, and slipped out into the street. Even more careful now, he sprinted from one doorway to the next alley, hugging the wall, waiting at corners to be sure there was no sound of traffic at all. He had the pistol in his hand—what good, hiding it?—and moving this way, it took him almost fifteen more minutes to get to the corner of Via Sospiri, where Aldo lived. By the time he turned onto that street, his shirt was soaked with sweat, and the sweat went cold when he made out the shape of an Italian military vehicle halfway up the block. Open in the back. Just the kind of vehicle the Nazis' Fascist helpers were using to transport Jews and young men to the train station. He ducked into a doorway, squatted on his heels, peered around the stone doorjamb. It was impossible to be sure, but there didn't seem to be any men in the back of the truck. No prisoners. No soldiers, German or Italian, standing guard. There might have been people in the cab, it was hard to tell. Aldo's apartment was a third of the way between him and the truck, twenty-five meters at most, but he squatted in the doorway a long time to make sure there wasn't any movement around the truck, soldiers coming or going. He wondered if they'd turned onto such an out-of-the-way street in midafternoon only for a nap beyond sight of their officers, or a tryst with a young woman in one of the basement apartments there.

Fingers prickling, breath coming in short gulps, Giuseppe counted backward from ten and, still not seeing any movement near the truck, sprinted up the block. Aldo's front door—dented metal—sat one step below the level of the sidewalk, partly out of sight from the street. It was locked. Whispering a prayer, he jammed the pistol back into the top of his pants, knocked hard on the metal twice, and waited. After one endless moment, the latch snapped inside, the door swung open, but, instead of Aldo in front of him, he saw the grizzled cheeks of a man he didn't know. *"Perfetto,"* the man said. "Spectacles and all." He reached out, took Giuseppe by the shirt collar, and pulled him roughly inside.

Lucia's father was sitting on a chair. Keeping a hold on his shirt, the man maneuvered Giuseppe into a second chair, facing Aldo, and stood there at the same angle to them both.

"This is Zozo Forni," Aldo said to Giuseppe in a tone that seemed almost, but not quite, amused. As if he were making an introduction at the Archives, a scholar looking for books on a certain period in Italian history. "You may have heard of the Forni family. Zozo heads it now. His brother, Giovanni, was killed last week by the Nazis."

Giuseppe was staring up into the face. The three-day growth of beard, the plump cheeks, the short, curly, well-trimmed hair that came down into a blunt V in the middle of his forehead and was touched with a few strands of gray. An ugly man, altogether. A face without mercy in it. Something in the eyes made Giuseppe terribly uneasy, and he remembered, suddenly, that Cilento had mentioned this man. A Camorra boss. Another demon.

Aldo spoke again. "Zozo seems to think you pocketed one of the weapons we stole last night."

Moving very slowly, Giuseppe lifted up his shirt, reached into the waistband, brought out the pistol, and, holding it by the barrel, tried to hand it over. Zozo didn't so much as blink. Giuseppe lowered the pistol and set it on the table, pointing it carefully toward the wall. After a long half minute of eye contact, Zozo said, in the most terribly matter-of-fact tone, "People don't steal from me."

"I'm sorry. I . . . didn't know. I hadn't ever . . . I'm worried about the Germans picking me up."

"There are worse fates."

"I know. I'm sorry."

"A pleasant word, *sorry*," Zozo said icily.

Giuseppe swung his eyes to Aldo, who was sitting back in the chair in a posture of neutrality, watching him. So Aldo had reported him to the Camorra. A father who'd send his daughter's lover to his death. "I came here because I have no place to go," he said, but the words made no impression.

Zozo pursed his lips. "Bad timing."

Another endless moment and then Lucia's father shifted his eyes to the standing man. "You're taking five and six weapons at a time, Zozo. Giuseppe here knows where there are hundreds. I think you might consider forgiving him."

"At the armory, sure. We know that as well. How are we going to storm the armory?"

"Not only there," Giuseppe said. "I'm making a map. I work in the Archives, and I walk around."

"You walk around."

"Yes, to see. In the Archives—I work there, I—there's a book that shows the interiors of all the nonresidential buildings in the city. The Nazis are using buildings for storage that you wouldn't expect them to use. Some were used by the Italian Army, and they—"

"Such as."

"Such as the school on Via Recco in the Vomero. Guarded by two soldiers."

"A school."

"Yes! But not used by students anymore."

"Guarded by two soldiers."

"Yes. During the day when the others are on patrol."

"And how do you know what's inside?"

"They wouldn't guard a school if there was nothing important inside."

"And you have a map showing the doors and stairways?"

Giuseppe nodded. "I've been working on it since . . ."

"Since his parents were killed," Aldo put in.

No sign of sympathy crossed the jowly face. Zozo didn't even look at Aldo. He hadn't taken his eyes from Giuseppe's for so much as a second. "Where's the map?"

"Lucia has it, my girlfriend. His"—he gestured toward Aldo—"his daughter. She's bringing it to . . . a woman. Because . . . we wanted to get it to someone . . . The woman knows of a spy, an American, hiding in the monastery in Ercolano."

"Which woman? There are several women in Napoli. Maybe even more than several."

"I don't know. I . . . But I could . . ."

"I know," Aldo said.

Giuseppe couldn't keep his head from snapping to his left. Lucia's father, the man with no mercy, was lying for him.

Zozo looked at Aldo, too. "Don't play."

"I'm not playing. I know the woman."

"How could you?"

"Rita Rossamadre. My Rita. You mentioned her the last time you came here, remember? She lives on Vico dei Bianchi, near the Spirito Santo church, in the Spagnoli. I visit her there. I've visited her for years. 241 is the number, second floor. There's a yellow door at the street level. The last time I spoke with her, she said something about a spy. And she has a brother who's a monk there. In Ercolano. There can't be two women like that. I don't know how Lucia knows her, but we can go there and get the map, and then you'll have every location in the city where the Germans have guards stationed and guns stored. If nothing else, you could sell it to the Allies."

"Right, if your friend Rita hasn't already *given* it to the Allies."

"Let's go see," Aldo said calmly.

Instead of answering, Zozo simply reached down and took the pistol, then walked to the door. Aldo stood up to follow him and motioned for Giuseppe to do the same. They went through the door, turned left on the sidewalk, and when Giuseppe saw that the truck hadn't moved, he stopped and stood still. It had all been a ruse. They were turning him in to the Germans. For pay, no doubt.

But Aldo took hold of him roughly by the elbow, pulling him forward. "Zozo's people are driving it," he hissed between his teeth. "Don't be stupid now."

When they came abreast of the truck, Zozo said, "We climb in the back, all three of us. Vito and Ubaldo are in uniform." He gestured to the open cab. "German uniforms. In an Italian truck. The idea is for them to look like they're out picking up Italians for shipment to the Fatherland. A brilliant plan, I must say. For now, those Italians are us, the three of us. Take back your pistol," he said, handing it to Giuseppe, "because the brilliant plan has one flaw. If we get stopped, it's important to know that Vito and Ubaldo barely speak Italian, never mind German."

When the three men were seated in the back, Zozo reached over his shoulder and tapped a fat knuckle twice on the window of the cab. "Where?" the driver asked, spitting the word quietly out the window and back to them.

"241 Vico dei Bianchi, in the Spagnoli. And don't take the road along the port. There's something going on there, I can hear bullhorns. If you see a Nazi, wave, or nod, or fake a salute. If they stop us, shoot."

Forty-Three

It was a day Naples would remember, Scholl thought. He'd given the order for the evacuation to begin midday on a Sunday because he wanted people to be in their homes. Let his men go through the neighborhoods near the port with their bullhorns, rousing the Italians from their tables or interrupting them at Mass, telling them to get out, leave, move, or be blown to bits the next day by German artillery.

Now it was just before noon, and from his perch on the office balcony, pair of Steiner 8x30 binoculars in his hands, he could see much of the city center and a long stretch of the port. The *Obersturmführer* he'd inherited here, a band of meek half men, seemed to have thought it would be impossible to put his plan into action, to move a hundred fifty thousand people from their homes in a day. He knew differently: so far in this war, much more difficult things had been accomplished by the forces of the Reich. The city would be destroyed as his troops departed, that was a given, but before the destruction commenced, the port area had to be made uninhabitable, the shores and harbor rendered as inhospitable as possible for landing craft and Allied ships, and a strip of the city nearest the water had to be left without defilade of any sort.

Even with the naked eye, he could see the main avenue that led away from the port—his map said it was Via Toledo—but not many people walking along there. Too soon for that, he supposed; his men would still be closer to the water, in the Chiaia neighborhood at the port's northern edge. He noticed one bus moving into town from the southwest and laughed quietly. Another two days and there would be nothing left of that part of the city; he'd give them twenty-four hours to evacuate and then tell the artillery battalion on the hill called Capodimonte that tomorrow, at exactly 0700 hours, they should begin their shelling. He'd see if he could arrange for two naval ships to draw close, and their SK C/34 guns would level whatever the long-distance artillery had left standing. Forty-eight hours from now, there would be a swath of destruction along the entire length of the Bay of Naples. The piers, many of them already damaged, would be useless. The homes, inland for three hundred meters, would have been reduced to rubble, so that any Allied soldiers trying to make a landing there would be naked, without cover, open to merciless German artillery and machine gunners perched in the upper floors of the nearest buildings. The citizens of this horrid city would be terrorized and obedient, awaiting only its final destruction by fire. Where the survivors would go then was no concern of his. Into the countryside, perhaps. To caves. To cemeteries. Into the arms of the Americans. It didn't matter. What mattered was that, when the Allies came marching into the city, proud and apparently victorious, they'd find only ashes, dust, death, an unusable harbor, and a million starving Italians begging to be fed.

A champion chess player in his youth, Scholl often thought of war—of life—in terms of the chessboard. The pawns were useful but expendable, infantry in the service of the king and queen. The bishops and knights represented machine gunners, perhaps artillery or the Luftwaffe or submariners. But the castles—*die Türme*—were his favorite, the great, hidden powers that came in late in a match and wreaked havoc on the enemy, trapping the opponent's queen and choking his king. He thought of them as his tanks and tank commanders, really the most valuable weapons at his disposal. It was important to save them for actual combat, not merely the keeping of order in a city. So, in the past two days, without asking Kesselring's permission, he'd arranged for two-thirds of his tanks to leave Naples and move north toward the Volturno River. The German retreat was the most temporary of things, one piece of the Führer's brilliant chessboard strategy. The forces of the Reich would fall back as far as the mountains and, from the high ground, form a line of defense there that would be impenetrable. The Allies would try to continue north up the narrow peninsula and be decimated. What would have been lost would be only this city of filth and depravity, nothing more, and tens of thousands of Allied lives.

As he was alternately glancing in the binoculars and musing about the near future, Scholl heard footsteps, first in the stairwell and then slapping hurriedly across the tile floor of his office. Nitzermann, the Handsome One, burst through the glass-paned doors and just caught himself before rushing onto the balcony. He saluted there, on the threshold, and said, in an extremely agitated voice, "*Mein* Herr Colonel, a situation."

Forty-Four

As Rita watched Aldo's daughter unroll the map on the kitchen table, she noticed that the girl's fingers were shaking and that the muscles of her beautiful face were pinched tight in a mask of distress. The paper beneath her hands showed a detailed, almost-complete drawing of Naples's neighborhoods, with the larger streets sketched in and named, various buildings marked with stars and numbers, and even some interior details. "The stars," Lucia told her, "are places where the Germans are most likely storing weapons. Arms depots for the Italian Army, some of them. And others just buildings they guard in a way that makes Giuseppe suspicious. The numbers show how many soldiers were at the gates or in the courtyards when he walked past at different times of day."

Rita ran her eyes over the map again and again, the neat squares and careful lettering, the sense that great care and time had been taken in its creation. But she knew also—Lucia's face, unsettling disguise, and shaking hands forced the awareness upon her—that the sheet of paper could easily turn into a death sentence. No German officer would fail to understand what the markings meant. And there could be only one explanation why a woman—in a nun's habit or otherwise—would be in possession of it. By instinct, she reached out and held on to Lucia's shoulder, to comfort her, to connect them to each other in risk. The girl's whole body was trembling.

"My friend's sister lent me—" Lucia started to say, pinching the material of her sleeve, then she stopped and shook her head. "Can you get this to the American?"

"Yes. I'll go today, now. If the Allies are close, they'll want it as soon as possible. My brother won't be expecting me, but I can ring the bell at the gates and he'll be called."

"Do you want to wear the habit? We could switch."

Rita shook her head. "I couldn't, no. For you, it's fine. For me, it would be . . . I'd feel it was . . . not right." She paused, squeezed the girl's arm. "And you're so much taller and slimmer anyway."

"Should I go with you, then?"

"I'll go alone," Rita said. "Better one of us than both get caught. You can wait here if you want. I can get some clothes from Eleonora downstairs. She's taller."

Now Lucia had one hand on the cross that hung around her neck. "I have to get the habit back to Rosalia. It belongs to her sister. They'll worry if I don't."

They embraced, held each other for a moment, then Lucia turned, long skirts swirling, and went out the door and down the steps. As she often did when Aldo visited, Rita stood at the window and watched. The girl went quickly to the corner, turned, looked behind her once, and disappeared.

Rita rolled the map tight, tied it with the same string Lucia had used, then stood there for a long time thinking about how best to carry it to her brother without getting caught. The nun's habit would have helped, but she'd been right to say no to it (even the sight of it on the sinless girl had given her the chills; how much more sacrilegious would it be on her! And it wouldn't have fit her, in any case). Lucia had suggested she place the map, as she herself had done, against her ribs, but Rita wasn't tall or slim enough to allow the map to fit comfortably there. It would stick up into her armpit. Instead of Lucia's inward curve between hip and shoulder, she had, even in these hungry times, a roll of flesh. She thought of attaching the map to her upper leg, but how, with legs not nearly as long as Lucia's? And how would she walk all the way to the bus stop and then up to the monastery without bending her knee?

At last, having gone through every scenario she could imagine, she knelt on the floor beside her bed, the tiles cool and hard against her knees. She held the map with one end in one hand and one end in the other and prayed to Santa Agata. Her beloved saint had an answer for her almost immediately. The answer took the shape of one word: Joe.

Rita hurried down to the first-floor apartment, and, as she'd hoped, Joe was home, still had a supply of thread, still had his needles, and, of course, had not lost his skill. It took him less than fifteen minutes to attach the rolled map securely to the inside of the front middle of Rita's longest dress. If someone looked very closely, they could see the four sets of thread loops, attached to the bands on the inside, but who would look that closely? She could walk with a natural gait. Her hands would be free. When she saw Marco at the monastery, it would be a simple matter to snip the loops of thread—she wouldn't have to disrobe—and let the map fall to the ground.

She kissed Joe on each cheek, said a prayer of thanks to Santa Agata, and set off.

Sometimes the bus to Ercolano arrived just as she'd reached the Maritime Station and taken her place under the sign there. Sometimes she'd not made it quite that far when she saw the 622 lurching away from the curb, leaning to one side, spitting black exhaust. That would mean a wait of two hours or more. Sometimes she stood there for that long and the bus didn't arrive at all: no service on that day, no explanation, no gas maybe, a driver who'd been killed, injured, or taken prisoner.

On this day, on the walk from her house to the port, she sent up a steady stream of prayers that the Sunday buses would be running and the wait would be short. She could feel her heart thumping against the ribs behind her left breast, and she didn't know if she'd physically be able to perform the errand or if she'd die of fear at the first sight of a passing German vehicle. Aldo's daughter had so much courage—dressing as a nun and walking through the streets with what amounted to a ticking bomb against her skin! Even protected by the saints as she believed herself to be, Rita didn't feel anything close to that brave. With every step, she expected the map to slip out and fall to the ground just as a Nazi soldier or Italian Fascist was walking past. The man would bend to help her pick it up. The string would come loose, it would roll partly open, the marks would be clearly visible, the fact that she'd been hiding it obvious, and that would be the end. She'd heard enough stories to know how much mercy the Nazis would show her.

She stood nervously at the stop, noticing odd noises off toward the Chiara, farther north along the port. Trucks there, someone shouting through a bullhorn, too far away for her to understand the words. A strong noon sun was beating down on her. Sweat was running along both legs; a talkative woman with bald spots on her head was standing beside her, going on and on about the curfew. How could her daughters get home from work in time, and what if her son was arrested, and how long would it take the Allies to get from Salerno to Naples, and what if they didn't come, what if the tiny amount of food available now disappeared, what if the typhus or cholera struck her? What was to keep that from happening? Why wouldn't she catch it as so many others had?

Because it won't want to listen to you every second, Rita thought, but she kept to a policy of nodding and mumbling agreement. The woman's stream of talk served to distract Rita a bit from her fear, and when the bus came—after a ten-minute wait—she made sure the woman got on first, and then found a seat as far from her as possible, and was happy to wave to her and smile when, instead of riding all the way to Ercolano, the *chiacchierone* left the bus near Piazza Angelica.

Forty-Five

On her way to Rosalia's from Rita's apartment, heading east, her back to the water, Lucia hadn't gone a full kilometer—ten minutes—before she realized someone was following her. The awareness of it reached her slowly, like the awareness of illness: fine at first, then seemingly fine, then small symptoms that might mean nothing, and then the sense that things are not right, and then the certainty of it. There weren't many people on the streets in that neighborhood—the men afraid to show their faces, or already serving in Russia, Greece, or Albania; the women at a late Mass, or out in the countryside struggling to find food, or at home trying to make a half-decent Sunday dinner out of what little food they'd found. Rosalia's mother had been making nettle soup. Nettle soup! Unimaginable.

The buses were running, but sporadically, and there was almost no gas for private cars, so the vehicles one encountered were mainly ambulances or military trucks and jeeps and German motorcycles, sometimes a lorry with a machine gun on its flatbed, or towing a long-barreled piece of artillery. There were tanks in the city, but she didn't expect to see one in the narrow streets of this neighborhood. She'd decided it would be better to stick to the side streets and alleys rather than take the faster route and risk running into someone who recognized her from work, or a priest or nun who might sense something wasn't right and question her. Or, worst of all, another Nazi patrol.

The first thing she noticed was the sound of footsteps, echoing against the stone walls of houses. Her own, she thought, for a moment. But then she turned a corner and paused and heard the steps behind her. She didn't dare to look around the corner but picked up her pace and turned whenever she could, hurrying through blocks she didn't know well, looking all the while for a courtyard to duck into. She passed an elderly couple sitting out on the sidewalk, their faces like those of twin ghosts. The woman made the sign of the cross as she passed, and Lucia nodded to her, almost stopped to say there was someone following her, could she take refuge for a moment in the couple's home? But she'd have to explain. And she'd be risking their lives. And if they were afraid and said no, the person following her would have caught up. Another turn, this one onto a totally unfamiliar street, narrow and so full of rubble that it seemed no one could ever have lived there. She saw a church ahead, miraculously intact, but when she ran up the front steps, she found the doors locked . . . and on a Sunday! Still, she didn't look back. Another corner, an even narrower alley, this one, too, blocked with piles of rubble and three cars that had been stripped of anything salable or usable—tires, antennae, lights. She glanced back and thought she saw someone, a man in uniform, slip behind an empty kiosk, a place where, in the old days, square slices of pizza or the cream-filled *sfogliatelle* she loved might be sold.

She went on, turned a corner into an alley, and after walking another fifty meters, realized she'd gone into a dead end. There was nothing to do but turn around, and the second she did so, she spotted the limping German officer there, the fiend, the rapist, coming straight toward her. Either he'd been attracted by the nun's habit, or had caught a glimpse of her face and recognized her, but the closer he came, the clearer it seemed that he knew who she was. She looked up to see if someone might be sitting on one of the balconies, but what was she going to do, call out? Ask them to risk their lives to help her fend off an armed Nazi? Now the man was only twenty meters in front of her. She wished for a knife, a gun, a stick, anything besides her hands, which were small and delicate, the hands of an office worker.

Heaving his bad leg along, the man came right up to her, very close, and stopped with his feet spread and his arms out wide to keep her from running. In his butchered Italian, he said a word Lucia was surprised he even knew, *"Travestimento." Disguise.*

She was too frightened to speak. A tremor, a series of twitches, ran across the man's face, as if some evil, bottled-up energy were boiling inside the column of his neck and spurting up toward his eyes and mouth.

He smiled, lips together, a twisted grin, leaned forward and took hold of her shoulders with both hands. She tried to wrench herself away, but he held her more tightly, pressed his face against hers, and pushed his tongue between her lips. She twisted her face to one side. He grabbed hold of it and twisted it back so forcefully that the wimple came loose and sagged back against her neck, and the wooden cross broke from its string and went clattering onto the stones. He was reaching down and pulling up the long, heavy skirt, pressing her back so hard against the wall that it knocked the breath out of her. She tried to scratch at his face, but he slapped her across the cheekbone, and she cried out. He'd lifted her dress, had reached one hand between her legs, and she was trying to kick him, trying to swing her arms, but the man was twice her size.

Just as he started tearing at the buckle of his belt, she heard the *tick* of something against the wall behind her head and felt a small, hard object brush her face. The soldier paid no attention, pressing against her, his belt loose now, his pants undone. But then a larger stone struck the wall, and another one hit him in the back. He let out a grunt. She heard the voices of children, boys, a small gang of them. The soldier turned, and she swung an arm and hit him as hard as she could between the shoulders. He jammed an elbow back against her ribs, and the force of the blow bent her in two and knocked her sideways against the wall. Leaning over, gasping, looking to the side of the man—his belt hanging loose—she could see the gang of boys. Street boys. They were picking rocks from a pile of rubble and firing them at him. One of them hit her instead, cutting her above the eye. The German was facing them, cursing in his own language. He reached down to his belt, but there was no pistol in the holster. He cursed again, picked up one of the stones, and threw it back at them in a gesture so clumsy, the boys started taunting him. He had his back to her now, and she wanted to hit him on his neck, but she was paralyzed with fear, wrapped in it, as if he'd encased her in ice and pain. When he bent down again for another stone, she was somehow able to shove him with both hands, and, with his bad leg out sideways, he lost his balance and fell on his face in the dust, his hat slipping off. The boys were upon him like a pack of wolves. Pummeling him with their small fists, kicking him, picking up stones and smashing them against the back of his body. One of them lifted a rock the size of a soccer ball, held it with both hands, then smashed it down directly on the back of the man's head. Lucia saw the soldier's skull break like the shell of an egg, and a huge spurt of blood in the dust, and then two of the boys were reaching into his pockets, and two others had her by the arms and were rushing her out of the alley. "Here, Sister. Run, Sister!"

They moved like some kind of sea creature, a woman in nun's clothing surrounded by pilot fish, boys of various ages, dark-headed, some barefoot, one of them acting like the boss. He led them quickly out of the alley and to the left, around another corner and down onto a main avenue. A church there, its door partly open. They brought her just to the entrance, then two of them scattered like phantoms. She was heaving for breath, bleeding from the cut above her eye, her face already swelling where the Nazi had hit her. The leader opened the door and said, "Go in, Sister. He's dead, that Nazi. Tomaso and I will keep watch out here to make sure no other soldiers come, and if we see

233

some, we'll lead them the other way. Pray for an hour, and then it will be safe to leave." He touched her near the bleeding cut, tentatively, his forehead pressed up into worry lines, dirt on his small triangular face. "Go, Sister."

She managed a single *grazie*, but the word came out in the voice of a terrified child. And then she was in the shaded nave, sitting at one end of a back pew, leaning over with her face in her hands, consumed by a wild, desperate weeping.

Forty-Six

Before he took his place in the bed of the truck with Aldo and Zozo, Giuseppe glanced into the cab. The taller Dell'Acqua brother was behind the wheel; his bald, shorter brother in the passenger seat, both of them hatless but in German uniforms now, not Italian. The three ununiformed men climbed in and sat with their backs to the cab, and the truck started off, moving slowly, as if the driver and his passenger were actually searching for more Italian men to catch and handcuff and throw into the rear.

Up Via Medina they went—some kind of commotion visible far behind them near the port, a crowd there—through a section of the city that should have been bustling with people leaving the late Mass and stopping for an espresso, but was now deserted.

Beside Giuseppe sat Lucia's father, the man's right knee pressed against his left, silent, preoccupied, it seemed, as if he knew what was about to happen but couldn't speak of it. To his right, driver's side, Zozo Forni rested his spine and shoulder blades against the back of the cab in a posture of relaxation. He'd told Giuseppe and Aldo to sit with their hands between their knees, as if they were tied or cuffed there, a trio of prisoners. He was sitting that way himself, but from the expression on his unshaven face, he might have been headed to the beach for a late swim and then a meal with a lovely woman. Without looking at

Giuseppe, Zozo said, "The Germans killed your mother and father, yes?"

"Yes."

"They killed my brother." It was a question asked and a sentence spoken without emotion. A couplet of facts, as brutal and pitiless as the war itself.

"And many others," Giuseppe said.

Zozo grunted, as if the others were of a lesser importance, or as if killing was. And then, after a few seconds of what might have passed for contemplation: "You afraid to die?"

Giuseppe had told himself, many times, that he wasn't, but his body's reaction to the question—a stiffening of the muscles around his jaw, a prickling along the skin of his neck—argued otherwise. He said, "Not anymore," and partly believed it.

Zozo grunted. "A good thing," he said. "Maybe soon, a very good thing."

At that remark, Aldo looked away from them and spat a bloody wad of mucus over his side of the truck bed.

"Are you taking me to be killed, then?" Giuseppe couldn't keep himself from asking. The truck went over a bump and threw all three of them up into the air. Hearing his own words, he felt ashamed, afraid, a boy with men.

Zozo turned his head very slowly, ran his eyes over Giuseppe's face, and then turned them straight back again. "For stealing a pistol? If I killed people for such things, I'd have no men. Correct, Aldo?"

"Correct," Lucia's father said, in a voice lined with nervousness. Afraid, too, Giuseppe realized.

"Instead"—Zozo pushed his legs open, taking up more space, forcing Giuseppe's right leg away—"I put them in my debt."

Against the sound of the truck engine, the phrase sounded six terrible notes. *Nel mio debito.*

Which is where you have put me, Giuseppe thought. *Or where I have put myself.* And then: *And where you must have put Aldo Pastone and scores of others.*

Zozo brought his legs closer together again, leaned forward slightly to keep his back from the bouncing metal. "It was Ubaldo who saw you take the pistol. You thought Aldo told me, yes?"

"Yes," Giuseppe admitted.

Aldo let out a bitter laugh and shifted his weight a short distance away. He coughed, and spat over the side again.

"It was Ubaldo. You're not a clever thief. If I were the type to kill people for such an act, Ubaldo would have known that and killed you himself. Out there in the countryside. You would be at the top of a long list of such victims. Your body would be rotting in the sun in the tomato field now or drifting down the river."

Giuseppe listened to the boastful note in Zozo's voice and kept silent. What he wanted to say but couldn't was: *You don't have to brag to me about being a killer; I can feel it. I can see it in your face.*

As they rolled and bumped along the broken streets, swerving every few hundred meters to avoid another pile of rubble, a dead horse, an abandoned car or bomb-battered tram, Giuseppe noticed a solitary nun half a block behind them, just the back of her black-and-white habit as she turned into a *vico*. All three men looked at her, but Aldo turned his face away, as if the sight made him uneasy. Another few meters and Giuseppe thought he saw a German soldier going the same way.

"Big courage, that nun has, walking alone now," Vito called back from the driver's seat. *"Grande noccioline."* Big little nuts.

Zozo grinned and shook his head.

They zigged and zagged through the Spagnoli. Another minute and Aldo was telling Zozo where to turn, a series of lefts and rights on the smaller streets. Zozo passed the directions on to the driver. Giuseppe saw a church with two walls standing, two walls gone. Spirito Santo.

"Here," Aldo said. "At the yellow door."

The truck came to a stop a few meters from an elderly couple sitting on chairs in front of the house, watching with a silent intensity. Giuseppe could instantly detect the fear on their faces—*terror* was a better word, he thought, an expression identical to that of the woman in whose home he'd hidden an hour earlier. Aldo jumped over the side, and when the old couple recognized him, their expressions moved from terror to suspicion. "Eleonora, Joe, is Rita upstairs?" he asked.

"No," the woman answered, shifting her eyes to the driver in his German uniform. "Why?"

"They're with us," Aldo said, swinging an arm back toward the cab. "We're . . . It's a trick, don't worry. Where is she?"

The couple stared at him, waited, then the man made his decision and said, cautiously, "She left an hour ago. To visit with her brother."

"Her brother the monk?"

"The only brother."

Aldo thanked them, climbed into the bed again, and put his hands between his knees. "Gone to the monastery," he said to Zozo.

Zozo's lips stretched downward in a tight frown. "How does she go? What route? Do you know?"

"She takes the bus to Ercolano. From there, a farmers' road, and then, higher up, a narrow path. She meets him outside the monastery walls, in a small building where the workmen keep their tools. She's told me about it. The visits are brief."

"The truck can't go that way," Zozo said.

"Right. But there's a paved road from the back, through Portici Bellavista. That's how they get their supplies."

Zozo leaned out over the edge of the bed and said to Vito, "Take the road from Portici that leads up to the monastery the back way. Do you know it?"

"*Sì, capo,*" Vito called back.

"Once you get on it, there should be no Germans to worry about. There's nothing they care about up there. Go as fast as you can."

"*Sì, va bene.*"

They pulled quickly away from the curb, and Giuseppe watched the eyes of the old couple following them until the truck turned the corner.

"She makes such a trip for a brief visit?" Zozo asked Aldo. "Every week?"

"A woman of faith."

Zozo turned his head toward the street, as if to hide another smile at the stupidity of lesser souls, Giuseppe thought. "We may get there after she's gone," Zozo said, thinking aloud. "We may have to ask permission to enter the monastery enclosure and speak to the good monk in private." He laughed, another bitter sound. "Do you think they'll refuse us?"

"I don't know them," Giuseppe said. "I've never been."

"It's not about knowing them," Zozo said, and suddenly the ease had disappeared, as if a sour breeze had blown away a fine coating of sand covering dark stone. The trip would take longer than he'd planned—to the monastery instead of just to Rita's house. More chances to be caught. And a delay in whatever it was he was planning.

Not long before they reached San Martino, halfway there, a German truck passed them going in the opposite direction, the driver holding out one stiff arm and calling back to them a forceful, *"Heil Hitler!"*

Giuseppe turned to see Vito's huge arm out the window and then heard the vulgar reply, *"Vaffanculo, Hitler,"* but not loudly. He watched the truck disappear into the city at a high rate of speed. Four armed men riding in back.

"Not a good day for them," Zozo said. "See how fast they go?"

"Yes, something's going on," Aldo said. "Just as we were leaving the Santa Lucia, I caught a glimpse of it. There was a big crowd behind us. Near the port."

Zozo squinted and smirked as if this were old news, and said nothing. Less than a minute later, Giuseppe felt his back pressed hard against the metal of the cab and the truck skidding violently to a stop, twisting slightly to one side. Zozo and Aldo turned to look over their shoulders, and Giuseppe did the same . . . and saw that a pair of SS officers in their black uniforms had waved them to a halt and were approaching in a slow, confident walk. Ten meters from the truck. Five meters. Giuseppe saw the first soldier reach down and unsnap his holster. The soldiers parted ways, one to each side of the cab, and came right up to the doors. *"Wo gehst du hin?"* the one on the driver's side asked. *Where are you going?* His eyes were jumping from the men in the back to the men in the cab, and just as the soldier seemed to sense something was wrong and was reaching for his weapon, Giuseppe heard an earsplitting blast, saw the one on the driver's side go flying over backward, his throat bursting blood. An instant later, another gunshot on the passenger side, and the truck was in motion, Vito ripping through the gears as they sped along. Heart thumping, ears ringing, Giuseppe realized that he'd pulled his own pistol from the waistband of his pants and was staring behind them at the two men lying like black-uniformed mannequins on the paving stones. Zozo put a hand on the pistol and made him lower it again. Not one word was spoken.

Another three minutes at the breakneck pace and they were in San Giorgio, at the far southeastern edge of the city. They passed a flattened house with three palm trees standing near it, the green crowns bending over what remained of the building like mourners over a grave. Just there, turning his eyes down one of the side streets they were passing, Giuseppe caught a quick glimpse of what appeared to be a blockaded roadway, a handful of ununiformed men crouching behind an overturned bus. He leaned forward and to the side, straining to see if the men were armed, but the truck made a sharp left and began to climb a series of hairpin turns, and the air was rushing past the sides of the bed and the bumps throwing them higher. In the distance, off toward Nola, he could see a plume of gray smoke. He was about to ask Zozo what was happening—the crowd near the port; the killing of Nazi soldiers, apparently without concern about vengeance; the blockaded side street, the smoke—but just then, Aldo's boss let out a huge belch, as if they were speeding away, not from two murders, but from a huge meal. He laughed at himself, then shook his head. "A monastery," he said aloud. "Why would anyone want to become a monk?"

There was no answer. Shaken to his core, Giuseppe was watching Zozo in a kind of disbelief, studying the unattractive face, trying to read the pinched eyes, wondering why the danger—and the killing—seemed not to have any effect whatsoever on the man.

Zozo turned and met his eyes. "You know," he said in his laconic way, "I think we need to get your map from this monk and get back to Napoli as fast as we can." He belched again, not as loudly, then looked back and down over the city.

"Why the hurry?" Aldo asked in a nervous voice.

"Because," Zozo said, peering at the column of smoke, squinting, "the people of our city are rising up."

Forty-Seven

For a moment, as she was stepping off the bus in Ercolano, Rita felt the rolled map press up uncomfortably against her dress, pushing the material into a raised point. The driver sat behind the wheel and couldn't see it; no one was ahead of her on the sidewalk; it wasn't the kind of thing anyone would likely have noticed in any case, but, for a moment at least, unused to any kind of deception, she felt the icy talons of fear grip her more tightly. She waited for the doors to close and the bus to start off, then crossed the street, touching the top of the map once through the material, as if it were a talisman, and then began the climb.

It was the warmest part of the day, and within seconds, she could feel the sweat on her skin. She could also feel a line of trouble running through her thoughts. As she placed one foot after the next on the stony road, rosary in hand, she struggled to understand what the cause of it might be. The map would be passed to her brother, and from her brother to the American spy hiding in the monastery, and then, most likely, the American spy would either memorize the places where the Germans kept their weapons or he'd carry the map back to his superiors, sneaking across the battle lines at night. She wondered what immense faith a man like that must have, to take such a risk with his life: without question, if the Nazis caught him, they'd torture him to death. And she wondered, too, what the Allies would do with the information. Maybe the bombing would start again, and they'd try, from thousands of meters in the air, to hit the buildings Lucia's boyfriend had marked with small, neat stars and squares of ink. How many innocent people would die in those bombings? How much more suffering would they bring? So was she doing a good thing or an evil thing by sneaking the map up to the monastery? Would the Lord shine on her for it, or would it be added to the list of her transgressions?

Breathing hard, she paused on the road and looked to her left, across the top of a grove of olive trees and as far as the rooftops of the southeastern part of Naples. Why was it, she wondered, that her city had suffered so much? Why was it that men like Hitler and Mussolini rose to power and then used that power to excite whole nations in the direction of war? How was it that the Nazi soldiers—some of them must have wives and children at home—could line up a hundred Italians and machine-gun them to death, or pull a girl or woman into a room and ruin her forever? What spider of evil crawled about in the brains of men like the officer who'd come to her home and tried to violate her? And how could the good Lord allow it?

Answers to these kinds of questions, she'd long ago decided, would have to wait until she passed over the river of death into the next world. Everything would be explained then. The evil ones would pay for their sins, and the good ones would have rest and comfort. To believe otherwise would be to lose hope, and to lose hope, in these times, would mean to die.

She went on, climbing to the end of the unshaded road in the strong sun and then continuing onto the path. Small blue moths flitted about as if welcoming or warning her, and she could feel the slight weight of the map in the cloth between her knees. A tiny snake, brown on top, black beneath, crossed the dirt in front of her feet. She bent over from the waist—careful not to wrinkle the map—and studied the beautiful creature. Even snakes don't make war on each other, she thought. Even snakes don't torture and rape.

Though she didn't want to scandalize her brother with specifics, once she'd relieved herself of the map and the fear that went with it, she planned to ask him what the moment of love with Aldo might mean, that strange new sensation between them in bed. How could a man capable of such moments be so cold to his own daughter?

A morning of questions, she thought. Perhaps they were born of fear.

She walked on.

Once she crested the hill, she paused again, looking down and back over the sunny, suffering expanse of Greater Naples. A tower of smoke lifted into the air near San Giorgio, bubbling up in a great twisting cloud. The Nazis burning the house of one of their "enemies," she suspected. Working her beads, she said a prayer for the people there, turned right on the narrow alley, and approached the stone monastery wall.

Rita sounded the bell and had gone to the outbuilding and was sitting on a crate, running the beads through her fingers, when her brother stepped inside. The sight of his face—narrow and light-skinned in comparison to hers—chased away whatever worries remained. Here was a man of holiness. If he thought that passing on the map to the American spy was correct and good, then it was correct and good.

They embraced and sat opposite each other.

"I'm sorry to bother you on a Sunday, brother, but I have something for your American," she said, and she leaned over and began to lift the hem of her dress. In a moment, the bottom of the rolled map was revealed and her brother had knelt before her and, pinching with his fingernails, was snipping away at the stitches. When they were cut through from the outside, he lifted her dress farther, reached under, and tugged the rolled map free of the top loop that held it. By then, the dress had been lifted to expose half her thighs, and Rita noticed how pure her brother was, as if the sight of a woman's body—after so many years without—did not even begin to trigger the sin of lust in him. He

244

worked his hands as a surgeon might, a pure act, then sat again, pulling his crate closer so they could unroll the map and spread it across their knees.

"This is an incredible piece of work, Rita. Who did this?"

"The lover of Aldo's daughter. My Aldo."

"It shows everything so clearly, the streets, the buildings, the entrances and stairways. Even the number of guards is marked, both during the day and at night."

"Lucia told me that Giuseppe—he made the map—walked past these places at different hours but couldn't be sure about the soldiers."

"Still, this is incredible!"

"Will it be used for bombing targets, Marco? I was worried—"

Her brother was shaking his head. "I don't think so. I think the Allies are so close, they'll make an assault on the city soon. They wouldn't want bombs falling on their own men. They'll just want to get to the arms before the Germans do."

"There will be more killing, though."

Marco held his eyes closed for just a moment, then opened them and looked at her. "You can stay here if you like, when the fighting starts. I can arrange it. You can sleep in this outbuilding. I'll bring you a blanket and some food."

"I'll be safe at home," she said, but just as the word *safe* was out of her mouth, as if to test her faith in the protection of the saints, the door was thrown open, and the first thing she saw there was a huge, hatless man in a German military uniform. Her brother turned and saw the man, too. Then another soldier, shorter, bald, also a German. And then, to her absolute horror, Aldo. She'd made the mistake of telling him about the American spy, and, desperate for money, he'd gone to the Nazis with the information! Nothing, nothing on earth, could have surprised her more than that. Behind Aldo, all of them squeezing into the small space, came someone with a face she thought she recognized. It belonged to a man of medium height, wide as a piano, with unshaven cheeks, fat lips, and small, evil eyes. Behind him, a younger, bespectacled, and much more handsome man, not far into adulthood. Rita squeezed the rosary tight and stood up.

"Rita," Aldo said, "this is not what you think."

"May God forgive you if it is."

Her brother had stood to face them, too, as if to defend her. They were all almost touching each other, and the small room smelled of sweat and something else. Death, she thought it was, death from the cloth of the uniforms, or from the souls of the men wearing them.

"Take what you need and don't harm her," her brother said.

The wide man stretched his lips into a thin smile. "What we need is in your hand."

Marco looked down at the map, and with some hesitation passed it over. "It's *my* work," he said. "No one else's."

The wide man laughed.

Aldo pushed forward between the soldiers and held out his hand to Marco. "I'm Aldo Pastone. This is Zozo Forni and . . . Giuseppe DiPietra, and these two men aren't Germans at all but Italians, Neapolitans. Vito and Ubaldo. They dressed this way so we could drive through the city, all of us, and not be shot at. Zozo needs the map, to get guns. Naples is rising up."

It took Rita a moment to digest this information. "But why now? The Allies are coming."

"We can't wait for them," the handsome young man piped up, but he seemed to Rita shaken, anxious, his eyes unsteady and his voice too loud for the small room. "My girlfriend saw a telegram," he went on. "The *bastardi* are going to burn the city to the ground before the Allies arrive. *'Reduce the city to ashes and mud,'* the telegram said. *'Ashes and mud.'*"

A terrible silence fell over them, a second, three seconds, a silence filled with screams and wailing. "Rising up," Aldo had said. *Rising up!*

How could that be? Rita could see that the men were in a hurry, about to turn and leave, taking the map and their foolish plans with them.

"You're Catholics, yes?" her brother asked them. "Baptized?"

The wide man—Zozo was his name—shrugged. Aldo looked away. The handsome one nodded. And the two men in German uniforms stared blankly at the monk in his brown robe, as if the question held a trick, or as if the word, *battezzato*, had never before entered the air around their ears. "No time now for prayers, Father," Zozo said. "We need guns, not prayers."

"Yes, I understand," her brother said. But he reached out and put his hands on Zozo's shoulders, causing the wide man to flinch.

"Most people don't touch me," he said.

Marco kept his hands where they were. "You are not afraid of dying, I can see that."

Zozo's face twitched. For a second, Rita thought he might raise a hand.

"I'm not, either," her brother said. "It gives one a great power. Use that power for good."

Zozo's face twitched again. It seemed to Rita that he wanted to smirk but couldn't quite manage it. Her brother was taller, thinner, dressed in his heavy robes, but he was absolutely unafraid, she could sense that. Zozo could sense it, too. For several seconds, the wide man seemed to be frozen in place, baffled. His mask of confidence had slipped to one side, and though his eye contact didn't waver, there was about him a sense, very subtle, of confusion. "Thank you, Father," he said at last, in a voice that might have been sincere. "For the map. We'll use it well."

As the others turned to leave, Aldo stepped over to Rita and took hold of her in a tight embrace. A very short and awkward embrace, yes, but an embrace all the same. No kiss. No words. But he'd done it in front of other men, a moment of public affection. Nothing, not even the betrayal she'd first guessed at, could have surprised her more.

When they'd hurried out the door, she heard a truck engine and then tires on gravel, and she plopped herself down on the crate again, thoughts spinning. She looked up at Marco. "Say one word to me now, my beloved brother," she said, moving the beads in her fingers. "I feel that I'm drowning in a great confusion. Say one word."

Marco stepped over and kissed her forehead, rested his hands on the tops of her shoulders for a moment, and said, "How much I love you!"

Forty-Eight

Lucia sat for a long while in the rear pew of the church, dabbing the hem of one sleeve to the cut on her forehead and trying to keep her mind from replaying the assault again and again. Most likely the limping captain had been killed—she could still hear the sound of the stone cracking his skull, still see the spurt of blood—but he haunted her thoughts, even here, and she suspected he would for many years.

When her breathing finally settled and her hands had almost stopped trembling, she pushed herself forward and knelt, elbows on the top of the next pew forward, head down, eyes pressed shut. The fear seemed to be filling her whole body, coursing through the blood vessels, pushing out against her skin. But she discovered, beneath it, an enormous burning anger. In the face of the violence, in the actual moment, she'd been all but paralyzed. Maybe it came from worrying that if she hit or hurt him, he'd hurt her even worse. Maybe it was the shock of the assault—imagining it beforehand, talking about it, hearing stories from other women, none of that was in the same universe as being actually attacked that way; the horrific threat of rape right there against her flesh; the feeling of vulnerability; the evil in the man, almost a stink; the sense of some force in him, some intense urge to get what he wanted no matter what harm it caused. She knelt in the pew, praying for women who'd been attacked that way, and giving thanks for the street boys—would she ever see them again?—who'd saved her.

But beneath all that, rising slowly to the surface, bubbling, spitting, steaming, like burning lava in the cone of a volcano, there was anger. Fury. Wrath. No word captured the feeling. It made her want to have a weapon in case she was attacked again, by a different German soldier. She'd speak to her father about it, tell Giuseppe. She'd be ready next time.

At the front of the church, she heard the tap of an interior door closing and opened her eyes to see an old priest, robes swirling around his ankles, step up to the altar and start to prepare it for midday Mass. He smoothed the altar cloths, set out the chalice—which, she supposed, was kept hidden in a back room between services to prevent someone from stealing it and selling it for food. A few women and one old, stooped man had come through the front door and taken their places in the pews. Before the priest could catch sight of her and inquire about her spiritual life or ask why her face was cut and bruised, Lucia made the sign of the cross and stepped back out into daylight. She stood in the stone doorway, timidly at first, not quite fully visible to the people on the street, and noticed that she was hunching her shoulders, lowering her head; the fear was still sending currents through her bones. With a pure exertion of will, she forced herself to stand up straight and step into the sunlight, then walk onto the sidewalk. She adjusted the wimple. The habit would have dirt on it now, on the back, where she'd been pushed against the wall. Blood from the cut on her forehead. She should clean it, or somehow find a way to buy Marcellina a new one.

But she decided she wanted to find Giuseppe first. She wanted to be held by him, just that.

As she walked, glancing behind her every few steps, a knot of fear still tightening her midsection, she became aware of a strange noise behind and to her right. Voices, hundreds of footsteps, some kind of clamorous chaos. She wondered, at first, if the officer had survived and gone to report the assault, and now his comrades in arms were out en masse, searching the city for little boys they might kill and the woman they all might assault.

But when she turned another corner, she realized the voices were Italian. And there, at the western edge of Piazza Dante, she saw a sight that made no sense: a massive crowd of people moving toward her, away from the water. Every single one of them was carrying something— bags, chairs, little children. One couple was lugging a mattress between them. Lucia stared for a moment in shock. The wave of humanity, like nothing she'd ever witnessed, was still several hundred meters away. She turned down a side street, went three blocks aimlessly, confused and frightened, and then, in a panic, circled north and east, away from the crowd, in the direction of Giuseppe's house. She stopped there, head spinning, not really sure where she was, and then she felt her legs buckle and she sat down hard on the stones.

Forty-Nine

Aldo had always been able to sense trouble before it arrived—anticipating police raids, keeping his workers' tempers in check, knowing when it was wise to leave a gathering of a certain kind of men. It was part of what had made him so successful at the port, and what had kept him alive all these years in the midst of the company he kept. And now, riding down from the monastery into the city in the back of an Italian Army truck with Lucia's boyfriend and Zozo Forni beside him, he felt a cloud of trouble, dark as charcoal, slide in over his thoughts. The Dell'Acquas had killed two Nazi soldiers. From this truck. They'd be hunted now for that, and they were in possession of a map with markings on it. *"A rebellion,"* Zozo had said.

A rebellion!

They had five pistols against the German army.

Aldo couldn't see the future, but he did have a street instinct for trouble, and the beast that lived inside him was awake now, circling its territory, the hair on its back standing straight up. What, exactly, was happening, he didn't know—what kind of rebellion? But he'd seen the barricade on a side street, then two fresh columns of smoke below them as they left the monastery, and now far to the east, in the direction of the airport, he was sure he heard the sounds of artillery or tank shells exploding. Could the Allies have reached the city already? If not, why were big guns firing there?

Zozo had stopped pretending to be a prisoner. He'd unrolled the map across three sets of knees and was studying the marks. Aldo was certain of this: Zozo Forni didn't waste his own time, didn't take an action unless it led to something he wanted. In this case, it appeared that what he wanted was a cache of arms. The question was: Why? Maybe, impossible as it seemed, the city *was* rising up against the Nazis. If so, if there were such a movement, a real rebellion, then Forni would be the first to know about it and probably be deliriously happy to join in: not out of any patriotism or moral sense, but because the German presence had strangled the Camorra's profits. And profit was their religion. Maybe that was it. But maybe not. Zozo's brother had been shot to death by the Germans, but who knew the true story? Maybe one of the other families had set him up to be captured and executed. And maybe, now that the Forni family was trying to move in to new territory—the procurement of military supplies—they were stepping on the toes of one of the other families, and soon a war-within-a-war would break out. Not something Aldo wished to be part of. Even a small part. It also occurred to him that if he got Lucia's boy-friend any more involved than he already was, if Giuseppe were hurt or killed in a battle between one branch of the Camorra and another, then Lucia would never speak to him again.

But maybe the wariness had other roots. It seemed he was starting, if not to like Giuseppe, then at least not to mock him in his mind. The boy had displayed a certain amount of *coglioni*, of balls, of spine. He was smart, too, seemed to be learning when to keep his mouth shut.

And what had happened with Rita? He'd hugged her in front of everyone. So unlike him. They'd had that strange moment in bed, too, he and Rita, different from the other times he'd been with her. He wondered if he was starting to care too much and therefore making himself vulnerable. In his world, nothing could be more foolish.

As they bounced and swerved through the streets, the deadly map wrinkled now under Zozo's sausage fingers, Aldo listened and watched, alert as a hunted fox. The sound of artillery, or tanks, or whatever it was, had ceased for the moment, but, if it was the Germans, why would they be using heavy guns like that within the city?

Keeping his hands low, he held one end of the map in two fingers and tried to pay attention as the truck bounced along and Zozo made his inspection, pointing out various marks, talking to himself, apparently looking for the easiest place to get weapons.

Not far into the city, Forni tapped a fat knuckle three times on the window of the cab, and on that signal, Vito Dell'Acqua turned into the Sanità neighborhood and pulled up in front of a house there. Ubaldo jumped out and disappeared through the door.

"Reinforcements," Zozo said, turning to him with his spiritless smile.

Aldo nodded. Giuseppe, he noted, looked puzzled but strangely unafraid. His look of puzzlement—he was trying too hard to hide it—only increased when Ubaldo Dell'Acqua came back out of the house leading a scraggly band of six men, one or two of whom Aldo recognized. They leaped into the truck like chimpanzees ready for a brawl, grinned, nodded, and took their places around the edges of the bed. Zozo said that four of them were army deserters and the other two "associates." Now, truly, with all nine of them crowded into the back, they looked like a group of men who had been corralled and was about to be sent north. But with the killing of the two soldiers, Aldo realized that keeping up the ruse didn't matter anymore. They were beyond that now. As he was thinking this, Zozo pointed to one spot on the map—a school it seemed to be, in the Vomero—turned his face to Giuseppe, and said, "In this building, only two guards, right?"

Giuseppe nodded. "It's a school. It was. Now it's—"

"And it's hard to get tanks way up there, right?"

"Next to impossible."

"Rifles there?"

Vito was waiting for instructions. The truck hadn't moved.

"I believe so."

"'Believe so' isn't good enough. The Vomero is the middle of it all."

"All what?" Aldo couldn't stop himself from asking, but Zozo ignored him, kept staring at Giuseppe. "You made this map. Why did you mark this building like this, with a circle around it?"

"Because my uncle heard something from a woman who lives across the street from the school. She was out on her balcony, and she saw a truck come into the school driveway. And then the soldiers were unloading boxes. At first she thought they were caskets, but one of the officers pried open a box—she could see from her balcony—and checked. Rifles."

"Thirdhand information, then."

Giuseppe shook his head. "When I heard it, I went up there and walked past the building three times, at three different hours. There were Nazi guards at the door each time. I think only three or four stay there, sometimes only two, but they were obviously guarding something. There's no fence. Before the war, it was a school. But the schools are all closed now, so why the guards? Last summer, the Italian generals started using it for storage, and when . . . things changed—the Germans took over."

"Maybe they don't have a lot of men guarding it because there's nothing there. Just a school."

"The Italian Army was using it before, and there are guards now. That's all I know."

Zozo peered at him, drilling his eyes into the young man, making a study. Aldo had seen that piercing look before and knew that it went only one of two ways. You pleased the Forni brothers and they promoted you based on their infallible instincts. You displeased them, and you no longer had any need for a promotion. Or money.

Or food. Or air to breathe. Zozo kept staring at Giuseppe, and Giuseppe kept staring back, eyes steady behind the glasses. "You want a job with me?" Zozo asked, when the inspection was finished. "After?"

Giuseppe shook his head. "I *have* a job. But I'll fight, if it's the Nazis you're fighting. Now, I'll fight."

"Who else would we be fighting?" Zozo asked, and at that moment, Aldo heard a spray of machine-gun fire, then answering single shots. Two blocks away or closer. He felt the skin on his arms crawling, the beast within him, the killer, showing its teeth. There was little doubt now what was happening. He saw, on Giuseppe's face, what he must be showing on his own: there was the reality of death, right there with them in the truck bed. And next to it, beneath it, something else. Something so Neapolitan, so familiar to him, that it seemed to be the place his own breath came from. Pride. Dignity. A fierce belief in their way of life. He couldn't find the words, but he understood then that there was no patience left in them, no more submission. They'd been terrorized to the point of not caring anymore if death caught them. They were going to fight.

Zozo swung his eyes out the back of the truck again, seemed to be considering something for a moment, and then rolled up the map and held it between his ankles. He leaned his head over the side, toward the driver's door, and said, "Vomero."

Up past Villa Genzano they went, climbing from the crowded Sanità around to the base of the Vomero hill. No one else tried to stop them, but at one point, in a place where they had a view down toward the port, Aldo saw the strangest sight: a mob of people, an enormous crowd, moving away from the water as if expecting a tidal wave, or as if a thousand infected families had come ashore and the mob was fleeing them in panic. Just a glimpse. Two seconds. "Did you see that?" he asked Zozo.

The *Camorrista* nodded. "A new order from the Nazi boss. Everyone who lives within three hundred meters of the port has twenty-four hours to move out. Anybody found there by tomorrow noon will be shot."

"How? When? How'd you hear?"

Zozo put the fingers of one hand to his right ear. "I heard just before we came to your house. This is why we took the inland route."

"It's impossible," Aldo said. "That has to be a hundred thousand people. In one day. Where will they go?"

Zozo shrugged as if he didn't care. "Friends. Relatives. The underground shelters. The churches. The streets."

"Why, though?"

"So the Nazis can blow up the port."

"It's already blown up!"

"It has to be made completely unavailable for an Allied landing."

"My house is within three hundred meters," Aldo said.

Zozo shook his head and almost smiled. "A little more, I think."

"Ashes and mud," Giuseppe said.

Zozo adjusted the map between his ankles, then squeezed both wrists between his knees. "Not something that can be permitted."

Aldo had been to the Vomero countless times. The district stood above the city's northwestern flank, an egg-shaped hill with a mix of houses and undeveloped land, and one enormous castle. From the heights there, he knew you could see everything: from Capodimonte to the port, from Chiaia to Poggioreale. When they reached Sant'Elmo, the medieval fortress that had been turned into a military prison, the truck slowed, edging its way along the railing near the Pedamentina stairway, a spot that offered a view down over the port. Zozo rapped on the window again and Vito pulled toward the curb. *"Eh, merde di Dio."* Vito's voice came wafting around from the driver's seat. "Look, boss!"

The truck came to a full stop, and they all turned their eyes over the railing. Far below, Via Console and Via Medina were choked with people moving along at the pace of a beetle. Behind them, as if herding a million sheep, came the German trucks and foot soldiers. Aldo couldn't stop looking, wondering if Lucia and Rita were there, if half the city was about to be torched, or shelled from the batteries on Capodimonte. They'd destroy the port, sure, and kill tens of thousands of Italians along with it.

Zozo tapped on the window again, and the truck moved forward, turned away from the castle and down into the lower reaches of the neighborhood. Three more taps and they stopped at one corner of Piazza Vanvitelli, in front of Café Sangiuliano.

"Now," Zozo said, and all the faces of the men in the bed of the truck turned to him. "Now you see why we can't wait. Their soldiers are occupied, busy herding Italian cattle. If my sources are correct, then there's going to be a big battle on Capodimonte tonight. Also, the Nazis have hostages in the stadium here, a few blocks away, and once the Nazi boss starts getting worried, they'll kill all of them . . . if we don't stop them. Now's the time. We're two blocks away from the school. We're leaving the truck here. Inside the back door of this café, there are enough rifles for everyone." He clapped Giuseppe on the shoulder. "Thanks partly to this man, who stole them from a German car in the dark of night! Take the guns, one each, follow him to the school, and do as he instructs."

Giuseppe pushed his glasses back against the bridge of his nose. "As *I* instruct?"

Zozo smirked. "I'm betting most of the soldiers will be gone, supervising the magnificent exodus below. I'll give you twenty minutes—I have to pass on this map to a friend of mine who will be very happy to have it—and then I'll drive there, to the school, and meet you. Collect whatever weapons you can find. Machine guns first, bullets, then rifles, then pistols. As much as you can carry."

Through a twinge of jealousy, Aldo was watching Zozo as he spoke, and then he came to understand, admiring the evil perfection of putting Lucia's boyfriend in charge: If Giuseppe was wrong about the school, who would be killed first? Giuseppe.

"And then?" asked one of the army deserters—a burly, poorly shaven man with arms the size of the trunk of a ten-year-old tree.

"Simple," Zozo said. "We bring the weapons to our friends waiting near the stadium. Partisans. Then we fight."

Fifty

Thanks to the excited shouts of a young *scugnizzo* running past them, word of the evacuation at the port reached Armando ten minutes after they'd left the Nazi soldier bleeding to death in the alley. He and his *coro* had taken whatever they could: he had the officer's knife tucked carefully into the side of his shorts, covered by the bottom of his T-shirt; his friends Antonio and Roberto carried a boot each and would try to sell the pair or trade them for food. Some kind of brass insignia had been ripped from the man's shirt, and Tomaso had clipped it onto the fly of his pants. The Nazi bastard had been left there on his face, bleeding into the stones, probably dead by now, and Armando felt not the slightest drop of sympathy for him.

The information about the evacuation could be just another rumor, so he knew he and his choir had to go and see for themselves. Now they heard noises—*boom, boom, ba-boom*—from the other side of the city, in the direction of the airport. The knife, the rumors, the sounds of fighting, the rescue of the nun—it all filled him with a prickling happiness, made him feel like he was at last breaking out of the prison of childhood.

As they started off toward the port, not far from Piazza Dante now, Armando saw a nun on the sidewalk directly in front of them and, after another few steps, realized it was the same nun they'd rescued from the Nazi. Even from this distance, he could see the stains on the back of her dress, and something about the way she was walking reminded him of the way he himself had walked after the times he'd been beaten. Her back was bent; she was forcing herself forward, reaching up every two steps to touch her face. As Armando watched, her legs gave out, and she crumpled to the pavement. He and his friends broke into a run, and he scampered up next to her. He and Tomaso took an arm each and lifted her up. She flinched at first, looked down at him, tried to smile. There was a cut on her forehead, but the bleeding had mostly stopped.

"Sister, you're all right now," he said to her. "The Nazi won't hurt you anymore."

She nodded, and a lock of her hair broke free from beneath the wimple. "Thank you. You saved me. You—"

"You thanked us already, Sister! For Armando and his choir, one thank-you is enough!"

"I'm not a nun. I borrowed this"—she pinched the fabric of her dress—"from someone."

"A sin!" Armando said and felt his face break into a big smile. "But very wonderful!"

"I have to return it. I have to find my boyfriend. Can you help me? Do you know Via Telesino, in the Materdei? The house where the hunchback sits out front?"

"Everybody knows the hunchback. *Zio* Donato!"

"My boyfriend lives there. That's his uncle."

"Lucky!"

"I'm going there now. Can you and your friends walk with me?"

Armando was shaking his head. "Something's burning near there. Look, you can see the smoke! It's not safe."

He watched Lucia look up. She seemed unsteady on her feet, as if she might faint a second time. "I have to find him," she said.

"We'll go to *Nanella*'s," Armando said. "In the Spagnoli. Not far. She'll help you find him, you'll see." He lifted the T-shirt and proudly showed her the handle of the knife. "We'll protect you!"

"But I just came from the Spagnoli."

"We have to go back, Sister. It's not safe the other way. The Nazis must be blowing up houses there! You can hear shooting—listen!"

Fifty-One

"What kind of *situation*?" Scholl demanded of the captain who stood near him on his balcony. "What are you talking about? The evacuation? The port? What's wrong?"

Captain Nitzermann shook his head and seemed for a moment incapable of producing a word.

"What, then!"

"Is your radio not working, Colonel?"

"I've been out on the balcony. It's been scratching, making noise. What is the problem!"

"You sent six tanks north, sir, yesterday, but now the tanks that are left, they're at Capodichino, the airport, and they've come under attack. The artillery on Capodimonte, too. And other places in the city."

"The Allies?"

"No, Herr Colonel. The Italians."

"What Italians?"

"The Italian people, sir. In the streets."

"Impossible!"

Scholl went over to the radio—it was squawking out a string of staticky syllables. He turned the dial and called one of his tank captains. "Mersom, you're at the airport?" More static. The sound of big guns firing, perhaps a grenade. "What's happening?"

"They have . . . Herr Colonel. I don't know—" The transmission was interrupted by a huge blast. Then silence. Then: "They have machine guns, antitank weapons. We're trying to advance, sir, but they've set themselves up in—"

Another furious *boom*.

"Mersom! Mersom, speak!"

Scholl looked sideways and up at Nitzermann, who immediately turned his face away, as if ashamed to make eye contact with an incompetent superior officer. A burst of machine-gun fire sounded directly below them, not on the radio but in the street. Scholl turned the dial again. "Pitsiak. Is Capodimonte secure?"

A very faint voice: "We're fighting, sir . . . Reinforcements, please."

Scholl called in reinforcements from the Vasto barracks. He grabbed Captain Nitzermann by the arm and practically threw him toward the exit and was following when the radio squawked again. "In the Vomero, Colonel," was all he heard. Then silence.

He was down the stairs and out the front door in fifteen seconds. From everywhere, it seemed, there were the sounds of gunfire, some as close as a block to their west. Renzik was behind the wheel of a different jeep, one with four good tires. Scholl climbed into the passenger seat, pistol in one hand, and began working the radio with the other. Nitzermann jumped in back.

"Where, Colonel?"

"Wait." He adjusted the dial. Nothing but static. A muffled voice that sounded like Pitsiak or Saggau. "Capodimonte, then," he yelled to the driver. "Go!"

They rocketed through the city, east along Via Duomo, then a quick left and a right and they were flying over the Sanità bridge, a large highway running beneath one part of it and a pitiful slum the other. At last, the radio came to life on an alternate frequency. "Too many . . . with the evacuation, Colonel. We're stuck between the mob of people and the port. Can't get to the Vomero. Trouble there, I think . . . Stadium."

Static.

A kilometer ahead, Scholl could see the raised bump of Capodimonte, the long brick palace on the hill there, and he knew they had three artillery units, Feldkanone 38s facing southwest, northwest, and due west. Manned by the best crew that had been left to him. He picked up the handset and started to speak the name of the captain in charge there—Pitsiak, an excellent officer—but what orders should he give? Fire on the city? The shells would land in the crowd of evacuees and kill scores of his own men.

They went along at top speed—Renzik could drive, if nothing else—then skidded to a stop a hundred meters short of what appeared to be a roadblock. Two trucks, both flying the Italian flag, were angled across the road nose to nose. Scholl aimed his service pistol and started firing at them. "There!" he said, pointing to a road on the right. Renzik made a sharp turn, and they went racing along and came up the hill from the south. Scholl heard firing all around now, a pitched battle. A bullet glanced off the jeep's windshield, leaving a long, thin scar in the glass. He could see his men crouching behind their semicircle of trucks, firing handguns and rifles, the Kanone unmanned. A nightmare.

Fifty-Two

As she started off down the path from the monastery, Rita replayed the last thing her brother had said to her: *"How much I love you."* The sentence rang in her mind like a church bell on Easter.

And just before that, Aldo had embraced her. In front of others! For a few minutes, she felt a sense of being loved, by men, by God. It was almost as if the war had never happened, she hadn't carried the infected girl to the hospital, hadn't risked her life with the map, no homes had been torn apart by the bombs, no families by the fighting overseas or the Nazi executions. But it didn't take long for the feeling to evaporate and the clouds of fear and worry to cover her thoughts again.

Farther down the hill, near where she'd seen the snake, she stopped and looked toward the city. Off to the east, near the airport, she saw a cloud of dust, and above it, thin towers of smoke, as if tanks or trucks were moving in circles there, or bombs were going off. There was a thinner plume of smoke in what she guessed was the Materdei, also. She said a prayer, worked her beads, hurried on.

All the way back to Naples in the bus, she tried to imagine what was causing the plumes of smoke. The young man with Aldo had said the Nazis were planning to destroy the city; maybe they'd already started. Maybe people *were* rising up. Marco had offered to let her stay at the monastery, but she felt an urgency to get back to her own neighborhood, whatever the danger.

The other seats were empty, and the man behind the wheel—too old to be of interest to the Nazis—kept swinging his head nervously from side to side, looking out the windows. "Do you know what's happening?" she asked the driver.

"Fighting everywhere," he said over his shoulder. "I'll take you as far as I can. Then I'm leaving the bus and going home to my wife."

When they reached San Martino, the driver turned a corner and suddenly brought the vehicle to a stop. The road was closed. Two jeeps were parked sideways, mostly blocking it, and three German soldiers were standing with rifles held across their chests, waving the bus to the right, east. *"La porta è chiusa; la porta è chiusa,"* they yelled. *The port closed.*

The bus driver made a ninety-degree right—there were various routes back into the city—and just then, Rita saw a trio of Nazi jeeps speed past, heading down the closed road, flying right past the soldiers without so much as a second's hesitation. Something was happening, yes. Love—human and divine—was a fine thing, but now wasn't the time for it. Gentleness, kindness, vulnerability—now wasn't the time. It felt to her that a certain moment had arrived, not so different from the moments she'd witnessed—rare, to be sure, but not unheard of—when a mistreated woman decided she'd suffered enough at the hands of her man. The woman would wait until the night, slip away, and never be seen or heard from again. Such an act of courage was difficult in Italy. The laws, written and unwritten, and the tight bond of family made it next to impossible for a woman to leave. Guilt and shame and poverty would follow her everywhere. But it had happened: she'd known such women herself.

So perhaps, after all their suffering, the people of Naples had arrived at just such a moment. But could Zozo and Giuseppe and Aldo and the two huge men with the empty eyes, could they really put up a fight against the German army with its fit and well-fed soldiers, its tanks and rolling artillery, its men like the man who had tried to rape her, its mad fascination with killing? She lifted up a prayer that it might be so, that some miracle might save Naples before it was obliterated by the Nazis, or before the Allies came, chased the Germans away, and in the process blew up what was left of the city.

Eyes darting this way and that, the nervous driver took a more inland route, along Galileo Ferraris. He dropped her five blocks from her house, saying, "This is the best I can do, woman. God protect you."

Rita thanked him, hurried onto the sidewalk and along the back-streets, staying close to the housefronts and listening to the *pock, pock* of rifle shots and larger explosions, like bombs, off to her right.

She made it safely to Vico dei Bianchi, and as she stepped through the front door of her building, she found Eleonora waiting for her, standing on the threshold of her apartment, holding the door open so that half her body showed and half was hidden. She cupped her hand and clawed the air downward and toward herself, then ran a finger lengthwise across her lips, the sign of silence.

Inside, it was all whispers. Fighting in the streets. The port evacuation. Cousins were going to stay here tonight—*could one of them use Rita's extra room?*

Joe was sitting at the table, his bald head glowing in a ray of sunlight that slanted in above the window curtains, hands folded in his lap, his handsome old face set in an expression of calm. On the table in front of him lay the pistol the vile Nazi had thrown against the wall when it had failed to shoot a bullet into his temple. *"Riparata,"* Joe said to her. *"Fixed.* One bullet was jammed. I took the mechanism apart and removed the bullet very gently, the way you would remove a stone from a toddler's mouth. There are still seven bullets there. He must have shot one. Here, let me show you how it works."

Without even looking at the gun, Rita stepped over and hugged old Joe where he sat, nearly suffocating him in her ample bosom, rocking his head back and forth. She didn't care so much about the gun; she cared that Joe and Eleonora would help her with anything, anything—the map, the pistol. She told them what she'd seen—the smoke, the road-block, clouds of dust at the airport. She said Eleonora's cousins could stay with her if they came. Of course they could stay.

She stood there while Joe gave her a brief lesson in firing the gun. How he knew this, the quiet tailor, she had no idea . . . From the war, perhaps. Or perhaps he'd learned it in America.

"Can you protect us if they come?" Eleonora asked her.

Rita almost laughed. The impulse rose up into her throat and mouth and drowned there in a sea of fear. She could no more protect them with a German pistol than she could raise the blessed dead. But Eleonora was old and tired, and Joe had little strength, so Rita nodded. She'd use the German gun to protect them—of course she would.

When she carried the pistol up the stairs to her home, hefting it in her left hand the way she might have hefted a melon in the prewar *fruttivendolo*, it seemed to have a spirit of its own, the kind of spirit she wasn't sure she should bring into her rooms. She did bring it in, though, and set it on the sill of the window like an icon from some religion of death and destruction, a bad saint, a devil. *"Use that power for good,"* her brother had said to the ugly man. She wondered, in this case, if the words could possibly apply to this metal creature now in her possession. She opened the window that faced the port and looked out. Rooftops, water tanks, wires. Nothing to be seen from this vantage point. But she could hear, even more clearly, the firing of guns in the distance. Then two larger explosions like the thumps of thunder or the explosion of huge bombs. Shouting below her in the street. The *tat-tat-tat-tat-tat* of a machine gun. Voices. Sirens.

She removed the beads from around her left forearm and began to pray.

Fifty-Three

Giuseppe noticed that, not ten seconds after Zozo Forni gave them their instructions to make an assault on the school building, he disappeared. There was something animalistic about the man—his facial expressions, the way he moved—as if part of him existed in the human world and part in some other dimension where he operated by instinct, wordlessly, his whole being out of reach of any moral code. He noticed it again when Zozo stepped away from the truck and disappeared down a nearby alley, carrying the rolled-up map with him. It wouldn't be exactly correct to say that the man walked. He *slinked*, he *slithered*, he sidled away as if his thick body were supported by eight legs, not two, and as if his other senses—smell, taste, touch, hearing—not only the sense of sight, were guiding him. When he looked at you, the animal inside him made a soundless snarl.

In any case, animal or human or part of each, in seconds Zozo was gone, and Giuseppe was left to slip into the back door of the café with Aldo, the two uniformed Dell'Acqua brothers, two Camorra henchmen, and four army deserters. In the same back room where he'd sat with Avvocato Cilento the day before, they found six rifles, standing neatly against a wall, one beside the next, as if in a museum display. But the kitchen and café tables were empty, Salvatore and Lena, the owners, gone, the front windows covered with blinds. Zozo seemed to have set everything up long before deciding they should, in fact, make an assault on the school. Or maybe he had weapons stored like this in other places around the city, other men *in his debt* who were willing to ride out into the countryside to steal, and then ride back into Naples to fight. Or let him use their café for the storage of weapons.

Giuseppe felt the men looking at him, Aldo warily, the soldiers and *Camorristi* expectantly, accustomed to having orders given to them; and the Dell'Acquas blank-faced, also awaiting orders but without so much as a spark of intelligence behind the eyes. How valuable men like that must be to Zozo Forni, Giuseppe thought. You could tell them to do anything—kill another human being, steal, stand in front of a bullet, run out into a street during a bombing raid—and they'd do it out of blind loyalty, the way so many thousands had given their lives for Mussolini. Even in the few seconds they stood there, Giuseppe realized the irony of it: the utterly loyal *Camorristi* had joined forces with soldiers who'd abandoned their loyalty to Il Duce in his moment of need. They'd stripped off and disposed of their uniforms and waited in hiding for a summons from an underworld boss, and then for the world to unravel.

And now they awaited the orders of a twenty-six-year-old Archives worker.

They were all looking at him. Vito and Ubaldo had unsnapped the flaps of the holsters at their hips, leaving the handles of their pistols exposed. The others held the rifles. Giuseppe realized that never in his life had he been in charge of anything besides the burial of his mother and father, and now it seemed he was being asked to give life-and-death orders. He hefted the rifle in his right hand, the metal cool against his skin. *"Allora,"* he said, trying to stall but feeling the seconds piling up against his back. "All right. Vito and Ubaldo, you're in uniform, so if you appear at the door of the school, they'll unlock it for you. Just show up there and don't say a word. If they don't open, pound on the door and keep pounding. When they open it, shoot them. These three men"—he pointed to the ones nearest him—"and I will be at the south side of the building. The other three of you and Aldo will be at the north side. Do what Aldo tells you to do. We'll walk up this alley together. The rear of the school is just opposite the end of it, so you, you, you, and I will go right, and Aldo, you and the others left, around the building. Wait at the corner. Vito and Ubaldo, you take the street, not the alley, and walk as if you have orders. No one should bother you. Left at the end, then left again, and you'll walk right up to the doors. The windows are high up. I'm thinking there will be two guards there, maybe one. We'll get in, find the rifles and ammunition and whatever they have, carry out as much as we can, and Zozo will come around with the truck to meet us. Let's go."

Giuseppe could feel his heart slamming hard in his throat, and as he was giving the instructions, he half expected Aldo to mock him, shove him aside, give different orders, take over. But Lucia's father raised no protest. Giuseppe led the three soldiers, or ex-soldiers, to the end of the alley and then around the back corner of the school. If his research was faulty, if there were more than a couple of soldiers guarding it, then they wouldn't live until the next hour. But he'd seen the guards himself, and this thick-walled building in this neighborhood would be the perfect place to keep a cache of weapons in case the Allies bombed the usual storage facilities—the main and secondary armories, the barracks, the police stations.

And what Zozo had said made sense: scores of German soldiers would be supervising the enormous crowd below, pushing people away from the port. Most of their men would be engaged in that, trapped there between the water and the mob, leaving the school lightly guarded.

So he hoped.

His heart was a wild creature in a cage; the rifle, held in both hands now, was slick with sweat. They had to time it perfectly. Up the side of the building they went, staying tight to the wall so anyone looking out the windows would be gazing over their heads and not see them. Three meters shy of the front corner, he stopped, waiting for the Dell'Acquas to walk past. There they were. He crept forward as far as the corner, crouched with his shoulder against the concrete, three men behind him. He watched Vito and Ubaldo march up the front walk like the confident thugs they were. He heard them pound on the door, and for a moment he worried his legs wouldn't work. The door would swing open, he'd try to move toward the entrance, but his legs would refuse to obey and he'd be locked in a cube of shame for the rest of his days.

More pounding on the tin door. He heard a latch, a squeak of hinges, a question in German, which, of course, the *Camorristi* couldn't answer, and then two single shots, as if from a pistol. Trained killers, the Dell'Acquas hadn't missed when they'd shot the two Gestapo officers from inside the truck. They wouldn't miss now.

His legs lifted him and pushed him forward. He felt the men behind him, saw the three others coming fast behind Aldo from the far corner. In a blur, he was up the stairs and into the building, the two German soldiers lying bleeding and still to either side.

He pointed to the Dell'Acquas. "Close the door and search the classrooms on this floor." Then to Aldo and the three men who'd been with him, "Search upstairs." And then to his own three, "We'll look in the basement. If you see a German, shoot."

They hurried down the stairs. He listened above him for the sounds of gunfire, but there was none. In the basement—he knew from his research that it was one large, open storage area with smaller rooms to either side—he saw four billets rolled up at the base of one wall, and small piles of personal equipment. Books and school supplies, left over from the days when there had been pupils here. But no weapons. He and the army trio split up and searched the smaller rooms. And came back empty-handed.

So much risk, he was thinking, and for nothing. He took the stairs two at a time and saw immediately, from the faces of the Dell'Acqua boys, that they hadn't found anything, either. All of them together went up to the second floor. Classrooms there, set out along the hallway—he remembered the layout perfectly. They began searching the rooms one by one. Nothing and nothing and nothing.

And then a shout from the far end. A voice in Italian. One word, *"Qua!" Here!*

In the last classroom, in a storage closet there, the Italian and German soldiers had been keeping at least a dozen Karabiner rifles, one machine gun, and boxes of ammunition. The men took two rifles each, left another handful, grabbed some of the boxes, and trotted down the stairs, with Giuseppe in the lead holding the machine gun. He kicked the German bodies aside, pulled the front door open, and saw that there were no vehicles there in front of the school, none at all.

He began, for some reason, to count. Eight, nine, ten seconds. Nothing. A trick.

And then, at the count of eleven, the truck rounded the corner at top speed, with Zozo Forni at the wheel looking delighted, a boy at play. He pulled up in front of the building, and they ran out with their treasure. This time, the Dell'Acquas ripped off their German army shirts and sat in back with the Italian deserters. Giuseppe climbed into the cab with Aldo and Zozo and slammed the doors. They started off. "Where?" Giuseppe asked, but Zozo was grinning, shifting, spinning the wheel, and didn't answer.

Fifty-Four

Rita had gone through the first ten Hail Marys of her rosary when she heard an urgent tapping on her door, not one or two or three taps but a continuous quick knocking. When she opened it, the first thing she noticed was the nun's habit, and the second thing, the face of Aldo's daughter. The face was marked with dust, swollen on one side and cut above the other eyebrow, the eyes full, the wimple thrown back over her head and the habit itself wrinkled and torn. The girl practically leaped across the threshold and, without a word, held Rita in an embrace so tight and for so long that Rita had trouble breathing. She closed the door behind them and listened to Lucia's story.

She knew what rape felt like, and knew what an attempted rape felt like, and as the girl spoke, Rita first took hold of her hand, then her arm, and then held her against herself again and let her weep there. A German captain with a limp and a craziness in his eyes. The same man.

It was only another few seconds before she heard the latch of the door, and then its hinges' quiet complaint. She turned and saw *Skutchamenza* standing there, shoulders thrown back, chin up. "We saved her. We killed the German," was the first thing the boy said. Those words shocked her, but the sight of Armando and his friend in her doorway seemed somehow unsurprising, just more evidence of a belief she'd held for many years now: that the people you met in this world were part of a mystical plan. It wasn't by chance that, out of the million citizens of Naples, she'd met and come to know Aldo and *Skutchamenza* and Lucia. They'd been brought together to help each other through the sometimes overwhelming challenges of human life. God had arranged it that way, so you didn't have to battle the demons alone.

"Roberto and Antonio went back to check, but he's dead by now, *Nanella*. We made sure no one followed us here."

At the sound of the boy's voice, Lucia's sobs, which had quieted for a moment, started up again. Rita could feel Lucia nodding against her shoulder and feel her tears running down beneath the fabric at the back of her own neck.

After a time, Rita heard the younger woman say, "Give it to me," and didn't know what she meant. "Give it to me. Let me have it," Lucia repeated. Rita held her at arm's length and only then saw that Lucia was facing the window where the pistol sat on the sill. "I don't ever want to be like that again, that way, that easily taken. If the boys hadn't . . . Give it to me, please. I have to go back out. We saw smoke in the Materdei. I have to find Giuseppe. I don't want . . . Please!"

Rita reached up and gently tugged the wimple forward until it fit around Lucia's face and hair again. She didn't know why she'd done that—a vain attempt to erase the past hours, maybe. She smoothed the girl's wet cheeks and said to the boys, "There's some fish and rice on the stove, eat," and heard their feet as they moved into the other room.

"I don't want you to have it, my sweet one," she said quietly, running one hand along Lucia's face and then using her index fingers to wipe the tears from under her eyes.

Lucia shook her head violently, almost crazily. "I have to find Giuseppe. I have to go out into the city. There's shooting everywhere. If that man had—"

"Calm, be calm. He's gone, dead. He'll never bother you again."

Lucia pulled herself away and fixed Rita with a terrifying glare, her eyes pinched tight, her mouth trembling. "I want to kill them all. All of them!"

"*Sì, sì,*" Rita said. "Yes, of course. We all do. But we should leave that to the *Americani.*"

Armando and his friend came into the room from the kitchen, the friend sucking the tips of his fingers one after the next, taking every last bit of taste from them. "*Nanella*, we heard shots *everywhere*! We saw smoke near Poggioreale. Everyone is being moved away from the port now. If you can walk to the port in ten minutes, you have to leave your house."

"How can that be?"

"It is," Armando said. "I told you about it before."

Rita turned to see Lucia nodding and nodding, the tears gone now, replaced by the pinched eyes, the tight line of her mouth. "It's true, it's true."

"But how can it be?"

"It is!" Lucia shouted at her, the voice so loud and fierce that Rita closed her eyes for a moment. "But people are fighting back. You can hear . . . everywhere . . . These boys"—she swung her arm toward the two *scugnizzi* standing in the middle of the room, staring at her—"they beat the soldier who tried to rape me. They killed him. No one is going to be quiet anymore! We have to fight them now!"

Rita stared at her for a moment, then reached out and put both hands on the tops of Lucia's shoulders, feeling the coarse fabric of the nun's habit against her fingers and remembering, all too clearly, the wild fury that had come over her after a man had first taken her against her will. The terror, then the shame, then, later, fury, raw hatred. She could feel now that something in the girl's voice was lifting those horrific memories back into the light. She understood the emotions, understood them all too well. "All right," she said, surprising herself, as if the memories were living creatures and had risen up against the weight of the years and at last found their voice. "All right. But if you go into the city with the gun, then I'll go with you."

"And *we* will, too, *Nanella*," Armando said. "We'll all go. We'll all fight."

Fifty-Five

At Capodimonte, Scholl leaped out of the jeep and immediately found Captain Pitsiak, manning a machine gun beside a truck with desert camouflage. "Get some of your men on the big guns, Captain. We have reinforcements coming. There's a tank battle at the airport. Get the coordinates from Mersom and fire."

"Our own men are there, Herr Colonel."

"Get the coordinates and fire!"

"Yes, sir."

It took fifteen minutes for the German reinforcements to arrive at Capodimonte. During that time, Scholl himself manned one of the machine-gun emplacements—with Nitzermann feeding him the belt of ammunition, and Renzik crouching behind the jeep, aiming a rifle—and kept firing at the pair of Italian trucks and then down into a restaurant to his right from which shots were coming. It took too much time, but the coordinates from the airport were eventually called in, and then one of the big guns went to work: the tremendous concussions, the heavy shells lifting up and out in a *crack-boom* and a blast of smoke. Scholl leaned away from the machine gun long enough to train his binoculars in the direction of Capodichino, saw the explosions there, one man actually flying into the air in a somersault of arms and legs. Another shell. Three more. Then he went back to firing at the trucks in front of him.

Once the reinforcements arrived and were in radio contact, they had the Italians pinched between them, and Scholl gave the order to obliterate them. It did not prove easy. Word of the battle had spread, and reinforcements had arrived for the Italians, too, and they were shockingly well armed: rifles, at least one machine gun, grenades. The battle went on—pauses, spurts of firing, crazed periods of furious exchanges—for several hours. The Italian trucks were sliced to bits, bodies everywhere, but there were German casualties, too, and a few of the Italians escaped down toward the restaurant, how many he didn't know. Eventually, the shooting paused and sputtered and stopped. Scholl sat there with the trigger against his finger, breathing hard, soaked with sweat.

From the airport, Mersom called in a halt to the artillery support. "Mopping up," he said.

And the company around him was mopping up, too, the German reinforcements walking among the bodies near the trucks and firing a shot here and there to make sure the wounded were now the dead. Except for those shots and a few muted rounds fired well below them, the air was quiet.

"Get the wounded to the field hospital," Scholl told Pitsiak. "Get your men some food. This was a last gasp. Tomorrow we start the destruction of the city in earnest, and if there are any more of these spots of trouble, have no mercy."

"Yes, Colonel."

For a long while, Scholl sat with Renzik in the jeep, trying to get in touch with captains across the huge city, using various frequencies with mixed success, cursing the radio. He could see a few twirls of smoke below them, but on this hill, at least, all was calm. The airport situation was under control—how was it that the Italians had been foolish enough to engage with tanks there? The port area would be empty of people. He'd give the artillery battalion a night of rest, and tomorrow they'd begin the shelling. The port first, and then, block by block, the rest of the cursed metropolis. Ashes and mud.

The fickle radio sparked to life again. One frequency—the FuG 3—seemed untroubled. He asked his captains for an assessment, and soon it arrived: eighteen men lost, in all, twenty-four wounded. One tank at the airport completely disabled, another damaged. The three big Capodimonte guns intact. All was quiet in the palace behind them, only a single window lit there. Scholl sat with a circle of men, eating and drinking, talking in quiet tones, staying there long after the red ball of the sun had disappeared into the sea. This was his special talent, mixing with the men, not standing above them, the talent that had allowed him to rise in the ranks. He'd risked his life just now, when, as commanding officer, he could have kept his distance from the battle, and he knew they appreciated that and respected him for it. A combat veteran himself, he was more or less unfazed by the events of the day. A last gasp, it had been, just as he'd said. Somehow, the Italians had broken into an armory, and apparently a platoon of Italian soldiers had set themselves up at the airport and made a surprise attack. That was the extent of it. The city seemed quiet, the men almost relaxed. Tomorrow, they'd begin. He'd order his troops out of certain sections—the Chiaia, the Materdei, the Spagnoli—and set the big guns on those neighborhoods, without mercy. Artillery first, then he'd send in the tanks and flamethrowers. If the masses who'd left the port happened to be in the wrong place, so be it. He'd lost eighteen men. No number of Italian deaths could compensate for that.

Quite late, after a last conversation with Pitsiak and a last radio exchange with Mersom, Scholl took Nitzermann aside, strolled up to the large park near the palace, and asked if he knew how many Italian men had surrendered as ordered by the proclamation. The moon had risen by then, casting them in a yellowish light.

Nitzermann turned his face aside and broke eye contact.

Scholl took him by the shoulders. "Captain, I don't care how tired you are. Look at me. Answer me."

The eyes swung back. "Approximately one hundred and fifty, sir," the captain said.

"One hundred and fifty!"

Nitzermann nodded.

"One hundred and fifty! Out of the thirty thousand we expected?"

"Yes, sir. People are hiding them, apparently. In one case, a mob of women attacked one of our trucks with Italian men in the back and . . . freed them."

"You're making a terrible joke, yes?"

Nitzermann shook his head.

"And where are the hundred and fifty?"

"Being held at the stadium in the Vomero, sir, as you ordered."

"Then send out word to have them shot."

"When, sir?"

"Tomorrow. First light. And by then, the number had better be far larger. Spread the word."

"Yes, Herr Colonel," Nitzermann said, but something in his face and voice sent a whisper of bad feeling through Scholl's thoughts. He wondered if there could possibly be German soldiers refusing orders, or at least fulfilling them sloppily. A hundred and fifty out of thirty thousand! Women fighting armed men! Freeing prisoners! What kind of soldiers had he inherited?

He turned away in disgust and, over his shoulder, told Nitzermann to stay with the artillery brigade. Let him sleep here, in the dirt. Let him toughen up.

Scholl made a last tour through the encampment, encouraging the men, complimenting them, preparing them for the next day's work. And then he called for Renzik to drive him back into the city. Their route took them in a southward loop around behind the huddled crowds, so Scholl could ride in along the empty port, get a sense of the situation there, and return to his hotel. Tomorrow, if possible, he'd have the artillery avoid the Parco and his headquarters. If they couldn't manage that, he'd simply move up to the palace on Capodimonte and oversee the operation from there.

Just as they pulled up beneath the **ALBERGO PARCO** sign, something occurred to him. He said to Renzik, "We still haven't had any direct word from the Vomero, have we?"

"No, Colonel. There's something wrong with that frequency, or with the radios there."

"Who's in charge?"

"Major Saggau, sir. We've been holding men there before shipping them north. Italians. In the stadium. A hundred or more."

"Yes. A pitiful number, a joke. Is Saggau any good, do you know?"

"Very good, sir, from what Captain Nitzermann told me. One of our finest."

"Then it must be under control. I'm going to get some sleep. You do the same. Tomorrow we begin."

Scholl returned Renzik's salute and marched into the hotel. Eighteen men lost, he was thinking. Only a hundred and fifty prisoners. Radio troubles. And, apparently, some kind of mysterious delay in the collecting of the Jews. Himmler would not be happy. Nor would Kesselring. No mercy, then. No mercy at all.

Every honest soldier he'd ever known who'd seen actual combat said there was a certain bodily reaction after the fighting was over. A huge increase in sexual appetite. Everyone said so, and he could feel it now in himself. The quiet, opulent lobby seemed to work a kind of spell on his mood. The garish maroon carpet, the marble front desk with the pretty young girl behind it, the one who'd given him the matches and understood German. He was exhausted from the day. Not physically, but in some other way. As if his willpower had run a hundred miles carrying the weight of command on its shoulders.

As he went toward the curving stairway, he couldn't keep his head from turning left. In the sitting room of the bar, he noticed the usual loiterers. All looking at him.

Fifty-Six

Holding the wheel tight with both hands, Zozo Forni sent the Italian Army truck racing and bouncing down along the middle part of the Vomero hill. Aldo had his hands between his thighs, holding the rifle with his wrists and gripping the bottom of the front seat tightly to keep from being thrown up against the roof. Beside him, Lucia's boyfriend had the machine gun between his knees, too, but was holding on in a different posture, one arm out the open window, pressing himself against the door, and the other palm pushing up against the roof. From the moment Aldo had first climbed into the bed of the truck (filled now with the Dell'Acqua brothers—stripped of their shirts—the two "associates," and four men who'd formerly been soldiers in the Italian Army), the day had taken on a very strange aspect for him: everything was sharper, more immediate, astonishingly real. It made him understand that over the past two years, he'd fallen into a kind of hypnosis. Instead of looking forward to meals, as he once had, he simply wanted to eat. Instead of the satisfaction of working and earning money, he'd scavenged small jobs here and there and been grateful for a few lire in his pocket when, in the past, he'd been able to afford luxuries. Instead of moving from pier to pier, ship to ship, warehouse to warehouse, quietly arranging the accumulation and transport of various materials, he'd become a solitary middle-aged bachelor, lounging near the port, smoking cheap cigarettes, waiting for the day when he could at least enjoy his visit to Rita. It was as if all his senses had been dulled, as if he were sleepwalking, hypnotized, drugged, trying simply to survive for another day, thinking about nothing beyond that.

Now, suddenly, he had an army rifle between his wrists (he'd stolen enough of them at the port to know that it was a Carcano M1891, an outdated weapon with a six-round magazine of outdated round-nosed bullets) and his wrists pinched between his knees, and he was sitting in a truck careening along a street in the Vomero toward some conflict that made sense only in the mind of Zozo Forni. They were going to fight the Germans! Well-armed, professionally trained, veteran soldiers. It felt to him like a suicide mission and so, strangely enough, faced with what might very well be its imminent end, his life had taken on a new clarity. His shoulder and hip bumped hard against the man to his right, someone he'd dismissed as recently as two days ago, but now someone on whom his own life might depend. To his left, Zozo appeared to be on the verge of a fanatical hysteria. The *Camorrista* looked like he might throw back his head and let out a crazy howl. He wrestled the wheel left and right, dodging piles of debris, turning up onto the sidewalk, crashing through and flattening a sapling that had somehow been able to survive there, then bumping off the curb and down onto the street again.

They careened into a sharp left at Via Consalvo, and beyond the corner, Zozo slammed his foot down on the brake and skidded the truck to a sideways stop. Three meters in front of them stood a roadblock made of two disabled cars and what appeared to be a pile of household furniture. Chairs, a broken table, one huge mirror frame with the glass shattered into pieces. Four men in ordinary workers' clothes stood there, two of them swinging an arm in a circular motion. They appeared to have been expecting the motley crew of fighters. *"Uscite! Andiamo!"* they were shouting. *"Get out! Let's go!* The Nazis have hostages at the stadium! Leave the machine gun. Bring a rifle you can shoot and leave the rest here for the others!"

Zozo jumped out one door, Aldo followed Giuseppe out the other. Behind them came the soldiers and the shirtless Dell'Acqua boys. Aldo knew exactly where the stadium was; everyone who'd ever gone to a soccer game knew: two blocks downhill and one block north of them, a large oval with two stories of seats set opposite a narrow park along a stretch of Via Rossini. On the opposite side of that street stood a row of elegant six-story apartment buildings with rooftop gardens and private courtyards. On foot now, he followed the four men—partisan fighters, Aldo assumed, a species he'd heard about but never actually encountered—and was aware of the sound of shooting before they'd gone twenty steps.

At the first corner, they stopped, crouching together. Aldo recognized one of the fighters now, Marco Pacella, a fisherman who had simply disappeared a year or so ago, leaving his pilotless boat in the port and a confused and angry wife at home. Pacella was a giant of a man, well over two meters tall, with broad shoulders and a face dominated by an enormous curved nose and pocked skin. *"Sentite,"* he said in the voice of a commander. *"Listen.* The Nazis have hostages in the *stadio.* Our men. Thirty, fifty, a hundred, no one knows for sure. Just outside the main entrance, they've parked three of their trucks at the curb, and across the street, we have a line of our trucks, parallel, with men taking cover behind them and firing at soldiers in the doorway and the windows beside it. We're in a standoff. But now you're here—at last—more guns, and the people in one of the houses have promised to help. Four houses down. Number 31. You'll go in there. The front door is wide open. Climb up to the top floor as fast as you can and see if you can get an angle on the *Nazisti* from the roof. There's extra ammunition there but—"

"We have some, too," Aldo said.

"Okay, but don't shoot unless you have a clear shot. The rifles are simple to use. Look through the sight, squeeze the trigger, pull back the bolt, do it again. Go!"

Aldo, Giuseppe, and the others crossed the street and, bent nearly in two, trotted single-file close to the buildings, moving toward the bottom of the shallow hill. From there, Aldo could hear the shots more clearly, and it seemed he was moving against cables that wanted to pull him back in the other direction, away from the loud reports—a machine gun, it sounded like now—of bullets striking stone, and panicky voices shouting words he couldn't understand. He could taste the fear in his mouth, but there were men behind him and Lucia's boyfriend in front of him, and he willed himself forward.

At the corner where Via Console met Via Vincenzo Gemito, the noise was deafening. Shots, shouts, an explosion. He could smell cordite, stone dust, his own rancid sweat. He crouched there, waving the men behind him to do the same, waiting for even a slight pause in the firing. Behind one of the trucks, he heard a wounded man screaming repeatedly; from far off came the sound of an ambulance Klaxon, then a German word shouted into a brief quiet moment. And then Giuseppe was up and sprinting. Aldo followed, ten meters to the doorway, a series of single shots, chips of stone flying everywhere. He was inside. They were all inside, sprinting up a dark flight of stairs, one floor, two, three, five, someone there—a white-haired woman in a house dress—waving them across the hall, through a door, up narrower stairs—wooden, these were—and onto a flat rooftop garden that was empty save for a radio antenna, a water tank propped up on three legs, and a metal table and chairs where the families here had no doubt spent many quiet afternoons.

This afternoon—evening now—was the last thing from quiet. The machine gun started up again below them, the yelling, a frantic confusion there and across the street. He waved an arm. *Down, down!* Giuseppe went one way, he went the other, both of them crawling over to the knee-high wall at the edge of the roof that faced the stadium. The yelling and shooting made him want to lie flat, but he forced himself to lift his head far enough to see. The curving wall of the stadium just opposite, its concrete pocked with the scars of bullets, a sign in front: **Campo Sportivo del Littorio**. At its base, a dark square opening, round-topped, with two sets of windows to either side. A German machine gun was firing from one of the windows. Just as Pacella had described, Aldo could see a wide strip of street between two parallel lines of trucks, parked grille to bumper, one line—German vehicles—near the stadium entrances, and the other—Italian Army trucks—directly below him. He counted seven men, crouching behind the Italian trucks and firing rifles around the sides, over the hoods, then ducking back to safety. One man lay there on the stones, writhing in agony, blood pooling beside his shoulder. To the right of them stretched a small park, ten meters across, with a few old eucalyptus trees and one ragged palm, scraps of grass and dirt and one lonely trash barrel and one lonely bench. At the other end of the building's roof, he saw Giuseppe peek up over the wall, and the shirtless Dell'Acquas and the soldiers and Zozo's men spread out to his left. Everything was happening in slow motion. At first, the Germans didn't seem to know there was anyone on the roof, but they knew now: bullets *ping*ed against the low wall two meters from Aldo's face. He ducked, crawled, waited. The soldiers started firing first, lifting their rifles over the wall, aiming, shooting, then ducking back down and crawling sideways to reappear in a different spot. Zozo's men imitated them. The Dell'Acquas imitated Zozo's men. "Can you see anything to aim at?" Aldo called to the boy. Giuseppe shook his head, eyes just above the top of the low wall. Then he pointed with his chin. "There. On the right side of the opening."

Aldo saw a soldier in a German uniform step into the fading daylight and fire a burst of bullets, then duck back in. Aldo aimed, held the rifle sight on that place, and when the soldier appeared again, he fired all six rounds in a row, the butt of the rifle banging back against his shoulder, but couldn't even tell where the bullets ended up. Giuseppe seemed to be having as much trouble. The others were all more experienced and more confident, holding their weapons steadier, aiming and ducking and moving, and Aldo tried to mimic them but felt he was accomplishing nothing. As he watched, another Italian Army vehicle raced onto the scene and skidded into place at the end of the line of trucks; the machine gun Giuseppe had just taken from the school had been mounted on its bed. A man there, Pacella himself it was, barely protected by a metal shield that looked like a pair of wings, began firing at the stadium windows, obliterating the little glass that was left. A hand grenade was thrown toward the German trucks. It bounced and rolled on the paving stones and lay there, mute.

When he'd ejected the empty clip and banged another into place, Aldo peeked over the wall again and spotted a German soldier at the top of the stadium seats, directly opposite him and a few meters below. Vito Dell'Acqua stood up like a wild man and started firing at the man, bare-chested, crazily, then went flying over backward onto the wet concrete, knocking one of the chairs sideways. Aldo fired a stream of bullets, too, saw one of them make a small spray of concrete just below the German at the top of the seats, saw the German look up at him. Aldo ducked, heard the *ping* of bullet against stone, crawled along to a different part of the wall, put his last clip into the rifle, peeked over again, and saw a strange sight at the east end of the park: two boys, each thin as a door edge, sprinting across the dirt and then diving, headfirst, onto the dirt this side of the German army trucks. Another *ping*, closer this time, and Aldo crawled to his left and stayed low.

Fifty-Seven

From the Spagnoli to the Vomero, it was a steady climb along the Pedamentina stairway. Rita could hear their breaths and feel her own sweat streaming down both sides of her body. Halfway up, she started to be able to hear shooting. They reached the top of the stairway, the Castel Sant'Elmo opposite them, a street running slightly uphill to their right. "The noise is coming from near the stadium," Rita said, looking sideways at Lucia, whose sweat had soaked the bottom of the nun's wimple. She tried with some success to push it back off her head, nodded, pointed a few meters in front of them to where Armando and his friend, Tomaso, were striding along, *Skutchamenza* holding a German army knife out in one hand like a grown man about to go into battle. If what the boy said was true, they were killers now, he and his friends. The two other boys had gone back to check, but if the limping soldier was dead, then they were killers, and at such an age!

Rita looked at Lucia, both of them worried, but there was nothing to do: Armando, so determined to prove himself an adult, was leading them straight toward the sound of the shooting. They were not about to let him go there alone.

Other people were heading in that direction, too, a trickle of men, mostly, three or four of them holding rifles, trotting along with their faces set in a grim concentration. No one in uniform. One army truck sped past, with what appeared to be a machine gun bolted to its bed.

A large man was sitting there behind it, three more men squeezed into the cab. Rita was out of breath, sweating through her bra, unarmed, accompanied by two twelve-year-old street boys and a beautiful woman in a borrowed nun's habit. A thin cable of fear curled around her belly and behind her breasts, but there was not even the smallest thought of turning into a side street and hiding, not even a moment of doubt. She felt a sense of being connected to everyone else in the city, every good soul, at least. It had become, in her mind, a simple confrontation between good and evil, fear and bravery, selfishness and sacrifice. They were going to save their men and their Jewish friends from the work camps, their neighbors from execution, save their city from destruction, or they were going to die trying. And so she went forward toward the sound of gunfire, calling on Santa Agata to protect them.

Left past the castle and down through Piazza Vanvitelli they went, the air filled with the smell of smoke and the loud reports of machine-gun fire and small explosions. Lucia had her pistol, Armando had the knife, and she had her prayers: But what could they do against soldiers?

They turned a last corner onto Via Vincenzo Gemito, and from there they could see the scene spread out before them: two lines of trucks on opposite sides of the street, one line flying the swastika, the other with a small Italian flag sticking up from one roof. Men with rifles had taken up positions behind anything that would protect them—the stone column of a fountain, the corner of a building, the trunk of a tree. Others were crouching at the end of the side streets, waiting, watching. The late-afternoon sun was casting its last long shadows, and the air was filled with horrible sounds—wails, shouts, gunfire, bullets smashing windows or singing against stone—and the smell of smoke. She, Lucia, Tomaso, and Armando circled around the fighting, along Via Paisiello, reached the edge of the small park, a safe distance away, and knelt in the dirt behind a bench, watching.

The noise was deafening, horrifying, and in the last of the daylight, it took Rita a minute to understand what she was looking at: German soldiers were firing from inside the front of the stadium. Italian men were firing from behind the trucks and around the corners of whatever was protecting them. She heard an ambulance coming up the hill behind them, Klaxon wailing. She saw a German soldier appear at the top of the stadium wall and point his rifle at the building across the street. She thought she saw men there on the roof, appearing and disappearing like fish surfacing and diving. And then Lucia grabbed her hand and, to her horror, she heard Armando let out a savage cry and watched him and his friend sprint down the length of the park, into the open street, and dive behind the cover, not of the Italian trucks but of the German ones. She could see the soles of their shoes, the ragged pants legs. They were crawling on their bellies, working their elbows.

With his friend just ahead of him, bare hands on a truck tire, Armando stopped at the first of the trucks, and she saw him push the point of the knife into the rear tire, bang on it with his other hand until it pierced the thick rubber, then pull it out, crawl forward, do the same thing to the front tire on that side. The tires of the second truck were already sagging. Both boys spun around, crouching, ran as far as the last meter of cover, then looked up. *Skutchamenza* caught her eyes. There was the devilish smile she'd first seen in the bomb shelter. He waved to them with the knife, so proud, waited for a pause in the firing, then both of them started sprinting back toward the park. Lucia had taken out the pistol and was aiming it at the top of the stadium, holding it with both hands and shooting, trying to protect them. But almost all the way to safety, first Tomaso and then Armando were hit by shots from high up there. The impact of the bullet ripped open the back of Tomaso's head and knocked him flat. Armando went flying through the air, spinning completely around, landed hard and skidded on the dirt at the far end of the park, and without even the thought of hesitation, Rita went running toward him, Lucia waving the pistol and sprinting ahead of her.

Fifty-Eight

In the confusion and noise, Giuseppe found himself fueled by an enormous surge of energy and moving according to some overwhelming survival instinct. He'd push the sweaty, slippery eyeglasses back against the bridge of his nose, raise his head up only far enough to see across the road in the quickly fading daylight, wait until he spotted a target, then he'd lift his rifle, aim, squeeze the trigger three times, working the bolt, then duck down again.

His breath was coming in gasps. A shallow pool of water had formed at his feet, and he realized the water tank had been hit by a bullet and was leaking. After one quick verbal exchange with Aldo, he wasn't paying much attention to the other men spread out along the wall, though he could glimpse them out of the corners of his eyes: lying low, popping up and firing just as he was, ducking down again, and scurrying to the next position, farther down the wall. Suddenly he saw a figure standing up and bracing himself with his knees against the wall. It was Vito Dell'Acqua, bare-chested, either crazy or unbelievably brave, standing tall and firing down at the Nazi trucks. Giuseppe saw two truck windows disappear in an explosion of glass, and then realized Vito was shooting at the gas tanks, trying to get the trucks to explode. He could see a rough circle of bullet holes there, and then the Dell'Acqua brother went flying backward in a way that was hideous and absurd, landed hard on his back, and Giuseppe could see a fountain of blood spurting from the top of his chest. For a moment, Giuseppe crouched in place and stared, horrible memories of his parents' bodies filling his mind. The blood mingled with the water leaking out of the tank, and a pink flood of it came flowing down the tiles and against Giuseppe's feet. Instead of tending to his brother, who was clearly not going to live, Ubaldo stood, sprinted to the doorway, and disappeared down the stairs. Giuseppe peeked over the wall, expecting to see him stand out in the open street and fire crazily at the soldiers in the stadium, taking his revenge. But no, he was gone.

Another German bullet hit the water tank, springing a bigger leak. Giuseppe could hear shots striking the wall just in front of him, an exchange of machine-gun fire below. Every time he had to raise his head, it required another leap of willpower. He crawled left, to the edge of the wall nearest the staircase they'd climbed, near the door through which Ubaldo had just disappeared. A concrete urn stood there, tall as a man; it afforded more protection. He kept his rifle out of sight at first, just peering with one eye. From this vantage, he could see that trucks, Italian trucks, had blocked both ends of the street now. Plainclothes drivers stood beside them, leaning against the fenders, rifles raised, firing away, reloading.

And then, in the midst of the chaos, he saw something that at first seemed impossible to believe: two skinny boys racing out of the park from right to left below him. The boys stayed low, sprinting, then dove behind the trucks Vito had been firing at, and were sheltered there from German bullets. One of the boys was holding a combat knife. He crawled forward, stabbed the rear tire of the first truck, crawled forward again, and did the same thing with the truck's front tire. His friend was ahead of him, releasing air from the tires of the second truck but using only his hands or a small stone. Giuseppe ducked, bullets singing off the wall in front of him, and when he was able to look again, both boys were sprinting back toward the park. He fired at the top of the stadium, hoping to protect them, but he could tell his shots were missing the soldier there. The boys made it most of the way to safety before Giuseppe saw one of them fall facedown, spurting blood, and the other go suddenly airborne, spinning around, landing flat on his spine and skidding a meter or two backward.

Giuseppe looked away to fire again at the soldier at the top of the stadium, one round after the next, sighting, working the bolt and firing, sighting, and firing. At last, one of his shots, or one of someone else's, hit the target. The man slumped sideways onto the wall there, then slipped from view, his rifle falling straight down to the sidewalk, bouncing into the gutter. Giuseppe watched for someone else to appear in the soldier's place, then turned his eyes for two seconds to the wounded boys and saw a nun and another woman running out from the park to help them, unprotected, clearly in the line of fire. Giuseppe put in a new clip and fired into the mouth of the doorway across the street, working the bolt like a crazed man, hitting nothing but hoping to keep any German from appearing there. He ran out of ammunition again—no more clips in his pocket—and glanced again at the scene below. Holding an arm and a leg each, and with their backs to him now, the nun and the woman took hold of the boy who was still alive—blood on his upper left arm—and carried him into the park. The other boy lay there with blood pouring out of his skull and running in a stream along the gutter.

Giuseppe sprinted down the stairs, hoping he could help, but the second he reached the street-level doorway, an ambulance squeezed past the Italian trucks. Red cross on its side, it pulled to the edge of the park. Protected by a burst of machine-gun fire from the big man in the bed of the Italian Army truck, two men emerged and loaded in the wounded boy. Giuseppe watched them turn their eyes to the other boy, still in the line of fire, still bleeding, and decide there was no hope.

Crouching and sprinting and under fire, two men carried over one of the Italian fighters who'd been there before they arrived, also apparently badly wounded, and loaded him into the back. The women climbed in after the two patients. The ambulance made a tight U-turn and went off, Klaxon sounding. For an instant, Giuseppe wondered if it was the same brave nun they'd seen from the truck bed hours ago, then he noticed the man firing the machine gun slump sideways and fall from the truck to the ground, and Giuseppe tossed his rifle aside, sprinted toward the truck, and leaped onto the bed. He took his place behind the metal wings, found the trigger, swung the barrel to his left, and sent a stream of bullets into the stadium opening and the windows beside it. The man he'd replaced was moaning. Two others came up and carried him off. Giuseppe kept firing.

The sun had disappeared, leaving a smoky dusk. Another military vehicle—Italian—pulled up tight against the third one in the line. Four more men, four more rifles. They climbed out of the truck and all began firing into the two openings. One of the men was hit immediately and fell hard, straight backward.

For another hour, with a yellowish, not-quite-full moon rising beyond the stadium, the battle went on—pauses, spurts of shooting, yelling. Someone from the fourth truck threw a hand grenade into the doorway. This one exploded, sending out a puff of gray smoke. Silence. A pause. And then, to Giuseppe's complete astonishment, a white flag appeared, held on the end of a rifle, the soldier invisible. Giuseppe watched, waiting for a trick. He heard someone come up close beside him, and moved his eyes. It was Aldo. They watched the German soldier step out as far as his trucks, which were tilting strangely now on their flattened tires. *"Lasciali andare!"* the man said, waving the flag back and forth. *Let us go!*

"Have your men surrender and we'll let you go!" Aldo shouted back in a voice so low and full of hatred that Giuseppe turned to look. Aldo's cheeks were shaking, and he had sweat covering every inch of his face and neck. "Give over your guns, free our men, and we'll let you go!"

"Non sono autorizzato!" the German shouted back. *I'm not authorized!*

The man ducked back inside, and the firing began again. The battle went on for another hour, a shadowy, moonlit darkness enveloping all of them now, flashes of light at the muzzles, sparks showing where bullets hit stone. "If they kill our men in there . . . ," Aldo said, and left the thought unfinished.

Another hour of shots and pauses, two more Germans at the top of the stadium now, and then a fifth Italian truck drew up on the other side, and a second automatic gun opened fire there, ripping into the Nazi trucks, sending glass and shards of metal flying. There were two more explosions, one beneath the first German vehicle and one to the side of it. Giuseppe fired bursts into the stadium opening, glanced over at the new Italian truck, expecting to see Zozo or Ubaldo, but someone else was driving. Two men stepped out of the protected side, one with the automatic weapon. They sent a fusillade of bullets into the farther opening. Another spate of silence, and then the flag again, eerily white in the half darkness.

"Enough!" someone behind Giuseppe shouted. "Let him come!"

Another voice: "A trick!"

"No!" Aldo yelled. "Let him come!"

Fifty-Nine

They were crowded so tightly in the back of the speeding, bouncing ambulance that Lucia thought all four of them would suffocate. Rita had her hands wrapped around the boy's wound, blood oozing between her fingers. "It's flesh," she said between her teeth, as if trying to convince herself. "Flesh, not bone. No arteries."

Looking at the amount of blood, Lucia wasn't sure. She peeled Armando's fingers from the knife he was still clutching, cut a strip of cloth from the nun's skirt near her ankles, and tied it tightly around the boy's upper arm. The man beside Armando, lying so close that their legs touched side to side, had been shot in the lower chest and was bleeding in a strange way, the blood draining out slowly beneath him, as if the bottom of the ambulance were leaking. Lucia could see that his eyes were glazing over. "Sister," he said very quietly, "pray." Lucia started to say the Our Father, took hold of his hand, and watched the last flickers of life leave his eyes. Rita was praying over him, too, a stream of Hail Marys. Armando was bravely clenching his teeth, but his face was coated in tears, and he was taking small, quick, panicky breaths, closing his eyes against the pain and then opening them and looking at her. "Sister Marcellina," he said. "Sister Marcellina. Tomaso?"

"You'll live," Lucia told him. "We've mostly stopped the bleeding in your arm. You'll live."

"I want to," the boy said weakly.

"Keep your eyes open."

"They killed Tomaso," he whispered, and Lucia did not have the heart to tell him he was right. The ambulance attendants had taken one look at Armando's friend and left him facedown on the street.

"You're going to come stay with me after this," Rita told Armando. "Enough of the living on the streets. You'll get well. You'll live with your *Nanella*."

Lucia watched something resembling peace come over Armando's triangular face, a slight change in his breathing. He tried to say something else, winced, closed his eyes. But she could see, when the ambulance came to a stop at the hospital, that he was still breathing.

Sixty

If it wasn't for the lack of female company, Spinelli thought, the monk's life might actually suit him. The meals were small but much tastier than C-rations, and the men were quiet, peaceful, kind. He had a bed with a real mattress, in a tiny, rectangular, stone-walled room on the third floor. There was one window, barely as big as a single volume of his mother's Encyclopedia Britannica. It faced south over olive groves and barren vegetable patches and a few widely spread tile-roofed farmhouses of the kind they'd been seeing from the day they landed on Licata Beach in Sicily, two long months ago.

It was time to leave. Sunday. One day past the full moon, just after dark—they'd be expecting him by sunrise. One of the monks had promised to procure some kind of map, showing the German positions, armories, and barracks—but something had gone wrong with the plan and that hadn't happened. Even so, he'd made two trips into the city for inspections, gotten a sense of the place, and tonight was going to be the night he headed south, through the German lines and back to file his report with Colonel Accetullo. The moon was a mixed blessing.

Unfortunately, he'd have to tell his colonel that they were facing a nightmare. He'd never seen anything like Naples. Catania and Palermo looked orderly in comparison. Naples had a few major boulevards wide enough for tanks, true, but shooting off in every direction and at every possible angle were side streets lined by five- and six-story apartment buildings. And off those side streets, a crooked maze of what the Italians called *"vicoli."* Alleyways so narrow and crooked that you could no more run a military vehicle along them than he could fit a pencil into the bowl and around the bent stem of his dad's pipe. Stairways running off the alleys, going up, down, and sideways. Handmade stone houses of every shape and size. It looked like the city had been built, piece by piece, over hundreds of years, without the smallest idea of a plan.

What were you supposed to do, send tanks and men into those streets so they could be shot to pieces? The Nazis would have snipers in the apartment buildings, machine guns on the roofs. Not to mention the artillery brigade he'd glimpsed up on the hill with the big brick palace and parks. Capodimonte, it was called. *Head of the Mountain.*

Crazy. It wasn't his decision, of course. Eisenhower would figure something out. And the Brits would likely be first into the city, in any case, according to the plans he'd heard. But he wondered if it would be smarter just to avoid Naples altogether, surround the city, put battleships in the port, and starve the Germans out. But the Neapolitan people were already starving, so that would basically mean torturing them.

For once, he was glad to be a corporal. On his way up, for sure, but a corporal all the same. The question of what to do about Naples would be made at much higher levels. Under the cover of darkness, helped by the light of the moon, he'd slip across the farmland and through the olive trees, use the question-and-answer password ("Where do the Red Sox play?" "Fenway Park"), get through his own lines, make his report, and go on to the next assignment.

The monks were at prayer and had been since right after dinner. It seemed that was just about all they did. An odd thought captured him: maybe, before leaving, he'd go and join them. Pray for his brothers-in-arms, for the family back home, for his safe crossing. But then, as he was about to head down to the chapel, he heard a series of explosions, a *boom, boom, boom* that was so well known to him now. Familiar as bread, in fact. The huge sixteen-inch guns firing from American battleships. He'd been hearing them since Licata, a welcome sound, as long as the shells landed on German positions, which they usually did. The Allies controlled the skies now, so the Huns had next to no defense. The big ships would draw in close enough; the FCs would get their info from spotter planes, make their calculations. The sailors would set their guns, load the massive shells into them, cover their ears, and fire. And the shells would arc up into the Italian sky and rain down on the Nazis like the freaking wrath of God.

He listened. A long pause. Then *boom boom boom boom boom!* Glued to the small window, he could see, on the southern horizon, bursts of scarlet and then columns of smoke, gray feathers lifting lazily into moonlight. The Allies were that close. A day at most and they'd be on the doorstep of Naples.

Probably made more sense to wait, then, rather than risk being shot at in the olive groves or blasted to bits by his own naval guns. The colonel knew where he was. Spinelli stared out the window, hesitated a moment, then decided: he'd wait for the jeep to drive up the road behind the monastery. He'd meet them at the gate and give his report, just in time to save them from moving into a death trap, the city his grandparents had always called Napoli.

Sixty-One

At first, warm in the hotel bed, Colonel Scholl wasn't even fully aware of the noise at the hallway door. Something had drawn him out of the deepest sleep he'd had in months. He'd assumed everything was under control: the area inland from the port had been emptied out, the skirmish at Capodimonte had ended well, at the airport everything was now quiet. The destruction of the city would commence in the morning. Jews and young men shipped north, everyone else made homeless or killed.

It had been a tense and dangerous day, the most combat he'd seen since Narvik, three years ago. Between Capodimonte and the airport, eighteen men had been lost, and another six elsewhere in the city. It occurred to him that perhaps he'd made a mistake with the port evacuation, committing so many men, but the area would soon be rendered completely unusable, the coastal zone impassable. There had been pockets of resistance, yes, more of them and more troublesome than he'd expected, but at the end of the day, he had returned to the hotel, confident all was quiet, Naples subdued. No word from the stadium in the Vomero, but that was merely a radio issue; they'd solve it soon enough. His other captains and majors had either not reported—a good sign— or reported that things were as they should be. So he'd given himself the small reward of a night of pleasure.

He blinked, breathed, gradually became aware of the sensation of bare skin to either side of him, the fragrance of sweat and sex and alcohol, the warm sheets, the dark room, the sense of being linked in love—or at least a temporary affection—to the creatures on either side of him. For a few seconds, still half-buried in sleep, his consciousness was filled only with the delicious memories from the night, the first thrill of anticipation, the sense of being desired, the first touches and kisses, the release.

A sound in the other room. He looked at his watch and thought at first that it had stopped. Twenty past two in the morning. No light shone through the curtained windows. The noise in the hallway went on. Something wasn't right.

And then he realized that someone was knocking—urgently, it seemed—on a hallway door. His door. The sound was muted because the door that separated the outer sitting room from the inner bedroom had been closed by one of his companions. It was the last thing he remembered before the lights went out and the feast of touch began. For half a minute, he was able to pretend to himself that the knocking came from farther along the hallway, and he could remain there in the warmth of the bed. Soon, though, cold reality seeped into the room. Naples, wartime, the massive responsibility that weighed on his brain every waking hour. The troubles of the day before. Malfunctioning radios, damaged tanks, lost men.

Now 2:20 in the morning. Outside the windows, the feeling of deepest night. In the bedroom now, a thin scent of shame.

As carefully as he could, Scholl climbed over the sleeping body to his right, found the hotel bathrobe, and wrapped himself in it, opened and quietly closed the middle door, and went across the sitting room toward the sound of knocking. He unlocked and opened the door, and there, hand raised in midknock, stood Captain Nitzermann. The captain's mouth was twitching.

"Very sorry to disturb you, Herr Colonel. May I step in?"

"Is it urgent?"

"Most urgent, sir."

For a few seconds, Scholl considered going out into the hallway and closing the door behind him, but he wasn't dressed, and the expression on Nitzermann's face—anxiety bordering on panic—pushed the thought away. He motioned the captain inside and to a chair, closed the hallway door, glanced at the bedroom door—shut safely tight—then took a seat at one end of the divan, opposite the anxious captain. Scholl put a finger to his lips and gestured toward the bedroom with his chin. Let the captain think what he wanted . . . as long as no one appeared from behind the glass panes and curtain. "Quietly, please," he said.

The captain nodded, not even glancing at the door, squeezing his hands together, tapping at the carpet with the heels of his boots as if he were anxious to be off on a morning run. "Sir," he managed. He appeared to be absolutely exhausted.

"Speak, speak."

"There's a—there has been a problem. Our men took hostages at the stadium yesterday, in the Vomero."

"I know that," Scholl said impatiently. "I ordered them killed starting at sunrise. I went to sleep with the radio quiet. Everything there has been taken care of."

The captain's face was shaking now, eyes flickering, hands squeezed tight. Very quietly, he said, "Herr Colonel, the men at the stadium, our men, met with an assault . . . more resistance than anticipated. From the nearby streets. They had radio difficulties, and for a time were unable to communicate, and are now unable to complete your order. A squadron, it seems . . . Italian irregulars . . . very well armed. Our tanks were unable to climb the Vomero hill to support them."

"How? Why?"

"Roadblocks like the ones we saw yesterday, sir. Trams pushed across the roads, furniture thrown from windows, piles of stone. One tank was disabled at the airport, a long way off, and the other damaged."

"Yes, but—"

"Hand grenades, sir. Heavy machine-gun fire."

"You're joking. No other vehicles could get there? No—"

"Not joking. Not at all, Herr Colonel. Major Saggau is here, downstairs."

"For what reason?"

"For the reason that . . . for . . . He has surrendered."

"To whom?"

"To the Italians. At the stadium. He surrendered to save the lives of his men, sir. Forty-one men there, seven already killed in the fighting. Eleven others wounded, four seriously."

"What fighting? What are you talking about?"

"Sir, we don't know how, but the Italians are well armed. Machine guns, grenades, trucks, riflemen. Streets have been blockaded all over the city. As of twenty minutes ago, our men at Capodimonte are under siege again."

"The Allies?"

"No, sir, the Italians, as I said. The Neapolitans. Their leader, or one of them, is here. There seem to be different leaders. It all seems unorganized, spontaneous, but . . . effective. He's downstairs. He wants you to agree to terms."

"What terms? What are you talking about, Captain? You woke me in the middle of the night for this? Kill them—it's that simple. Kill them all!"

"Sir, we're not in a position to. Not any longer. If we fight every single one of these battles, we'll end up having very little to take with us to the new positions. The Allies will arrive—apparently they're less than twenty kilometers away—and we'll be unable to defend the city."

"Then raze the city! Burn it! Today we were—"

"The situation, sir, has changed, sir. Can you please come downstairs in uniform? I think the fate of our men is in the balance, or I wouldn't have awakened you. We tried everything to get men up there to help. Major Saggau negotiated for two hours, hoping help would arrive, but instead there were more and more Italian irregulars. We waited as long as we could . . . Their leader is offering to let us leave the city without being fired upon. It's that, Herr Colonel, or I'm afraid we'll be fatally weakened and facing the full might of the Allied advance."

Naked beneath the robe, arms crossed over his chest, Scholl leaned his face forward and peered at Nitzermann. He could feel a torrent of insults rising into his mouth. They had tanks, artillery, the most highly trained soldiers in the world, and this moron captain and his moron underlings couldn't fight against a few Italians with stolen rifles! Couldn't give him half a night's rest without losing the city entirely! Was he supposed to personally supervise every minor skirmish across all of Naples, to remain awake at the radio—two-thirds of the frequencies out of order—twenty-four hours a day?!

Just as he was about to spit words into the captain's face, he heard the sound of a door opening behind him. The captain looked up. Scholl turned his head. *Let it be the woman, at least,* he thought. *Let it be the woman.* And it was. Naked, apparently, she opened the door only wide enough to show her face and drooping black hair, one bare arm held across her right breast. "What's this?" she said sleepily, grinning. "More fun?"

Sixty-Two

At the hospital, Rita watched the ambulance driver and his assistant carry Armando inside on a stretcher. The boy was in a state of shock— skin clammy, breath fluttering—and as she and Lucia waited with him just inside the emergency entrance, Rita asked the nurse for a blanket. When it came, she lay it over *Skutchamenza*, praying a steady stream of Hail Marys, watching the thin little chest rise and fall and the eyelids flicker. The room in which they waited—large enough for two rows of five beds each—was filled with men, women, and children, some standing, some sitting, some lying on the floor, all the beds occupied. She remembered these smells, sights, and sounds from the time she'd carried Anna to the Palazzo Fuga, Anna with the burning skin and typhus in her blood. In her mind's eye, she could see *Skutchamenza*'s friend's head exploding, and she prayed she wouldn't have to watch another child perish. The man who'd shared the ambulance with them was dead, his body wrapped in a bloody sheet and lying in a corner. One woman she could see appeared to be dead also; beside her, another woman was quietly weeping. There were smudges of blood on the floor, the smell of antiseptic and decay, grunts of pain and the wails of an infant.

One by one, patients were taken from the waiting area into the treatment rooms behind. When the nurse at last signaled that it was Armando's turn, she helped Rita and Lucia carry the boy inside and lay him on a cot. Another wait—perhaps half an hour, Armando writhing in pain now, breathing heavily, eyes still closed—and a white-haired doctor arrived, removed the tight black bandage Lucia had fashioned, made his examination. "Flesh wound," were the wonderful words he spoke.

He ordered Armando to be taken into yet another room, where the boy had a mask of some kind of anesthesia put over his mouth and nose while the doctor first cleaned and then sewed up the wound. "A hand's length this way, it would have gone through his heart," the doctor said grimly. Armando stirred but didn't wake. They carried him into a large ward, filled with men of various ages and in various states of pain or recovery, and once he'd been settled in place, Rita and Lucia stood on either side of the bed, saying their private prayers.

With each new arrival of the ambulance, every new wounded man carried into the ward, another burst of news reached them, traveling mouth to ear. There were two nurses in the ward, both nuns, and, as they made their rounds, one or the other of them would whisper something to Lucia in her tattered habit, as if she were in fact a fellow member of the religious, and Lucia would pass on the news to Rita. Fighting all over the city. At the airport, at Capodimonte, in the Materdei, the Vomero, Poggioreale. Germans killed. Italians killed. More and more wounded being brought in to the hospital.

From time to time, Rita would go downstairs to the waiting room and check the faces there, looking for Aldo. And then Lucia would take a turn, looking for Giuseppe. No sign of either.

They took turns standing watch at Armando's bedside, too, trying to sleep sitting on the floor with their backs against the wall. But sleep was impossible. With every new report from the city, the air in the ward and waiting area filled with a sparking mixture of fear and hope, as if the possibility of the occupation's end—dreamed of for so long—might actually be taking shape around them. But at what cost, Rita wondered. And why hadn't the Allies arrived?

She watched Armando's chest to make sure he was breathing, studied the bandaged arm to make sure there was no fresh blood, and from time to time looked into Lucia's eyes, too, seeing there a reflection of her own sorrow. Her Aldo, and Lucia's Giuseppe, could be anywhere, alive or dead, safe or in mortal danger. Rita had a sense of what so many other women had gone through all these years, worrying about a husband, son, or boyfriend in combat. The tragic waste of war weighed so heavily on her just then. Millions killed, maimed, tortured, widowed, or made homeless, and for what? To satisfy the ego of a few madmen.

Finally, just after three in the morning, the nurse came by, checked Armando carefully, and assured the two women that he'd survive. The wound, she said, had been thoroughly cleaned and neatly sewn, and there had been enough antiseptic to prevent infection. He'd be in pain for a week or two. Once the wound healed and the stitches were out, he'd have a scar. But he was young and strong. "Most likely, he'll be up and walking around by lunch tomorrow."

At the edge of complete exhaustion, having eaten nothing since breakfast the day before, Rita discussed it with Lucia for a moment, then decided to walk to Rita's house, two kilometers, sleep there, and try to find their men in the morning.

They touched Armando's leg in farewell, and then out of the building and down the driveway they went, along Via Santa Teresa in darkness so complete, they had to pick their way very slowly. The moon was gone. An eerie calm had settled over northeast Naples. They didn't see a single German vehicle, but here and there, they came upon families huddled together, sleeping in alleys, some surrounded by their belongings. Far in the distance, they heard a series of pops, gunshots certainly. A few louder explosions. Klaxons off toward the train station. But the farther they walked toward the water, the emptier the streets. They could hear their own footsteps echoing against the buildings as they went.

"They spoke to me as if I were a real nun," Lucia said. "I never could live such a life, I know that. But I wonder what it's like. To have that much faith, I mean. Right now, on this awful day, I feel my faith has been shaken to the core. Watching that boy killed, seeing these people sleeping outside, thinking constantly about Giuseppe—my mind has no room for God."

"Nuns and monks suffer," Rita answered, "just as we do. But half their spirit lives in another world."

"A real or imagined world?"

Rita shrugged. "One day we'll know."

"Do you think they're alive? Our men?"

"I feel that they are, yes. I feel it."

By the time they reached the yellow door and climbed the steps to Rita's home, they were so tired, they only sipped from glasses of water and undressed in darkness, without making conversation. Lucia took off the heavy nun's habit and they lay down side by side in the big bed. Rita felt Lucia reach across and take hold of her hand, grasp it, and let go, and then she stepped over the edge of her fears and worries, into sleep.

Sixty-Three

The sitting room of the Parco Hotel bar was filled with men. The smell of sweat, cordite, and stale tobacco, in every corner a strange mix of triumphant Neapolitan pride and a bubbling anger. Giuseppe sat in one of the armchairs, with the stolen German pistol—its safety on—held lightly in his right hand and resting on top of his thigh. Directly across from him, the Nazi major, Saggau, who'd been in charge of the men at the stadium, sat in the middle of a brocaded sofa, elbows on his knees, face in his hands. A former Italian soldier—out of uniform but armed—stood to each side of him. Aldo was there, still holding his rifle in one fist, pacing back and forth behind the couch like a wolf in a cage. The rest of the seats were occupied by others who'd fought at the stadium, and elsewhere—there were stories of battles from every neighborhood in the city—but there was no sign of Zozo Forni or the surviving Dell'Acqua brother. They had disappeared into the night.

No one spoke. Fifteen minutes earlier, the German captain had gone upstairs to fetch Colonel Scholl, because, at the second waving of the white flag, after endless hours of fighting, Saggau had said he wanted to surrender but didn't have the authority to release the Italian hostages. The major had stood there—bravely, Giuseppe thought—exhausted, bleeding from his right hand, the white flag drooping beside him on its rifle. *"Non sono autorizzato; non sono autorizzato!"* he kept saying.

"Who is authorized, then?" Aldo pressed. He'd leaped forward and taken the German major by the collar of his shirt and was shaking him with one strong arm.

"Only Colonel Scholl!"

"Then take us to him."

But for a long time, the major stalled, arguing, discussing, threatening, hoping for reinforcements that never came.

On the ride in from the Vomero, all of them squeezed into the bed of the truck, it was Aldo who'd come up with the idea of letting the German troops leave the city in exchange for the release of the stadium hostages. A brilliant stroke, Giuseppe thought.

Which was how they'd come to be sitting in the hotel bar in the small hours of the morning, a stone's throw from the water, the buildings around them emptied of residents, with reports of battles erupting spontaneously all over the city, with the rumor of the Allies' arrival by sunset the next day, with a German major at their mercy, and a German colonel soon to be. Giuseppe hoped only that Lucia had survived the fighting, Lucia and his uncle. There was no more room inside him for the death of someone he loved.

At last, monocle perched absurdly in one eye, Scholl appeared at the door, in full uniform, accompanied by his captain. There was a defiant look on his face, and it caused Giuseppe to see, once again, his parents' bloody bodies on the Ministry's stone steps. He tightened his grip on the pistol. He had a terrible urge to simply stand up, shoot the man, then walk away without saying a word.

"*Was ist das!*" Scholl demanded, the captain beside him translating.

"This," Aldo said, stepping around the end of the couch so that he was half a meter in front of the colonel, "is your moment of choice. Your men at the stadium are surrounded and outnumbered. Others are in gunfights around the city. Dozens have been killed. As of half an hour ago, the batteries at Capodimonte are under our control. What tanks you have left are stranded in alleys or disabled by grenades. And your major here raised the white flag to save his men's lives."

Scholl turned and glared at Saggau, who spoke to him in German. There was no translation.

Scholl began to speak again, spitting out the words, the captain beside him translating immediately but looking like he wanted nothing more than to be allowed to walk through the door, into the Italian night, and out of the war forever. "*We* have the hostages," Scholl said defiantly, as if he hadn't heard Aldo's words, or wouldn't let himself believe them. "*Your* people. I will give the order to have them shot as easy as—"

Giuseppe took three steps across the room, lifted the pistol, and pointed it directly into the middle of Scholl's face. His hand was shaking. In a voice that came out of him as a low growl, he said, "*Your people* killed my mother and my father."

The monocle slipped off and bounced on its string near Scholl's chest medals. His eyes moved from the tip of the pistol to Giuseppe's trembling mouth.

"We're in a generous mood, take advantage of it!" Aldo shouted in the most bitter tone Giuseppe had ever heard. Frightening in the best of times, Lucia's father looked like a killer now, a roaring beast. "We're offering you a deal. Give your men the order to stop fighting, all over the city, and we'll let you leave Naples without being fired upon. Don't be an idiot!"

"Your other option," one of the Italian soldiers said in a slightly calmer tone, "is for you to die here, tonight, now, and for your men to fight us *and* the Allies tomorrow. We'll draw up the order. Sign it, and you leave at sunrise."

The captain started to translate, but Scholl held up his hand and stopped him.

"Understand?" Aldo asked him.

Squinted eyes. No answer.

Giuseppe's hand was shaking so violently that he put his other hand up and held the pistol out in front of him, careful to keep his finger from the trigger.

Scholl's eyes went from him, to Aldo, to Major Saggau—who could not make eye contact with anyone. The colonel's mouth was twisted in scorn—he looked as if he were about to spit—but Giuseppe could see the tic in the muscles of his left cheek. Standing beside Scholl, his captain made a small movement, almost invisible, a very slight nod of the head.

Scholl waited and waited, as if expecting a team of German commandos to burst through the door and rescue him.

Giuseppe flipped the safety off. He saw the skin beside the colonel's mouth start to twitch violently. The man ran his eyes around the room one last time, hesitated, took in and let out one breath, then another, blinked twice, and pronounced this sentence in broken Italian: "As one man of honor to others, I agree."

Sixty-Four

Having signed the agreement—literally at gunpoint, what choice was there?—and having extracted from the Italians the solemn promise that he and his men wouldn't be fired upon as they left the city, Colonel Scholl told them he had to notify his superiors, and he had the captain requisition a vehicle and take him directly to his office. Not a word passed between them as they made the short trip. On the top floor of the darkened building, he ordered Nitzermann to stay in the outer room, then sat alone at the teletype, trying to find the correct way of passing on the news to Kesselring in Rome. He had failed in his command, that was clear. The arrest and collection of Jews would not be accomplished—Kesselring would realize that soon enough; let *him* pass it on to Himmler.

Not only had the city not been subdued, he and his troops would have to abandon it to the Allies at least somewhat intact. But Nitzermann's argument had been a solid one: fighting to the last man in Naples one day before the Allies appeared would achieve little, weaken any line of defense to the north, and result in a useless loss of life and matériel.

After considering various versions, Scholl repeated that argument in the teletype message, choosing his words with care, typing them in with two fingers in the lamplight, while Captain Nitzermann paced outside the door. He informed Kesselring that he was making a strategic retreat in order to preserve men and matériel for future battles. And then, as an afterthought, hoping to soften his disgrace, he added this: "Will place timed explosive devices in this building, the post office, the hotel, the Municipio, and other locations around the city. Will be departing in orderly fashion at 0700 hours tomorrow. Will not be available to receive return message at this address. Will consult further upon reaching our offices in Sperlonga. Heil Hitler! Scholl."

Nitzermann met him at the door, and they went down the five flights of stairs side by side. Scholl couldn't escape the conclusion that the captain blamed him for everything that had gone wrong, for sending some of their tanks north ahead of time, for committing so many men to the evacuation of the port, for failing to make a proper assessment of the resistance, failing to secure the arms depots by giving the order before he arrived, failing to be awake and on the radio instead of frolicking in his hotel room on what would likely turn out to be one of the key nights of the entire Italian campaign. No doubt, the captain would make a report to their superiors in Rome and Berlin. Perhaps the unfortunate moment in the hotel room would be mentioned, a second black mark on his record, or what was left of it. It was possible he'd see the Russian front after all.

At the bottom of the stairs, before they stepped out into the night, Scholl said, without turning to make eye contact, "Give the order to place timed explosives in this building. The most powerful ones you can find. Also in the Municipio, where we have the names of the Jews, where Marshal Bruni works. In the Central Post Office. The hotel. Any public place where we can still put them. Now, in darkness. Before we depart."

There was a too-long hesitation before the captain's "yes, sir." Scholl turned and met his eyes. Disdain there. Disdain and disrespect. Very thinly disguised.

Sixty-Five

It was a twenty-minute walk from the Parco Hotel to Aldo's apartment in the Santa Lucia. Weary to the marrow of their bones, he and Giuseppe set off together in darkness, this part of the city empty of people, abandoned in haste, at gunpoint. The agreement had been signed. The official orders had been sent out by both Italian military radio and personal couriers to at least a dozen places around the city where there was fighting. A man named Maci, who'd been one of the first to arrive at the stadium, had been sent back to the Vomero with the German major to make sure the order not to fire was understood and the Italian hostages freed. There was nothing left to do besides get a few hours' sleep, but Aldo wondered if he'd be able to sleep at all. The scene at the stadium and the scene at the hotel played themselves over and over again in his mind's eye. He'd experienced so much in his life, from the cells of Nisida to the bomb shelters of the port. But never anything like what he'd seen on this day.

"You can stay with me," he said to Giuseppe.

"Fine."

For a time, they walked along without another word. Aldo squeezed the rifle in one hand. In the middle of him—his belly, his lungs, his heart—he could still feel the rush of the battle, a current running beneath the tiredness. It made him want to talk. "I'm not someone who trusts," he said quietly into the darkness. "It's fine for Scholl to scratch his name on a piece of paper—you noticed he used only his last name, not his first?—but tomorrow he could change his mind, get reinforcements, and start shooting people in the streets again."

"Not with the Allies a day away," Giuseppe said. "He'd be a fool to fight the Americans and British and New Zealanders with their tanks and planes and ships, and with Neapolitans like you and me shooting at them from the rooftops at the same time."

Neapolitans like you and me. Aldo worked that over in his mind, reviewed the scenes for the fiftieth time. He didn't trust the slimy major who'd waved the white flag and then argued with them for hours with armed men behind him in the stadium, and he didn't trust the tall colonel with the superior attitude and the twitching cheek. Yes, the colonel had agreed—in broken Italian, and with such an odd phrase—but only because of the pistol in his face, the rifles in the room, his men trapped at the stadium. Giuseppe was right, though: the Allies were coming.

"You're smarter than I am," Aldo said, without knowing he would say it. "Braver, too, it seems."

The boy didn't answer for a minute, then, "What happened to your friend Zozo?"

Aldo let out a bitter laugh. "Friend, ha! There are no friends in that business. If you can put money in their pocket, they let you live. Maybe do you a favor now and again."

"You worked for them all these years, though."

Aldo ground his teeth together, watched the sidewalk for holes and rubble. He glanced at a young couple, recently made homeless. They were sleeping against a stone abutment, wrapped in a blanket. He turned his eyes to Giuseppe. *And I was just starting to let myself like you,* he thought. "Grow up the way I grew up," he said, bitterness streaming out of him. "Live the way I lived. Spend two years in Nisida dealing with what I dealt with. Raise a daughter on your own. Then judge me."

"Not judging."

"No?"

"I've just never been able to think of Lucia having any connection to the Camorra. Any at all."

"I had no education when I got out. Zozo's brother, Giovanni, found work for me. Put money in my pocket. Kept me from getting killed. Did other things."

"What other things?"

Aldo turned his face to the side, coughed, and spat. He resented the conversation, resented it, resented it, felt a hatred rising inside him and turning its face toward the boy his daughter slept with. And then something else. Some other face that was mysteriously connected to what they'd both been through that day. He began to speak in another voice, long buried, unstoppable now. "One day," he said, then he bit down on the insides of his cheeks and tried to push the voice back down. Unstoppable. "One day, I was walking in the Vasto. Going to see a girlfriend. A long time before Lucia was born. Before I met her mother. Long before. In one of the alleys in that neighborhood, I saw a man I recognized . . . a man who'd been a guard at Nisida when I was there. Short and fat. Bald here." He touched the top middle of his head. "He had pulled a little street boy into the alley, behind a stairway there, and I could see that he was going to do to the boy what he'd done to me. Something exploded inside me. I went into the alley, I took hold of the man. I beat him senseless, and then I put my hands on his neck and I choked him until he stopped breathing." He held out his free hand, as if the mark of the murder might still be on it. "Left him there in the dirt. The boy ran. I ran."

Giuseppe was quiet for a few steps, waiting for more. "And then?"

"And then, an investigation. The man had friends in the prosecutor's office. All the guards at Nisida had friends there."

He went along, waited. Giuseppe wouldn't look at him. "Before you, I told exactly one person about this."

"Who, Lucia?"

Aldo shook his head. "Giovanni Forni. Who I knew from Nisida. Who had already given me work by then. I was afraid of going back to prison, so I told him . . . everything. I don't know what he did, who he talked to, how much he paid. But no one ever connected me to that dead man, and people saw me running out of that alley, I'm sure. And Forni never told anyone else the real story, I'm sure of that, too. Because of him, a *Camorrista*, I was able to stay out of jail. Because of him, I had my life, my work, my daughter. Because of him, I was able to give her food, and clothes, and encourage her to go to the school she went to, so she could go to the university . . . So she could meet someone like you!"

When Aldo finished, he realized he was squeezing one hand around the rifle stock and had made the other into a fist. He was walking faster, pressing his teeth together. Another minute and he was going to take the rifle and smash it down on the head of the boy who had drawn the story out of him.

"She appreciates it," Giuseppe said. "All of it. She can't say it to you, but she appreciates it. She's grateful. What you just told me, you should tell her. And you're smart, too. You should find another way to make a living if you can. Zozo left the fight today. Left us to die kicking the Nazis out of the city, so he could make money again. And it was his brother who helped you, not him. Once morning comes, once the Germans are gone, Naples will start to return to normal life. You should find other work."

Aldo snorted, spat. "Sometimes," he said. "Sometimes I wonder if the university teaches people anything at all."

They reached the place where he lived. He opened the door and told Giuseppe to take whatever food he could find if he was hungry, take a blanket and sleep on the floor. "First thing in the morning, we'll go watch the Nazis leave. But we'll carry our guns, just to be sure."

He took off his clothes and lay on top of the sheets, staring up at the ceiling, hungry, worked up, unable to sleep. Even now, in the midst of his exhaustion, he went back over everything that had happened that day, everything he'd said, everything Giuseppe had said, searching for ways in which he'd made himself vulnerable. Stupid of him to have told that story. He'd sworn he never would again. Not to Lucia, not to Rita, not to anyone. So stupid.

The room was dark and quiet, the air warm. He reached out and touched the cool stone wall to his right and held his fingers against it. Now Giuseppe was going to tell Lucia, and there would be more trouble between them, more disrespect. It was possible she'd never speak to him again, her father the murderer. The raped boy. So stupid!

But then a twist of something else found its way into the room. Not in his thoughts but in his chest and belly, he could suddenly feel something—not nameable—that he'd felt the last time he'd slept with Rita, and then again, just now, on the walk from the hotel. He was proud of being unafraid, but this new *something* carried with it a taste of terror, left him unguarded, unprotected, a naked boy.

He was trying to understand it, but the exhaustion caught him. The violence of the day. A single ray of pride: it had been *his* idea to make the deal, to convince the Germans to leave. On the edge of sleep, he remembered what Giuseppe had said. "Once morning comes . . ." That things would be different once the Germans were gone and the Allies owned the city. That he should find other work.

Impossible as it was, the thought was like a breath of air in his mind. Cool sea air on a hot September night. A surprise. A gift. Rita, he knew, would call it a "blessing."

For a few seconds, he could almost picture a resurrected Napoli, and his new life in it. And then the vision left him, and he slept.

Sixty-Six

Lucia awoke to the sound of voices. Rita and her neighbor from downstairs—Eleonora, she thought the woman's name was—were standing in the doorway, speaking in excited tones. *"Se ne stanno andando!"* the woman was saying excitedly. *They're leaving!*

A dream, Lucia supposed. She closed her eyes, drifted back toward sleep for a few minutes, then heard the door click shut and saw Rita come into the bedroom. Rita sat on the edge of the mattress, black hair tousled around her face, eyes still full of sleep. "Did you hear?" she said, putting a hand on Lucia's arm and squeezing once. "Eleonora doesn't tell stories. It's true. The Nazis are leaving Napoli!"

"How? When? I have to find Giuseppe."

Rita shrugged, tried to smile. "Leave the habit here. Wear my blouse. Eleonora is a little taller, she can lend you a skirt that's long enough. Go find him."

They breakfasted—five minutes—on three stale crackers and a glass of water each, but the skimpy meal only served to make the hunger gnaw more insistently at Lucia's insides. She felt nauseous, too, a new trouble. Against Rita's wishes, she kept the pistol with her, sliding it into the pocket of the skirt Eleonora lent her, then hugging them both and stepping out into the warm morning. It was very early. No one was out. No German patrols. No neighbors sitting in front of their houses. No sound of shooting, or ambulance Klaxons. Not so much as a single bus running on Via Toledo when she reached that main road.

The only thing that mattered to her now was finding Giuseppe. Seeing him alive, taking him in her arms, telling him everything that had happened to her in the past day and a half, and finding out what had happened to him and his uncle. But where to look? It seemed impossible that he'd be at the Archives, and only a little more likely that, with everything that was happening, he'd have remained in hiding or gone back to his house. She hoped he was sleeping at her father's, or had found some other safe place to stay, but walking along in the sunlight, she realized he'd have chosen to fight. If he had survived, and if it were true about the agreement and the retreat, then *he'd* be looking for *her*— at her apartment or at the office. The office was closer. She'd go there. If Bruni and the Austrians on the top floor were gone, then she'd know the rumor was true. Maybe she'd see Rosalia, explain why she hadn't yet returned the nun's clothing to her sister. Maybe Rosalia—queen of news—would tell her what was really going on.

She turned in the direction of the Municipio, aware now of people sleeping in strange places—in the square, against the walls of the churches. Furniture and mattresses and blankets strewn about. A few of them were awake and seemed to be heading back toward the neighborhoods near the port. She thought of Armando and his friend, the boys who'd saved her, one wounded, one gone forever, and wished she'd had something to give Rita, who was heading back to the hospital to see him. On the next corner, she came upon a *carabinieri* vehicle with two uniformed officers standing beside it, looking south, as if watching for the Allies to march into their city and silently rehearsing what they would say. *Signori, why did you bomb the neighborhoods and churches and shops, and machine-gun people from your planes?* Or, *Signori, thank you for chasing the Germans away, we hope you'll be kinder.* Or, *Signori, please find us something to eat.* She went up to one of them. "It's not true, is it? About the agreement?"

The taller man looked down at her, his face a mask of suspicion at first—typical of them—and then the mask broke open and a wide smile stretched the bottom of his face, cheeks unshaven, a gap between his top front teeth. "We've been ordered not to shoot them as they leave," he said. "Imagine. *We* have been ordered not to shoot *them*!"

"Then it's true?"

"The war here is over," his partner said. "Go celebrate with your boyfriend, if you have one."

"I'm looking for him."

"Look without worry, signorina."

She thanked them and walked on, feeling something different deep in her abdomen, a bubble, a swirl. Hope, it felt like. She wanted to hold it down, but couldn't, not quite. It pressed up through the hunger there on another wave of nausea, rising up against the back of her throat. On the corner of Via Medina and San Tommaso, she came within sight of a familiar café and was surprised to see that it was open. People returning to the port, the café open, the *carabinieris'* kind words. Maybe the news was true, then. Maybe it had traveled that quickly through the night. As she went past the door, the old owner waved her inside. "Coffee," he said. "For you, beautiful girl. Not the tastiest coffee but free. Drink, please. Here." He handed her a small ceramic cup. Bitter, diluted, no sugar, but it was enough for her to see the expression on the man's face, as if there had been a resurrection of the very best of the Neapolitan spirit, the crazy generosity, the reflexive caring for every other human being, the joy in simply being alive. When she had drunk, the man leaned across the counter, put his hands on her shoulders, and kissed her on both cheeks, and she let him.

She was within a block of the Municipio, her building. She decided it made sense to stop there. If it was true that the war was over, at least in Naples, then there might be something on the teletype confirming it. And it might be wise to take the files the Nazis had compiled on the Jews and at least hide them, in case the Nazis or Italian Fascists returned. Or hand them over to the Allies. And maybe Rosalia had gone in to work, or to say goodbye to her lover.

By the time she reached the square, on the far side of which her building stood, Lucia had more evidence of a new mood in the city. Signs of life. Here and there, the upstairs windows were open, a few women on the balconies. Two men stood on the corner, waving their arms and arguing like friends. She came upon a vendor selling mushrooms from a cart—the price was so high! There was even one optimistic soul already making repairs on an apartment building—his or someone else's—with a gaping hole in one wall. The man was lifting stones the size of loaves of bread from a pile of rubble nearby. He'd managed to mix up a bit of mortar and, using his hand as a trowel, was slapping it down, wiping the hand on his trouser leg, then setting the stones, fitting them tight together, closing the hole, bit by bit. It seemed to her a Sisyphean task, but it was a sign, nevertheless.

As she drew closer to her building, she saw someone sitting on the main front steps. Closer still and she realized it was Giuseppe's uncle, Donato, back hunched, hands folded in front of him as if in prayer, and a spasm of worry caused the nausea that had been swirling in her belly and throat to rise up even farther. It very nearly choked her. She quickened her pace. Donato saw her and stood, and she peered at his face, looking for news. He smiled, and she let out a sound she'd never heard herself make, half cry, half spurt of laughter. She hurried up and held him tight. "He's alive, then, yes, Uncle?"

"*Sì, sì,*" he said. "Alive, well, looking everywhere for you. I told him I would be the one to find you and that I would bring you to our home. I knew you'd come here. I saw it in a dream. There's no one in the building now. I'll take you to him."

"I want to go up to my desk for a few minutes, to get some files and—"

"No, no," he said with an insistence that surprised her. "Not now, Lucia. I had . . . an evil dream about this place. One of my dreams.

Don't go in now. We'll go home and find Giuseppe. Perhaps your father is searching for you, too."

She resisted for a few seconds but couldn't change his mind. Wrapping one arm in his, she turned and started east again, in the direction of the Sanità. Walking at his slow pace, they'd gone only three-quarters of the way down the block when there was a tremendous roar behind them, a deafening sound, and then, half a second later, a blast of hot air that knocked them forward onto the pavement. Lucia sat up, hands and face scratched, and looked back to see one whole side of the building, right where she'd worked, slipping out of itself in a cascade of smoke, dust, and stone. The material gushed down onto the street as if dumped from an enormous truck, and she felt a fine rain of particles falling on them and heard Donato say, *"Madre di Dio."* He reached out to take her hand. The pistol lay beside her in the dust, and she discovered that she had no urge, none whatsoever, to pick it up.

Her stomach pulsed again, and she put a hand there to settle it. Sitting in the eerily gentle rain of dust and grit, watching the smoking building and realizing how close she'd come to her own death, a thought occurred to her. More than a thought: a realization, a surprise. *We should have been more careful, Giuseppe and I,* she nearly said aloud. *More careful making love.*

But she kept the words in her mouth and thought: *Not really, no. Not at all.*

Sixty-Seven

Because of all the many people who'd been wounded in the street battles, the hospital nurses were very busy. And because they were so busy, Armando noticed that they came to the large, crowded ward only once every hour or so and walked along the rows of beds, checking on the men and boys who were sick or wounded, then moving on to the ward that held women and girls.

He waited until the nurse had taken away the tray that had held his breakfast—brown-edged pieces of old apple and a cup of weak tea. "The Germans are leaving us," she said. When he asked her, she told him she didn't know why. Something had happened during the night. They were already on the move, she said, this morning, marching out along Via Castellino. "A lot of people are going to watch." And then, "Are you in pain, little one?" she'd asked, and he'd lied and said, "No, not at all," and bit down on the anger. The "little one," he wanted to tell her, had lost his best friend in the battle. He was wounded. *Ferito.* Wounded by a Nazi bullet. A fighter now, perhaps a hero.

But instead of getting angry at the nun—she'd been kind to him—Armando waited until she'd finished her checking and left the big room, and then he sat up and very quietly placed his feet on the floor. The arm hurt terribly, pain radiating all the way down to his wrist and up into his neck, but the blood on the bandage was dried blood, not fresh. He touched it lightly with one finger to be sure. Not fresh. Before doing anything else, he knelt beside the bed and said a prayer for his lost friend, in heaven now, certainly in heaven, probably with a girlfriend already. He kissed the mattress three times, thanking it, whispering that he knew he would sleep on a mattress again one fine day, but until then, he was grateful.

It seemed to him that he remembered *Nanella* saying something to him, asking him to come live with her. It seemed that Sister Marcellina had been there, too, but it all could have been a dream. The last thing he remembered with absolute clarity was the sight of Tomaso's head exploding in an eruption of blood.

His clothes were folded neatly on the marble shelf of the window. The old shoes. A pair of tattered pants. The shirt with American writing on it, a stain of blood on the sleeve. He dressed without making the smallest sound and, holding one shoe in each hand, went silently to the door. He could see the nurse walking there, away from him, and when she'd gone far enough, Armando crept through the door, down the corridor, and out into the cool morning air before anyone noticed. He went a little way to be safe, sat on a low wall, and put on his shoes. The arm hurt so much, with his heart pumping hard, but the sun was up over the buildings behind him. He had slept, he had eaten, the day would be warm, he was *ferito*. One of the brave ones who'd chased the Nazis out of Napoli! Against all that, the pain was nothing. Almost nothing. And there was something he had to do now. Tomaso would have wanted it.

He went quietly down the driveway, stepping behind a shrub when an ambulance came rolling through the gates, the cross on its side so large and red that he blessed himself and whispered a few words of one of the prayers the nuns had taught him.

And then he was out in the city again, free. From the moment the nun had told him about the Germans leaving, he'd known exactly where he wanted to go.

Down along Via Fontanelle he went, the sun burning yellow light into the morning, a few people out on the streets, looking around cautiously as if watching for German soldiers and hoping they wouldn't see any. One cart, drawn by a horse, came clopping happily along. Armando walked into the Materdei and climbed the steps of the church there, next to the ruined orphanage. The door was unlocked. He went inside and hurried around to the room where the priests dressed for Mass. There, as he'd hoped, he came upon Padre Paulo sitting on a bench wearing only his black pants and black undershirt, the prayer book open on one knee and his lips going quietly.

"Padre!" Armando whispered.

The old priest straightened his back and spun his head around, his face breaking into a smile.

"Padre, have you heard? Is it true?"

The priest nodded, the smile shrinking. "Your arm!"

"Wounded," Armando told him, and then, in the dialect, the language of men, *"Ma nun fa male."* It doesn't hurt. "Tomaso is dead, killed in the fighting. Can you pray for him, Padre?"

"Of course. I'll say this Mass for his soul. I'm very sorry, Armando. Come. Take communion for him. I'm so sorry."

"I can't stay for Mass, Padre, but I'll come tomorrow. I promise. Can I have the hat?"

Without arguing, and without standing up, the priest reached to his right, pulled open a drawer, and took out the German soldier's hat. He handed it over. "A promise is a promise," he said, and Armando couldn't be sure whose promise he was talking about—the priest's own, for keeping good care of the hat, or Armando's, about Mass the next day. It didn't matter.

"They're leaving, Padre. Along Via Castellino in Arenella. I'm going to say goodbye."

"Then for me, say also a goodbye."

Armando nodded, thanked him, hurried back out into the day, not bothering to hide the hat now but holding it tightly in one hand.

He spotted an old man in a horse-drawn wagon, the kind of person he might have tormented or stolen from before the uprising. He waved a hand. The man tugged on the reins and stopped.

"Going to Arenella to watch?"

"Everyone's going. Climb on." The old man helped him up and nodded at the bloody bandage. "You're hurt."

"Nazi bullet," Armando told him. "I fought at the *stadio*."

"Is that where you got the hat?"

"*Sì, sì,*" Armando lied.

"You should keep it for a souvenir."

"*Sì.*"

It took them fifteen minutes to get to the bridge on Via Fontana where it crossed the larger Via Castellino. Three times they passed notices on the sides of buildings, announcing that an agreement had been reached, that the Germans should be allowed to leave without trouble. No guns should be fired. He noticed that these announcements had been scrawled in large letters over the other ones, the posters from the Nazi colonel.

By the time they made it to the bridge, where Armando thanked the old man and climbed down, a long column of soldiers was already moving along beneath it in orderly rows. The tanks had gone first—he could still see them far in the distance—and then the trucks towing artillery, and then trucks carrying men (he wondered if any of them had recently had their tires repaired), and then only soldiers on foot. People lined the roadway there, jeering, making vulgar hand signals, but not shooting or throwing stones.

He wouldn't throw stones, either.

The old man had parked his cart a short distance away; the horse was stamping its hooves and snorting. Armando watched, waited, and at a certain moment, hurried over and found what he had been waiting for: a pile of *merda* still steaming in the cool morning air. Being careful to avoid the horse's kick, and with only one arm working properly, it wasn't an easy job, but he managed to drag the firm black circle of the hat brim along the ground just so and collect a good portion of it inside. The smell was horrible. He held the hat out with a straight arm and turned his face the other way. By the time he reached the railing again, he could see the end of the column, men eight or ten across, and then one last vehicle, a jeep with the Nazi flag waving, surrounded on all sides by motorcycles. An officer who looked important was sitting in the front passenger seat of the vehicle, one arm resting out the open window, eyes forward. Armando balanced the hat on the top of the railing, pinching his nose with his free hand and trying to measure the pace of the column. He moved sideways two steps to align himself properly. When the last ranks of soldiers were moving beneath him, he tipped the hat over the railing and released it, then leaned far over and watched as it shot straight down. A kind of bomb, he thought. But he could see right away that he'd released it one second too early. It landed, not on the officer but in front of him, on the metal hood of the jeep. He saw the officer flinch, saw the dark brown fly in a wet spray across the metal in front of him, perhaps a bit of it reaching his uniform. Armando hurried to the other side of the bridge and noticed that the officer hadn't moved. Perfect. He'd ride like that all the way to Germany, smelling Neapolitan horseshit.

"From Tomaso," Armando said quietly, water in his eyes now, the whole scene gone blurry. "From Tomaso and me and our *coro*, and from Padre Paulo, and from *Nanella*, and from Sister Marcellina. *Ciao, bastardi!* Die like dogs."

Sixty-Eight

When Rita made it to the hospital and saw someone else in Armando's bed, she worried, but only for as long as it took her to find the nurse on duty. "He sneaked away," the nun told her, and Rita wasn't surprised. As she'd walked through the city, with doors and windows open on the day and a cautious sense of celebration in the faces she passed, she'd been dreaming about having Armando come and live with her. The bed in her other room could be cleaned off and made ready. He'd have his privacy, be able to come and go as he pleased. She imagined herself cooking meals and buying clothes for him, even taking him with her to Mass.

But it was foolish. Of course it was. What would she do with the boy when Avvocato Cilento or Aldo came to visit? And how would she survive if they didn't come, find a job cooking pasta at Orlandello's?

No, the life she had lived would go on until she was too old to live it. When that happened, she'd have to depend on the saints to support her or she'd end up sitting at the doors of the Duomo with her hand out, like the Gypsy women and the legless men. Other children of God.

She walked down the hospital driveway, held in a quiet sorrow. As the morning warmed, she could sense more and more signs of happiness in the faces she passed. One or two shops were open for the first time in years; she even saw a few expensive pieces of fruit in the windows, as if they'd grown magically overnight. No German trucks or motorcycles. No soldiers on the streets.

She walked as far as the Centro, breathing and praying, trying to shed the thick cloak of sadness, trying to let the air of freedom wash her skin clean of old sorrows. She wondered if she should continue on in the same direction, toward the Arenella, and watch the Nazi soldiers leave, but some other place called to her. Not far from Piazza Bellini, another good sign: instead of standing closed but unlocked, the doors of her favorite place on earth, the Church of Perpetual Mercy, had been propped wide open. She climbed the steps and sat in her usual pew, halfway up the left side, opposite the statue of Saint Anthony and the row of votive candles there. One of the candles had been lit. Its flame flickered proudly in a breath of air wafting in from the street.

Rita knelt, resting her arms on the pew in front of her, and gazed at the mural above the altar. The angels, the Lord, the Lord's mother: these figures had been painted hundreds of years before the war, before Mussolini, before Hitler, before she herself had been born and before she'd been abandoned and before she'd been abused. There had been cruelty and sadness and disappointment even then. There had been war and misery and death. Her saintly brother had reminded her, more than once, that in the midst of suffering, it was important to remember one thing: everyone suffered. Some more, some less; some now, some later; some in one way, some in another. But no one was exempt. It was, he said, a lesson, not a punishment. She closed her eyes and bowed her head. Some women were given children; others were not. Some women had parents and then a husband; others did not. She would try to do what she had been trying to do for years now, take the love of God into her and pass that love on to others.

She only wished, on this day when the city was swelling with joy, that she did not have to return to an empty house.

Rita knelt and prayed for half an hour, asking especially for comfort for the friend of *Skutchamenza* who had been killed. The sting of loneliness passed, as she knew it would, leaving only a faint, mild ache. She stood before the statue of Saint Anthony, took one of the thin brown candles, and touched its wick to the flame, then set it in place and said a prayer for the murdered boy, and also for little *Skutchamenza*. That he would be safe. That he would find love. That one day, he would leave the life of the streets and have a warm bed and a job and a family.

She touched a finger into the font of holy water, made the sign of the cross, and stepped out through the open door. She looked around her. Women walking with bags folded under their arms, scouting for food. An old man with a cane, limping past, a gray growth of beard on his face, his lips working in a silent prayer or complaint. The city alive again, half in ruins, bathed in sunlight.

On the far side of the piazza, a hundred meters away, she saw someone sitting on a stone bench, part of which had been broken apart, no doubt by the Allied bombs. She looked closer: the person—a thin, black-haired boy with a triangular face and a bandage high up on his left arm—seemed to be waving to her.

Sixty-Nine

It was a small thing, she knew, but Lucia hadn't wanted to return the habit to Rosalia's sister without cleaning it. The cross was gone—left in the stones of an alley, beside a dead Nazi soldier—but the black dress and white wimple were stained with dirt and sweat, two small blood-stains on the sleeve, and she'd cut off a piece of the hem to help the wounded *scugnizzo*. There was water but very little soap, so she'd soaked the habit in her deep, rust-stained sink overnight, hoping to make it at least somewhat presentable, and was squeezing the heavy cloth dry when she heard someone knocking on her front door. Giuseppe, she supposed. She smiled to herself, remembering the sight of him in front of his house the day before. He'd been watching for her, waiting for Uncle Donato to return, and the second he spotted her, his face broke open in the most beautiful smile. They'd spent a perfect afternoon and evening together, kissing and talking, strolling hand in hand around the Materdei, and they'd agreed to meet today and do a couple of impor-tant but painful errands. All morning she'd been rehearsing the words, thinking up different ways of giving him the news that seemed to be swelling inside her. Now that the Nazis were gone, beneath the surface of celebration and relief lay a current of concern: Where would they get money to buy food? How would they live?

She worried Giuseppe wouldn't be happy about what she had to tell him. And then what would she do?

While Lucia was drying her hands, the knock sounded a second time. She hurried across her tiny living room. The door opened directly onto the street and, for a second or two, still haunted by the memories of the limping German, she wondered if she should peek through the window to make sure it was Giuseppe and not a Nazi or a Blackshirt, seeking a last revenge.

But she told herself that chapter was past; it was important to be brave now, to face the future in whatever shape it arrived, so she opened the door without hesitating. Her father stood there in his leather jacket, an envelope in one hand and on his face an expression she'd never seen. Something, some little spider of emotion, was running through the muscles around his mouth; his eyes, steady on her as always, seemed half a degree softer. She wondered if he'd come to tell her that, now that the Germans were gone, he'd finally had the chance to see a doctor about his bloody cough—something she'd been asking him to do for months—and the doctor had told him he had only a few weeks to live.

"Come in. Come in, Father."

He shook his head, feet set wide, body still, and after a second's hesitation handed the envelope to her. "Open it," he said.

"Yes, but come in. Sit with me."

He shook his head again, blinked, watched her.

Money, she thought. The envelope was square, made of yellowish paper, a bit larger than an ordinary piece of mail. Lucia ran her thumbnail under the flap and saw that it held two fifty-lire bills and a photograph. She drew out the photograph slowly and turned it right-side up. A photo of a woman, dark-haired and dark-eyed and so beautiful, Lucia thought at first her father was giving her the odd gift of an autographed picture of a film star, something he'd stolen long ago, something he thought she might now be able to sell for food money. Slowly, though, as she studied the eyes and mouth, an understanding reached her. She looked up into her father's face.

"Your mother," he said. "Vittoria DeMarco. She was from a small village called Parolise, between Avellino and Benevento." He hesitated, flexed his cheeks as if to keep them from trembling. "She died giving birth to you." To Lucia's astonishment, he leaned over and kissed her quickly on one cheek, then turned and walked off down the street. She knew it was useless to call and try to stop him. She stepped across the threshold and watched him walk away, arms out, head up, chin slightly forward . . . a man pushing his way through a chest-high ocean of pain.

Seventy

Late that afternoon, sitting in the back seat of the Willys with some very tall, skinny private he'd never seen before manning the wheel and Colonel Accetullo occupying the passenger seat directly in front of him, Spinelli couldn't quite make himself believe that Naples had been taken without bloodshed. No American bloodshed, at least. From the stories he'd heard as they'd made their way cautiously into the city—one incredible tale layered upon the next, rumor, exaggeration, truth, who knew?—a hundred, or five hundred, or a thousand Italian fighters had perished. The Brits had led the way, early this morning, and from their reports, one or two German snipers either hadn't gotten the news or had decided to make their own last stand from the windows of a bombed-out building near the railway station and take a last few Allied lives. Two tank shells had ended their dreams and sent what was left of the building crashing to the ground. Now, as the jeep in which he was riding careened along Corso Umberto, Spinelli half expected there to be an ambush, to discover that the rumors were incorrect: the Nazis had played a trick and were waiting inside buildings and on rooftops for the Americans to come.

But no. The city was eerily tame. A few people wandering around, carrying chairs on their heads and babies in their arms. Lots of cafés open. Women on the balconies. How, exactly, it had all happened, he didn't know. The businessman who was helping them now had come to greet them on the outskirts of the city with all kinds of heroic stories. An uprising, he said. Mostly unorganized. Ordinary people fighting Nazi soldiers in the streets, throwing rocks, firing stolen rifles and machine guns, tossing homemade hand grenades, dropping furniture out of apartment windows into the narrow streets to make it so the tanks couldn't reach certain neighborhoods. If the stories were true, then it was certainly the strangest and most remarkable thing he'd ever heard, and in a war full of strange and remarkable things.

Still, it was hard to think of another explanation for why the Germans had abandoned the city in haste, without burning it to the ground. There were some mined buildings, yes, and booby traps; the engineers were doing their best to take care of them. But nothing like what he'd imagined on his two trips into the city: no German tanks in the piazzas, no artillery firing from the Capodimonte Hill, no machine-gun emplacements in the mouths of the narrow alleys in Spagnoli or Materdei.

"You know how to find the house?" Colonel Accetullo asked him, swiveling his head a few inches and throwing the words back over his shoulder.

"Yes, sir."

"You're sure?"

"Very sure, sir. I have the address. I got directions from our friend."

"You don't lack for confidence, do you, Spinelli?"

"No, sir."

The colonel grunted. They turned right onto Via Duomo, went toward the huge cathedral—undamaged, it seemed—turned left on Tribunali before reaching it, and bumped over the stone pavement, through the tunnel there, past Piazza Dante (the statue hadn't been damaged).

"Take the next right," Spinelli said to the driver, and up into the Materdei they went, turning onto a street so narrow, he could have reached out and touched the walls of the houses on his side. The driver—no Neapolitan blood, Spinelli could see—hesitated at every intersection. A left and then another right, and he tapped the driver on the shoulder and they pulled up in front of a house with a man sitting calmly out front in what looked like a broken lawn chair. Spinelli jumped out and saw that the man had a badly curved back. *"Mi scusi, signore, ma Giuseppe DiPietra abita qua?"*

The old man looked at him quizzically, and Spinelli expected a response like one he'd get to a similar question in New Haven: *Who's askin'?*

But the man only turned his crippled body and yelled over his shoulder to a knot of men at the corner. *"Oy, Giusepp! Lu cavone ti chiam'!"*

Spinelli smiled—the tone of voice, the slang, the dialect; it carried him all the way back to New Haven. *Hey, Giuseppe,* the old guy had said. *Some big clown askin' for you!*

At the summons, a young man wearing glasses stepped away from the conversation on the corner. He looked to Spinelli like an unimpressive specimen, certainly not soldier material. An intellectual, it seemed. An intellectual with big shoulders. Spinelli wondered if their Italian contact had been playing some kind of trick on them, or if this bespectacled guy—a hero, supposedly—was some other DiPietra; it was a common name. Still, the glasses, the square, nice-looking face. The description fit. And it seemed to be the right address.

"Giuseppe DiPietra?" Spinelli asked.

The man nodded and stood facing him.

"This is Colonel Accetullo of the United States Army. He has a proposition for you. I'm going to translate."

"I speak some of the English."

"You speak well! You worked at the Archives, yes?"

The man nodded, reached up with one finger, and pushed the glasses back against the bridge of his nose, then shook the colonel's outstretched hand, a bit reluctantly it seemed. Accetullo eyed him up and down. Speaking slowly at first, as if to a second grader, the colonel said, "I'm in charge of the Allied occupation of the city . . . on the American side. We're looking for a local person to act as liaison with the US Army. A connection between us and your people." He waited to make sure Giuseppe understood, then went on, gaining momentum, speaking now almost at a normal pace. "There's a lot of work to do, as I'm sure you know. The hunger, the sickness, the mines, the rubble. We have to get the sewer lines patched up, people sprayed against typhus, the rats taken care of, hospitals up and running at full speed, and so on. We'll pay you, of course, but we need someone right away, someone with leadership skills and local knowledge. You were highly recommended. Willing?"

Giuseppe squinted at the colonel. His face showed no emotion at all. He seemed suspicious at first, half-interested. Spinelli was on the verge of giving him a full translation but decided, instead, to say something to the young man in the dialect. *"È 'nu brav'omm,"* he said in Neapolitan, leaning his head sideways toward the colonel. *A good man.* And then, *"È 'na bona fatica." A good job.*

At the words, Giuseppe's face registered surprise, seemed to soften. He moved his eyes back and forth between the two Americans. "I will to do it," he said. "If I can to choose the helper. I know somebody who knows the port, has a lot of connection."

"Done," the colonel said. "You live here, correct?"

"*Sì.* Yes."

"You start day after tomorrow, then. We'll have a vehicle here for you at 0800 hours."

Giuseppe looked puzzled. "Eight o'clock in the morning," Spinelli told him.

Giuseppe nodded, still, it seemed to Spinelli, not exactly excited about the proposition. He moved his eyes from one of them to the other and back again. Two *Americani* in uniform, welcome enough, but, even so, another group of strangers come to take possession of his city. "Who give you my name?" he asked, staying with English.

The colonel had already turned back toward the jeep, so Spinelli stood there and answered in Italian. "A businessman. The guy who was there to meet us as we came into the city. In an American car. A Ford. Not far beyond Poggioreale where the big cemetery is. He's been helping us with several things. He recommended you."

"This man," Giuseppe said. "What is his the name?"

"A strange name," Spinelli said. "Zozo something or other."

Seventy-One

Later that afternoon, on the day of her father's unexpected visit, Lucia and Giuseppe rode the bus together in the direction of the small city of Nola.

Already, it seemed, she could feel, like the first hints of a change of season still weeks away, the end of the war in Naples. The Germans had left; the Allies were pouring into the city now, British and New Zealanders and Americans, met by cheering crowds, handing out chocolate, receiving kisses. It was a miracle, certainly a miracle, but, hungry and wary, remembering the bombing raids, the Neapolitans seemed to Lucia to have just the smallest touch of reticence to their celebrations. After all the noise and fighting, there was a measure of normal life on the streets, people walking around freely, young men going about their business, unafraid of being picked up and shipped north. A few more buses had started running, as if German soldiers had been guarding the municipal garages and, hearing the news, had abandoned their posts. She was sitting in one of the buses, at the window, Giuseppe beside her, his right hand clasping her left.

South and east they were going and, because of the damaged roads, not much faster than they could have walked. In her purse, Lucia held the photograph of her mother, and she took it out and gazed at it as the bus bumped past Poggioreale, the cemetery where Giuseppe's parents were buried. He'd said he had something important to tell her, and she'd said she had something important to tell him, as well. But they'd agreed to wait until this errand was finished. They'd visit the cemetery on the way back, say a prayer at the grave, then have their talk.

It wasn't a happy errand. She knew what they'd find at the end of the bus line, and Giuseppe knew it, too, and it caused a heavy silence to hang between them. She squeezed his hand tight. Just as they arrived on the outskirts of Nola and stopped to let an elderly couple board the bus, she turned and looked at Giuseppe's face. It was set in a mask, expressionless. She could sense that the old tenderness she'd loved had been buried beneath that mask—he'd told her that he'd tried to kill people and had seen people killed—but there was nothing to do about that, not for the time being, not now, not today.

The last part of the ride seemed to take hours. When the bus at last pulled up to the stop at Bel Sito, they stepped down, still holding hands, and started off in the direction of the villa. From a kilometer away, they could smell the smoke, and then, a bit closer, behind a row of houses, they could see a few thin trails of it still lifting into the sky like the faint weeping of exhausted mourners. Giuseppe was squeezing her hand so tight that it hurt, his lips pressed together, eyes narrowed. Turning a last corner, they saw the gates of the villa, the long driveway curling in a gentle arc behind them, and then what remained of the building where the precious documents had been stored. They went through the gates and walked up the drive in silence. Lucia could see the jagged, still-standing portions of the villa's front walls, the windows like empty eyes, the charred rafters lying about as if some giant had tossed them there in a fit of anger. The trunks of two large eucalyptus trees in front of the main door were blackened on one side, the leaves on that side burned and drooping.

As they drew closer, Lucia noticed a middle-aged man sitting on a block of concrete not far from the entrance. When he heard their footsteps, the man turned, glanced at her, and then locked his eyes, wet with tears, on Giuseppe's face, and stood. Still without speaking, Giuseppe walked over, and he and the man held each other in an embrace. "I'll spend the rest of my life trying to replace them," Lucia heard the man say, but it seemed to her that, brave as they were, those words had little connection with reality. It was possible that, for Naples at least, the fighting was finished. But the suffering wasn't. Rebuild the city as the living might do, the dead could not be brought back to life; the deep wounds of bereavement would not be healed for decades, if ever, and the seven-hundred-year-old documents could never be re-created.

She wanted at that moment, in the midst of their sorrow, only to find the right way to tell Giuseppe her happy news. *Their* happy news. She wanted only to make a life with him, to raise a family they could feed, to live in the city they loved. Staring at the green leaves of the half-burned trees, she held to the dream of that future, and part of her was at peace.

There was, though, another part. Much as she wanted to, she couldn't deny it. She looked up at the charred remains of the villa and thought: We can build a new life, yes. And we will. But none of this will ever be forgotten.

Epilogue

When the Nazis marched out of Naples at dawn on September 30, 1943—with Colonel Scholl riding in a black Ford—the Neapolitans' suffering was eased but not ended. Not long after the soldiers left, German bombers targeted the same city their troops had once occupied, a sporadic and brief air campaign that resulted in more death and destruction. Despite the best efforts of the newly arrived Allied forces, starvation and disease persisted in Naples, and the job of rebuilding the thousands of damaged and destroyed buildings would not begin in earnest for years to come.

One week after the German retreat, a series of explosions rocked the Palazzo delle Poste, the city's main post office. People who'd been made homeless by the Allied bombings had taken refuge there, and the October 7 explosions, caused by time bombs the Nazis had planted just prior to their departure, resulted in the deaths of more than one hundred men, women, and children, including members of the American 82nd Airborne Division. Other buildings in the city had been sabotaged, too, though some of the explosives were defused by the Allies, and waiters at the Parco Hotel found the bombs there before they exploded, and saved many lives. The epidemic of rape and pillage in Naples did not stop with the departure of the Nazis.

The Germans did, in fact, retreat north to higher ground, bombed by the Allies as they went, and yet committing unspeakable acts of sadism and viciousness at the same time. North of Naples, they formed defensive positions, the Gustav Line. Battles along that line would result in the deaths of tens of thousands of soldiers, but eventually, in June of 1944, the defenses were breached and Rome was taken. Even then, nearly a year of fighting and death lay ahead before the rest of Italy was liberated and the Nazi scourge ended.

Heinrich Himmler's plan to arrest all the Jews in Greater Naples and ship them north was thwarted by the Neapolitan uprising. But two weeks later, a similarly hideous plan was executed in Rome—still under German control—and over one thousand Jewish men, women, and children were arrested in the ghetto and sent by train to Auschwitz, where all but a handful of them perished.

Italian Fascist generals Pentimalli and Del Tetto, who had turned their authority over to Colonel Scholl, then fled Naples in civilian clothes, were arrested. Each was sentenced to twenty years in prison.

To acknowledge the bravery of its citizens in the spontaneous uprisings that have come to be called the Four Days of Naples, the city was awarded the Gold Medal of Military Valour, an honor established in 1793 for outstanding gallantry in war. Today, one can find plaques in various neighborhoods commemorating the many acts of heroism that occurred during the Four Days, but very few of the participants remain alive to tell their story.

ACKNOWLEDGMENTS

For twenty years, though my wife, Amanda, and I made a dozen trips to Italy, we avoided Naples. I'd heard it was a dirty city, plagued by street crime, the Mafia, garbage strikes—not the place we wanted to spend our vacation time or, later, bring our two daughters. But then my good friend, the painter John Recco, made a visit to the city (some of his relatives, like some of mine, trace their roots to that part of southern Italy) and insisted that continuing to avoid Naples would be a mistake. He assured me that the tales of crime and mess were exaggerated, and that the kindness and generosity of the Neapolitans were remarkable, even by Mediterranean standards.

So, in March of 2016, Amanda, our daughters, Alexandra and Juliana, and I spent a week in Sardinia, then took the overnight ferry to Naples. ("You're brave!" a Sardinian friend said when she heard we'd purchased the ferry tickets. I didn't ask her why she thought so.) The voyage went without trouble, but once we arrived in Napoli, things didn't start out very well: in addition to peppering us with a dozen offers for his paid-in-cash tours, the ebullient middle-aged taxi driver who took us from the port to our Airbnb on Via Duomo offered to purchase our older daughter—eighteen at the time—to be his wife.

Shortly after that unsettling exchange, the gentleman who met us at the rented apartment showed us how to work the front door's three different locks and two dead bolts. In answer to my first question, he said, yes, the neighborhood was safe . . . then added, *"Durante il giorno."* *During the day.*

That first night, we huddled in the apartment, wondering if we'd made a terrible mistake. But the next morning, we ventured out to a bar in Piazza Bellini owned by John Recco's eighty-five-year-old friend, Vincenzo Fiorelli. We arrived unannounced, strangers, but Vincenzo sat us at one of his sidewalk tables, served us coffee, juice, and snacks, and refused payment. Later in the day, he took us on a walking tour of that section of the city, brought us by some historical sites, treated us to gelato, and showed us the best place to buy fruit and vegetables. That night, we went out again and, instead of dark and dangerous alleys and legions of pickpockets and mafiosi, we found a city filled with people of all ages out for a drink or a meal, laughing, singing, gesticulating, talking loudly and enjoying each other's company.

We ate dinner on Via Tribunali, at a place called da Carmela, and the waiters there—especially a man named Gennaro—were as kind as uncles to our girls. The rest of the week included one act of spontaneous generosity after the next. (On the crowded train to Pompeii, a college-aged young man got up to give me his seat. I'm not infirm, and not elderly, and I can't remember anything like that ever happening in New York or Boston.) The phenomenal museums; the streets lined with what the Italians call *palazzi*—palaces—but what we'd refer to as townhomes or narrow apartment buildings; the crooked alleys leading to crooked side streets and vibrant neighborhoods both poor and elegant. It was a visual feast, and the Neapolitans' joyful attitude was contagious.

The city we'd once avoided had quickly become one of our favorite places on Earth.

Back home, to hold on to the good memories, I started reading up on the City of the Sun and happened across a story about something called the Four Days of Naples, a chapter of World War II of which I was completely ignorant. The story intrigued me from the first.

So Amanda and I went back in 2018 and did some on-the-ground research, hiring a wonderful guide named Alessandra Raio, who walked us around the city center and the Vomero, and took us to some of the many places that figured in the story. At home again, I wrote up a rough draft, and then we went back to Naples for a third visit, in October of 2019, and hired another wonderful guide, Ricardo Cicatiello, who drove us to important locations farther afield. This research refined the characters and events I'd imagined, and provided a clearer sense of both the suffering and heroism of those four days in September 1943.

I'm indebted, most especially, to my wife, Amanda, for her unfailing encouragement, steady love, and for her marvelous photographs, which made remembering the look and feel of certain places much easier; to my daughters, Alexandra and Juliana, for their love, support, and wisdom; to my friend, Peter Sarno, who helps me with so many aspects of the writing life; to a Neapolitan historian, Alessandro Fava, who, in response to the inquiries of a curious American stranger, put together a small encyclopedia of valuable information on conditions in Naples in 1943; to the actor John Turturro (who made a beautiful film, *Passione*, about Neapolitan folk music) for connecting me with Alessandro Fava; to Simone Gugliotta for ongoing Italian language lessons; to an elderly bookseller at Porta Alba who, when asked about the Four Days, rummaged through his shelves of printed material and came up with a treasure: Pietro Gargano's exhaustively detailed series of commemorative magazines put out by *Il Mattino* to mark the seventieth anniversary of the events; to Simone Fogliano, for invaluable assistance with the mysterious intricacies of the Neapolitan dialect; to Jeff Matthews, an American resident of Naples, who has spent decades putting together an online encyclopedia called *Naples: Life, Death, and Miracle*; to Chris Wronsky for helpful information on antique automobiles (in that area and others, any factual or linguistic errors are my own); to the aged Boston terrier Buddy Merullo, who, lying on the floor near my chair, accompanies me while I work; to my wonderful agents, Emma Sweeney and Margaret Sutherland Brown, for their editorial advice and encouragement, and for placing the book in such good hands; to my fine editors, Christopher Werner and David Downing, production editors Laura Barrett and Nicole Burns-Ascue, Stacy Abrams, James Gallagher, and everyone else at Lake Union; and to the many kind and helpful people we met on Naples's streets, in its alleys, and on its Metro, trains, and buses, all of whom responded to my curiosity and questions with the hospitality for which their city is famous.

Begun: June 22, 2019, Naples, Italy
Completed: June 22, 2020, Conway, Massachusetts

ABOUT THE AUTHOR

Photo © 2019 Amanda S. Merullo

Roland Merullo is the bestselling author of more than twenty works of fiction and nonfiction, including *Once Night Falls*; *The Delight of Being Ordinary*; *The Talk-Funny Girl*, an Alex Award winner; *Vatican Waltz*, a *Publishers Weekly* Best Books of 2013 pick; *Breakfast with Buddha*, an international bestseller now in its twentieth printing; *Lunch with Buddha*, selected as one of the Best Books of 2013 by *Kirkus Reviews*; *Revere Beach Boulevard*, named one of the "Top 100 Essential Books of New England" by the *Boston Globe*; and *Revere Beach Elegy*, winner of the Massachusetts Book Award for nonfiction. Born in Boston and raised in Revere, Massachusetts, Roland attended

Brown University, where he obtained a bachelor of arts in Russian studies and a master of arts in Russian language and literature. A former Peace Corps volunteer, he's also made his living as a carpenter, college professor, and cabdriver. Roland, his wife, and their two lovely daughters live in the hills of western Massachusetts. For more information, visit www.rolandmerullo.com.